# the last best thing

### A Classic Tale of Greed, Deception and Mayhem in Silicon Valley

## Pat Dillon

SIMON & SCHUSTER

 SIMON & SCHUSTER
Rockefeller Center
1230 Avenue of the Americas
New York, NY 10020

SIMON & SCHUSTER and colophon are registered trademarks
of Simon & Schuster Inc.

Designed by Brian Mulligan
Illustrations by Reid Brown
Manufactured in the United States of America

10   9   8   7   6   5   4   3   2   1

Library of Congress Cataloging-in-Publication Data
Dillon, Pat.
    The last best thing : a classic tale of greed, deception, and mayhem in Silicon Valley / Pat Dillon.
        p.   cm.
    I. Title.
PS3554.I433L37   1996
813'.54—dc20                                    96-42452
                                                       CIP


ISBN 0-684-83614-9

Portions of this work have been previously published, in slightly different form, in the *San Jose Mercury News*.

# acknowledgments

I want to acknowledge my debt to my colleagues at the *San Jose Mercury News:* reporters, editors, artists, designers, researchers, online specialists and clerks who generously contributed their knowledge and patience in helping me write a newspaper serial that eventually found its way into a book. In particular, I thank David Yarnold for taking the risk, Reid Brown for adding extra life through his wry illustrations and Ann Hurst for being my champion and for proving time and again that an exacting editor and friend can be one and the same.

Also to Carol Pogash, whose wit was a great well for me.

And to Annie, my wife, who imagined the story alongside me, read my raw material, added her own spirit and grace and otherwise prevented me from making a complete fool of myself.

Also to Joel Fishman, my literary agent and magnificent warrior, and Bob Mecoy at Simon & Schuster, who gave my words another home and kept everything in order and did so with a firm, steady hand and sense of humor.

Finally, to all the sources whose expertise, insights, perspectives and good cheer I was able to harvest for these pages. I owe them the biggest debt of all.

# chapter 1

**Brad Roth was in no shape to drive to work.** Even looking at his hands made him wince in pain. At least she had loaned him her Range Rover. His Porsche would have killed him. He would have needed both hands on the wheel. The Rover had power steering and an automatic transmission. It was more forgiving than the Porsche. He could steer with his wrists, his only recourse since both hands were fully swathed in gauze. A flash fire had sautéed his fingertips and palms the night before. His hands throbbed as if he were still holding the embers. His right eyebrow was missing.

Elizabeth, Brad's wife, had her own early client meeting at the firm. She couldn't drive him. She could barely spare the time to fix the kids' school lunches, knot his Ralph Lauren rep tie and remind him in that patronizing way of hers that he was in California now and needed to loosen up his wardrobe.

All that mattered was the pain and the boss's words ringing in his ears: "Be there by 8 A.M. sharp. Show time. It'll be a killer." The call had come late the night before, just after Brad got home from the ER at Stanford Hospital.

Now, it was the morning after and Brad gingerly headed south on Interstate 280 ("The World's Most Beautiful Highway," according to Caltrans), checking out his tie in the rear-view mirror and listening to the KCBS traffic reporter chirp about a jackknifed big rig near the Shoreline exit on Highway 101 and the normal backup on the Nimitz from Newark to Milpitas and cheerfully remind probably a million solo commuters to carpool and "spare the air."

As he turned onto Highway 85 heading toward Cupertino and entered the diamond lane, the pain flared up. Brad whimpered and tried to breathe as if he were leading a Lamaze class.

His passenger sat erect and silent in the shotgun seat, conveying not one bit of sympathy. She had been silent from the time Brad maneuvered the hunter green Rover out the driveway in Old Palo Alto and onto the Oregon Expressway and into the impossible traffic that Xerox PARC had spawned years ago along Page Mill Road.

"This is unbee-lee-vable," Brad shouted angrily and pathetically. He was feeling a bit disconnected.

The night before, the night of the accident, he'd come in late, as usual. Elizabeth had gotten home much earlier. The kids were in bed and so was she, propped up and scanning a letter to the SEC on behalf of a deep-pockets client. The latest copy of *Vanity Fair* lay on the floor.

"Brad, is that you?" she called when he came into their bed-room.

"Who the hell did you think it was? The contractor?" He had been in a foul mood all day. Maybe weeks. Maybe a couple of months.

When a forty-year-old white male with a deadly jump shot but lacking an MBA or EE degree gets fired for making a joke, the world becomes a worse place. That's how he saw it, anyway, and he was more than a little bitter.

He'd been on the Team. The team for the Windows 95 launch. As a marketing guy, he'd helped spend the $200 million Microsoft had devoted purely for advertising for the roll-out. Some of his ideas had actually sailed, although he wouldn't publicly take credit for the inspiration to secure the rights to use the Stones' "Start Me Up" for the launch's anthem. It was against company protocol to take credit for anything. But privately, at the kids' soccer games or over wine with nonindustry friends, he was not above letting loose a few details. After all, the August 24, 1995 launch had been the biggest single thing to hit the Seattle area since Ken Griffey, Jr. Maybe ever.

Only a week before the launch date, Brad made the fatal slip of the tongue. Chalk it up to fatigue. Or his penchant for self-destruction, as Elizabeth had suggested. Who knew? But obviously, he had let his guard down.

Over satay with two R&D guys in a cool new pan-Pacific place in a strip mall not far from Microsoft's Redmond campus, Brad had said simply, "Windows 95 equals Mac 89."

That's all.

The waiter took the check and Brad noticed that he took his sweet time returning. When he did, he wore a sheepish look. "Sorry, Mr. Roth, your company credit card has been declined."

Brad got a bad feeling.

Back in the marketing pod of the leafy, lawny Microsoft campus, he could tell the pink slip in his mailbox was a different shade from the ones that showed up randomly and usually contained stock options.

Alone in his office, Brad shut the door and started his 166 MHz multitasking Pentium-processor PC with the 6X CD-ROM, Vibra 16-bit sound card and 80-watt amplified speakers. Usually, the first thing that greeted him on the screen after the insipid "Where do you want to go today?" slogan was the WinQuote—the hourly update of Microsoft NASDAQ stock prices.

This news item often inspired him to call Elizabeth.

"Honey, we just made four grand," he would announce.

"How much did Bill make?" she would reply, pretending to be disinterested. Brad chalked it up to the inhuman demands the firm made on his wife, an up-and-coming securities lawyer.

This time though, there was no WinQuote. There was only a single e-mail:

    You have not been selected to fill your current
    position. If you wish to talk further, I am always
    available through billg@Microsoft.com. Bill.

Which led to the move south to Silicon Valley.

It had been relatively quick. The Valley was booming again, and Brad didn't even have to hit the employment section of the *San Jose Mercury News*. Old buddies from San Jose State had been surfing the Net and had come across a remarkable home page of a startup being put together by one of the all-time legends of the Valley. The guy, J. P. McCorwin, had worn a diamond-stud earring and black leather since way back before *Wired* made cyberpunk fashionable. This guy was going around saying, "Nothing in this world is so powerful as an idea whose time has come," which Brad vaguely remembered hearing in a college lit course. In any case, his buddies, who were all more or less in the industry, insisted that this guy was one of the hippest fifty-year-olds left out there.

The motto on his company home page was: "You fail, you fail, you fail, and then you KILL!"

The guy'd had a couple of spectacular failures already. Venture capitalists love that. He was probably due for a hit. That's what Brad's buddies told him.

As head of product development of Infinity Computer, the Valley's tabernacle of technological theology and digitalized human potential, J. P. McCorwin had always been out there. When he jumped, he wore the longest bungee cord. His newest products were built with one thing in mind—to change the world. In other words, to change client-server interface with reality for all time. His products were always touted sincerely as the very latest next best things.

"Come on down, Bradster. We see a red Ferrari in your future," his buddies chorused and broke into "It's now or never," and made plans to get together for a little bachelor reunion at Gordon Biersch brewpub in Palo Alto.

Brad e-mailed McCorwin and was surprised to get a return the very same day. He was on a plane to San Jose the next. Elizabeth was a bit more dubious. But then, she was employed. Still, she called some old Stanford Law School chums at Wilson, Sonsini, and they were all encouraging. She could land anywhere in the Valley, they reassured her. Business was exploding. There were more than enough billable hours to go around.

Which led, in dizzyingly short order, to Brad having a rather impressive Chinese takeout lunch with J.P., who explained he needed a savvy marketing type for an idea ahead of its time. "Something that kisses the Internet full on the lips, unlike Microsoft, which keeps turning the other cheek," he said.

Brad felt the hot twinge of revenge and said, "Yes." He was anointed head of marketing right then and there, even before he finished his lemon chicken.

"We'll discuss the terms later," J.P. said. "There'll be plenty of incentive bennies, I assure you." This led to Elizabeth making a lateral move for an even bigger salary at one of the Valley's high-powered law firms and to an $898,999 three-bedroom, two-bath bungalow "loaded with possibilities" on one of those streets named after dead poets in Old Palo Alto, to a bumper sticker on Elizabeth's Rover that proclaimed the operator to be a "Proud Jordan Middle School Parent," and to the kids feeling short-changed. If they were going to move to Silicon Valley, their dad could have at least gone to work for a "really cool company" like Silicon Graphics, which made 3-D dinosaurs and graphics for MTV and presidential candidates.

So Brad was now shooting down the diamond lane on a dusky October morning with his passenger, an inflatable, human-looking, plastic dummy riding shotgun, heading for his nearly two-month-old job in Cupertino. The dummy was anatomically female, but her ethnicity was open to interpretation, in keeping with the start-up's quest for a "perfect balance of racial diversity." The dummy, the Human Resources person pointed out, was part of the Essential Employee perk package, along with a cell phone, mobile fax, tickets to Sharks games, a schedule of in-house tai chi classes, his nomination to the in-house Values Task Force, a book of coupons for Round Table Pizza ("you have kids, right?") and a laptop, the latest of Infinity Computer's FirePower 9500 line, with the 1.1 GB hard drive and 32 MBs of RAM, not to mention a really huge power management system that gave the battery six times the endurance of any competitor, including the Apple PowerBook, all in an indestructible-looking, cobalt-colored plastic carrying case.

"It is essential that you be punctual," she had said, with what Brad took as a little too much authority. "The chairman has vowed to do anything to enhance essentiality and punctuality. If it means circumventing the traffic tie-ups...we are all entrepreneurs, aren't we?"

That first day he was shown through the teal, mauve and black carpeted hallway to his small corner office, where he had a view of his neighbors in a strip mall along Stevens Creek Boulevard. There was a Safeway, a Longs Drug, an Egghead Software, a Noah's Bagels, Starbucks, Chili's, basically nothing to suggest that he had just left one place near the West Coast of America for another. Even his own building was generic: low-slung, three-story, white, trimmed in Canyonlands Red, with a band of tinted glass orbiting the middle level like wraparound shades.

Not long after he finished loading application software and

began making file transfers, one of those life-changing events occurred. Brad got his first e-mail, a come-hithergram, and it was rather explicit and shocking.

He fired back, playing it completely straight, although he had never been above being playful.

```
Sorry, got this by mistake. (BRoth).
```

```
No Brad. I've had my eye on you since you signed
up with payroll. I like the cut of your Calvin
Kleins. By the way, no use reporting this to the
big boss, he encourages it. It's more efficient
than going to lunch or to the Ramada. So just go
with it. (RoseD).
```

He called Human Resources. Which D had the first name Rose? "No one."

His curiosity was aroused.

About a month into the correspondence, Brad was more than a little distracted and peeved at RoseD. Through e-mail, they had made at least half a dozen dates, all broken. He had reserved a table at Fontana's. She never showed. He had waited in the parking lot of the Decathlon Club. No sight of her.

Always an excuse. Always elusive. He didn't even know what department she worked in. He didn't know what she looked like, at least not specifically, although she e-mailed:

```
My personal trainer says I'm gorgeous. So does
my rock-climbing coach. (RoseD).
```

He roamed the hallways when he should have been assisting with the birth of a business plan. He tried not to look as though he was on the prowl. But he was definitely checking out the women and they could probably tell. There were four or five, all in their midtwenties, all fit, all wound pretty tight. He could guess they were intelligent. But which one was leading him on? Which one was RoseD?

Elizabeth was pretty much like them. Such incredible self-assurance. You could hear it in the clack of the heels of her Bruno Maglis every weekday morning as she strode across the terracotta floor of their fabulously lit gourmet kitchen, with European cabinetry and top-of-the-line appliances, including the six-burner Wolf range that was the pièce de résistance for buying the house in the first place. That and the terrific school district, which the Realtor from Coldwell Banker had assured them was worth at least an extra $100,000. The house still needed some work, such as a second story. But, hey, the market was heating up. Appreciation would solve everything.

Brad walked in. Elizabeth didn't look up. He leaned over and gave her an obligatory peck on the cheek.

"How was your day? Any cold wine in the fridge?" he asked without breaking stride on the way to the kitchen. He pulled the cork from a half-full bottle of 1993 Hacienda chardonnay, weekday stuff that Elizabeth had picked up for $4.99 at Trader Joe's, and padded into his corner of the family room, which doubled as a study when the kids weren't watching MTV or lobbing flamers over the Internet.

Brad half-closed the door, cradling his FirePower laptop in his lap, sat back, booted up, moved his finger along the trackpad until he came to AOL, and clicked. A password, a few clicks later, and she was there.

    SUBJ: SEX
    DATE: 95/10/30 1:30 EST
    TO: BRoth
    Well? I'm waiting in People Connection, Lobby
    37. (RoseD).

He clicked open the door. She was there, all right.

BRoth: Rose, ready to go private?

RoseD: Of course, silly. With what I'm wearing, you wouldn't want me too public. Would you?


Brad could feel his chest get heavy and his breathing accelerate. He was obtuse and fumbling at first, even trying humor. But she reminded him that the meter on his Visa card was ticking.

So he let loose and she responded in kind.

Faster and faster his fingers flew at the keyboard. His sentences got shorter and she matched him, stroke for stroke. It was totally transcendental. He could feel something building, an inner fire, a flame.

That's when the pain struck.

"Elizabeth!" he screamed. "Help me. My laptop blew up. I'm hurt."

# chapter 2

**Brad was two minutes late to the conference room.** He slid into a seat, joining the handful of other so-called department heads at the oblong conference table without drawing attention to his hands. J.P. was already at the whiteboard. With a dry-erase marker, he drew a time line, marking off performance in vertical slashes. As he drew, the events began bunching closer together and the line headed in an ever-steepening decline.

Everyone knew the events by heart. But this exercise was becoming a ritual, like daily tai chi on the lawn and take-out Chinese food in the reception pod:

There was the birth, twenty years before, of Infinity Computer, when two post-adolescents emerged from a garage, shading their eyes from the sun and holding a clumsy-looking gray box they felt certain would change the world. Then there was the birth of the Cynthia, the first so-called upgrade, which crashed in flames, followed by another, the Layla, which was beautiful but barely had enough market strength to leave the nest. That was old history. As head of product development, the boss had been part of the old history.

"Creating art is one thing," he said, paraphrasing Apple co-founder Steve Jobs, whom he had once described as his archenemy. "Shipping is another. Great artists ship."

Now, John Peter McCorwin, founder, chairman and CEO of this emerging company, would make new history with the help of some like-minded individuals. And this history would spring forth from a moribund company: Infinity.

"For now, we'll be so lean and mean and quick, we won't even carry a name," he said with intense self-certainty, acquired during a grueling weeklong Outward Bound management retreat at the Golden Door in southern California. And he began paraphrasing one of his fifty or so favorite authors, Victor Hugo. "For we are after supreme happiness. The supreme happiness of life is the conviction that we will be loved."

A fit, cannily casual-looking bachelor in his early fifties, he looked ten years younger, partly because he had a full head of tousled blond hair that just might be gray when observed in the right light. "More gorgeous than handsome," the women said, and the men did not argue. Most men did not understand him. Why, if he was so damn charming, wasn't he married?

J.P. had a way of making everyone suspicious, even those who were charmed by him. He was blessed with expressive eyes that could turn merry or threatening in an instant, just as he could make them sincere, sad and tearful on command. He exuded a magnetic sense of sorcery, a reality distortion field that could change anyone's belief platform if they listened long enough. He also possessed the essential element common to all the Valley's major players—an enormous ego—and was not beneath comparing himself to the next coming of Voltaire, "another epoch."

Indeed, his moral construct was assembled between early Jesuit seminary training in Los Gatos, engineering school at Stanford and a graduate student cell at the Sorbonne, where he met Pierre Coupole, his alter ego and friend for life, who persuaded him to toss over Catholicism, polish his French, accept existentialism, and refocus. If there was a moment for his self-construct, it would have been during a virtual stroll in the garden with St. Francis or sometime between the post-Napoleonic era and the day Jim Morrison died, to be updated every so often, say with Jerry Garcia's death, as he was "always open to inspiration."

He had intrigued the broad thinkers at Xerox PARC in the hills near Stanford and landed a job that required him to do little more than look and listen. When the guys at Infinity announced they were going to change the world, he persuaded them he could fit right in as head of the social implications division of R&D. Later he took over product development itself.

His tenure had been fabulously tumultuous. He had convinced the chairman to let him run free and unfettered by any budget. During his dozen years, he had overseen a dazzling array of ideas that arose out of his own intuition and that of his French anarchist friend. Their ideas were transformed into products that defined both narcissism and overpricing and excited everyone except consumers and financial analysts.

Through Infinity, J. P. McCorwin acquired something of a rogue reputation, which he encouraged with his signature stud earring, a rainbow array of T-shirts and a black leather Armani jacket. Once, he had been invited to guest-conduct the San Jose Symphony, but declined when the musical director would not allow him to slip in a number by Sinead O'Connor. He did, however, accept an invitation to toss the coin at an Oakland Raiders football game, and even the unruly drunks stood and applauded him as one of their own.

Finally, with the board of directors closing in, and after pleading his case passionately and eloquently to the press in what seemed a reenactment of *Les Misérables,* he was marched to the corporate gallows and handed his head. "Thrown out like the end of a fine cigar," he said in an interview with *MacWorld* magazine.

He dropped out of sight. It was rumored he had gone to a remote corner to work in a mission with Mother Teresa. It was also said that he became a yak herder, a wildlife photographer, a Zen novice, a road manager for Eric Clapton, a melatonin addict, and later that he was reposing in a monastery on a Tibetan mountain flank overlooking the Jokhang Temple in Lhasa. When he showed up in the Bay Area again, it was as a talk show host for a Green FM radio station in Berkeley, and people speculated that he might be ready to launch a political career, which his father, a former heavy in the state Democratic Party, had urged him to do.

But he had recently reread *The Agony and the Ecstasy,* the biography of Michelangelo, and *The Fountainhead* by Ayn Rand, and concluded it was his destiny to restore order and dignity to technology. That would be like serving God.

He recruited Pierre, who had changed his name to Baba RAM DOS and acquired a 1947 Indian motorcyle (burnt red) and a ponytail just before he, too, had been offed in the bloodbath at Infinity. "We'll share our bitterness and channel it toward a right and proper and prosperous revenge," he promised his old friend and named him his No. 2.

J.P. bought a house in Woodside near enough to Neil Young to call himself a neighbor, outfitted it with an industrial-strength workstation, a Bose sound system, a Soloflex, and some fiber-optic cables. He discovered some back alleys on the Well, the possibilities of interactive television and voice recognition, and collected himself once and for all. When he came down from the mountain, it was with his ever-present charm, sanctimonious self-assurance and the ease with which he could summon Hugo: "I am for religions, not religion," or borrow a line from RAM DOS: "We forgot that a life of Infinity was not made of a series of orgasms, but also of love," and he created the biggest buzz in the Valley since there were blossoms and bees.

And when he roared up and down Highway 280 in his cobalt Mercedes 600 SL convertible with LUVBYTS personalized plates, people would recognize J. P. McCorwin and they would say, "There goes a visionary scorned. At least he's kept his sense of humor."

John Peter McCorwin was now taking his sense of humor all the way to the venture capitalists on Sand Hill Road in Menlo Park and in San Francisco's Financial District and to anyone else he thought was worthy enough to recognize the gleam in his eye.

It was rumored that some of his money had come from France or a rock star he had been dating or from Steven Spielberg, or from equally questionable sources, possibly in Marin County. It might have been his well-reported line about Bill Gates and Andy Grove ("the only remaining dictators besides Castro in the entire Western Hemisphere") that eased his reentry. But that was just one of hundreds of things to speculate on when J.P. let word that he was starting a startup with a quote from Voltaire:

"I have never made but one prayer to God, a very short one: 'Oh, Lord, make my enemies ridiculous.' And God granted it."

J.P. was back in full voice and black leather jacket. Once again, a pirate flag was flying over the Valley. And it was probably no coincidence that the Raiders returned to Oakland from Los Angeles. This distracted people for a few moments from the panic caused by Infinity Computer's troubles combined with the on-slaught of the Windows/Intel Axis, aka Wintel.

The once-high-and-mighty computer company had released its quarterly earnings report just the week before. And the company's death rattle vibrated across video display screens throughout the world.

J.P. noted this on his time line. Earnings were down nearly 50 percent from the previous quarter, which analysts had declared a disaster—this was worse than anyone had predicted. Stock prices had been dropping steadily for months. Infinity couldn't get key components. It couldn't get its computers delivered. It couldn't even keep its highly respected No. 2 guy from telling anyone who would listen that if the world were truly a good place, the board of directors would focus on the horizon and sell the company for salvage. And then the company couldn't even keep its No. 2 guy or the next No. 2 guy. Its product development guys hadn't come up with a next-best-thing in years, since J.P. and Baba RAM DOS had left.

And if that weren't enough, there was a grotesquely embarrassing problem with the FirePower 9500 high-performance laptops. They kept spontaneously combusting.

Brad started to raise both hands. But the chairman was on a roll, holding forth, dancing around the conference table and back to the whiteboard as deftly as Deion Sanders doing a bump-and-run.

He also reminded his fledgling management team, "All we have to do is glance northward toward Seattle, or across the Valley to Santa Clara. What do we see? The long shadow of the Microsoft-Intel Axis. It is getting longer. Go into any Peet's Coffee or the software section at Fry's or CompUSA. What do you find? Terror. We are in dark times.

"We are as Paris was in 1940, waiting for the jackboots to march down the Champs Élysées. Listen. Can you hear? They're coming down El Camino Real. They are threatening to squeeze the joie de vivre out of every single operating system that isn't Wintel."

His disciples sat spellbound, except for RAM DOS, who'd heard it all before, and Brad Roth, who was distracted by pain and wondering how he was going to finally meet RoseD. Maybe he'd tell her face-to-face that the laptop fire might have been a sign from God. Maybe they should end their e-mail romance. Or so his head told him.

"We are at a time of terrible peril. We are at a time of solemnity and fear. But also of great romance and heroism," J.P. continued, looking around the table and summoning a nod from RAM DOS.

He looked at his communications chief, an attractive woman in her early thirties with a Stanford MBA and experience at IBM, Sun Microsystems, and Infinity. Maria Isabel Cisneros also happened to be Mexican-American and able to converse in Japanese.

He looked at a couple of guys who passed for the R&D department, who looked up from the games they were playing on their handheld personal digital assistants just in time to meet his eye. And he looked at Brad Roth, who sensed his cue and held up both bandaged hands.

"It got me last night," Brad said, forcing a smile. "Right in the middle of a file transfer."

Everyone gasped. Except the chairman. He seemed delirious with glee.

"You mean one of our, I mean their, FirePower test models actually did it for one of our own guys? Blew up right in your lap? Brad, come up here and share everything."

# chapter 3

**Brad Roth was the fifth victim of laptop combustion.** Or rather, he had participated in the fifth such incident. But he was the only one injured and the only one to have suffered the hazard at home. Two other laptops had gone off during remote product testing at Infinity. Two had gone off in J.P.'s office within days after he borrowed them to figure out what the bug was all about.

But that was enough to make the industry watchers murmur "epidemic." Which was exactly why J. P. McCorwin had persuaded the Infinity folks to let him secretly take a crack at extinguishing things before there was an outbreak of potentially fatal publicity.

And now, Maria Cisneros was summoning all of her considerable self-control as Brad shared how the company-issue laptop more or less blew up in his lap. He was obviously in pain and laboring to tell a coherent, believable story. But she was at the threshold of bursting into uncontrollable laughter, wondering which parts besides his hands and face got burned.

The guy had a wandering eye. She often felt herself in his radar lock. And so did her female colleagues. They joked about him at lunch, comparing notes, and each of them told of at least one instance of either being approached by him in the hall or being asked furtively over e-mail: R You Rose?

So he thinks in cliches, thinks that because I am obviously Mexican-American that I have this sultry *nombre de amor*? That I'm some sort of generic Rose? she thought. He thinks I live a double life—that I sing in a Tejano band, cruise El Camino in the back seat of a low-rider?

Actually, Maria's DayRunner contained the phrase: "Get a life!" spaced at appropriate intervals, along with the reminder: "Floss!"

She was just thirty-two, sinuous and beautiful, like her Aunt Evelyn, prima ballerina of the San Francisco Ballet. All her friends told her that.

"You should get out more," they told her. Usually it was at her place in Los Gatos on Thursday nights, when she and her friends gathered for potluck and watched *Friends*, followed by *ER*. Or worse, when they all ended up pumping iron and hitting the Stairmaster on Friday night. (The seriously upscale Decathlon Club was not her workout hangout of choice, but it was, her friends insisted, "the best place in the Valley to network while you puff and buff.") Actually, the only part of her life that really gave her unguilty pleasure was Fuego, her leased chestnut Thoroughbred. She reserved Sunday mornings for him and tried to jam in another ride at least one weekday morning. But she knew it couldn't last. Her new work schedule was seeing to that. She and her horse were becoming estranged. Fuego deserved better. Both of them knew it.

She was the daughter of a retired vineyard foreman who had worked all his life for the Messalini family on land that was under lovely and prosperous bloom when Maria and her two sisters were growing up.

Her sister Paula, thirty-six, was born the same year the microcircuit was born at Fairchild Camera in South San Jose. Her younger sister, Alessandra, was twenty-nine. As the sisters grew up, the high-tech boom took its toll on the orchards and vineyards that their father, Ramon Cisneros, and his friends had worked. The farmland beneath the east foothills was steadily being parceled and sold to developers. Much of it became known as "the Evergreen," a malapropism once the trees and vines were gone.

In any case, Maria, Paula, now an engineer working for a high-tech company outside Boston, and Alessandra, now married with two kids and living in Contra Costa County, grew up with farm animals and friendly ranch hands and work routines that taxed everyone. "We were needed," Maria remembered saying during one job interview. "That's how you felt. Needed. It was a privilege to feel needed."

Ramon Cisneros insisted that his daughters study hard, and all three graduated from San Jose State University. Maria, with chiseled facial contours and open, fiery green eyes, was judicious with her warmth and quick wit and won people over. She had an active social life and still managed to graduate with honors. On half a lark, she applied to Stanford Business School and was elated, but not totally surprised, when she was accepted. When she graduated, she traveled to Europe and Asia. She took a job working for IBM in Tokyo, where she improved upon the Japanese language skills she had pursued as extracurricular self-enlightenment at Stanford and became adept in the Japanese workplace.

Maria had been stimulated by the business pace but felt buried socially in Japan, because women were an underclass. She longed to come home. When a position opened up in the communications department at IBM in Almaden Valley, she took it. She renewed friendships, dropped in on her parents, leased a horse and bought herself a red BMW 325i convertible.

At work, she acquitted herself well but worried from time to time whether her looks, her gender, her ethnicity had given her some advantage, just as they might have helped open the door to grad school. Which bothered her. She kept worrying even after she was snapped up by Regis McKenna, the dean of the Valley's high-tech marketing gurus, best known for his ability to polish the image of Apple Computer and that of Infinity, the account to which she was assigned.

Immediately, she learned the value of networking and gained a full appreciation for what her boss evangelized as the "essentials of respecting the infrastructure of the Valley," which meant ideas and how to market them and make everyone feel better about themselves if their ideas made money.

She also learned the value of illusion, particularly when she was told that once an editor at *Forbes* magazine had written a short note saying: "Please drop us from your mailing list. . . . We are simply not interested in covering small companies such as Intel," then one of McKenna's emerging clients. So she learned to stage events—pitch circus tents, make things seem bigger than they were. When things went right, at least in the minds of the press, things actually did get bigger—Intel being chief among the beneficiaries of such early illusions.

She was lured away by Scott McNealy himself, whom she bumped into one night at the pool table at the Dutch Goose in Menlo Park. She thought he was cute. He bought her a beer and extolled Sun Microsystems' workstations as well as his prowess as an amateur hockey player and golfer and enlightened human being who had personally discovered the last best bottom line at his company's campus in Mountain View and needed someone to help tell the story of his fabulous, emerging wisdom: "Life's like hockey. You shoot. You score. Or you don't." He offered Maria a job. She took it with reservations, then left after about six months.

She worked as an outside consultant and had a hand in drafting the initial prospectuses for two small companies that went public. One bombed. One launched. The one that flew, the one someone said was like "using Jet Skis to surf the Internet," made some people, some of them much younger than herself, very rich. That broadened her mind.

It was about this time that J. P. McCorwin began calling around to find out who put together the Internet IPO deal.

When he contacted Maria, he was very charming.

"Lunch." It was not a question. He suggested Birk's in Santa Clara. "Great grilled chicken Caesars."

It was her baseline meal. How'd he know?

"Let me try something out on you," he said, his eyes dancing. "I'm thinking of asking Danielle Steel to write for one of the software programs I'm planning. It will be called 'How Do You Know When You're Really in Love?' "

That made Maria laugh. "She already has her own vanity press." She didn't let on that she was very familiar with the frothy romance novelist through books on tape.

"No, I'm serious," J.P. said. "If I can bring Danielle in, I can probably land her boyfriend, Tom Perkins. You've heard of him?"

She pretended not to be offended. Of course. Mr. Venture Capital had launched Tandem Computers and, as one of the heads of Kleiner Perkins Caufield & Byers—KP as it was known in the trade—had bestowed millions on startups, including Genentech, Lotus, Sun and dozens of others occupying the roster of the Fortune 500.

"I want to congratulate you on your part in the prospectus. Such economy of style and yet so moving," J.P. had said, leaning across the table. "By the way, did you get in on any of the stock?"

"No," she said, embarrassed and feeling exposed. She poked her fork at a piece of romaine.

"Hmmm," he murmured, pausing significantly, studying her. "I feel sad for you. Is it because you're not a gambler? You're afraid to play the game?"

"What do you mean?" she asked.

"Are you afraid? To gamble? Do you or do you not believe in the value of your own sweat equity?"

Maria started to answer, but J.P. leaned closer.

"Look, I'm putting together a company that will have one mission—to come up with the last best thing. Not peripherals. Not some pissant little server like Netscape. I mean a platform to end all platforms, to do what Infinity and Apple and all the others promised they would do: Change the world."

His eyes were aglow.

"How would you like to own a piece of this new world? It's the company I'm forming. Toss in maybe $10,000 or $20,000 for seed money, add some sweat equity and we're partners. Think about it."

"Look, I'm a farmworker's daughter," she said, borrowing a line from herself that she used only when feeling cornered.

"Come off it," J.P. said. "We both know you've got star potential. The question is, do you have ambition?"

The words sounded threatening. But his eyes were not.

"So how are you going to change the world?" she asked.

"I'm not ready to say," he answered. "I will, though, after I've gathered a critical mass of brains and energy. Together, we can leverage our ideas into a big payoff—for our clients, our investors and us."

He leaned closer still. "So. Are you game?"

Maria sensed it would be the last time he would ask. She was struck by his spiritual intensity, drawn to reading his lips, even as a voice in her head said, A killer IPO. Everyone's doing it. This is the Valley.

J.P. was kind of sexy, a thought she quickly pushed out of her mind. But she was aware of her head moving up and down affirmatively. Without actually speaking the word *yes*, she took the job.

And now, a couple of months later, she was listening to Brad

Roth finish the account of his injuries, and she was feeling some urgency toward the road ahead. She also made a note to herself right after Brad said, "And boy, was Elizabeth ever p.o.'d. She had to get the kids out of bed and drive us all to the emergency room."

*Not getting along at home*, Maria doodled. And she was going to have to work with this guy.

# chapter 4

**J. P. McCorwin thanked his wounded**
**marketing director** for demonstrating just what
laptop combustion could do.

"And now, we have arrived at a moment I almost couldn't wait
to share with you," he said, switching off the main light and booting up the Power Mac, which projected an image onto the whiteboard. There, bearing the circular Infinity logo, was a contract.

"This is top secret," he said, fiercely glancing around the room and looking like General George Patton must have on the eve of leading the U.S. Army across the Rhine. "It has been worked out between the chairman of Infinity Computer and me. It calls for our company to put out the fire burning in the belly of their equipment. Again, secret. If the word gets out that they outsourced to get things taken care of . . .

"The real point is that we just got $2 million from Infinity. This may not sound like a whole hell of a lot, but there's a nugget here that could lead to the whole damn mother lode. I've worked for that company, I know where their desperation threshold lies. They're approaching it. They've got a poison Tylenol problem; they've got a Pentium meltdown problem," he said, not laughing.

"They're manufacturing laptops that go *whomp* in the night. We've product-tested them, am I right, Brad?"

Brad arched a nonexistent right eyebrow and saluted with his gauze-swaddled right hand.

"What they've got is a terrific PR problem, and what we've got is a terrific PR gestalt," nodding toward Baba RAM DOS, his No. 2 guy, and Maria Cisneros, head of his communications team of one. "This contract means more than scoring a secret alliance with Infinity. It should prove that I am back in the game."

He let the gravity of all that sink in for a moment.

The night before, he and RAM DOS (who J.P. still privately called Pete) had celebrated with a three-hour dinner at the semi-discreet Le Mouton Noir in Saratoga. They embellished the meal with a bottle of '87 Heitz Martha's Vineyard Cabernet, followed by a distinguished Griotte Chambertin "for old times' sake."

"To think they tossed me out like the dregs of this bottle," J.P. muttered, draining the last drops of the Burgundy just as a half-bottle of '86 Barsac arrived for dessert. "You know, Pete, I thought about becoming a hopeless alcoholic or a survivalist for revenge. But this is better. It shows that hearts are big. It shows that anything is possible in this Valley. You can take any leap of faith."

J.P.'s eyes welled with tears, and he struggled for control.

Baba, a onetime est trainer, sensed his duty to console. "They squeezed the orange and threw away the skin," he said, invoking Voltaire.

J.P. surrendered what was left of his composure. He grabbed his old friend in a clumsy hug, passion propelling his words. "God, I love this place."

"Suit yourself," Baba-Pete said, pouring another glass of the pricey sauterne. "You always do."

Now J.P. stood before his disciples, his eyes still moist and repeating the lines he'd tested on his friend.

Sounds like he's rehearsing for his own press conference, Maria thought. But she couldn't discount the charge J.P. had generated. Energy was flying around the room like loose electrons.

As if on cue, a red light blinked on the interoffice phone. Absentmindedly, J.P. clicked on the conference button.

"Fire in R&D! Fire in R&D! We've got a flaming laptop down here!"

"Let's go!" J.P. said.

The entire department head group—"the J.P. Pod"—filed out briskly but in an orderly manner so as not to panic the two-person support staff. Down the hall they went, down the stairs, past the workout pod, past the kick-back pod, to R&D.

Brad and Maria were striding nearly shoulder to shoulder behind J.P. when Brad turned and said, once again: "RoseD?"

Maria ignored him. Besides, the sharp, metallic odor of an electrical fire was already assaulting her senses as they reached the doorway. Inside, hazy blue smoke hung close to the floor.

"Where are the damned extinguishers?" a panicked voice shouted from somewhere in the smoke.

A silhouette appeared, beating its chest in a primordial manner. J.P. grabbed the figure and threw it to the floor. Heroically, he peeled off his own leather jacket, which he used to smother what looked to be a thousand points of light.

"My God," Maria said. "His chest hairs are on fire!"

The victim turned out to be one of the new programmers J.P.

had hired to develop software for a speech recognition application. At least that was the cover story. But everyone in the building knew that the guy was developing software for decoding any Netscape-preemptive avatars Wintel might be experimenting with. The project was supposed to be top secret, but at least around the building the word was out that he had found a virtual path into the Wintel coders' pod. It was only a matter of time before J.P. would have his hands on a trophy trade secret.

"What in the hell were you doing in the laptop quadrant, trying to turn it into Chernobyl?" J.P. asked, rather harshly, when the smoke had cleared.

The guy, Jason something-or-other, buttoned what was left of his aloha shirt, straightened his ponytail and his orange shorts and mumbled: "Hey, I just wanted to check out how fast I could make the thing run Flying Toasters."

J.P. regained his composure and tossed his jacket toward a trash can, where it landed Armani label up.

"Everyone, stay in your own quadrant unless you check with one of us first," barked Baba RAM DOS, his French accent sounding unequivocal.

Maria and Brad looked at each other. This was a side to the startup neither one had seen before.

J.P. ordered one of the other R&D guys to stand watch over the still-smoldering laptop and to call him if there were any other outbreaks. Then he invited the J.P. Pod back upstairs.

"We just had combustion number six. Do you see? If we don't act on this opportunity, there may be nothing left for us to save," he said, sipping an Odwalla superprotein drink and looking saintly once again. His eyes were wide and fierce but not menacing. He looked intensely intimate, as if he were wooing each of them over candlelight and wine.

"We will succeed in putting out these little fires," he assured them. "But if we succeed with a bigger stroke of genius, who knows? We may be asked to save Infinity for all time."

This drew nervous laughter. But J.P. appeared deadly serious. He squared his jaw in determination and narrowed his eyes. For a moment, Maria thought his eyes looked crazed and menacing. No, she told herself, sitting up stiffly and squaring her shoulders. She dismissed the thoughts as quickly as they came and chided herself for her inclination to see a dark side in everything.

At J.P.'s urging, she and Baba hung back as the others left the conference room.

"How'd I do?" he asked.

"You moved them," Baba said.

Maria nodded. She had been moved, especially when J.P. smothered the fire with his jacket.

"Seriously, if we can do this, if we can restore faith in Infinity, its earnings ratio, its respectability, its soul, we may be able to help turn back the Axis and retake some market share."

He paused, locking his eyes on Maria's. He began again, slower now, drawing out each word, riveting each one in Maria's mind.

"At least, if people believe that we are doing this, then they will love us. I promise this. If we can make them love us . . ."

He hesitated again, letting the words dance into Maria's consciousness and remind her why she had signed on in the first place.

They were participating in a risk of the highest order. But the one thing J.P. had told each of his disciples was probably the most right-on thing about the whole Valley: Risk was the coin of the realm.

Even a failure, if it was brilliant enough to burst across the Valley sky, could be reason enough for being.

"Pretty soon, my friends, we are going to start hiring. Maria, talk to each department head. Let's get ready to go with some employment opportunity ads, but we'll be deliciously vague: software, hardware, Net applications, especially Net applications.

"Let's say something about relational databases that will no longer confine people to their desktops. Let's use words like 'new social order' and 'interface rapport,' stuff like that."

He gestured toward the door and Maria took her cue.

Baba stayed behind.

"We must win hearts and minds before the wallets, eh,

*mon vieux copain?*" J.P. said. He put his arm around his friend's shoulder.

"I want you to draft a memo to leak to the press. Make sure you mention the new fires in the FirePower and make them sound very mysterious and mention the secret contract between us and Infinity. Make this whole thing sound desperate on their part, heroic on ours," J.P. instructed. "I'll give you a couple of quotes, such as how I feel like the Red Adair of Silicon Valley, you know, riding around like a cowboy putting out infernos."

Baba cocked his head and gave J.P. a nonplussed look that J.P. knew well.

"We'll give Maria a trial by fire, so to speak. When the press starts calling, we'll see how fast she is on her feet.

"And one more thing.

"I also want you to do something else. Call the FBI Unabomber Task Force in San Francisco—if it still exists—and ask them if they have ever remotely considered asking their computers at NASA whether Bill Gates had any beefs against authority figures or ever got beat up on the school playground. I'm not suggesting that he'd be that ruthless," J.P. said, running both hands through his short-cropped hair and staring at the ceiling. Thinking. Then laughing. "It might plant a seed. Throw it out there against the wall. See if it sticks. If the press gets hold of that, sees it as a possible competition thing, if the press even got to considering out loud whether Bill Gates would plant a virus . . .

"He's certainly smart enough. Just ask the FBI that. Is Bill Gates smart enough to plant a combustion virus? Let's just get the wheels turning. We could use a little smokescreen right about now."

He patted Baba on the shoulder and winked. "Know what I mean, Pete?"

Baba RAM DOS grinned. He knew indeed. More than anyone, he knew just how savage his old friend could be. And Maria Cisneros was about to find out.

# chapter 5

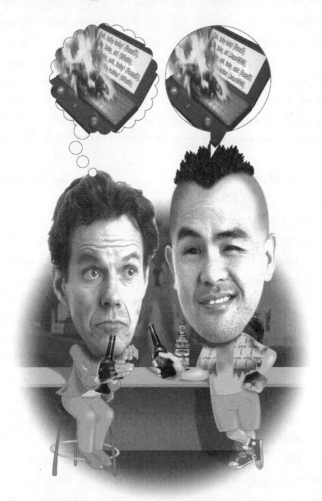

**Brad knew he should have gone home early.** But his hands hurt, and fighting the commuter traffic with the steering wheel in his wrists would have been too risky. He could have caused more havoc out there than normal.

At least that was the excuse.

"Hey, Jason, you want to go out for a drink after work?" he

asked the programmer who, like himself, had been wounded by a combusting laptop.

"Sure thing, dude," Jason said. And Brad thought that he had heard this very accent coming from the television in his very own family room during the kids' very own shows.

"Pete's Pale Ale with a shot of Cuervo Gold," Jason told the bartender at T.G.I. Friday's in the Vallco Fashion Park not far from work. He also beckoned him to lean across the bar. The bartender obliged and Jason spoke to him in low tones. "Pete's Brewing is gonna go public in a couple of weeks. My guys tell me they'll be coming out at $14 or $15. If they're not at $30 by the end of the month, you can shoot me."

The bartender laughed. Jason did not.

Jason turned to Brad, who had ordered a Pete's but no tequila. "I didn't need this hassle."

Brad thought Jason was talking about the remnants of the aloha shirt the laptop had incinerated.

Actually, Jason seemed to enjoy displaying his ashen wounds. And so Brad held up his bandaged hands, asked the bartender for a straw and proposed a toast: "To brothers in flames."

"Cool," Jason said, after downing the tequila in a gulp and chasing it with a prolonged swig of ale.

Brad was curious. *Just who was this guy?*

"I grew up in Santa Cruz," Jason said. "Surfed. A lot. And painted houses. But I had this thing, you know, I could do algorithms. I had them running through my head all the time the way some people do music. You know what I'm saying? Instead of playing the Stones or Nirvana, or counting sheep, I'm like going two to the twenty-fourth equals what? Or I'm saying one, zero, one, zero, or oh, zero, or I'm multiplying twos by twos by twos and coming up with righteous numbers."

He turned to order another drink, and when he did the light shone off the flesh of his scalp, where the hair would have been. At first, Brad thought Jason's hair had been burned away. But upon closer examination, it was obvious Jason had shaved both sides of his scalp. He had the perfect hacker's Mohawk, punctuated by a short ponytail.

"How old are you, anyway?" Brad asked, finding himself slightly lightheaded from drinking through a straw.

"I don't like to give that away. I still have fantasies about getting into the cast of *Baywatch*. Actually, that's only a means to an end. I've got the hots for Pamela Lee. I've actually had fantasies about having modem sex with her. Can you imagine that, having fantasies about virtual sex? I e-mailed her a letter letting her know about it. And she writes back, telling me she's touched."

Brad could not tell for certain whether Jason what's-his-name was putting him on.

"Actually, I'm into an e-mail relationship right now," Jason continued. "Someone in the office. Someone very sexy and elusive. She's really dominant."

He ordered his third shot of tequila. As the bartender poured, Jason confided something else. He told the bartender to bet against the spread in Sunday's game between the Colts and 49ers.

"Steve Young won't last the game. He shouldn't be playing at all," Jason said.

"Why?" Brad asked.

Jason told him what he knew. Everyone knew the All-Star QB had been playing with a sore shoulder. But what Jason knew went beyond common knowledge. He had learned it straight from the doctor's mouth.

"So I've got this place in Santa Clara. It's really too small for all my stuff—couple of Power Macs, big-screen Sony TV, sound system, CDs up the gazoo, Sega Saturn, mountain bike, the usual. But I also have this little gizmo. It's pirated. Basically, it's a receiver. So I've programmed it to scan cell-phone calls. Better yet, I have it programmed to pick up certain cell calls."

Jason stopped talking as a couple of dwerbs still wearing their ID tags from Apple and Tandem elbowed their way to the bar. They ordered beers and started to lean against the oak and polished brass, until Jason shifted aggressively in his seat, squaring his shoulders like a defensive back confronts a runner. This made things uncomfortable, and the dwerbs took their beers elsewhere.

"Anyway, as I was saying, I can pick up certain cell-phone calls. Did you know, for instance, that Steve Jobs plans to take Pixar public on the Monday right after *Toy Story,* the movie they animated, hits the theaters? Lemme tell you something, Jobs owns like 80 percent of the company. So he's planning to price it at $14 a share, initial offering, and this guy from Robertson Stephens, the investment bankers who are handling the thing, comes on and says demand is already so high that they should start at $22. So, Jobs is driving down Highway 280 and the investment banker is telling him he's gonna be worth more than $1 billion in less than a month, and I'm like eavesdropping."

Brad took a big suck of ale. He was impressed.

"What about Steve Young?" he asked.

"Oh, yeah. Well, it seems that one of the 49ers' doctors likes to dictate the results of his examinations to his office machine while he's driving from one office to another or from the training facility. I don't know from where. But I do know that at certain times of the week, I can dial in and get the complete lowdown on various injuries. Lemme tell you, from what I heard last night, Young shouldn't even be playing against the Colts."

The next question was obvious. Jason anticipated it.

"This is valuable info. I know that. I also know that I am a sports fan second, an entrepreneur first. So, if I were you, I would bet now cuz the line's going to start dropping minutes before kickoff when the bookies get into the final action. I can help you make the bet."

They looked directly at each other. Jason was grinning.

"Dude, can you do me a favor in return. OK?"

"Sure, what?" Brad replied.

"You've got some juice in Human Resources, otherwise you wouldn't have that inflatable doll that only the essential employees get, am I right?" the programmer asked.

"Right, I guess," Brad answered.

"So find out something for me, will you? There is this person. Her name is RoseD. Only that's not her real name, OK? That's her screen name. RoseD.

"Find out her real name, OK? We've been having this relationship for a couple of months. But she won't let me get close. I think she's afraid of intimacy or something. Anyway, I almost had her image up on the screen. But just as the pixels were coming together, poof, the laptop goes off. . . . I gotta talk to this RoseD. I'm like crazy about her."

Brad nearly choked on his drink. He felt as if the burn in his hands had flooded his guts. He felt rage. He felt faint.

"I'll try," he sputtered. "But no promises."

# chapter 6

**Brad was too preoccupied to deliver himself wholeheartedly** to the self-congratulatory mood that was raging wildly through his house, his neighborhood, and, he guessed, the entire town.

What set things off was a story on page one of the *Mercury News*. A magazine called *American Demographics* had named the Stanford community the nation's smartest spot. The report stemmed from the percentage of adults twenty-five and older with at least a bachelor's degree.

This was a dangerous provocation, virtually waving a red cloth in front of a bull. No, like waving a red flag in front of an entire herd.

The way Brad read the story, the way it appeared in the newspaper, was that the status the magazine heaped on Stanford was because the campus was considered a separate community, census-wise. So its resident population of professors and grad students pretty much skewed the results. Palo Alto, he pointed out at the breakfast table, ranked seventy-first, not first.

This observation was not without hazard, which he had already calculated before he offered the caveat.

"Palo Alto and Stanford are the same. It has always been that way, except during the Vietnam War protests," Elizabeth snapped, a little reflexively, Brad thought. He had expected this reaction. He also caught the familiar look of contempt in her eye, just before her head disappeared under the cardinal and white sweatshirt she was throwing on dramatically over her white J. Crew polo shirt.

"You actually going to wear that to work?" Brad asked, grinning. "It's only Thursday. I thought Friday was dress-down day."

She didn't answer. Instead she took up conversation with Winston, their golden retriever. Winston was the only household member Elizabeth talked to first thing in the morning. Winston was also the first to be patted in the morning and the last at night.

Brad tried to act indifferent to her displaced affection. In fact, indifference was a Zen-like defense mechanism he had been working on the past few months with help from his company's Human Resources department. He had laughed when he first heard the term "irreconcilable indifference" and used it to describe some couples he and Elizabeth knew. But now the concept was beginning to take shape, practically speaking.

It was his way of fending off situations that sometimes led to exchanges between them, which sometimes led to the inference that Brad might not be quite as smart as Elizabeth.

"You know," Elizabeth would tell him when Brad's temperature started to rise, "when I feel stupidity coming on, or when I am dead wrong, I usually keep quiet about it."

On this particular morning, the exchange went like this:

Brad to Elizabeth: "Where I am going to work, down into the Silicon Valley, now *that* is a smart spot. It may be the single greatest collection of intelligence since the Renaissance."

Elizabeth to Brad: "Are you talking about computer geniuses sending monosyllabic sentences to each other through the Net? Is that what you're talking about? If you are, you're talking about a bunch of messenger boys."

Brad formed his rejoinder. It was going to be something about Elizabeth and all lawyers being a service industry, the world's oldest profession, but he also had been battle-tested and knew when to retreat.

So he glanced out the window instead.

He saw John and Lucy, their next-door neighbors. John had prematurely gray hair and smoked a pipe. He was an engineering prof at Stanford and a Silicon Valley consultant, a mentor, John liked to say, to at least five dozen multimillionaires. She was a commercial real estate broker who found space for some of the Valley's giant corporations to stretch their elbows. Lucy was thus described as a true visionary.

Both John and Lucy were standing in the driveway greeting their nanny. John was wearing a blue and white Duke sweatshirt. Lucy wore a maroon one with VASSAR emblazoned in gray and white across the chest.

"Jeez, it was just a magazine article," Brad said. "But you'd think it was an invitation to some medieval pageant. The nobles are assembling, bearing their colors . . . or is it more like flying yacht club flags at some regatta?"

Brad liked the latter analogy but directed it through the dog, who acted as a medium for their conversations in the morning. That way, everything became oblique and seemed less hostile.

At least Brad thought so.

But Brad was not without cleverness. To embellish the point, he put on a Banana Republic blue denim work shirt and stonewashed black jeans, then gingerly knotted a $69.50 Façonnable silk floral print tie, all the while concealing the pain the exploding laptop had caused to his hands. "My migrant worker look, Wilson," he announced to the retriever, who appeared appreciative.

The dog's real name was Winston, but Brad had taken to calling him Wilson, after the maker of tennis balls, which the dog was obsessed by. Actually, he had become more obsessed than normal following their move from the Seattle area to Palo Alto—or, as Brad liked to say to mimic Elizabeth, the "Stanford area."

She actually had suggested making an appointment with a canine shrink, because there was a certain hostility in the way Winston-Wilson was mouthing tennis balls lately. He would juggle the ball in his jaws, rotating it as a bingo machine does little Ping-Pong balls. And then, when someone walked by, the dog would spit the ball, shoot it with his nose, in the path of the pedestrian. It seemed like a premeditated, hostile act, which was not normal for golden retrievers. Elizabeth had pointed this out.

"You're just trying to get more attention, aren't you, you poor underprivileged thing?" Brad would say to Winston. But he was really pleading his own case and Elizabeth knew it.

She would frown at her husband and rush to console her dog by kicking the tennis ball back to the retriever.

So on that morning, as Brad painfully weaved his red Porsche through their Palo Alto neighborhood and out onto the Oregon Expressway to head for work, he beheld a parade of color, domi-nated, of course, by the Stanford cardinal and white. There was also the green and white of Dartmouth, the blue and white of Yale and Columbia and Wellesley. Polite little schools such as Whitman, Oberlin, Bennington and Pomona were also well represented. There was the purple and gold of Williams (the little college town had also done particularly well on the survey), the orange and black of Princeton, the dark crimson of Harvard (the Stanford of the East), the blue and gold of Michigan. There was Haverford,

Middlebury, Vanderbilt, Cal Tech, MIT, Amherst. The neighbors were all turning out.

"Palo Alto's version of the Rainbow Coalition," he said out loud. "It's a great day to be white, connected and proud of it."

Brad felt in top form. He popped in his favorite tape: the Kingsmen. And his animal instincts were stirred by the very first note of a wailing sax. "Louie, Lou-a-y," he sang along, confident he knew all the words.

He stopped at a traffic light. A couple jogged by, each wearing a Stanford sweatshirt over black running tights. The guy was pushing one of those triangular, aerodynamic strollers that looked as if it was designed to set land speed records. And as the couple jogged past, Brad got a glimpse of their child. It was wearing a sweatshirt that said STANFORD BABY, BRED FOR SUCCESS.

"That does it," Brad said. He made a U-turn and sped home.

The kids had left for school. Elizabeth had left for the firm. Unimpeded and feeling diabolically correct, Brad bounded into the bedroom and dove into his side of the couple's walk-in closet. In the far corner, among his hoop togs, he found an old blue and gold T-shirt. It was full of holes. It was spattered with paint. He pulled it out and held it proudly, as a fisherman might a trophy trout.

The T-shirt said SAN JOSE STATE UNIVERSITY. He took it downstairs and got out a stepladder and climbed to the gable over the front doorway. At the peak, he hung his meager banner with thumbtacks.

He climbed down, walked backward into the front yard for a better view and congratulated himself. Hanging the proletarian emblem of the local state school in this town on this particular occasion was like sprinkling elephant poop in front of the parade.

Brad knew he was being a jerk. He knew Elizabeth would tell him so when he got home. Unless, of course, he managed to get home very late. Which was sometimes a very good trick.

Besides, he had plenty of catching up to do at work. He had a few things to clear up with RoseD. He'd find her if it killed him. That was for sure. He had even practiced his speech.

"It's either me or a post-adolescent hacker. Take your choice."

And he also reminded himself to take Jason's advice and put down some money against the 49ers.

# chapter 7

**"If it isn't Mr. Inferno,"** the Human Resources person cracked when Brad walked in. "Are we here to test the kindling point of another laptop?"

Brad despised her. He'd felt it right off, from the first day of work, from the very first moment she'd issued him the inflatable dummy companion for driving in the diamond lanes.

She'd made some comment about the two of them discussing

Kierkegaard or the philosophy of Regis McKenna. Really condescending, Brad thought.

On the other hand, he didn't have an excuse for visiting Human
Resources and she'd provided one.

"If that's possible, I would like to check out another laptop," he
said, with a contrived smile. "And, while you're at it, let me ask
you something else. . . . Do we"—he was careful with the pronoun
—"keep logs of people's sign-on names or their screen names?
Like, suppose I was signing on as *BRoth* and I changed it. But then
I forgot my previous name, *BRoth,* and wanted to reinstate it.
Would we have a record? . . . Of my previous name? Or any names?"

She looked hard at him. Through him, really.

"Personnel records are confidential. I already told you that," she
said, handing him a cardboard box that said INFINITY FIREPOWER
9500. "Here, keep it away from children and matches. We're starting to run out, in case you haven't noticed."

If she were a guy, I'd . . . Brad thought, and burst out the door.

And almost collided with Maria Cisneros.

"Hi. Got a minute?" he said, reflexively.

Maria hated those words. They were the rudest words in the
workplace, totally preemptive. Human Resources at more than one
company she'd been in had held seminars ad nauseam, all variations on the same self-management theme: "Got a minute? Help
turn it into seconds." It never worked.

"Only a sec," she heard herself say, regretting it.

The next thing, they were face to face across the table in the
company kick-back quadrant, each cradling a single low-fat latte.
As k. d. lang tunes played over the sound system, NASDAQ numbers marched across an enormous flat panel on one wall.

Both Brad and Maria noted how sharp the resolution was.

| Stock | P/E | Sales (100s) | High | Low | Last | Chg |
|---|---|---|---|---|---|---|
| Microsoft | 33 | 60078 | $86^7/_8$ | $85^7/_8$ | $86^1/_4$ | $-^7/_8$ |

Brad started to say how great it was to get away from Bill Gates
and Microsoft and to be part of the new frontier J. P. McCorwin

was going to carve out of the Silicon Valley wilderness. He was mixing metaphors. But that was the least about him that annoyed Maria. He just looked too anxious. She cut him off.

"What do you want to talk about?" she said, still watching the big screen.

"I just want to know. You don't have to be embarrassed about this, OK? I just want to know if you have like a sub-rosa sign-on, a *nom de* e-mail?" he said, looking around the kick-back quadrant for any eavesdroppers.

Maria took her eyes off the screen.

"What?" she said, immediately infuriated.

"I, I just wondered if you ever used the name RoseD," he said.

He looked like a dog before dinner, Maria thought.

"Look, Brad, you've asked me this before. Remember? You also asked other women. You know what? You're getting a reputation." Maria could feel her temperature rising.

"Look, we have to work together. So I'm going to be straight with you. It's for everyone's sake, so don't take this personally. No, take it personally. You can't just go around hitting on people like this. You're married, Brad. You are married. I'm sorry the laptop burned your hands. I'm even sorry about your marriage, if that's the problem. But don't drag us into your distractions. OK?"

"OK," he said, barreling ahead as if he hadn't heard her. "But are you RoseD?"

"No!" Maria hissed. She stalked off, leaving her latte.

k. d. lang was singing "Pullin' Back the Reins" when Jason what's-his-name walked in. He must have been lurking in the hall.

"Hey," Jason said, finishing Maria's latte. "Aarrgh. Low-fat."

Brad hated this. He was beginning to lose his dignity. He had to rally.

"Nice shirt," he said, noting that Jason was wearing a purple and black Pink Floyd T-shirt that actually looked clean.

"To the only two dudes in this whole space who have lit up the FirePower and survived to tell about it," Jason said, tapping Brad's paper cup with Maria's paper cup. "So, did you get the info?"

Brad felt rage welling up. He and this cybercretin were competing for the same virtual woman. Keep calm, he commanded himself. Jeez, don't let on.

"It's a little harder than we thought, buddy," he said. "The keeper of the records is a card-carrying pit bull. But I think I can do a little fieldwork."

"Like virtual elimination," Jason said, nodding in the direction of the hallway. "Like Maria ain't Rose. Am I right?"

Brad felt flushed. And nodded affirmatively.

"Bummer," Jason said.

Brad changed the subject.

"How about those Colts?"

Jason seemed lost in download. Actually, he was looking at the flat panel.

On the screen, two large robots were battering each other in a technological cockfight. Sparks and parts and spatters of grease were flying all over the place as the machines roared at each other, flailing away with spikes, hammers, blades, chainsaws, claws and spears. And the crowd, seated behind a Plexiglas screen, was in a grease-thirsty frenzy.

"Cool, huh?" Jason said, searching for the remote to crank up the sound. When he did, the noise assaulted Brad's senses, as if youth gangsters were slamming their skateboards all over his body. "It's a mosh pit for machines. They do this in a warehouse up in San Francisco. Even have corporate sponsors, although most of these things are totally freelance. There's even big-time betting. It's like the other side of the Valley. Basically your Raiders crowd."

Brad watched, dumbfounded, as one of the behemoths, armed with a spiked snout and a whirling-saw tail, pierced the armor and the hydraulic lines of its adversary. A cloud of evil-looking smoke poured forth as the crowd screamed the death count: "One, two, three . . ."

He reached for the remote and changed the channel to CNN, making a point of turning the sound way down.

"Listen, Jason, there's something I've got to ask you," Brad said sincerely. He was gulping for air, fighting to summon the courage to ask the question. "How do I get hold of a bookie? I've never made a bet in my life."

Jason's face softened. He put his hand on Brad's shoulder.

"Braddie boy, you're about to take a walk on the wild side of cyberspace."

# chapter 8

**Brad had never really hung out with hackers.** Even so, Jason's generic garden apartment on one of the main drags of Santa Clara was about what he had expected. From the outside, Jason's place looked like dozens of others, all in a squared-off honeycomb, vertically, horizontally and symmetrically aligned, giving the complex of pane glass and faux redwood stain the appearance of a giant Cost Plus wine rack.

Inside, it was a one-bedroom storage space, a receptacle for random accumulations. Judging from the empty Round Table Pizza cartons, beer cans, juice containers, yogurt containers, freeze-dried soup containers and assorted other empties, it was a repository for discards as well.

There were, however, two uncovered Pamela Lees on one wall, one a poster, the other crudely clipped from *Playboy* or something. On another wall, there was a giant poster of Eddie Vedder doing something barbaric with a microphone. Over it, a homemade banner said THE MEDIUM *IS* THE ENTIRE FUCKING WORLD. On still another, a mountain bike hung from the mouth of a gargoyle. Heaped in one corner were a neon windsurfing sail, at least three mismatched Asics cross-trainers and one stained Jansport backpack that had obviously held organic materials. In another was a huge pile of team banners—not just the 49ers and Raiders and Sharks, but Big Ten banners and Ivy League banners and banners from just about every professional sports team in existence.

Brad thought that was a little weird for someone who pronounced himself an entrepreneur first and a sports fan second.

Hard drives, memory cards, CDs, boxes of Sega games and back issues of *Wired*, *MacWorld* and *Bicycling* magazines were strewn all over the place. And Brad counted at least five pairs of Dakota Smith shades like the ones Tom Cruise wore in *The Firm*.

"No inoculations necessary. Honest," Jason said. "But, it's like when I'm here, I'm actually not."

He beckoned Brad into the bedroom which glowed like the inside of a mini—mission control.

There was a giant television monitor, two power conversion backup units, two hard-drive towers with five bays each, an HP LaserJet printer and three Radius monitors, one connected to a Power Mac, one to an AcerPower P166 and one to an Infinity Accelerator, all top of the line stuff. Each monitor had variegated metaverse screen savers that gave Brad pause as he watched their molten forms pulsate into various sexual contortions.

"A variation of the old lava lamp. But this stuff is museum

quality," Jason said, clearing a heap of clothing from the edge of a futon. He turned down his cell-phone scanner and motioned Brad to sit down.

"Here, put these on," he said, handing Brad a set of headphones and some wraparound goggles. He added what appeared to be a hooded sweatshirt. It was ribbed with wires, including one that attached to the power tower. "This is where I go when I'm home. Enjoy yourself for a sec. I'll get us a couple of beers."

Before he put on the goggles, Brad watched Jason fly at his Infinity keyboard. He signed on and moved through the various platforms onto the Internet. Once there, he typed http://www.dominatrix.com. And then he winked at Brad, signaling for him to put on the goggles and the headphones.

Almost immediately, Brad was jolted by the sound of heavy breathing. It was his own. The rest of his senses seemed to rush like a tide to what was being reflected into the goggles. In short order, Brad was swept away.

Then came Leslie. Only she very slowly and deliberately pronounced it "Lezlee." She was the most athletically fit, animal-like and totally uninhibited creature he had ever encountered. What's more, she was very accommodating. "Whatever you like," she whispered breathlessly into his ear.

Brad could hear his own breathing growing louder. He could hear his own voice imploring Leslie to take him where he'd never been before. He could feel his shoulders being massaged, the back of his neck, his chest. He could hear himself offering to take Leslie to Reno, to Mendocino, to dinner in San Francisco. He could feel himself ready to throw over the elusive RoseD.

And when he felt a tap on the shoulder, Brad had no idea how long he and Leslie had been gone.

"Pretty cool interactive physiokinectivity, huh?" Jason said, pulling the hooded shirt and headphones off his guest and handing him a Red Hook ale. "I coded the home page myself. This is what the government is trying to jettison from cyberspace. But, hey, it beats hell out of running into someone you know at the video store, right, dude? Or even worse, coming down with something none of us deserves. So I figure, why not code this stuff up right here, right now? There's bound to be a big black market for it."

Brad felt about as lifeless as an overdone linguini noodle.

"OK, sports fans, it's time to talk to the numbers dudes," Jason said, coaxing Brad to one of the keyboards and onto the Internet. "Use your own password, dude. That way, they'll know you're sincere—and it won't be on my Mastercard."

At Jason's direction, even though he still felt pain in his burned hands, Brad typed http://www.allsport.com and found himself on the home page of what appeared to be a sports memorabilia shop. With a simple point-and-click, he could scan the inventory of autographed trading cards, team jerseys, team warm-up jackets, team banners . . .

"That's it," Jason said. "Go to team banners."

There was a long pause as the computer seemed to ponder whether this was the proper protocol. But then the screen cleared and Brad found himself in the lobby of a conference center. There were at least a dozen others there already.

Within seconds, the screen assigned him a code name—D-34 —and asked if he would accept that name and if he wished to continue. Jason leaned over and clicked on OK.

And Brad found himself in a live chat room.

Host: Welcome D-34. You shopping?

Brad turned to Jason.

"Jeez. Say 'yes,' " the hacker urged.

D-34: Yes.

Host: What banner? What size?

Brad turned again.

D-34: I don't want a banner. I want to make a

Jason stopped him before he blew the whole scene.

D-34: Sorry. This is B-26. D-34 is new. But he's with me. He's OK.

Host: OK. . . Banner? Size? Over, under?

"Tell him Indianapolis and large," Jason coached. "That way he knows you want to bet the whole enchilada that the Niners don't cover the ten-point spread."

"Huh?" Brad said, feeling terribly nerdish.

"Just type what I told you," Jason commanded.

Brad obliged.

Host: OK. Indy big on Sunday. Let me get the size again.

"The Vegas odds are five to one. So he wants to know about how big your bet's going to be," Jason said. "Tell him medium."

"Why not large?" Brad asked.

"Dude, you want to bet five thousand bucks?" Jason asked, looking wide-eyed.

D-34: Medium-small.

Host: OK. Medium-small. On Indy. What credit card will you be using?

"That's the beauty of it," Jason said as Brad paused. "Go ahead. It's mail order."

Brad tried to stay cool, but he could feel himself flushing as he reached for his wallet. His instincts were trying to hold him back. But Jason had this guy on the line.

"Hurry up before someone else interrupts," he said.

Brad surrendered his Mastercard number.

Host: OK. Your banner will be mailed within five working days. Thanks for your business.

"How much did I bet?" Brad asked as Jason signed him off.

"Only a grand," the hacker said. "Shoulda listened to me. Remember, Steve Young's playing hurt. You shoulda bet medium —$2,500. At five to one . . . that's better than money down on Netscape."

"And if the Niners cover the spread?" Brad asked. "And I lose?"

"You're covered as long as your credit line isn't under $1,100," Jason said. "Either way, you still get a Colts banner out of it."

Brad added one more item to the growing list of things he couldn't even begin to explain to his wife.

# chapter 9

**It was well past noon and already the light was dusky** on the last Sunday in October when Maria pulled her BMW onto a gravelly farm road heading into the folding hills above East San Jose. On the audiocassette, Mary Chapin Carpenter had come to "Stones in the Road."

How appropriate, Maria thought, as the gravel became dirt and the road became rutted.

She knew this road and loved it. It serviced a small cattle ranch and led to the big vineyard her father had overseen. The road was part of her childhood. Maria and her sisters had chased birds and butterflies along it, raced horses up and down it, counseled each other about early love and other grave matters as they walked and skipped and hummed to each other, losing themselves and the sight of the adults as they followed its bends.

Now, with a turn or two left, she could see the wood smoke rising and knew exactly what to expect.

A dozen vehicles, mainly pickups, were parked in an open space studded with oaks. Maria recognized all of them. They belonged to her family and to the hands her father had supervised until his retirement last year as foreman for the Messalini family's half-dozen ranches and vineyards that strung from the east foothills in San Jose nearly to Morgan Hill.

"*Jefecito,*" Ramon Cisneros's men had called their former boss, and they did so with respect and affection. This once-a-year gathering celebrating *El día de los muertos,* one of Mexico's most spiritual holidays, kept their bonds warm and close.

Maria pulled in alongside her father's blue Chevy pickup and was instantly mobbed by her young cousins and nieces and nephews. To the three oldest girl cousins, she separately handed three white boxes containing pumpkin pies she'd picked up from Chiffonos Gourmet Desserts on University Avenue in Los Gatos. It was a break from tradition to bring prefab desserts to a fiesta. But then, Maria's whole life was a break from tradition. She hadn't gone to Mass that morning, hadn't gone in years. Sometimes she went to the Decathlon Club or Gold's Gym. Most often, she did what she had done this morning. She went to the stables and saddled Fuego and rode through the hills. Now she was late for the party and still wearing her jodhpurs and riding boots.

The lower branches of the oaks were festooned with papier-mâché skeletons. She made her way out of one clearing and into the next. There, her mother, Catalina; her grandmother Antonia; her aunts Carmen, Clara and Marilola; her female cousins; and half a dozen other women—wives and girlfriends of her father's friends—were seated at a weathered wooden picnic table. Some made tortillas, flattening, smoothing and shaping the dough by rotating and patting it between their hands as if applauding the tortillas' passage to the fire. Others, her mother among them, kneaded a *masa* of cornmeal, lard, salt and water that would cover a mixture of corn and shredded pork and would, in turn, be wrapped in cornhusks to be cooked over the open fire. The tamale recipe was more than 150 years old and had traveled northward from Ciudad Obregon over the mountains and along the Sonoran desert with Maria's great-grandmother. Maria's mother liked to say these tamales bound the families together as tightly as the church.

Maria felt a momentary remorse for being late. She rushed breathlessly into the clutch of women, exchanging embraces with each of them. She saved her mother for last and was mindful of the mild rebuke in her eyes. Sometimes this look transcended all the education, all the travel and the seeming successes Maria had chalked up. Sometimes the look said, "Why aren't you married?"

Today it said, "You're late. You haven't even changed. Go hug your father."

A frantic voice was coming from the boom box in a clump of trees about twenty yards away. The sound and the smoke gave away Ramon Cisneros's location. She had only to follow the charcoal aroma to find the men. They were gathered around a big pit that contained a mesquite fire. The men were laughing, singing and shifting their weight as they studied every nuance of the transformation of flame to coals. Nearby, on a spit, a baby goat was splayed and ready for roasting, along with a half side of beef. A huge iron pot of bubbling pinto beans hung from a makeshift A-frame support over the fire. Each man held a long-necked bottle of Dos Equis. An aluminum trash can filled with ice held more.

Everywhere Maria looked, there were preparations for a long afternoon.

"Papa!" Maria shouted, throwing out her arms.

"Maria, my little big shot," her father bellowed for the benefit of his relatives and friends. *"Cómo estás, hijita?"*

*"Bien, bien,* Papa. And you?"

"Hey, you know the 49ers are losing?" Ramon Cisneros groaned. "To the Colts. Aaiieegh!"

Ramon hugged his daughter and they held the embrace for a long time. Maria tucked her head against her father's muscular chest. She could smell cigarette smoke on his breath. Her father was maybe the only person in the world whom she would forgive certain vices. And it probably helped that he had few.

Her father asked about work and she gave him the usual answer: "I seem to be working day and night.

"But you know what? We got a contract, a couple of million bucks, Papa." It was news she thought Ramon Cisneros needed to hear. A month earlier, fueled by J. P. McCorwin's sales pitch, she had persuaded her father to take out an equity loan on his small home in east San Jose and contribute $15,000, which Maria had more than matched by cashing in some stock options. It all went into a seed fund for the startup she had joined as communications director.

J.P. had couched the whole transaction in spiritual rather than financial terms, saying, "This will prove that you believe in yourself and our partnership."

Ramon had balked at first.

She had explained what J.P. had told her and even tried to evangelize the concept of an idea whose time was about to come. But in the end, she knew the check he sent her had less to do with making her father feel like an entrepreneur than it did with how she batted her eyes at him.

"So what's my share? When do I get to be a rich man like your boss?" he said.

"Be patient, Papa. This is just the beginning. We're coming up with something unbelievably big," she said, leaning back in his arms and laughing because she felt happy to be right where she was.

She broke away and ran back to the women, settling alongside her mother. She took up a flour ball and patted it gingerly into a tortilla and set it with the rest. She made small talk and answered questions about her job. Everyone seemed genuinely interested, and no one asked if she had a new boyfriend.

When she and her mother were alone, Maria considered confiding in her. About the exploding laptops and the contract to extinguish them and of the married marketing manager who was hitting on her.

"Rose?" he kept asking her. It was weird.

Maria wanted to tell her mother everything, but she knew it was impossible. Her mother would not understand.

*"La cena esta lista,"* her father shouted from the barbecue. *"A comer!"*

Time to put the food on the table.

The women began heaping food into bowls and onto platters, and Maria helped round up the kids. For the next two hours, everything but the feast was forgotten.

There would be dancing later. For as long as Maria could remember, her family and her father's friends had repeated this fall harvest ritual. Occasionally, they were joined by her Aunt Evelyn, the great ballerina. When she danced everything would change. Sometimes Maria was glad Aunt Evelyn was too busy to join them. What she liked best was being held by her father as they danced by the fire.

Now in his arms, she could feel his contentment. Someone put on a Carlos Santana tape and everyone danced alone, as if they were hippies at the Fillmore Auditorium or Golden Gate Park. And again, Ramon told how he had seen the great guitarist before he got famous, performing with a street band at the old Poppycock in Palo Alto. "Now it's a Good Earth or something," Ramon complained.

They would drink mescal, and the trophy would go to the person who drained the bottle. It seemed they always rigged it so that Maria got to eat the worm lurking at the bottom. She went along, always. She even took part in the jalapeño-eating contest until it became too macho.

Someone broke out a guitar. Another a violin. They played the old songs. And Maria sang along with them, telling herself: The songs change everything. They almost make everything as it was supposed to be. Something to rely on.

She requested *"La Malaguena,"* and shed the accustomed tear as the mournful tune played itself out. This was her cue. With the fanfare expected of her, she took her leave.

It was long after dark when Maria wound down the hill. The lights of San Jose and the Silicon Valley stretched before her like jewels afire. She punched in the tape again. She knew the words by heart and sang along: "Another day, another deal before we get back home . . ." Maria shuddered with anticipation and fear as she headed the car down the hill.

# chapter 10

**First thing Monday,** Baba RAM DOS curbed his vintage motorcycle at a pay phone on Big Basin Way in Saratoga and dialed 1-800-701-BOMB, hoping to reach a tape. But when a live human being answered: "FBI Unabom Task Force, may I help you?" he hung up.

As soon as he reached his office, he used his secret override capabilities and called up Maria Cisneros's sign-on, MCisneros, and her password, Fuego. Then he sent an e-mail to unabom@orion.arc.nasa.gov, which sounded bureaucratic and anonymous enough.

His message was exactly what J. P. McCorwin had dictated: Ever wonder how far Bill Gates would go to kill the competition? Is he devious enough to plant a combustion virus?

Within two hours, someone was in the lobby to see Maria.

"I'm Lily Watanabe, with the FBI," the woman said, displaying a pleasant smile and a badge. A short black leather jacket hung smartly over one shoulder; she carried a supple black Bally briefcase. "May we talk?"

Maria was dumbfounded. All her internal alarms went off simultaneously. For a moment she felt nauseous, even as she ushered the woman through the hall, past the support pod and into her office. She noticed how confident the agent seemed, how jaunty her stride was and how the hem of her straight black skirt was well above the knees. She seemed too slight, too young, too pretty, too hip to be an FBI agent.

"I'm an affirmative action hire," Lily volunteered, as if she had read Maria's thoughts. Her voice was friendly, too friendly, Maria thought. "They needed someone with an engineering degree."

Agent Watanabe seemed relaxed as she took a seat on the beige-and-eggshell raw cotton couch along the far wall. Behind her hung Maria's Stanford MBA diploma in a dark walnut frame and a subtle wood-block print she had acquired from a shop in the mountains outside Tokyo. On another wall there was a poster that said:

Q: HOW MANY MICROSOFT ENGINEERS DOES IT TAKE TO CHANGE A LIGHT BULB?

A: NONE. BILL GATES WILL JUST REDEFINE DARKNESS ™ AS THE NEW INDUSTRY STANDARD.

The FBI agent regarded the poster and said, smiling, "It's a curious question about Bill Gates. I can't help but wonder what inspired it."

"What?" Maria asked.

"The e-mail that mentioned exploding laptops," Lily said. "You are MCisneros@McCorwin.com, right?"

"Yes," Maria said.

"This morning, the Unabom task force received a question from you asking about Bill Gates," Lily said.

Maria stared at her. "What are you talking about? I never sent any e-mail—" and somehow caught herself midsentence.

The FBI agent was not smiling now. "For the past year, I have been a member of the largest law enforcement task force ever assembled for the largest manhunt ever undertaken. This investigation has gone some strange places. That I can tell you. I can also tell you that, at this point, when computers are blowing up, no question is too weird."

Maria sat back, trying hard to stay cool and listen. She looked at the window and tried to deflect her attention to the far hills, which were bathed in soft autumn light.

But Lily could tell that Maria's guard was up.

"That's from Nikko, right?" she said, nodding at the print on Maria's wall. "I've been there. I have one like it."

The FBI agent, it turned out, was exactly Maria's age. She had attended Harvard, as had Gates. But Lily Watanabe had graduated. She went on to grad school at MIT, studying electrical engineering. "Technology was a big thing inside Route 128. My classmates wanted to work in software and make lots of money."

At the suggestion of an old family friend, Norm Mineta, a U.S. congressman, former San Jose mayor and nisei, like her father, she interviewed with the FBI. Because she could speak some Japanese and had an engineering degree, she was told she'd be valuable in the international war on trade secrets. That meant a fast track. Within a few years, the government would send her to law school. They also promised to assign her to the San Francisco area. That clinched it. She could be close to home.

The pot grew sweeter when the bureau transferred her to work with the U.S. Attorney's office in San Jose, she said. "They were up to their necks in trade secret and tech theft cases."

Lily softened her tone.

"My father was a flower grower," she said. "I understand your father was a farmworker."

Maria felt herself wanting to like this woman, wanting to forget the fear and confusion that were raging inside her. But then came the stab of reality.

"How'd you know that?" she said, stiffening.

Lily looked intently at her.

"Does anyone have access to your e-mail?" she asked.

Maria shook her head.

"Anyone have a grudge against you?"

Maria shook her head again.

"We know it was sent from your business e-mail. We can even check the time it was sent. We can probably find out who was here when the e-mail was sent. So we can start narrowing things down . . ."

"Maybe it was a joke," Maria offered.

"Look, computers have exploded. People have gotten hurt. The Unabom task force possesses the most sophisticated array of high-tech forensics ever assembled. You wouldn't believe what we have. We can go places and find out things about people and technology that you couldn't possibly imagine.

"You wanted to know how I knew your father was a ranch foreman? That's how I knew. A computer program. Very fast, very thorough.

"We need to examine the laptops," she continued. "It could be an engineering flaw. Or a very dangerous prank. Or something worse. I need the laptops."

"I'm afraid I can't just give them to you," Maria said, telling herself to stay cool. "I must ask my supervisor for clearance."

"Who's that? Present or absent?" Lily snapped.

"He won't be in until late this afternoon," Maria answered.

"I can be back here with a federal warrant before lunch," Lily replied. "It would be better, though, if you cooperated, especially if somehow the press were to find out about this."

Maria knew she had no choice. She dialed R&D. "Bring me the laptops," she directed, her voice flat, lifeless.

As soon as the agent left, Maria e-mailed J.P.:

`FBI here. Took both laptops. (MCisneros).`

She mentioned nothing about the Bill Gates e-mail.

J. P. McCorwin was at lunch at the Lion & Compass in Santa Clara with his old ally Jerry Sanders, the chief of Advanced Micro Devices, one of the Valley's biggest chip makers. The two had been the closest thing to centerfolds the Valley had ever produced, at least during the free-for-all years. Plus, they both hated Intel. That helped their relationship.

Sanders had wild white hair and a handlebar mustache. He resembled General George Custer, particularly when he was doing battle with Intel. Once, he'd dressed in a toga and ridden an elephant into an AMD Christmas party.

That was a dozen years ago, a long time past in Valley history but about the same time that most companies, Infinity Computer included, were staging elaborate corporate parties and drawing a lot of attention.

"It was a competitive thing," J.P. had proudly told Maria. "You were known for competitive lavishness. For one party, we wanted to reenact the entire chariot race from *Ben-Hur*. We rented the horses and the vehicles, had the track at San Jose City College booked and everything. It was going to be a Roman orgy unlike any orgy this Valley had ever seen. But our liability guys said mixing booze and horses and chariots was too risky. So we toned things down and hired the Chippendales to do a gladiator show instead. The support staff loved it."

With time and the downturn of the economy in the late '80s, even Sanders had cooled it. But he had been spotted more frequently recently at his old haunts—the Lion & Compass, Original Joe's in San Jose, MacArthur Park in Palo Alto—a sure sign that things were heating up. It was also rumored that Sanders was about to ink a deal with Nexgen, an up-and-coming chip designer over in Milpitas. Between them, they were looking to develop a whole new generation of chip speed and firepower to roast Intel's butt. At least that's what Sanders was saying.

"If Jerry can produce something faster and better, we might be interested in linking up somewhere down the road. . . . At least that's what I want the press to hear," J.P. had told Maria. "So, casually let 'em know that we took a meeting. . . . OK?"

J.P. picked up Maria's e-mail about the FBI visit on his Motorola Envoy mobile communicator. He was never out of touch.

Around 2:30 P.M., a return message flashed across the monitor screen in Maria's office. There was no mistaking what was on J.P.'s mind. She could feel the heat coming off her monitor:

Be in my office in 30 minutes. (J.P.).

"You gave up the laptops? To the feds? You actually turned them over?" The bulges of his neck veins and the purple in his face conveyed rage so great it nearly choked off his wind. Baba RAM DOS stood by his side, apparently ready to administer CPR.

J.P. bent backward at the waist and threw back his head as if trying to catch raindrops with his tongue. He breathed deeply and ran his hands through his hair in the familiar manner that Maria had come to know when her boss was trying to compose himself.

"OK, OK," he said, transitioning into warp-think. "Schedule a press conference for Wednesday. Let's say we've solved the mystery ourselves. And let's thank the FBI for offering to help. But get the laptops back ASAP!"

"But . . ." Maria stammered.

"Call the press or fax them tomorrow. Tell them we have been secretly working on this thing with Infinity and that we have the problem solved. I'll call the honchos at Infinity tonight. . . . Call Brad Roth. You, he, Baba and I are gonna drop by the chairman's first thing in the morning. We're gonna deliver the news in person."

With a wave, he dismissed her.

As Maria glanced back through J.P.'s picture window, her boss and Baba were both gesticulating wildly. J.P. was still agitated.

"Be more discreet," J.P. was telling his No. 2 guy. "I want her on our side. OK? She's still pure. Remember that. Don't go turning her paranoid. We need her."

But he was talking too fast. Maria couldn't make out a thing he was saying.

# chapter 11

**Brad Roth had barely gotten the gauze off his swollen and discolored hands** when he got the call from the office. He also happened to be standing in the bathroom, probing the inside of his son's right nostril with a pair of needlenose pliers.

Fifteen-year-old Damien had gone with friends to Santa Cruz. And returned with a nose ring.

At first, Brad and Elizabeth thought it was a fake, probably done with suction cups, just a decor option for Halloween. Damien had said he was going as a cybernaut, which Brad figured meant he was planning to stay in his room and terrorize the universe through the Internet. But then Damien announced that the nose ornament was permanent, that the little clamp that attached inside the nostril had been welded by a freelance street artist near the Boardwalk who specialized in microblowtorching. His girlfriend, Cola, had gotten one too. It was a symbol of their being forever together.

Elizabeth immediately broke into tears. "My boy. My God. We let him go off with those older boys and he . . . comes back . . . *pierced!*

"And in Santa Cruz. I've always hated Santa Cruz."

"Mom, I didn't come back with needle marks in my arm or anything," Damien whined. "You should have seen Drew and Megan. They even got chains to attach to their nose rings so they'll never be separated. And Kyle . . . you should see what he got for himself and where . . ."

"Stop! Just stop!" Elizabeth screamed. She picked up her Yamaha racquetball racket and her gym bag and stormed out of the house.

It was up to Brad to right the ship. "If a welder can seal a nose ring," he said, "anyone with a flashlight and an acetylene torch can damn well cut it off. Let's get the Yellow Pages."

"Dad, just kidding," Damien protested. "It comes off. You just have to unscrew it. OK?"

"Not OK," Damien's father said, casting a disapproving eye toward Damien's twelve-year-old sister, Alexus, who had come out of her room to cheer her brother on. "Let's find out."

Which was how Brad happened to have his needlenose pliers up Damien's nose when the phone rang. Alexus grabbed it. "Dad, it's Maria from work."

"How're the hands?" she asked.

"Operating," Brad said, without humor. "What's up?"

"J.P. thinks he has the combustible laptop problem figured out. He wants to tell the chairman of Infinity himself," she said.

"He wants you and Baba and me to accompany him. Meet us at the Woodside Bakery at seven tomorrow morning for rehearsal. Then we'll go to the chairman's estate around eight to deliver the news."

Brad started to protest, remembering that Elizabeth had fired a preemptive shot before the nose ring thing sent her storming out of the house. She had a 7 A.M. client meeting on Tuesday with a group of securities underwriters. "It's been in my DayPlanner for weeks," she had said from her closet while sorting through some Marc Jacobs silk blouses. It would be up to Brad to get the kids off to school.

"Great," Brad told Maria, disguising his momentary distress. "I'll be there."

For months, he and Elizabeth had been waging the war of the DayPlanners, and Brad was clearly losing. He had been losing to such a degree that he accused his lawyerly wife of overcompensating for the family's forced march south from Seattle.

For this, Elizabeth had a retort. "One of us has to have an adult job and provide a stable income for the sake of the children's college education."

At 7:30 A.M. on a Tuesday, Brad was doing his best.

He, Maria, Baba RAM DOS and J.P. himself all took separate cars to the chairman's Woodside estate. J.P. thought a procession through the gate would look more impressive to the Infinity Computer chairman, who was used to entertaining industrial big shots and movie stars and heads of state.

The chairman had been there from the beginning of Infinity, lending approbation, maturity and juice with the venture capitalists to the gimmick a couple of young geeks had come up with for putting a PC in every home and classroom. He had helped steer the fledgling company into the light of day and onto the NASDAQ. He had steered it through the shoals of false promises and faulty applications and always managed a steady hand, a hand that was steady enough to guide the company past J. P. McCorwin's seductive notions of marrying technology and love and giving birth to cool, exclusive, expensive things. The chairman's hand had lowered the ax on J.P. when the board of directors had had enough and said, "Get on with business." And now, not so many years later, the hand was extended. This, perhaps more than anything else, distinguished real time in Silicon Valley. It could be measured in terms of birth, ecstasy and desperation to stay alive.

"Only the paranoid survive," Intel Chairman Andy Grove had said in writing the code that was to be virtually embossed over every company's doorway. But the chairman of Infinity Computer operated at another level. Slightly imperious and a bit old school for a high-tech entrepreneur, he was also an adventurer, an outdoorsman, a member of the Sierra Club and Friends of Midpeninsula Open Space, with an unabashed admiration for Ernest Hemingway, Stanford's ex-president Don Kennedy (a fellow birder), and even Ted Turner (although he wished he'd acquire a little more humility, plus he didn't much care for Ted's "airhead, commie wife"). But he had insisted that there was always room for true gentlemen, even in cyberspace, men who practiced "grace under pressure," he was fond of saying.

This was why, before hearing of the cure for Infinity's laptop flameouts, he insisted on showing his guests around the estate. It could be described in breathless terms as "magnificent." But that was too shallow. "Seventy acres in Woodside" was all anyone really had to say. That meant meadows, bridle paths, stables housing fine hunter-jumpers, a vineyard of pinot noir whose vines had originated in Burgundy and a considerable forest of noble and feathery redwoods, all bordering the chairman's 18,000-square-foot, twelve-bedroom, $10^1/_2$-bath château that was still "evolving," as he put it with some annoyance.

It was no secret that the Woodside town council had been giving him a tokenly rough time of it, asking, for instance, why he couldn't settle for, say, a 12,000-square-foot house like everybody else, except Larry Ellison, the Oracle chief, who was planning an entire Zen meditation center, medieval weapons range, fifteen-car garage and waterfowl refuge nearby.

The chairman had been patient. He'd even attended the public hearings and endured the platitudes of certain members of the council ("housewives with too much time on their hands," he muttered to close friends) as well as the environmentalists and some of his neighbors who would never see the house unless he invited them over for cocktails or a political fund-raiser. He'd unrolled the site plans himself. And he'd set those plans alongside a blow-up map of his property, showing where everything was and what the scale was. And he'd patiently pointed out that everything was not in scale. That was precisely the problem.

"The redwoods dwarf any house that is not in scale. Twelve thousand square feet is too small. And, I assure you, I am an environmentalist and not inclined to cut down a single tree to rectify the situation."

The chairman repeated this to his guests that morning as they strolled the pathways. Maria noticed how the redwoods let in filigreed light and how the jays protested their presence with indignant screeches. It was magnificent, she thought.

"So how's the fight going with the town council?" Brad asked.

J.P. and Baba flinched.

But the chairman seemed upbeat about the whole thing.

"I have my people on it," he said. "If we have to, we'll put together an opposition campaign and simply run them off the council. Although getting involved in local matters is a bit beneath one's dignity.

"Hell, we've got good people in Washington, good, tough lobby-ists. If this thing doesn't go through, we'll just renegotiate the whole damn Louisiana Purchase and take over the town."

Maria waited for him to signal he was just kidding. But the chairman did not relent. He did just the opposite. He stepped up the tempo, beckoning for the three to draw nearer. "I could have just gone down to Morgan Hill or San Martin and built as much as I wanted.

"I could have gone to downtown San Jose. I could have built the Élysée Palace. I could have offered to put up an 18,000-square-foot piece of crap and called it art and they would have approved it. They would have bent over backward. But, you know what? I want to be right here, this close to Stanford."

Maria expected a long homily on old school ties, but the chairman reached higher.

"I want this property to be part of a venue for the 2004 Summer Olympics. I can see equestrian events here. We could build a swimming pool over there. We could run part of the marathon or a bike race through the property.

"What I want is for the 2004 Olympics to come to Stanford and the Peninsula. And what I want most of all is for us, Infinity Computer, to be the first corporate host in the history of the Olympic Games."

He was breathing heavily and his eyes had a faraway look. "I want an Infinity multitasking operating system at every venue—doing the timing, measuring, score-keeping, helping the TV guys and keeping everyone informed.

"That is my dream. I don't care about profits, or shipping the most PCs," he said somberly. "I want to outbid Stockholm, Rome, Lillehammer, Cape Town and anybody else who thinks they can host a better Olympics than we can.

"Actually, that's not my only goal. We could get a tidy government subsidy to cover our indirect costs, you know, bill the government the way Stanford used to bill the Defense Department. Plus, we could get unlimited publicity. And if I personally host some event right here, I'll get a nice tax write-off."

The chairman had drawn the foursome into his confidence now. Even J. P. McCorwin appeared stunned by his Delphic disclosure. "The Infinity Olympics." He seemed genuinely awed by the chairman's delusion. But delusions were what appealed most to him.

"Mr. Chairman, we can help you take that first step," he said. "We can tell you with full confidence that your FirePower laptops will stop combusting . . . if you do what we recommend."

J.P.'s timing was impeccable. His delivery, a tour de force.

"Tell me what we should do to stop this conflagration," the chairman said, his voice lowered to a conspiratorial whisper.

Maria could feel the quiet settling in on the estate. It seemed to ride in on the soft light. Even the jays shushed, craning for the news.

"Change the batteries, Mr. Chairman," J.P. said. "Just change the batteries."

# chapter 12

## On the third floor of the FBI office on the outskirts of downtown San

**Jose,** Lily Watanabe sat at her desk staring at the charred husk of what was once a laptop computer. Actually, it was a Polaroid snapshot of a laptop. The original evidence in question had been sent by special messenger service to the FBI forensics lab in Quantico, Virginia.

The lab had been in the news a lot over the past couple of years. It was there that specialists, using ultrasensitive microscopes and other classified devices, had pored over the remnants of exploded package bombs and letter bombs, leaving no fragments unexamined. From their work, they had drawn scientific conclusions as thoroughly as if they were mapping a genetic code. The bombs were the work of a single maniac—dubbed the Unabomber, because his early victims, going back some seventeen years, had been university staffers and professors and airline executives.

Even though she worked out of San Jose, Lily Watanabe had been assigned to the Unabom task force based in San Francisco because she was an electrical engineer and because the task force director, Jim Freeman, had a theory that ran contrary to the prevailing theory, or at least the one that was launched in the press. The portrait the bureau had been painting of the Unabomber, and partly one he had been painting of himself through various communiqués, was that he detested high-tech. That lead to the conclusion that he must be some sort of low-tech, Earth First!er type, probably holed up in some mossy cave somewhere in northern California or Montana, where he kept company with a spotted owl while he honed his exploding devices.

But what if he was exactly the opposite? What if he was just plain antisocial, like half the guys in Silicon Valley? What if he was actually working there and hating it or liking the work but hating his boss? Was that so unusual?

No, Freeman thought. Which was why he was not ruling out the idea that the Unabomber could actually be a disgruntled Silicon Valley geek. That could include anyone *without* stock options, probably. Thus, he had assigned Lily Watanabe to be the bureau's Valley connection. Which also explained why Maria Cisneros's seemingly ludicrous question of whether Bill Gates was capable of introducing a combustible virus into the Infinity laptops' operating system was not such a wild stretch.

To be certain, Freeman would have bet his pension that the Microsoft king was not motivated enough to cause the competition's hardware to burst into flames. He could destroy them through more conventional means, like creating a virtual monopoly on operating systems. But Freeman was still intrigued with the possibility that such a virus could actually be introduced into an operating system.

"Remember, we all sat around waiting for that Michelangelo virus to destroy the computing world," he had said. "Sure, it never happened. But that doesn't mean it couldn't."

When Lily Watanabe first persuaded Maria Cisneros to turn the latest combustive laptops over to the FBI, Lily had to restrain herself. She wanted to tear right into one of them. Undo those tiny screws, open its back and follow the course of the electrical current all the way from its power port to its lithium-ion battery right into its speedy 166 MHz 603 processor and on into the big 1.1 GB hard disk.

That would have been thrilling, even a little erotic. And also a breach of FBI protocol. She knew that and checked herself at the door, so to speak, confining her initial examination to the externals.

She unfolded the compact frame, which still gave off the flinty odor of an electrical fire. She glanced at the blank display screen, which was designed to be backlit and dual-scan, conveying high-resolution, 640-by-480 pixelated color. The screen looked dead. The only color was a rainbow smear resembling an oil slick.

She turned the case on its side, extracting the battery pack. It felt heavier and thicker than that of her own government-issue Hewlett Packard Pentium Notebook. It was then that she noticed something in particular. One end of the battery, the end that married into the laptop's internal system, was scored white. The other end was burned, too, but no more intensely than the rest of the battery pack. This led her to believe that the fire could not have been started by an external power surge; otherwise, the portion nearest the external power port would have been the most severely burned. The fire had to have come from the belly of the machine.

She checked the second laptop. Same thing. This she noted, sending her observations along with the laptops.

Within forty-eight hours, Lily got a call from Quantico.

The lab guys confirmed her theory.

The lithium batteries had combusted, all right. And it was not from an external power overload. It was from an internal engineering flaw in the system's BIOS power management system. Somehow, something, a virus of some sort, had been introduced into the software that governed the power management system. It was one of the great features of the FirePower that its unique power storage management allowed nearly instantaneous recharging of the battery. This gave it five or six times the legs of conventional portable laptops.

The system operated on a superconducting coil the size of a microcircuit, which kept energy moving in a circular motion. That created a powerful microelectronic field that could be tapped into any time through a tiny device called a "flex tank." This gave the battery its long life. It was also potentially combustible if certain protocols weren't followed in directing its release.

Apparently, at some point during operation, something in the software rearranged the gate array in the power management sequence, causing the current storage area to dump its energy. If this happened at the wrong time, if the gates of the flex tank weren't properly opened, it would be like overpumping a car tire. There would be a tremendous surge of electrical energy.

*Whomp!*

It wasn't the batteries. It was what went into the batteries, a train racing out of control through a tunnel.

"When that happens, the thing would be better for cooking waffles," the lab guy said.

He also said he was dead certain that this flaw in the circuitry had to have been engineered into the system to take its cue from the software.

"It was like a damn time bomb ready to respond to a certain set of commands," he said. "Absolutely ingenious."

"Was it the Unabomber?" Lily asked.

"Probably not. This was like nothing the Unabomber had ever shown the bureau," the lab guy said. And there was a measure of respect in his voice. "It was so much more sophisticated, it had to be the work of someone who really knew his way around an operating system. Not just any system. This system in particular.

"Had to be an inside job," the lab guy added.

Then he said something that caused Lily to sit straight up in her chair.

"The hard disks were not ruined. We were able to retrieve information off them right up until the time the machines flamed out," he said. "Whoever was using them was having e-mail sex. And get this. With the same person. Her screen name is RoseD."

Lily called her boss in San Francisco. And then she e-mailed Maria Cisneros.

Can we meet for a drink? LilyFBI.

# chapter 13

**There was a time in the Valley's very recent history** when it would have been considered presumptuous to hold a press conference to announce a mere $2 million business deal. But now, the way competition was heating up, the way ideas were flying around like loose atoms and actually sticking, it was de rigueur to share every incremental triumph, especially when it appeared you were reacting to a leak in the press.

A preemptive press conference was the best course, like artillery fire in the night. Even if you missed the target, the flashes, the thunder of it all, still caused the competition to pay attention. Sanders at AMD, Grove at Intel, Jim Clark at Netscape, Scott McNealy at Sun Micro and Larry Ellison, the combative founder of Oracle, the software database company, were all masters at converting corporate musings into headlines.

But there was no fleeter lip than J. P. McCorwin.

On this day, resplendent in his black Armani T-shirt, framed dramatically against a gigantic whiteboard as the cool sounds of Keith Jarrett's keyboard flowed like water from two Bose speakers small enough to hold in the palm of the hand, J.P. bounced on the balls of his feet, looking wide-eyed and ready to discuss his secret alliance with Infinity Computer. He welcomed every question the way Jerry Rice welcomed every pass. With his every answer, J. P. McCorwin would prove he was back in the game.

"What's the name of this new company, J.P.?" a reporter for the *San Francisco Chronicle* challenged him right off the bat. The reporter had been around awhile and was considered something of a wise guy. He had often been quoted by his fellow reporters as sneering: "Covering business is no different than covering sports, except the math can get a little hairier."

"That's a very relevant question, baby. At this point we don't have a name," J.P. said, clearly on the upswing and winking at Baba RAM DOS. "At this point, we don't even want one. A name would just slow us down. Bad sangfroid. We don't need that kind of baggage where we're going."

That led to a series of questions about his plans for exploring cyberspace, which he parried deftly, offering just enough so that the reporters took notes.

What they would lead with the next morning was essentially the same, whether the story appeared in the *Chronicle*, the *Mercury News*, the *Wall Street Journal* or the *New York Times*.

J. P. McCorwin was back. Anyone needing proof should consider his latest promise:

"In our camp, speed and efficiency and personal bandwidths are everything. We will be so efficient, we will establish interactive profiles of all our workers so that their every need is provided for. They need look nowhere else for care and comfort. We will develop a food consumption profile, just the right amount of biomass, vitamins, minerals and caffeine to fuel each physique. We will establish a needs matrix and virtually cater to each employee. We will encourage e-mail relationships. It's just so much more efficient than meeting outside for lunch or paying day rates at the Holiday Inn. . . . Think about it."

This drew laughter and showed up high in the articles the next morning.

But that was just J.P.'s warm-up act.

He cut the lights and booted up the multimedia operating system. It showed the guts of a computer. Its motherboard, disk drive, circuits, power switches, card slots. "The FirePower is a mighty machine," he said, taking a pointer and moving it along the labyrinthine circuitry. "But here is where we discovered that it was incompatible with the real world."

He stopped at the battery.

"The engineers wanted to use a new lithium ion. The concept was commendable. Coupled with its vast energy storage reservoir, lithium would give the FirePower much longer battery life than the competition, between 6.5 and seven hours. It is also lighter than the other nickel batteries. Lithium is the lightest known metal. It is also a very fast conductor. Two generations ago, scientists had so much respect for its speed, they used it in thermonuclear explosives. And that was the problem. With a surge of energy running through it, there was a tendency to . . . well . . . spontaneously combust.

"We discovered this only after extensive, but I would say intensive, product testing by our R&D staff," he said, still pointing at the battery.

Even from where she was sitting in the back of the room, Maria Cisneros had a good view of the demonstration. She had set up the press conference to respond to a leak about the secret research. And now she was feeling a touch of weirdness.

The only R&D guy who'd touched the thing was Jason what's-his-name in software, who claimed he had been loading screen savers. Just being there when the laptop blew up was hardly product testing. What's more, as far as she knew, the only other people to actually test the laptops were J.P. himself and Brad Roth, who got burned at home, and two guys from Infinity whom J.P. knew and didn't particularly like. That was it.

She started to fidget and felt the hand of Baba RAM DOS on her shoulder.

"He's doing magnificently, eh?" Baba whispered, squeezing gently.

"So we are here to say that our worst fears will be unrealized," J.P. continued. "There will be no virus epidemic, no outbreak. We have recommended to the chairman and to the president of Infinity Computer that, for the time being, they retrofit their FirePower with a more conventional nickel hydride battery, and they have agreed to begin immediately."

And the reporters took notes.

"When will they begin to ship again?" one asked.

"I can't speak for Infinity . . ."

"But you'd like to," another reporter interrupted, drawing laughter. J.P. even joined in. He appreciated irreverent wit. And the truth.

"I have consulted with the folks at Infinity," he said. "Following our advice, they should begin getting the product to market by just after Thanksgiving. In any case, it should be on the shelves at Fry's and CompUSA before Christmas."

The press conference wound down with questions J.P. refused to speculate on, questions about restoring Infinity's quarterly earnings and boosting its market share, not to mention even more pointed questions about Infinity's losing ground to Wintel.

On these subjects, J. P. McCorwin remained resolute.

"I can only say we will do whatever we can to help stop the

onslaught," he said. "Technology is not about monopolistic domination and enslavement. Technology is about love and anarchy and independence. That is what the founders of Infinity Computer set out to achieve more than twenty years ago. I was lucky enough to be part of that crusade. And I intend to do everything in my power to help restore it.

"I consider this a personal crusade. You guys can put that down. This is a crusade."

Maria found herself wanting to applaud. And yet, something was odd. She rolled back a mental tape of the press conference, pushing the pause button on all the disconnects between J.P.'s speech and what she knew to be reality.

Very weird, she thought as she and J.P. and Baba escorted the reporters out the door.

"Pretty good, wasn't I," J.P. said, as soon as they were alone. It was a declaration, not a question. "But that lightweight from the *Chronicle* . . .

" 'What's the name of your company?' " he said mockingly.

"That was . . . what is the word in English?" Baba weighed in. "A 4-megabyte question. These guys are all so much deem bulbs."

J.P. laughed. Baba laughed.

Maria followed the two into J.P.'s office and stood idly as J.P. fielded some phone messages.

There was already a congratulations from the chairman of Infinity, who seemed to have recovered fully from the loss of corporate face when word leaked that Infinity had secretly outsourced to solve its laptop problems. The chairman didn't seem the least put out that J.P. had, in fact, been speaking for them. The chairman proposed lunch the next day at the Silicon Valley Capital Club in downtown San Jose. The name spoke for itself. And the implications were obvious. This could be a score.

"Hooked 'em," J.P. said to Baba. "Maria, I can see another press conference in our futures."

There was another call. It was from Larry Ellison, the head of Oracle. He was one of the biggest sharks in the tank. Rumors were flying that Ellison, the onetime dead-end kid from Chicago and now one of the richest guys in Silicon Valley, was planning a breakout. He was thinking of a cheap "network computer" that didn't need its own software or hard drives or even a monitor. All it needed was a television screen and a phone line and presto, you were hooked into the Internet. The Internet would drive the platform Ellison envisioned.

"It's brilliant," J.P. pronounced. "Like harnessing the energy of the cosmos."

He knew Ellison to be a man of contradictions and delusions of grandeur. Ellison was, for instance, personally overseeing the excavation of 41,000 cubic feet of dirt from land in Woodside for his Zen spiritual center, where he could meditate and cut things down with a samurai sword without having to file an environmental impact report. J.P. admired him for that.

The Oracle CEO was also rumored to be trying to form a software alliance with Steve Jobs. J.P. despised Jobs, whom he had once called "psychologically impaired," and was quick to remind everyone that "Steven P. was adopted, which explains everything." But the hard rumors had it that Ellison and Jobs were plotting to merge their software alliance with Infinity's software division, apparently in order to establish a stronger line of defense against the Microsoft-Intel Axis.

This rumor had drawn predictable scoffs from Bill Gates. But J.P. thought it was all rather transparent. What they were really after was a takeover of the entire damn Infinity operation, which was worth billions. This did not sit well with J.P.'s business plan. If anyone were going to take over his old company, it would be him.

In any case, he returned the call. Ellison was also an old carousing buddy and fellow meditation devotee. They talked amiably and made a date to do some nightclub crawling in San Francisco next Wednesday night. Maybe they'd conclude the evening in the Japanese baths at the Miyako Hotel.

"Just like old times," J.P. said, vigorously rubbing his hands together as though he were trying to start a fire.

# chapter 14

**The cockpit-red dashboard digitals glowed 7:55** when Maria pulled her BMW 325i off the Central Expressway and into the packed parking lot of the Decathlon Club in Santa Clara. She made a point of noting the time, especially on Friday nights when she entered her workout zone. Solo.

It was a pattern.

Early in the week, she had made a weekend reservation for herself at the Joshua Grindle Inn, one of those gingerbread B&Bs in Mendocino offering ocean views, a studiously unhurried pace, organic scones and herbal teas. On Friday morning, she canceled.

It wasn't just the drive that daunted her. It was making the drive alone. But even that wasn't quite the whole of it. The pattern usually went something like this: After a nothing weekend, she would resolve on Monday morning to turn things around by the following weekend. Then work would intervene. Then it would be Friday. She would be drained, mentally and physically. The planning, the packing, the effort just to escape acquired the onus of a trek up Annapurna. She canceled ski weekends in the Sierra with friends. She canceled camping trips to the Lost Coast and to Big Sur. Not long ago, she even canceled too late—her reservation, plus massage, at the Sonoma Mission Inn—and forfeited her $200 deposit.

At work, though, Maria was tireless, attending to every detail, never too busy to talk to whomever might need her. But when it came to socializing, she was becoming reclusive.

Someone had said that the only good men still left in the world were either locked away in bad marriages or trapped in their lack of imaginations. But Maria didn't know about that.

She'd had a few episodic relationships, but none lasted more than a couple of months. One boyfriend, Nathan, was actually sweet and compliant. He sold commercial real estate and he talked about taking her on a bike trip across France.

"Sometime, I'll probably get married," he told her one rainy Sunday night as they sipped a low-tannin 1991 Duckhorn merlot (Three Palms Vineyards) while lazing by his fireplace, watching the blaze recede into embers.

"Don't laugh," he confided. "I think I'd be a pretty good Little League coach. Or soccer. That's a great sport for kids."

Maria refused to take the bait. "I'll consider marriage the day at least half the married couples I know are happy," she said, and launched into a litany of troubles her friends were having.

Soon, work demands intervened, and it became harder to set dates and keep them. They drifted apart. Now she couldn't bring herself to call and invite him to a movie, even if it meant staying home alone on a Friday night.

She had meant what she said about marriage at the time. But she also knew her words were harsher by far than she felt.

Maria knew she was becoming cynical. And she worried that she might be letting herself sink into depression.

She usually spent Friday mornings empathizing with Rachel, who had inevitably suffered some terrible travail on *Friends* the night before. By Friday afternoon, she was out of gas. She expected she would be and planned accordingly.

And so, Friday nights were becoming self-fulfilling prophecies. She had a choice. She could do "home alone": Buy herself an extra-special $14 bottle of Sonoma-Cutrer chardonnay and dive into one of her Joyce Goldstein cookbooks, sometimes concocting some little polenta-based thing with portobello mushrooms and an elaborate salad—usually enough for two or three, just in case somebody dropped by. This killed a lot of time.

Sometimes, if she was feeling up to it, she even ran her David Orrick eight-pound vacuum cleaner over the carpets and bleached oak floors of her condo in Los Gatos to stifle a rebellious burst of unbidden energy. But usually, she would conclude the evening alone with Carol Shields or Isabel Allende, Amy Tan or Jane Smiley (a sister horse person), and Maria prayed that each of them was finishing another novel to enable her to salvage her own tragic future Friday nights. And yet, no matter how much she loved their words and characters, Maria was aware that more and more she needed to reread entire chapters.

Concentrate, she'd tell herself. And, moments later, her mind would be racing again.

She worried about protecting her father's investment in the startup she was part of. She worried that she was not technologically savvy. She worried that her relationship with her engineer sister in Massachusetts was suffering neglect. She worried that her own body was suffering from neglect.

When she really got agitated, she forced herself to hit aerobics classes at Move-It, near her condo, or to go to the Decathlon Club, which, truth be told, she was using less as a fitness center than a Mecca for networking and deal-making.

On Friday nights, it became an aerobic Lonely Hearts Club. Which made everyone self-conscious and caused them to go into hyperdedicated workout modes. The Valley was not about sympathy. It was about survivability.

Judging from the number of cars in the parking lot on this Friday night, Maria took solace in knowing she wasn't the only one left holding her gym bag. Instinctively, she parked her little two-door convertible toward the middle of the well-lighted lot, surrounded by other inconspicuous vehicles. Such was the social convention of the Valley. Anyone who could afford anything starting around a BMW 500-series, Lexus, Mercedes, Porsche or Jag on up preferred to remain at work or at their home entertainment centers rather than be caught soloing with the other serfs in the club's workout complex on a Friday night.

Which caused Maria nearly to shout with joy when she crossed over the indoor creek and spotted Lily Watanabe limbering up in the workout area.

"Hi," Maria said.

"Oh, hi," Lily said, looking surprised. She shot Maria a "Come here often?" look and both shrugged and laughed.

Maria was impressed by how waiflike but totally taut Lily looked in her gray Nike cutaway halter top and electric blue Spandex skintights. She hit the locker room, changed quickly into tights and slipped on a thin sweatshirt that said NO FEAR. She returned to the workout area just as Lily said, "One hundred!" and concluded her sit-up routine. "Whew," Lily gasped. "I haven't been here in a while. But I used to come a lot to blow off steam when I was working on the Kevin Mitnick case. You know that one?"

"Vaguely," Maria replied as she sat on a mat and eased into some stretches. "Wasn't he the hacker who gained access to something like 20,000 credit card numbers and supposedly secure files at Apple and Motorola before he was caught through the Internet?"

"Right," Lily said, flashing a bright smile. "I brought in Tsutomu Shimomura, the programmer who tracked him down. We're cross-country skiing buddies. The bureau hired him as a consultant, and now he's famous. He's known as the 'Cybersleuth.' They're even making a movie about the whole case."

"Are you in it?" Maria asked. "You look good enough to play yourself."

Lily smiled but said nothing. She was scanning the workout area for a vacant StairMaster. One presented itself, but she demurred and continued to scan and stretch and make small talk. A few minutes later, two became available side by side, and Lily and Maria took their places among more than two dozen other StairMaster jockeys, all staring at a big-screen television tuned to CNN. Maria concentrated on her aerobic resistance, setting the controls well below max. She also set it on Interval Training to vary the speed and stride of her program and keep her from becoming bored. Lily, on the other hand, selected the Blast-off program and maxed her own resistance setting.

Lily stared at the TV screen, appearing to concentrate. This was the protocol for the exercise: Stare straight ahead, never at the control panel. Concede nothing. That's what it was all about, especially on Friday nights.

Lily kept up a steady banter without seeming to even breathe hard, which was beginning to irritate Maria until the FBI agent said, "By the way, we've found out something about the flaming laptops. You know, the ones you loaned me? Our guys have been over them pretty well. Our guys think the combustion was not caused by a virus or faulty batteries. Our guys think someone rearranged the gate array on the output for the power reservoir."

Maria sought to make eye contact with Lily. What was this about? But Lily continued staring straight ahead, betraying nothing.

"In other words, the predisposition to explode was engineered into the laptops," the FBI agent said.

But there was more. Lily ended her program and climbed down. She stood beside Maria.

"Our guys were also able to restore the programs that were running when they ignited," she said. "Both programs were exactly alike. I mean, both guys were on e-mail at the time."

Lily took her eyes off the TV screen and locked them onto Maria's.

"Here's the thing: Both guys were in the middle of a fast-and-furious dialogue. . . . That's actually too polite a term. They were both engaged in live online sex," Lily said. "And that's not all. The object of their affection was the same person.

"RoseD. She must be something. Does she work with you? Do you know her?"

Maria clutched hard at the support bars running from the control panel. She felt as if she was falling down the stairs she was supposed to be climbing.

"No. I don't know anyone by that name," she said.

What Maria didn't say was that Brad Roth had asked her the very same question—"RoseD?"—more than once.

Maria pushed with all her will against the StairMaster's pedals, wishing the machine would bear her upward and out of the club and Silicon Valley at that very moment.

# chapter 15

**When the 911 call came crackling into their black-and-white cruiser,** Atherton police officers Pierce Cullen and Chip Meyers already were performing triple duty. The two represented one-twelfth of the entire police force guarding one of the world's richest communities, and they undertook their responsibilities zealously—just as the 7,500 denizens of the 94027 zip code expected.

They had taken up a vigilant position under a spreading oak

tree on a quiet, curvy street, where they were hard at work waiting for anyone—including bicyclists—to violate the 25-mph speed limit. That was just one of their responsibilities. They were also vigilant for any of the other element who might have crossed over from East Palo Alto or Redwood City, or anyone who looked unfamiliar and who so much as slowed down to maybe case one of the French château-style or Mediterranean revival houses built to the scale of the booming stock market.

Officers Cullen and Meyers were not so well trained that they could not make allowances for the shabby station wagons and pickups of the nannies, gardeners, housekeepers and pool cleaners, who at times seemed to be the only inhabitants other than the watchdogs. (Atherton had more GUARD DOG ON DUTY signs posted per block than any other community in northern California.)

Cullen and Meyers knew their jobs were no different from those of their fellow officers: Their jobs were to keep the peace. A gate left open, a pair of Dobermans gamboling? Officers Cullen and Meyers to the roundup, often shutting the gate so that the owners would never know their guard dogs had gotten loose. A private alarm accidentally tripped (this happened a dozen times a night)? The officers were on it, assisting homeowners, including repeat offenders, to shut the thing off. No questions asked, and certainly no Breathalyzer would ever be administered on private property. When a party got out of hand, it was their duty to intervene, sometimes even using their patrol vehicle to escort guests who were, say, no longer welcome, out of the vicinity, just to minimize everyone's chagrin.

Cullen and Meyers were models of decorum, never above going to extremes to assure the neighborhood the peace and quiet residents believed they had earned.

When the 911 call broke the calm of the night with this bulletin: "All units, neighbor reports flames, possibly full-structure involvement.... Potential serious injury.... Menlo Park Fire Department responding..." Meyers acknowledged immediately. "Atherton Unit Two will arrive within two minutes!"

Cullen switched on the siren: "To hell with the speed limit!"

The cruiser rocked around every turn, but Meyers was able to check the address against the criss-cross directory and the Standard & Poor's Register. "Jeez!" he whistled. "The Hopkins place. Harold Hopkins. Young guy, hot venture capitalist. Board of directors of The Gap, San Francisco Opera, Pacific Lumber, National Semi, Infinity Computer, Williams-Sonoma, Wolfgang Puck Food Company, etc., etc."

"Maybe he was into too much BTU on the restaurant-strength range," Cullen said, as they careened around a final curve and headed up the long driveway. The gate was open; another patrol car had beaten them to the scene.

"Holy hell! Look at that!"

A pyramid of flame and smoke threatened to engulf one entire wing of the villa-style mansion. Against the glow of the flames, Cullen and Meyers could see the profiles of two other officers hauling two limp bodies out the front door.

"Anyone else in there?" one of the officers shouted.

"Yes, yes," one of the victims said, choking and sagging to her knees, "Daisy, Daisy, please, please save her."

Cullen and Meyers charged full-tilt into the burning mansion and did not hear the weak voice behind them whisper: "Daisy, our cockatoo."

"A goddamn bird," Cullen sputtered to the Menlo Park fireman who pulled him out five minutes later. "Is that what you're telling me? We risked our lives for a frigging bird? . . . I thought we were looking for some little kid."

He was choking and on the verge of tears.

The firefighter deposited Cullen next to Meyers, who was lying on the lawn beside the victims. He was vomiting and seemed dazed, but at least he wasn't burned beyond retaining his professional comportment.

"Sorry, Mrs. Hopkins," Meyers said. "We did all we could. . . . It was like a furnace in there."

A fire investigator was kneeling beside the man, presumably Harry Hopkins, as a paramedic, holding a respirator, patched in an

IV. He was badly burned, Cullen could tell. Little was left of the venture capitalist's shirt; bits were stuck to the flesh of his shoulders and back. His face was blackened; most of his hair was gone. His eyes looked glassy, and he wore an eerie, beatific smile.

Cullen had seen the look before in burn victims. It was shock, virtually a state of grace. Shock helped mask the pain, which would be nearly unbearable in a couple of days.

"I don't understand," the man wailed. Cullen had seen him before, possibly in a photo in the business pages of the *Mercury News*. He knew him to be in his late thirties or early forties. But tonight, Harry Hopkins looked ancient. "I don't understand. I just got this thing in the mail. I, I, just took it out of the box."

He half-turned to the fire department investigator and held up his hands: "I don't understand. I took it out, plugged it in and *pow*. The flame climbed right up the curtain."

"What thing?" the investigator asked. "What thing, Mr. Hopkins?"

"The, the computer. The new little computer—one of those portable ones," he said weakly as two paramedics lifted him onto a gurney. His wife was already in the ambulance.

"Boy, that's a lot of firepower, Mr. Hopkins," the fire investigator said, turning back toward the house.

"Precisely," the venture capitalist said. "FirePower. An Infinity FirePower. . . . I'm on the board, you know."

# chapter 16

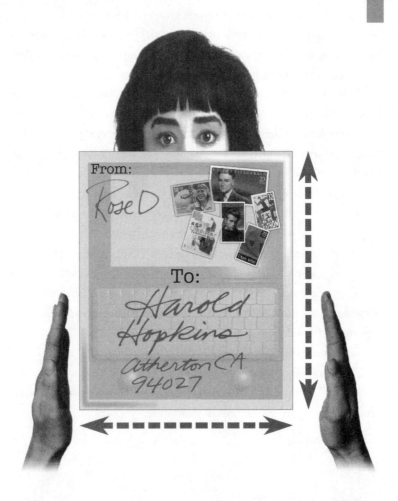

From:

Rose D

To:

Harold
Hopkins
Atherton CA
94027

**"Feeling OK?" Maria asked solici-
tously.** J.P.'s eyes were nearly as red as the digital clock that
glowed 7:56 A.M. Baba RAM DOS was leaning against the big
picture window, and his face betrayed a nurselike look of concern.

"That little old software shark still likes to play hard," J.P.
replied, massaging his eyelids. "Hey, Maria, do you know anything
about eyeball kneading? It's an old Zen exercise for redirecting

pain and anxiety. See, you use your fingers to manipulate the eyeballs to create centrifugal force . . ."

Maria had grown accustomed to J.P.'s obtuse, playful come-ons. This time she felt certain he had been unduly influenced by Larry Ellison, who had recently settled a lawsuit filed by an executive assistant who insisted she was fired because she refused to have sex with him. Maria did not care for the Ellison she knew through newspaper reports and rumors of his sporting life with women.

In any case, it was clear to her that her boss and Ellison had enjoyed quite a night in San Francisco.

J.P. started to regale Maria and Baba with the details: dinner at Bix near the Financial District with some venture capitalists ("In the old Barbary Coast days, the place used to feature girls swinging over the dinner crowd on trapezes"), hanging out in some alternative industrial-style dance clubs south of Market, then back to Bix for a nightcap or two.

"Dolce, made sauterne-style by Far Niente of Napa," J.P. said, looking to Baba for approval. "Eighteen-seventy-five a glass."

Baba shrugged indifference. Maria had heard Baba say often: "If one cannot have zee Château d'Yquem, one simply limits one's pleasure to nothing at all."

J.P. ignored him and pressed on. "We were joined by two really lovely—and, I assume, intelligent—women. After a while, I get up to go to the men's room and when I return I see Larry walking out with one girl on each arm."

He was mustering the energy to sound indignant. Maria knew he was not. It was all in sport. She began to disconnect.

"They leave me, *moi*, with the bill. And since Larry and I had driven up together in his SL, I'm stranded. . . . So I call a cab and tell the driver, 'Woodside!' My place. The fare's over a hundred bucks, but I give the cabby two hundred and tell him that's the tip. I give him the address of Larry's 12,000-square-foot pied-à-terre in Atherton and tell him to drive over and stick Larry with the actual charge."

Maria could tell that J.P. was building to the climax. She hoped it wouldn't be embarrassing. Baba was beginning to fidget, and Maria guessed he had already heard the rest of the story.

"So what happens? Guy comes back. It's like 2 A.M. and he's ringing my doorbell." J.P. was still rubbing his eyeballs. "He says he can't get through to Larry's house. The police and fire departments have all the streets blocked off. There's a big fire, or at least, judging from the number of red lights flashing, it's a big deal."

Baba hissed an expletive in French that Maria couldn't quite hear.

"It turns out it was a very, very big deal," J.P. continued. "It was Harry Hopkins's place. . . . Harry Hopkins, you know? Big VC, all kinds of boards."

"We know him well, eh, *mon ami?*" Baba said to J.P.

"He was on the board of directors of Infinity during the inquisition when Baba and I were let go," J.P. continued. He suddenly looked gray. "Humorless. Very unromantic, very bottom-line. He's still on the board, and we hear he's one of the movers for downsizing or selling out altogether."

"You know what VC stands for?" Baba asked Maria. "Vichy coward . . ."

Maria got the point.

"Was he hurt badly?" she asked.

"Bad enough," J.P. said. "At least that's what KCBS said this morning. But who knows? The announcer was one of those cheerful types who delivers the traffic reports."

Just then, J.P.'s intercom rang. He picked up the receiver and said, "Right. Put him through.

"Hi, Larry, hey, how'd you do last night, ha ha? Hey, you owe me a hundred bucks for a taxi. . . . What? He is? He is? . . . She is? . . . Hmmm."

J.P. turned from the receiver and winked directly at Baba.

"OK. Right. Yeah, I'll have one of my people send flowers over," J.P. said. "Hey, you still owe me a hundred bucks. . . . Wha? Wha? Well, same to you, buddy . . ."

J.P. abruptly hung up the phone. His face was even grayer. "You know what he said? He said that's all our stock will be worth—a hundred bucks. Boy, he can really be a jerk sometimes."

He got up and started to pace.

"Jeez, Margot, too."

"Well?" Maria asked. "What else? How's Harry Hopkins?"

"Yeah, Harry. Oh, yeah, both he and Margot, his wife, at least she was his wife," J.P. said, sending a grin Baba's way. "They're both in Stanford Hospital. Harry's upper body is pretty badly burned, but he's out of intensive care. Larry says, as a good neighbor, he's already scheduled him with a plastic surgeon. Margot swallowed a lot of smoke, but she's expected to be out by tonight or tomorrow.

"Hmmmm," J.P. mumbled, and then cursed and repeated, "Jeez, Margot, too," to Baba, who looked away. Maria had never seen J.P. so agitated unless he was trying to download something free off the Net. Plus he was twisting his body in an unnatural way, as if he was trying to corkscrew himself through the floor. Even more, there were the looks, the silent signals exchanged between J.P. and Baba and clearly meant for them alone.

She felt incredibly diminished.

J.P. paced around his office like a caged animal. Then he stopped and looked squarely at Maria.

"Lunch later?" he said.

"OK, sure," she said.

"Good, I have something serious I want to discuss with you," J.P. said. "By the way, on the way out, would you stop by the admin pod and ask them to send flowers and personal notes from me to Harry and Margot?"

On her way back to her office, Maria asked one of the assistants to order assorted herb baskets from Smith & Hawken at the Stanford Shopping Center to be sent to the hospital.

"Who for?" the assistant asked.

"Harry and Margot Hopkins," Maria answered.

As Maria started to dictate the notes from J.P., the assistant interrupted: "Harry Hopkins . . . hmm . . . he's popular."

"What do you mean?" Maria asked.

"We sent him a package just yesterday. Or at least, somebody did." She held her hands about a foot apart, maybe a little more, to convey the approximate size and shape.

Maria shuddered. She couldn't stop her thoughts. The assistant's hands were forming the shape and size of a laptop computer.

"It was waiting in the out-mail basket when I got here yesterday morning. All stamped and everything. Definitely had our return address on it," the assistant said. "But the name was weird. RoseD. We don't have anyone here by that name, do we?"

Maria shook her head and shuddered again.

# chapter 17

**"Look around," J.P. said,** sweeping his hand in
a beckoning motion around the peach and gold walls and picture
windows of the Silicon Valley Capital Club. The view was spectacular. Theirs offered a panorama of downtown San Jose and the
haze-filled valley and highway corridors that stretched to the Santa
Cruz Mountains. "No, over there. At that table. That's Gordon
Moore."

Maria recognized him instantly. Next to David Packard and Bob Noyce, if anyone deserved the title "patriarch of Silicon Valley," it was Moore. It was on Moore's office blackboard in 1959 that the blueprint of the world's first integrated circuit was drawn. "The sketch that changed the world," they called it. From it, the silicon chip was born. And the Santa Clara Valley became the Silicon Valley, and San Jose became the fastest-growing large city in the United States. And Maria's father was headed for early retirement.

Maria had heard the story many times, mostly from her father, who lamented the technological revolution because it signaled the end of an era. Farming would soon give way to office parks and housing developments. The Valley would change forever.

From the initial $500 monthly salary investments that Moore and some other scientists at Fairchild Camera and Instrument had pooled, along with a two-page business plan, a $100 billion high-tech industry was born.

"That's Andy Grove with him," Maria said, recognizing the president and CEO of Intel, which Moore cofounded in 1968. From her case studies at Stanford Business School and later, with Regis McKenna, when she worked on its account, she remembered that Intel's initial sales were around $3,000 in 1969. This year, its net income was supposed to be something like $3.7 billion.

"And look who's with them," J.P. growled. "The chairman."

As if on cue, all three—the chairman of Intel, the president of Intel (the Silicon Valley half of the Microsoft-Intel alliance) and the chairman of Infinity Computer (supposedly the sworn enemy of the other two)—turned toward J.P. and Maria. J.P. grinned and gave a half-wave, half-salute. They did likewise and turned back to whatever it was they were discussing.

"It has to be business," J.P. muttered. "Jeez. He's doing business with the enemy. He's that desperate."

It was the fourth time recently that Maria had seen J.P. come unglued. First, when he personally extinguished the fire that was raging on the chest hairs of Jason what's-his-name; second, when she told him that she had turned over the exploding laptops to the

FBI; third, when he heard about the flameout at the Atherton venture capitalist's house.

"Not such a great week, huh?" Maria said. "Loaded with contretemps."

She was trying to provoke J.P. in a code he might understand. Just what the hell was going on? Another fire, another FirePower connection? Her guts were telling her she needed to ask J.P. something. But what? Reveal that she didn't trust him?

Did she trust him?

*"Au contraire,"* J.P. retorted. "This week has the promise of being very . . . revenue-connected."

In spite of last night's abrupt ending and the bad news about Harry Hopkins getting burned, J.P. said he had accomplished what he had set out to do. He had gotten inside Larry Ellison's head.

"He really thinks the world wants a $500 Internet-driven network computer. Or is it his penance for nearly pushing his company over the edge back in the late '80s and generating so much stress? He really thinks he was put on earth to provide computers for the masses.

"He's talking about 4 megs of random-access memory, 4 megs of flash RAM for a few basic programs with a small RISC microprocessor, some kind of connection to the TV. He's talking about no hard drive. He's talking about having all the applications stored on the network rather than inside the machine," J.P. said. "But I'll tell you something. It isn't the price that will deliver; it is what $500 won't deliver. People will pay for performance—speed, precision, access, customization and socialization."

Maria remembered reading those very lines this week in the *Mercury News*, or maybe the *Wall Street Journal*. They had been spoken by her former boss Scott McNealy, the head of Sun Microsystems. She was beginning to lose patience. "Come on, J.P., we've heard that speech," Maria blurted, surprised at her own rush of courage. She kept pushing, knowing she shouldn't. "McNealy, wasn't it?"

He seemed unruffled.

"Yes, but McNealy runs a company that primarily makes workstations. Workstations are too cumbersome for the masses, even if they are fueled by Java language for the Net and can hop around all over the place. Even if they have forced Microsoft to take out a Java license. Although that's the key . . . the license."

Maria cocked her head.

"See, that tells me that Bill Gates understands what he's got to do next. He's got to get up and running on the Internet, like right now. Or he's dead. He instinctively understands that PCs are still the future. They are. But he also knows that software could be a thing of the past even well before the millennium. He's using Java to take some initial shortcuts. My guess is that once he's got the technology copied, he'll come up with something of his own, which will suddenly be the only application Windows understands. So he'll kill off Java. And go after Sun. . . . Think about it.

"So here's the deal," he said, looking as if he were expecting her to take notes.

Maria wondered if J.P. was a bit hungover. He rambled on.

"Gates doesn't get it. He's never gotten it. His time is about up, even if he does manage to hitch Microsoft to the Net. See, he really is a nerd. He really believes a relationship with a PC is like a lord and a serf. He loves giving a computer orders and having it obey, just like you and your horse."

Maria blanched. But she got the point.

"As long as Gates stays a little boy, and as long as his personal fascination with computers holds, as long as he thinks he can really control the universe, Microsoft will always be the same," J.P. continued. "Like a little boy, like Caesar and Napoleon, he'll keep fighting like crazy to hold onto what he has. In order to do that, to protect his borders, he thinks he has to claim new territory and kill off the competition. But he won't make any spiritual advances."

He's stalling, Maria thought. He knows I want to ask him something. He knows I want him to come to the point.

"This is where we come in. We stand for connectivity," J.P. continued, fingering his earring.

He sat back and gave Maria time to ponder and appreciate his sagacity.

"See, Gates is counting on computers staying dumb. If they stay that way, he stays in control. But we can help smarten them up. We can enlighten them, open them up. And when we do, the whole network becomes a galactic brain. Information is no longer passive; it comes at us like a meteor shower. The trick then is to navigate through it and to our destinations. That's what I was talking to the chairman about yesterday," he said, nodding in the direction of the table the Infinity chairman was sharing with Moore and Grove.

J.P. suddenly flinched, distracted. He started to rise from his chair. The three Silicon Valley giants were approaching their table.

Now standing, J.P. extended a hand to the chairman, who shook it and patted him on the back, congratulating him on his "lovely luncheon companion." Then the chairman decorously shook hands with Maria and introduced her to Moore, an avuncular man in his late sixties—Maria thought he looked like a deputy sheriff, which his father had been in Pescadero, where Moore was raised—and to Grove, who looked feral, telling them both that she'd been a key player in the successful joint venture to squelch the fires in Infinity's laptops. J.P. was obviously well known to the two Intel executives. They'd tried to recruit him once, before his wonderful failures at Infinity. Both seemed sincere in welcoming him back into the competitive loop.

"We could use a little entertainment," Grove said. Maria instantly picked up on his famous sardonic side.

"Andy, Gordon, I was just asking Maria to add another title to her business card," J.P. said. "I'm trying to persuade her to become my executive assistant."

The other men nodded their approval and saluted J.P. as they took their leave. "Call me tomorrow," the chairman said over his shoulder. "By the way, you hear about Harry Hopkins?"

J.P. nodded and looked sympathetic.

When they were out of listening range, J.P. said: "Maybe he had those guys give him an oral nondisclosure agreement."

"Or maybe the chairman was setting them up for a deal of his own," Maria offered. "Like looking to buy the Pentium chip. . . . Or offering Infinity for sale."

J.P. shot her a surrender-is-no-option glare and said: "So you want the job or not? Even longer hours, more connectivity with me. A 10 percent raise, 5 percent increase in preferred stock."

Maria tried not to look self-conscious as she considered his proposition.

"As far as I understand it, we don't even know what we're about. We haven't got a name for the company. We haven't even got a next big thing. And, don't get me wrong, but we haven't got a whole lot of money, do we? And there's another question. About those fires in the laptops."

"So is it yes?" J.P. interrupted, showing her his familiar, fervently charming side.

"Let me sleep on it," Maria said just as the waiter arrived with the curry Tillamook Bay scallop soup and small Caesar salad she had ordered. Things were getting intense and she was relieved to get a momentary break.

# chapter 18

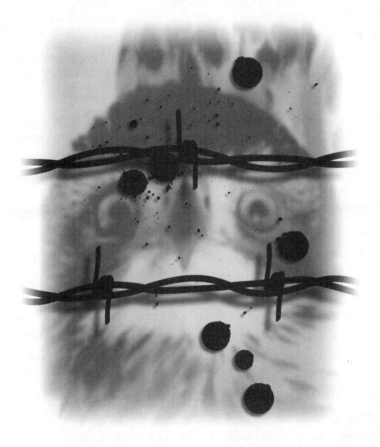

**The ground fog was lifting and re-treating into the hills** as the sun broke free of the eastern ridgeline. Maria was already in the ring, working with Fuego, guiding her Thoroughbred through easy figure eights, changing leads on the fly and working on her own form. But she could also sense her concentration lacking, and her horse could, too. He kept pointing his ears toward the gate, offering an antidote to their morning, and Maria could tell after half an hour that dressage exercises were fruitless. Better to go for a ride in the hills.

She eased along the fence, and Fuego instinctively checked when he came to the gate. Maria bent over, undid the latch and nudged her horse into a deliberate walk, setting off past the exercise ring, the barn and the paddocks holding other horses, who whinnied their envy as Maria and Fuego sauntered by.

She patted his sleek, muscular neck as they walked under a canopy of oaks leading to a wooden bridge that spanned San Francisquito Creek. Maria took comfort in her horse's rhythmic, cradling stride. He seemed so careful, dainty almost, as if picking his way around pebbles. Yet sometimes she imagined him approaching the starting gate at Golden Gate Fields or Bay Meadows this way, with all his power and speed deceptively coiled up inside—just waiting to be unleashed by the starter's gun.

Other times, more often times like these, she transcended into his rhythm, just swaying with her horse and welcoming the sounds of his hooves striking the earth in a rataplan clop and the soft snap-crackle of the leather saddle in motion. If her horse turned his head just so and if she followed his ears, Maria could spot mourning doves roosting in trees or a hawk, perched but poised, awaiting the movement of small game in the field ahead. And very often, Fuego's ears would point to deer that grazed with impunity as horse and rider approached.

"This is the way to bring on the day," Maria said out loud, stretching in the saddle. Fuego nickered in reply and picked up the pace at the slightest nudge of Maria's knees.

They ascended a rise along a line of eucalyptus and moved along a dry streambed, then up again, through a field of sun-bleached, white-gold grass that looked ablaze in the early morning sunshine. When they came to the crest, Maria halted Fuego under an oak tree and gazed down on Highway 280, which bisected the big meadow from the Stanford University hills. From here, the traffic sounded like surf, relentless and inexorable.

She felt a sudden pang. Or maybe it was her subconscious.

She followed the line of cars heading south, deeper into the

Valley. She could see others lining up for the Page Mill Road exit that would take them to Xerox PARC or the high-tech companies in Mountain View.

In an hour or so, she'd be surfing along the highway with the rest of them. She could be doing this for the rest of her life.

It was a morbid thought. But she knew she had potential for dwelling on morbidity. Although she never thought of herself as being depressed.

Just neurotic, she laughed.

She was, after all, in a strange spot. Here she was astride her horse, riding through the hills and getting pangs about what she was facing—a promotion, a raise, more responsibility, and most of all, the risk-reward of a Silicon Valley startup company. In the time she had taken to position herself atop this hill to begin a solemn exercise of quiet contemplation, there were probably two or three fortunes already being made.

Someone, probably younger than her, was meeting right now for breakfast over at Il Fornaio in Palo Alto with a couple of venture capitalists from Kleiner Perkins or investment bankers from Hambrecht & Quist or Morgan Stanley.

She could picture the VCs: studiously casual, hair a little long, Top-Siders, Dockers, cotton sweaters, looking comfortable, almost smug. Who wouldn't be if they were sitting on a pile of money the investment arm of Harvard University or Stanford or some pension fund wanted to wager in the high-tech game?

She could see the young would-be entrepreneur, conspicuous in a starched white shirt and Brioni tie and blue suit, looking very self-conscious.

She could see the whole scenario playing out, the initial polite conversation, the inside joking the VCs would do among themselves. Then the grilling would begin.

She could see the guy spilling his briefcase on the floor and the stifled snickers all around—until he pulled out the next big thing. And everybody would suddenly start concentrating. Maria had witnessed a few of these scenes and she imagined herself in the crossfire. How would she come off?

That depends, she answered, on what it was we had to sell. . . . Certainly not laptops that need "Caution, inflammable" warnings. . . . So what is it we are selling exactly?

She imagined her boss, J. P. McCorwin, in similar circumstances. She imagined him answering every question, parrying every concern, charming the VCs, cajoling them, challenging them, intriguing them and in the end, walking away with a soft circle—a conditional deal worth millions for something he had only dreamed up hours earlier.

The game wasn't completely about software or hardware or product or service anymore. Maria understood that. It had a lot to do with who you were and who you knew. J.P. had the cachet. She could tell by the way the chairman of Infinity Computer and Andy Grove and Gordon Moore had greeted him the day before at the Capital Club.

J.P. was probably in the office already, dialing for dollars. Maybe he'd begun a second round of seed money financing with Infinity. Maybe they were getting close to the brass ring.

If J.P. had the panache, Maria certainly did not. At least that was what she was thinking. But he was offering to guide her onto the path.

So what was she so bothered about? Wasn't this why she had gone to Stanford Biz School? Isn't this what she wanted?

Then why did she have the nagging feeling that something was wrong? Very wrong? It was a feeling she couldn't shake. Why did she long to be sitting on Fuego at the top of a hill outside of Ciudad Obregon in Mexico? Why did she wish the path through the arroyo led to her aunt's house where people she knew and loved would be making tortillas instead of computer chips? Why was she pining to ride her horse into a little Mexican village she could only imagine her parents coming from and exchange *abrazos* and sing songs in Spanish? And then ride her horse along the road toward Guyamas and to the great broad plain of flat white sand and turquoise water. It was her fantasy, fast becoming her obsession.

Stop it, she told herself. Get a grip.

Fuego stamped his hoof, impatient. Maria cleared her head. She was perched on the rim of a golden opportunity. Games like the one she was being invited to play were going on all over the Valley. Half the BMWs and Mercedes convertibles she saw roaring down Highway 280 were probably already paid off with stock options. Why shouldn't she share the present?

Mind games, she reminded herself. Approach-avoidance. You know all about this.

She wheeled Fuego around, actually guiding him to turn on his haunches, a dressage maneuver that called for the horse to plant his hind legs while making a half-circle with his front legs. The show exercise must have looked classy to anyone glimpsing it from the highway. Maria hoped someone noticed.

On the way back, she urged Fuego into a trot and then a controlled canter, talking to him all the while.

"We're going for it, boy. It's right there in front of us. All we have to do is reach out and grab it."

Suddenly, Fuego's ears shot out and he shook his head. He was staring at something. Maria looked hard. Then she saw it. She reined Fuego down to a walk. He shook his head again but she urged him on. When they were within twenty yards, she pulled up and then urged him forward again a step at a time.

In front of them was a magnificent red-tail hawk. His wings were fully extended and stretched four or five feet, tip to tip. His back was beautifully mottled, all brown and black and white. And his rusty red tail feathers were all fanned out. Even his fierce talons were fully extended, as if he were reaching out to snatch his prey.

And at that moment the hawk collided with a barbed-wire fence —and impaled himself. It was as if the force of his own will had blinded him—and then frozen him at the moment of truth.

Maria shuddered and took a deep breath. She couldn't take her eyes off the dead creature. Finally, she looked toward the sky, breathed hard and headed back for the barn.

# chapter 19

**"Download this," J.P. said the second Maria walked into his office.** His spirits were high.

"The chairman and I had a heart-to-heart this morning," he said. "Infinity Computer is reassessing. They're ripe for the picking. They know that. And that's exactly what Andy Grove and Gordon Moore were talking to him about yesterday at lunch. . . . And, oh, keep this offline: They were actually urging the chairman to surrender to Wintel . . . on a nonhostile basis. Said if it was done soon, it would be carried out with dignity and humanity and with a likely short-term uptick in Infinity share prices."

"And?" Maria said.

"And the bottom line is that this so-called friendly offer by the Axis only got the chairman's juices going. That's why he called *moi*," J.P. said, grinning. Then he went into his now-familiar meditative contortion, which signaled that he was about to erupt in rage, inspiration—or was trying to keep the morning sun out of his eyes.

"Here's the problem," he continued, squinting and shielding his eyes with his right hand as if saluting. "Until a few months ago, they had the superior products, laptop flameouts notwithstanding. They had a great operating system. But they overpriced, they under-forecast demand, they refused to license to the knock-off market, they want to be the first corporation to sponsor the Olympic Games, they want to find God through an operating system and . . . they got flaming laptops.

"I want to find God, too. We all want to find God. Right?"

Maria did not answer. She hoped her facial language would force J.P. to get to the point.

"So they have two disastrous quarters, back to back. Even though we doused the flames in the FirePower laptop, the world's confidence in Infinity has been shaken. . . . This is a true fact. According to the chairman, so keep it offline, no one wants to write software for them anymore. Do you understand what that means? It means they are no longer cool. That's what it means. It means that Stanford and Berkeley and probably all the public school systems in California are ready to pull the plug and rewire with PCs, Wintel PCs. Disasterville."

Maria nodded.

J.P. looked solemn. "That's a hell of a problem. To not be cool today is like . . . being middle-aged and not being cool . . . and therefore being thought of only as middle-aged. It's virtual hell."

J.P. was not one for gratuitous expletives. But this had obviously touched a nerve.

"Infinity and I went through our formative years together," he continued, letting his voice drop into a melancholic lower octave. "Not only are they losing their hot software writers, the chairman told me he's already gotten a warning that the bond rating companies are threatening to lower their debt securities ratings. . . . Jeez, there was a time when we had so much money we didn't even worry about debt securities. They were like restaurant bills.

"This is big, big trouble . . . and big trouble for us because we only exist if they exist."

Maria was just starting to sink into the doldrums along with her boss when he leaped to his feet, poised and taut like a Power Ranger.

"So the chairman asks me what he should do. . . . Imagine, after all these years of estrangement, he turns to me. And I can honestly tell you, I got a tear in my eye." She could see another welling. Suddenly, J.P. seemed older, sweeter, sort of like Ronald Reagan.

"So first I told the chairman to string a little barbed wire around the place, you know, shake up the PR department. He said he'd already thought of that. In fact, he just hired a new PR mistress. Her name's Gloria Godsend. You should get to know her.

"Then I gave him some tough-love advice. I told the chairman it was time to stick it to the president," J.P. said. "He should advise the president to fall on his sword, issue a blanket apology to Infinity's shareholders for leading the company into the dumps, and then resign. Sort of the Japanese tradition. Noble."

"How did the chairman respond?" Maria asked.

"He asked me if I would be interested in coming back and running Infinity, started talking about a ten mil package with stock and no-interest loans and all that," J.P. said, looking deep into his own face, which was reflected off the glass frame of a large photo of himself and Linda Ronstadt on safari at the base of Mount Kilimanjaro.

"And?" Maria said. She could feel her heart pounding and her throat tightening. She was having difficulty getting her arms around this.

"And," J.P. said weakly, sounding as if he was coming out of a meditative stupor, "I told the chairman I was interested in helping Infinity Computer, not running Infinity Computer."

It was then that J. P. McCorwin—for the first time ever—confided what he said were his deepest thoughts as to why he and Maria Isabel Cisneros and Brad Roth and some other hotshots were gathered together in a modular building in Cupertino and how they just might be on the brink of becoming terribly rich.

"I told him that Infinity needs to reassert its ideals, the stuff about changing the world, that got everyone hot and bothered in the first place. Look at how far things have come in the past ten years, hell, five years. Five months! The smaller, better, faster thing lives among us. Netscape has shown us the way. But before you sell people on changing the world, you've got to sell them a little sugar water. Everyone is missing that step. We've got to provide a technology that makes people feel better about themselves while they are using it. We've got to provide something for them that is truly *them*, a truly customized platform that knows them."

"You mean reads their minds?" Maria asked, picking up on the scent of a budding symbiosis.

"And their motivations and spiritual needs," J.P. added.

Maria's subconscious was searching for some reference point to J.P.'s apparent vision. It settled on Rilke's essays on love and other difficulties.

"This would be the crowning achievement, the next best thing to end all next best things, the once-and-for-all next best thing," J.P. said, staring out the window at the parking lot space he was planning to convert to a company lawn and recreation pod with a pool, basketball court—"the works"—once the next round of seed money rolled in.

"The ultimate killer application . . . a truly smart, compatible, companionable technology. . . . Think about it," he said.

"Did you try this speech out on the chairman?" Maria asked.

"Obviously."

"What did he say?"

"That it was worth something to have the Infinity name behind such a breakthrough. So, I gave him a ballpark figure . . . fifteen mil . . . and said he could have it on the shelves at Fry's and Comp-USA by the end of the third quarter of fiscal '96."

"And?" Maria stifled her urge to whistle.

"He said he'd get back to me."

"Any idea what this technology would be like?" Maria asked, trying not to sound pessimistic, because she was actually desperate not to become pessimistic.

"I have no idea," J.P. said. "That's the beauty of it. What we are building, with the help of Infinity Computer, I hope, and eventually the venture capitalists, is more than a company; it will be a true democracy, where the coin of the realm is ideas. Anyone is free to offer them, and none will go unvalued.

"For the here-and-now, though, we need to convince the chairman of Infinity Computer that it can be done and we can do it. For our own sake, we need to play some mind games. We line up Infinity seed money and the VCs fall in line."

Then he paused and drew in a deep breath.

"But first, we need to deliver a collateral-bearing illusion," he said.

Maria felt her insides tremble. So they were really starting with nothing. And the goal was to whip up a froth that would whip up the venture capitalists. It was, in effect, a virtual pyramid scheme. She couldn't imagine trying to draw up a business plan, much less a red herring—the critical initial prospectus of a new product—for that.

Her first instinct was to climb back on her horse and ride him as far as he would take her. But then, as if propelled by an uncertain force, she found herself interrupting her boss.

"I accept the offer to be your executive assistant," she said in a voice that was barely a whisper.

# chapter 20

**Lily Watanabe's blue Mazda Miata convertible coupe** and Maria Cisneros's red BMW 325i nearly collided in a parking lot off Bascom Avenue near the Pruneyard shopping center in San Jose, symbolizing their emerging relationship.

It was 7:42 P.M. on a Saturday, three minutes before they had agreed to meet. Neither wanted to be late.

Lily had called Friday and asked to hook up again at the De-cathlon Club. Maria begged off. But Lily persisted.

"What about dinner tomorrow?" she said.

Maria could not come up with an excuse. So they agreed on a place, Chez Sovan, a Cambodian restaurant, high on their mutual list of favorites.

Lily giggled at their near-miss as Maria held open the restaurant door. It was in a low-slung building at the far end of a commercial thoroughfare. Next door was a FOR LEASE sign. Pausing in the restaurant doorway, Maria noticed how attitudinal Lily looked in a skimpy black skirt flared over black tights and Doc Martens urban combat boots. She was also wearing a wonderful plum scallop-neck T-shirt that definitely was not from J. Crew or The Gap. Over it was an equally wonderful soft black leather jacket cut smartly to the waist.

Maria couldn't help herself. Too well-fitted for Banana Repub-lic, she thought. Was it a Calvin? Armani? Versace? How much do government employees make these days, anyway? Maria wondered whether her own DKNY wool slacks were too bunchy and whether the silver lapel pin on her oversized black wool blazer was big enough.

They slid into a table for two against the wall facing the en-trance and Lily immediately put Maria at ease, remarking how peaceful the place was, with its recessed murals of the soothing Cambodian countryside. The mixed ethnic crowd seemed to be there for one reason, the food. Then Lily asserted herself, grabbing the menu and falling into a parody of Meg Ryan's restaurant scene in *When Harry Met Sally*. Maria noticed that Lily was wearing more eyeshadow than when they first met, and thought: Even FBI agents go off duty.

Kellie, the hostess-manager and daughter of the owner, Sovan Boun Thuy, came to the table. They ordered without further con-sulting the menu and went with the recommended B.V. char-donnay.

"Her father was killed in a prison camp," Lily said in a low voice. "Her mom fled with the kids. When they started a restaurant, the banks wouldn't give them any money. But her friends did. Now she's got two restaurants."

Maria had heard similar stories. They were part of the California conscience. But she also thought she heard some anger in Lily's voice.

"My grandparents on my father's side were first-generation Japanese. They came first to Watsonville to grow strawberries," Lily said, taking her first sip of wine. "They and my father were sent to the camps at Manzanar. When they got back, their fields were gone, foreclosed. Now they are run by big companies that use Mexican immigrants as sharecroppers. To this day, my father says, 'Never trust the banks.'

"Anyway, my grandfather and father and other issei and nisei got together and formed a co-op. They pooled their money and were able to buy some cheap dairy land in north San Jose. I remember as a little girl, working in the fields with them, pulling weeds and picking the flowers they grew. I remember always feeling, even as a child, so essential to the work of my family. My father told me it was an honor. You sort of know the rest. . . . I'm not certain flowers would have paid for Harvard. But the land they finally sold was a different matter."

"Ever call up NetGirl?" Maria interrupted, not wishing to convey any more of her own family history. Instead she invoked the Internet connection for women.

Lily smiled. "You mean 'Pagans Online' and 'Secrets for Hotchatting' and 'Secrets for Dealing with Lurkers and Flamers'?" Obviously, she had.

"I love the morality stuff," Lily said. "Like, you know, when they ask, what's her name, Rosalinda R? 'Since it's just an Internet fling, is it OK if he is married?' And she comes back: 'How would you like it if you were his wife and you discovered him hotchatting with someone else?' "

Lily poured another glass of wine just as the dishes arrived. As they ate, they compared notes. They were both straight. They both had been in relationships with guys who adored them, relationships that had run their courses within a year.

"My parents are still holding out for a model Japanese guy," Lily said. "To be honest, maybe I am, too. Although I don't know what that means anymore. I only know I feel right now that if I found anyone, the quality of our relationship would depend on just how well I could fit him in. And that's probably not fair."

Maria nodded. "I always felt like it was my fault when things went bad. I probably should have seen things coming sooner, should have better intuition. . . . But that pertains to a lot of things. I just always feel, even at work, when things go bad, that it's my fault."

It was Lily's turn to nod. "Try the Federal Bureau of Testosterone," she said, dropping her voice. "Male bosses as far as you can see up the ladder. If you don't take care of them, they resent you. If they're not feeling like masters of all that lies before them, it's your fault.

"By the way, tell me about your boss. From what I hear, he's supposed to be the next big thing."

Maria laughed. But she gave Lily a brief character sketch of J. P. McCorwin. It was true, he did command a cultlike following. And you felt like you had to match his eternal optimism or risk losing ground with him.

"Is he cute?" Lily asked.

Maria smiled. "Uh-huh. I guess you could say he is charming."

"Charm can be like loose change," Lily said. "Some people have a way of jangling it in order to make every one else think they're rich."

"Or they think if they jangle it long enough and loud enough it will produce dollar bills," Maria added, thinking of J.P.'s plan to lure the venture capitalists."

They both laughed.

"Some people jangle it because they're nervous," Lily offered. She looked pensive.

Maria didn't quite know what to make of that.

"Is he married?" Lily asked.

"Nope."

"Is he hitting on you?" Lily asked, leaning backward, appraising Maria.

Maria blushed. "I don't think so." She sipped the chardonnay and pushed some ginger chicken around on her plate. "I really don't think women are too high up there in his obsessions. But I don't know."

"Didn't you work for Sun Microsystems when they were really getting hot? What was the president, Scott McNealy, like back then?" she asked. "And how come you quit?"

Maria thought it was an off-the-wall question and was even more put off. And yet she knew that Lily knew something.

"It was one big bachelor party over there," she said cryptically, and cast Lily a glance that said she was done being interviewed.

Lily suggested that after dinner they hang out at a club downtown for a while, and Maria welcomed the change of venue.

They drove separately to downtown San Jose. On the way, as she headed onto the Guadalupe Expressway approaching the renewed downtown, Maria felt a sense of pride as she looked at the radiant skyline. She picked out the recent additions and thought to herself how luminous and orderly everything seemed—the convention center, the Children's Discovery Museum, the Fairmont Hotel, the big arena, the high-rises—SimCity personified, even better.

They hit Toons on Santa Clara Street. But it was full of rowdy, whitebread, post–San Jose Staters. Then over to the Agenda in the old cannery district at San Salvador and First Street, where they listened to Jungle Biscuit and watched some vampish women shoot pool with a couple of Donkey Kong II types in white shirts and Jerry Garcia ties.

Over at the Cactus Club, they danced salsa to D.J. Radio Aztlan until one in the morning, which, they agreed, was very late for both of them, even on a weekend. As if on cue and with a mutual nod, they left their dance partners and made their way to the parking lot.

Maria was feeling a little better about Lily now. They embraced lightly and made a tentative date to work out together later in the week, or maybe over the following weekend, depending.

"Sometime I'd like to ask you more about the flaming laptops," Lily said, pushing the camaraderie that Maria had gradually begun to feel, "and if you have any more thoughts as to who might have used your e-mail to send the phony question about Bill Gates."

"I really haven't had much time to think about it," Maria said, immediately regretting it. It was a lie, and Lily knew it. The question had been dogging her, especially since the fire that seriously burned Harry Hopkins.

Should she tell Lily about the laptop-sized package that had been sent from her company to Hopkins the day before the fire? And the name *RoseD* on the return address? Was she guilty of covering something up?

"Anyway, I gave Tsutomu Shimomura, the programmer, a call and told him what the lab guys had come up with," Lily said. "He asked to see the reports, and he looked at the programs and the gate arrays on both laptops.

"His conclusion was the same as the lab's. Definitely an electrical overload prematurely released by the system's power manager. But the weird thing is that he thinks the release was directed by certain commands written into the software. In any case, something was introduced into the operating system that wasn't supposed to be there.

"He thinks it was an inside job," Lily said.

Maria tensed, every muscle in her body jolted by the blow. She remembered what J.P. had said at the press conference. That the fire in the laptops was caused by faulty batteries.

Her mind was racing, yet she was determined to show nothing. "Good night," she said. But she could tell that Lily had picked up a signal of fear.

# chapter 21

**Brad Roth was feeling newly em-
powered.** His Internet bet against the 49ers had paid off.
It wasn't so much the $4,000 he had earned by wagering on the
Colts, it was that he had entered a whole new space.

He had contacts— bookies—and he found this very liberating.

Just that day, he had read in the *New York Times* that some
people possessed genes that made them prone to risk-taking. "Aha!"

he exclaimed to himself, eagerly devouring the explanation. He had a precondition! No wonder he had gone to work as marketing manager for J. P. McCorwin, even though there wasn't yet anything to market. No wonder he was incredibly attracted to RoseD, whom he had only met through e-mail.

His risk-taking was inevitable. This had nothing to do with questions of character and personal strength. No, it was more than that. Fate? Predestiny? Did he have a choice in the matter? Not at all, he quickly concluded, smiling about the delicious inevitability of his new self.

How else to explain why he and Elizabeth were standing on opposite sides of the soccer field on a glorious late fall Saturday in Palo Alto, having a heated argument through their cellular flip-phones. Brad had provoked it, she had said, by acting out childishly, because of his insecurities from having attended a second-rate university.

He had done nothing more, he insisted, than hang his old San Jose State University T-shirt from the front gable of their house. It was a matter of pride with him, just as wearing Stanford cardinal and white to work at one of the Valley's most prestigious law firms must have been for her. Why else would Elizabeth make such a fool of herself, like everyone else on the day the local newspaper announced that the Stanford community was the smartest spot in America?

"Let it go, Brad," Elizabeth had said the previous night, long after the kids were in bed. "Just let it go. You don't have to be in a rage all the time for your own shortcomings."

That was an incendiary statement and Brad knew exactly what she was talking about—his dismissal from Microsoft. But there was something acutely hostile in the barrage Elizabeth was sending his way across the soccer field, even as they both tried to concentrate on the action playing out before them. This consisted mainly of a massing of colors: pink and black, the Flamingos, their daughter's team, against the green and white Clover Crushers, a team that seemed to have more of Alexus's friends on it than her own.

This perhaps explained why Alexus preferred to kibitz with the opposing players rather than attack them.

Alexus had said firmly that she did not want to play soccer, but Elizabeth had insisted. Since they were new to the neighborhood and since all the Jordan Middle School kids played soccer, it would be the best way for Alexus to synthesize, Elizabeth maintained. The matches also offered Elizabeth a chance to network with the other moms and dads.

"Deals are being opened and closed up and down the sidelines," she said.

Brad, on the other hand, prided himself on being a reconstructed ex-jock. He meant that spiritually, not physically. Once, he had condoned violence on the playing field, even practiced it. But he had matured, he announced to anyone who would listen. He had simply backed off. And if Alexus did not want to play soccer, that was fine with him. Which was fine with Alexus.

It was not with Elizabeth.

"She needs to hone her competitive instincts," Alexus's mother insisted.

"Kind of like a prelaw course, then," Brad quipped, making certain both his daughter and son overheard and appreciated both his cleverness and gumption. And to further his in-your-face attitude, Brad had worn his SJSU T-shirt to the soccer match, stood on the opposite side of the field from his wife and networked with no one.

He was actually calculating his next bet against the Niners. That is, if his source still had intelligence on whether Steve Young's shoulder was on the fritz.

But Elizabeth kept ringing him up just to pick a bone and to talk about his keeping up his end of their family symbiosis. That meant adhering to an agreement Elizabeth would draw up every Sunday night, outlining their separate and joint projects for the coming week. Who would pick up and drop off. Who would shop, chop, cook, wash, take out the garbage and walk the dog, whose various meetings were more important, whose week it was to be flexible in case one of the kids needed to go to the Palo Alto Urgent Care Center.

They would agree in principle on what the drill would be. They would sit in the family room and plug the "weekly manifesto," as Brad called it, into their separate DayPlanners, making certain that each entry was penciled in in both books.

"That way there will be no excuses," Elizabeth had insisted.

Actually, Brad liked this exercise. It provided another opportunity to rebel. But only in little, forgetful ways. This was better than before, when he would announce at the drop of a hat that he was thinking of leaving for Montana to work as a guide for the Nature Conservancy and would anyone like to come with him?

He'd consigned that gambit to private conversations with the dog after the kids had called his bluff and said they would be happy to join him in Yellowstone National Park or wherever Montana was, but only in the summer.

On this day, though, Brad was not thinking about Montana, at least not directly. He was thinking about how silly Elizabeth made him feel and whether the best way to avoid being made to feel silly was to move out altogether.

This brought a spasm of exquisite melancholy to his entire being. But then Elizabeth interrupted with another phone call from across the field.

"I suppose you forgot we're having dinner tonight with one of the partners," she snapped.

He hadn't.

"Otherwise, I wouldn't have this feeling of dread," he retorted.

Things went along like this through the whole first half and even during the break when the girls left the field to swill fruit drinks and suck oranges and to assess each other's wounds while their parents offered well-reasoned advice on such concepts as "give-and-go" and "covering on defense."

Brad appreciated his own vantage point and was beginning to drift off again when the cell phone rang for the umpteenth time.

"What now? You want to tell me what not to wear to dinner?" he said.

"Brad, this is Maria. I want you to know that I have accepted a new position as executive assistant to J.P.," she said. "And he just called me with some great news. The chairman of Infinity Computer called him this morning and said they were offering $10 million in seed money for us to come up with a whole new killer application for them. . . . And he wants you in first thing on Monday to talk about a major marketing strategy."

Brad could feel the rush of attention hitting every single tendril of his nervous system. He felt like a bird dog must feel when he hears the first whir of wings.

That's the analogy he used with Elizabeth when he called her back on the cell phone.

"Remember that early-morning appointment you have Monday?" he said. "Screw it, we just got ten mil to launch our new project. I think that takes priority over your priority. In other words, outta my way."

# chapter 22

**On the last Monday morning in November,** the world heard from Cupertino, California.

The president of Infinity Computer, Inc., made the first earth-shaking announcement. Projected earnings for the remainder of the quarter were very disappointing once again, he disclosed. But he didn't stop there. Stunningly, he apologized to the company's stockholders. Indeed, Infinity stock had declined from nearly $60 a share in June 1993 to $34.25 at Friday's close. The president looked the way he probably felt—with the vision of a guillotine in his immediate future.

"If this guy doesn't lose his head, there's no justice in the world," a portfolio manager for one of San Francisco's big investment banking firms muttered to a reporter for the *New York Times*. "He's resisted takeovers. He resists licensing for clones. He hasn't come up with one new product in three years. The products don't get to market on time. He's getting his fanny kicked by Wintel. His laptops blow up. He's toast."

All through the press conference, the chairman stood to the side.

And then it was his turn. He stepped forward, put his arm around the president's shoulder and said, "Now for the good news."

On cue, the president made an even more astonishing announcement. For the second time in months, and the second time in history, Infinity was going outside for help. The company was awarding $10 million in seed money to a Cupertino startup to develop a new platform that, he promised, "will launch a renaissance in personal computing."

Naturally, questions followed, especially when it was revealed that the company to the rescue was J. P. McCorwin's. The president tried valiantly to answer the questions, but there was a discernible vagueness about his answers. Which the business writers interpreted as a wholehearted effort to keep the new project buttoned up.

Which, of course, fueled wild speculation.

And that, of course, played to J.P.'s strength—his flair for gaudy drama.

At a press conference timed to begin seventy-five minutes after the announcement at Infinity, J.P. appeared onstage against a backdrop of hazy, diaphanous, dim light that was clearly intended to blur things. He trotted out a team of software programmers and hardware engineers. Because of the light, the team could not be photographed or readily described. But from her perspective in the wings, Maria could see them clearly. They all looked like Deadheads who had assembled for the Second Coming, even though she thought she recognized a couple of them from one of the places, probably Sun Micro, where she'd worked before.

J.P. introduced each one briefly, but with convincing familiarity. The team was, he declared, "totally awesome and totally up to the privilege and the challenge that Infinity has bestowed upon us." As he spoke, Maria felt a dull pressure growing in the back of her neck.

"We are setting out to create creativity," J.P. said. "The operating system we shall develop will allow anyone to actually live technology, not just use it. We seek to create the convergence of soul and intellect. Previously, we were content to let people use technology or be used by technology. Our challenge is to restore proactivity to the mind. We will create a technology that is companionable and will actually jazz up people's lives."

Questions came and J.P. deflected them by raising his hands. He called for quiet and got it. When he was certain he had captured everyone's full attention, J.P. took a deep breath, leaned across the podium and said: "This will allow each of us to become maestros of our own lives. It will be to technology . . . what the Manhattan Project was to World War II and the future of mankind."

And he rushed from the podium, stopping at the threshold of the doorway only long enough to say: "Thank you all, but I'm certain you can appreciate we have lots to do." He winked at Maria and Baba, who followed him closely down the hall and into his office.

"Why didn't you tell me?" Maria snapped as soon as the door slammed shut. "You offer me this job as your executive assistant. I take it. You say we are going to begin working closer than ever. Next thing, you have me line up a press conference and then you line up a bunch of people, most of whom I've never even seen in my life . . ."

"Imagine how this is gonna play up in Redmond," J.P. said, cutting her off. He was grinning. So was Baba. "If this doesn't get Bill Gates's glasses steamed up . . ."

"You kept this from me," she persisted.

J.P. stiffened. He gazed at her coldly. Maria had never seen this before.

"Let me tell you something," he said. "Let me tell you how bloody this business is. Let me tell you how I felt when I showed up for a meeting one day and walked into a room full of sharks and was told my resignation was a done deal. . . . At Infinity.

"Now, I'll tell you something else. The president over there at Infinity has been saying for months that the company ought to be sold. Hell, Oracle, IBM, Sony, Toshiba, Hewlett Packard, they've all put huge offers on the table. He's over there urging the chairman and the board to accept. But the chairman says 'no way.' It's the chairman who wants to run this company until it drops, not the president. You know why? Because the chairman wants to be the corporate host of the Olympic Games. That's it. Have you ever heard of anything so ego-driven?"

It was an interesting question coming from J. P. McCorwin.

"I'll tell you one more thing about the laptop contract we got, and now this big contract. The president didn't even know about it. The chairman and I cooked it up. When it was a done deal, the president was brought in. You know why his answers were so vague during the press conference? He didn't have a damn clue what this thing was about."

Maria started to ask another question. But she could tell that J.P. wasn't done yet. And he was clearly worked up.

"You think this is unusual? Listen, things move fast both inside and outside these companies. You want another example? You remember the deal Apple struck with IBM and Motorola a couple of years ago?"

Of course Maria did. It was a highly publicized event in which Big Blue and the Big Apple agreed to launch a joint product development venture using Motorola chips. It was their first allied counterattack against Wintel.

"Listen, John Sculley, the president of Apple, never knew about that deal until it was done. The whole thing got put together on a napkin at Maddalena's restaurant in Palo Alto one night. The guys who put it together were Arthur Rock and Harry Hopkins, who were on the board, Mike Markkula, the chairman and Regis Mc-Kenna, your old boss."

Maria was stunned, and she knew J.P. knew it.

"They draw up the deal and one of 'em catches the red-eye to New York and presents it to IBM. The next morning, Sculley calls a press conference and lays the whole thing out. Very smooth, very much seeming in control. And yet, you think he wasn't humiliated about being kept in the dark? So don't whine to me about being out of the loop. . . . You're not. You're my executive assistant. Therefore, you are."

He took Maria by the elbow and ushered her out of his office and into the hallway.

"C'mon," he said, his voice sounding confident, "we're going to meet our new R&D team."

Maria started to say something about the FBI investigation into the exploding laptops and RoseD. But she held back. Maybe it was best that J.P. himself be kept in the dark on this one. At least until she could sort things out.

# chapter 23

BRAD, ARE YOU HAVING AN AFFAIR?

## "Brad, are you having an affair?"

Elizabeth shouted the words from about seventy-five feet away, seventy-five feet below him to be exact.

Brad Roth was dangling from the side of a rock wall. Elizabeth was standing on the ground, holding onto a rope that secured him temporarily, assuming that he answered correctly.

Somehow, he had known he would be maneuvered into this position eventually and come to regret it.

This was the Saturday before the big announcement in Cupertino. What Brad had done, with great self-reproach, was put his life in his wife's hands.

This bold move came as an antidote to the escalating hostilities of unspecified origin he and Elizabeth seemed to be bringing down on their household. By mutual agreement, and after a camouflaged inquiry Elizabeth had made to a woman colleague at her law firm had yielded the name of a therapist in Menlo Park, they had gone in for a consultation.

The therapist, a considerate-looking guy in his late thirties, sat between them on a wide Persian rug. He listened for about forty minutes and made a quick diagnosis.

"You're both suffering from a lack of primitive trust and understanding," he said, scrawling what they both took to be a prescription on a piece of white notepaper. "Here, call this number and make an appointment." He handed the paper to them.

It read REI (408) 446-1991.

"I think you two need to hit the wall," the therapist said, laughing at his own metaphor. "I'm prescribing rock-climbing."

Brad looked at Elizabeth. Elizabeth looked at Brad. They both nearly burst out laughing.

"I'm serious," the therapist said. "It's done in pairs. It involves taking responsibility for your partner, teamwork in other words. And I think you both could use something outside the normal recreational milieu."

Brad wasn't certain what he meant by that and said so.

"Do you feel threatened by this, Brad?" the therapist countered. "Because it does involve fear—not just the fear of heights but the fear of real intimacy and dependency."

Brad looked at Elizabeth and could see she was listening.

"You could also use something that demands concentration on only one thing, just one foot after another, one hand over another. It's becoming dangerously dormant in all of us," the therapist told Elizabeth. "Besides, it's terrific for getting you limber and your body hard and it calls for quick and precise decisions, something we all need to sharpen."

Like when I'm commuting on Highway 85, Brad thought.

The next thing Brad knew, they were signed up to start beginning sessions Wednesday nights at Recreational Equipment, Inc. (REI), not far from Brad's office in Cupertino. This caused a major klong for Brad because Wednesday nights were supposed to be reserved for going over to Jason what's-his-name's apartment in Santa Clara and making sports bets with the bookies through the Internet.

Their male get-togethers also offered Brad a chance to try to find out whether Jason was still trying to hit on RoseD through e-mail.

So Brad had done some big-time rearranging to accommodate the shrink and his own wife, probably to assuage his own guilt or to cover his tracks for a time, at least until he finally got to meet RoseD. Besides, he remembered that she had mentioned her fondness for rock-climbing, or at least that her rock-climbing instructor said she was gorgeous.

Brad saw this clearly as a chance to not only get the monkey off his back at home but to ingratiate himself with the person he was becoming virtually obsessed with.

At first he felt silly when they put the harness on his waist and around his thighs and ran the nylon rope through some metal catches to the top of the twenty-foot wall and back down. But when his third step on his very first assault turned out to be a false one, he felt less ridiculous and actually grateful. The person on the other end of the rope—the belayer—held tight and caught Brad, who simply dangled eight feet above the safety mat.

As it turned out, both Brad and Elizabeth took to rock-climbing, especially Elizabeth, who seemed to channel her natural obsessive-compulsiveness toward every crag and cranny and overhang in her way to the top.

Brad saw this as a purely competitive challenge and the chance to maybe one day prove to RoseD that he was a pretty well-rounded guy.

So they both graduated within a few weeks, bought nearly $1,000 worth of ropes and shoes and tights and other gear and made plans for an assault on the vaunted granite faces at Pinnacles

National Monument down by Hollister. Elizabeth seemed so turned on by the whole thing that she was already talking about joining a women's climbing club and hitting Half Dome in Yosemite in the spring.

On the way down to Hollister, the talk in the car had been pleasant enough as long as it stayed focused on the technical angles of climbing. Elizabeth led the discussion and, because she did, it eventually got around to Brad's fear of becoming an adult.

"This will be good for you," she said. "Climbing doesn't help you conquer fear, it helps you work within the framework of fear. It's what we all have to do to survive."

Brad cut her off and said he had already read that somewhere, in *Outside* or *Climbing* magazine or something.

But when the moment of truth arrived, when they were standing at the base of the sheer hundred-foot wall, when they were facing the real thing, Brad balked.

"I dunno," he stammered, fiddling with the rope. "I dunno."

"Look, I'm on belay, OK?" Elizabeth said, moving right up next to him. "I'll have the rope. I'll have you. Don't you trust me?"

"I dunno," Brad repeated.

She moved closer to him until she got right up into his face.

"Jeez!" That's all she said. And began dusting her fingers with chalk to enhance her grip.

Brad looked hard at his wife and could see that her face was contorted with disgust. Or was it rage? Or was she masking her own fear?

Nonetheless, Elizabeth started gingerly up the face and Brad took up the rope and dutifully planted both feet on the ground. He was also to scout the face above Elizabeth for pitons, metal spikes with eyes that had already been drilled into the rocks and through which climbers could thread their safety ropes. Elizabeth's task was to find the pitons as Brad pointed them out, secure the rope and explore the rocky avenues to the next piton.

It took the better part of an hour before she reached the top, and when she did she let out a triumphant, primordial howl Brad had never heard from her before. It scared him a little.

It scared him even more when he watched her descend. At times, she would kick loose the catch break for the rope running through her climbing harness and allow herself to swing outward and downward in a controlled fall. It was only for a few feet, but it terrified Brad to watch.

When she hit the ground, Elizabeth looked wild and exhilarated, got right in his face again and shouted, "Go for it!"

There was something so resolute about her that it scared Brad even further. He felt an urge to bolt. So he chalked his hands and began scrambling up the face, splaying his feet, his hands, his fingers. He was already beginning to hurt.

Once he looked down and nearly swooned. Elizabeth screamed out the location of the next piton. She was also talking a blue streak about how disconnected he had made himself from everyone lately and that maybe he should hug the rock in front of him and think about things while he had the chance.

Brad was thinking he felt weak. But Elizabeth cajoled him and he could feel her paying out the rope behind him, which unnerved him all the further. So he kept climbing. Up. Up. He looked away and could see a hawk floating on an updraft. It was floating parallel to him and watching him. Brad felt good about this and for a moment, he tucked his head against the granite and thought about his next move—hang tight, left foot over right. There was a slight crevice he was trying to get to . . .

Elizabeth shouted something out of the blue. He looked down and craned to hear what she was hollering about.

What she was saying was that if he was having an affair or thinking about having an affair or thinking about thinking about having an affair, she didn't care which, he'd better damn well come clean and he'd better do it pretty damn soon.

There was a tone in her voice that led Brad to a single conclusion. He was not coming down off the mountain while she was in that state. So he tucked his head back into the rock face and closed his eyes and tried to transcend this whole thing.

"ARE YOU HAVING AN AFFAIR?" Elizabeth shouted out again. "ARE YOU?"

Brad neither answered nor looked down. He looked up, and when he did, his foot slipped. He started to slide even as he grabbed hold of a narrow ledge with his right hand. He could feel his hand losing its grip. He could feel himself slipping. He could feel an adrenal rush that only made him weaker and nauseous. He tried to renew his grasp, and when he did, he let go and did slip. And felt the rope snap tight.

"I've got you," Elizabeth shouted. "Don't worry, I've got you on belay."

But there was no way that Brad could not worry. She had him dangling.

She shouted something that he did not hear and then he smacked against the rock. He reached out, took hold, steadied his body and found a foothold. It was solid. He felt the rock against his cheek and tried to bury himself against it.

"You OK?" Elizabeth shouted. "Hang on for a minute and catch your breath."

This made Brad angry. What the hell did she think he was doing, singing something from *The Sound of Music*?

"Honey, I'm scared," he heard himself saying. "I can't go up anymore."

And furthermore, he thought to himself, I'm not coming down.

Minutes went by. How long? Brad didn't know, he'd lost track.

"Having an affair? For God's sake, no," he said out loud. "I've never even seen this person."

Then he repeated the phrase: "I've never even seen this person."

And he was thinking how ridiculous this sounded just as Elizabeth reached him.

Brad looked at her and then looked down. Jeez, there was no one on belay.

"You're crazy," he shouted.

"I've got your rope secure," she said. "Just back off the safety catch a little at a time and back down. OK?"

If she had said this in a soothing, reassuring, yes, loving way, Brad would have felt better about things. But she was shouting at him and her face was even more contorted. She was not very attractive, he thought. And told her so.

"Just back down," she snapped.

"No. I'm scared. Just leave me for a bit, will you?" he said.

And she did.

It was near dark when Brad finally descended with Elizabeth on belay. She offered him a slug of water and after he'd swallowed three-fourths of the bottle, she cast him what he took to be a condescending glance.

"No, I'm not having an affair. OK?" he said. "I'm not even thinking about having one."

They coiled their ropes and packed up and drove back to Palo Alto in silence, as if they had agreed to one of those pacts that certain circumstances sometimes forge between people.

# chapter 24

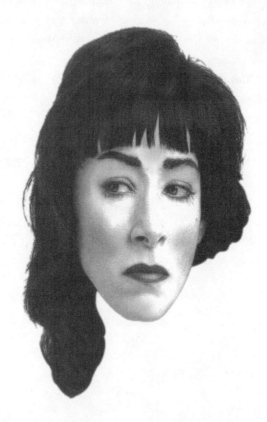

**The glowing responses to J.P.'s news**—that he was launching an expedition to technology's cutting edge and beyond—reached the fledgling company's R&D department before he and Maria did.

Even as they descended two flights of stairs to meet the new programmers and coders, they could hear triumphant bellows rising from various pods.

"Look at this," one of the new geeks was shouting. "It's already out over the Net. The financial wire is quoting Marc Andreessen, the Netscape wizard."

J.P. hustled Maria to the big Radius monitor in time to see the words flash: It has been a long time since Infinity has produced anything insanely great. So if J. P. McCorwin can create even a perception of momentum, it would be self-fulfilling.

"That's a testimonial to take wing," J.P. said, grinning. "What are they trading at this morning? Eighty-nine? Ninety? And that's while everyone is still trying to figure out what Netscape is supposed to be."

"Yeah, yeah, and the market's still bettin' he'll come up with an answer," said a tall, lean guy with the sharp, predatory features of a snapping turtle. He was wearing the standard uniform: Stüssy ball cap turned backward, extra-large T-shirt with the word THINK emblazoned across the chest, and baggy pants that appeared to be falling in a bunch from his hips to his Airwalks.

His quip drew unintelligible, tribal-sounding snorts and the mashing of plastic Odwalla juice bottles from the others. The pod was inhabited mainly by guys in similar MTV-skateboard plumage; Maria vaguely recognized two of them from her days at Sun Micro. They had parked cars at company parties. She had thought they were freelance valets.

But one of them, J.P. whispered with undisguised awe, was a physicist who had been to Cambridge and had worked with Stephen Hawking. The other had an engineering degree from Caltech and had worked for Ross Perot on some nonpolitical project.

But the focus of J.P.'s attention was the snapping turtle.

"Maria Cisneros, meet Rick Raptor," J.P. said, putting his arm around each of their shoulders and pulling the two together, as a referee would convene two boxers to the center of the ring before the bell sounded to open Round One. "Rick's gonna run one of our two new R&D pods."

"We're the killers," Rick announced loudly, thrusting out his jaw. "We're doing the killer-app thing to wipe out Wintel. You should make up some T-shirts for us, like maybe a Microsoft-Intel logo with a mushroom cloud rising."

Maria felt herself recoil as J.P. applied some pressure to her back. He was clearly intending for her to shake hands with this overly octaned, post-adolescent cybernaut.

"Rick's a full-fledged engineer. He's worked for NASA, Lockheed and the Livermore Lab," J.P. said, sounding like the emcee on *The Dating Game*.

"When I heard what J.P. was looking for, well, I would have killed for the chance," Rick said, laughing at his own double entendre. "My grandfather spent years working as an engineer at Los Alamos. Teller, Oppenheimer, they were my grandpa's mentors and my heroes. My grandpa worked on the Manhattan Project with them."

A soft look crept across his face.

"I mean, how many people actually sat on the knee of someone who helped build the A-bomb? This gives me my sense of humility," he volunteered. "I mean, how many people do you know who have been that close to someone who had been that close to total destruction?"

Maria was considering the question when J.P. broke in.

"Rick gave me the inspiration to suggest the Manhattan Project analogy for our endeavor during the press conference. I think it was real effective at getting everyone's attention, don't you?" he said, looking directly at Maria.

She knew J.P. sensed her aversion to the whiz kid. She also realized that she'd better go with the flow.

Meanwhile, the other guys—there were half a dozen—were busy arranging their work stations into a configuration with five angles. Everyone would be facing outward.

"Are you all protecting each other's butts?" Maria asked, facetiously dropping her voice half an octave. "Or facing the enemy?"

"Both," said Raptor. "We're calling this the 'Pentagon Pod.' We're trying to build something here that will be bigger, I mean smaller, brawnier, faster, better bundled and more preemptive than anything on any desk or workstation anywhere. People are gonna try to steal our ideas. So from now on, it pays to be paranoid."

It was clear to Maria that Raptor was, if not a rising star, at least a meteor shower.

Already, his crew of programmers and coders was launching into variations of phony German accents accented by aggressive-sounding verbs. She guessed this was meant for her, and her instincts told her to get out before the towel-snapping began.

"Hey, J.P.," Raptor half-shouted. "You gonna talk to Jerry Sanders and that guy Atiq Raza at Nexgen about getting hold of those new superspeed NX686 chips they're supposed to be coming up with? We're gonna need speed, man."

"Righto," J.P. said, reverting. "We're gonna outbrowse, outretrieve, outstore, outnavigate, outmanipulate and outunderstand anything Bill Gates, Andy Grove, Jim Clark, Marc Andreessen, Larry Ellison or Scott McNealy could dream of. We're gonna make the future arrive. Now. We'll try a bunch of chips. The ones that aren't fast enough to meet our processing-power demands, we'll serve them with guacamole."

Maria could see that J.P. was cruising on the fraternal spirit of the moment. She could tell she was headed for a delayed funk. She was thinking of her horse and the hills and that she couldn't get back up there fast enough.

"Another thing, J.P.," said Raptor, who apparently didn't possess the maturity to let his host leave the party while everyone was having a good time. "When are we gonna get a juice bar in here so we don't have to swill this old bottled stuff?

"And, oh, yeah, a name? When are we gonna come up with a name? I mean, it's important, marketing-wise, right? It sends a signal. We could name ourselves something like 'Fat Man' and 'Little Boy,' you know, after the first A-bombs. Something that packs a way-cool punch."

J.P. gave Maria a "get-ready-to-start-earning-your-humongous-salary" look. Instinctively she pulled out her "To Do" planner to write NAME, big enough to satisfy everyone in the Pentagon Pod.

On the way out the door, J.P. conceded that Rick Raptor could be a pain, but he had good Defense Department contacts. "You just never know where this thing could go," he said. "As Dickens said, 'It is the whole essence of perspective that comes quickly to a point.' "

# chapter 25

**Almost by accident,** Maria stumbled into her company's Affirmative Action R&D pod.

At lunch in the dining pod, she came upon a curious array of people she did not recognize. They were clustered around a hefty, baldish man with wise eyes, webbed crow's-feet and a rusty white beard framing a boyish face. Maria took him to be either a lot older or a lot younger than he looked. He was speaking softly in a kind of organic way and quoting lavishly from Joseph Campbell and Robert Bly and Robinson Jeffers.

Intrigued, Maria took a seat nearby and listened hard while consuming her usual grilled chicken Caesar salad and scanning the Big Board above the kitchen, which said:

```
AppleC 30¹/₂ + ⁵/₈ . . . InfinityC 28³/₄ − 1 . . .
Microsoft 98 + ¹/₈ . . . OraclesS 46 + ¹/₂ . . .
SunMics 48⁹/₁₆ . . .
```

And then it followed with the message of the day:

```
For every Infinity sold in 1996, nine new Wintel com-
puters will be sold. If every owner has $500 to spend
on new software, the potential market is $500 for a new
Infinity program, $4,500 for a new Windows program.
Guess which one offers the better return on invest-
ment? Have a great day.
```

The guy with the beard and those around him seemed to pay no heed.

"Just follow your bliss," Maria heard the man repeating in response to various questions from the others who had assumed certain deferential bodily attitudes that, taken as a whole, conveyed the appearance of a gathering of disciples.

But one of them, a woman with flamboyant salt-and-pepper hair held in check by a blue bandanna worn in reverse, Chechen-rebel style, was not so deferential as the rest.

"I simply object to a dogma that anything has to have the word 'killer' as its defining value, even in technology," the woman said. She wore six or seven oversized silver earrings on the right, only one on the left, an oversized teal-colored cotton sweatshirt with HERBAL WISE stenciled across the chest, black tights and urban combat boots. She also looked tremendously self-assured, Maria thought.

"Remember what J.P. told us, remember the reason we signed

on as programmers and coders," the woman continued. "We have been given a chance to develop the ultimate creative application. To me, this is the antithesis of a 'killer app.'"

The others nodded and so did the bearded man, who seemed to heavily consider her suggestion and in doing so, appeared statesmanlike, even in a ridiculous flaming chartreuse O'BRIEN SURF SHOP, SANTA CRUZ T-shirt that did not hide his protuberant belly and baggy shorts that did nothing for his pale knees and skinny ankles.

"Precisely," he said. "When we are ready to launch, it should be seen as more of a Gaia app . . .'"

"How about birth instead of launch?" the herbalism woman broke back in. "How about this being called a birthing app? A natural birthing app. Could you all go for that?"

Maria was paying great attention to this debate and found it curious that no one seemed to challenge the woman's proposition. In fact, the entire group seemed rather sanguine and considerate of one another. She was beginning to get into them when her beeper sounded. She could tell by the flashing number that she was being summoned to J.P.'s office.

Reluctantly, she made her way upstairs, telling herself the whole time to resist throwing a flamer at her boss for surprising her again with still another mystery R&D pod, if that's what this group she had just encountered was all about. And she guessed that they were.

"I stumbled onto some interesting folks downstairs," she said, even before J.P. told her why he called her. She tried to make her voice sound steady so as not to reveal her sense of growing humiliation at being kept continuously in the dark. "I think they were programmers because they were discussing an application for an operating system. Anyway, what they were discussing was an application that would be intended, right from the beginning, to give birth to creativity rather than killing off the competition. What do you think?"

J.P. gave a heavy laugh and pulled at his earring, which he always did when he was feeling more or less himself.

"The Birthing App Pod, right," he said. "You meet the elder statesman, the guy in the white beard?"

Maria said she had only tapped in on their discussion.

"Ethan. Ethan Daniels. He used to call himself Brother Land-mass back in his Bolinas days. He's an admitted former user, for-mer true believer, former baby vegetable grower. He's actually a friend of Timothy Leary and Stewart Brand and Jean Luis Gassee. He helped John Vasconcellos go statewide with the whole 'Self-Esteem Movement.' He was housesitting Stewart's houseboat in Sausalito when I called him, told me I was interrupting a deep moral e-mail discussion he was having with Guy Kawasaki over the existential meaning of the & being paired with the 7 key at the top and middle of the keyboard. Seven is a very metaphysical number . . ."

Maria tried to get a read on J.P.'s face. Was it mockery? Yes.

"You ask him, Ethan will probably tell you he sprang full-blown from the *Whole Earth Catalog*," J.P. said, laughing at his own sardonic wit. "Birthing app, give me a break. He ought to change his name again, to Bio Diversity."

Maria stood her ground and stayed silent. She had come to learn that her silence was evocative. J.P. went for the bait every time.

"OK. OK. It is another pod. I brought them on for two reasons. The first is that I want to avoid getting a lot of heat from Computer Scientists for Social Responsibility. I needed to pack in a totally diverse group of programmers that would reaffirm that we really are about affirmative action. You get me?"

"Not quite," she said.

"Look, Ethan is an over-fifty white guy, a dinosaur in the work-place, the emerging minority," he said, impatiently. "I hire him, I look good in the eyes of guys like Pete Wilson and Newt Gingrich. We could use their help."

"I get it," she said.

More than Maria could ever let on. Here she was, making a high salary, with debatable credentials except for the fact that she was a woman, a Latina, with an MBA and completely out of J.P.'s loop. No one was hipper to this and felt more conflicted about it than she did.

"The other reason is that they are all willing to work cheap," J.P. said. "Partly because they are all Infinity disciples and believe, as you and I do, that an Infinity can do God's work. Acts of God don't come cheap. Therefore, as acolytes, we might be entitled to becoming fabulously wealthy by merely following our beliefs."

J.P. said he first met Lisa, the woman Maria heard advocate the birthing app concept, when she was working as a biofeedback technician at the fabulous Golden Door spa in southern California, where he had gone on an Infinity executive Outward Bound retreat years earlier.

In the intervening years, she had also been a baker at the Tassajara Zen Center in the Carmel Valley; worked as a midwife in the Santa Cruz Mountains; had fought with the Sandinistas; had co-founded a lesbian think tank in an old farmhouse near Los Gatos that had branched out, with some support from some corporate wives, into the "Home and Hearth" hospice for terminal family pets. It had been a thriving concern until somebody had complained to the county health inspectors that dogs were escaping and wandering onto the neighbors' property, where several had actually expired in full view of children at play. So the county had shut them down. J.P. thought the whole thing smelled of politics.

There was another woman, Bindhu, in the group, J.P. pointed out, just in case Maria had missed her. She was a promising young engineer from the Punjab of India with great connections to an already well-established network of Sikh engineers and entrepreneurs.

"I met her family when I was doing good works," J.P. said. "Her uncle helped show me to the path of enlightenment. I'm hoping she can show me the path to some more seed money."

With an overtone of undisguised self-congratulation, J.P. continued to run through the alternate R&D group.

There was an engineer, Terence Toyota, who was also a Buddhist monk and originally from Osaka, Japan, where J.P. had met him and been influenced by him during his self-imposed pursuit of the truth, which eventually led him back to Cupertino.

There was a young Vietnamese man, now a programmer, who was attending graduate school at San Jose State. His mother had put him on a boat, along with his three brothers and three sisters, to escape the war in 1974. All six had graduated from college, which impressed J.P. mightily. Besides, the family restaurant was one of the best cheap eats in the Valley and allowed J.P. to run a tab.

The final member of the team sounded like something of a wild card. J.P. said he possessed incredible hacking skills that let him break into the supposedly secure Microsoft psychological profile indication program for all prospective employees. With the answers in hand, on a lark, he easily maxed the test by e-mail and was told to come on up—stock options awaited. This guy wasn't so sure he wanted to go all the way to Redmond. So he stopped in San Francisco on the way north, hoping to get a gig on *The Real World*. But on the first day, he got into a hassle with Puck, the kamikaze bicycle messenger bully on the show, and got discouraged. So he went north in his '72 VW van plastered with Dead decals and drove straight to the edge of Puget Sound. He didn't stay.

It wasn't so much that this guy hated being a Microserf, but that there was no surf to speak of up there. The guy felt cheated. He felt he was losing his creative edge.

"Actually, I'm thinking about utilizing his cybersleuthing skills over in the Pentagon Pod," J.P. said. "But first, I'm hoping he'll give the Birthing Pod a bit of an edge."

"Any more secrets you want to tell me? Or do I wait to stumble onto them myself?" Maria said firmly after J.P. had gone through the roster.

He looked wounded.

"None that I can think of right off the bat," he said. "Some things just self-disclose. No timeline. Everything's seamless. Remember what Kesey said: 'There are times when we can't wait for somebody. Now, you're either on the bus or off the bus. If you're on the bus, and you get left behind, then you'll find it again.' "

Maria tried to follow, but her brain seemed to lack the RAM to download. Maybe it was a form of self-protection, like shock is for someone who has been wounded worse than they should care to know.

# chapter 26

**Above the whiteboard in the Affirmative Action Pod was posted the following:** OUR MISSION IS TO COMBINE MYTHOLOGY, THEOLOGY, MORALITY, SELF-WORTH AND INTUITIVE CONNECTIVITY INTO SOMETHING THAT WILL FLOURISH AT 98.6 DEGREES, TRAVEL FASTER THAN LIGHT, BE WINDOWS-COMPATIBLE AND SHIP ON TIME.

The words were written unevenly, whimsically and in multicolored Brite Liners, conveying a virtual *Sesame Street* influence.

"We felt we needed a mission statement, it's a kind of leftover from the late '80s, early '90s. Sort of a security blanket thing. Everyone worked on it," Ethan, the pod's elder statesman, was explaining as he escorted Maria around the birthing app work space. "It makes everyone sort of nostalgic."

"Nostalgic for what?" Maria asked.

"Uh, whatever," he said, twinkling his eyes. "Myself, personally, I sometimes trip back on the days running with Kesey and the Pranksters. Did you know that I was also a personal friend of Tim Leary and John Vasconcellos?"

As politely as possible, Maria said she had heard all this.

Ethan flinched. He projected heavy internalization.

Touchy, Maria noted to herself. Tread light.

She glanced around the pod, taking in its hodgepodge charm and Ethan must have picked up on what it was she was processing.

On one wall was a blackboard with the schedule of each pod member's housekeeping chores posted, which felt weird to Maria since the company already had a maintenance crew that cleaned up daily. Against the same wall were parked three cross-trainer bikes with big hill-climbing treads. There was a large black-and-white Ansel Adams "Sunrise over the Sierra" poster on another wall and on one partition there were the words NOTHIN' AIN'T WORTH NOTHIN' BUT IT'S FREE. In the middle, away from the work spaces, which were scattered haphazardly, was a trampoline and under it, in an obviously submissive position, was a life-size, blow-up Bill Gates plastic doll. Also, there was a three-foot-tall rosewood Buddha flanked by a statue of Luke Skywalker of equal size. The statues were holding a multicolored banner that read PERSON, FAMILY, COMMUNITY, PLANET, ELSEWHERE.

"We're trying to recreate a group house effect here," Ethan explained. He was wearing a dashiki, which Maria found distracting.

Ethan picked up on this and said, "The Reverend Cecil Williams gave it to me one night after a big fund-raiser for Glide Memorial Church. He's a spiritual entrepreneur, just like me."

Not wishing to appear to be discursive, Ethan continued.

"So everyone feels they own and share a piece of the overall responsibility for our little development community. For instance, Lisa wanted to bring in an AK-47. She said it had been autographed by Daniel Ortega and was very personal and enabling. We took a vote and settled on a framed snapshot instead. And she was OK with that.

"And Donald, the surfer guy who came from Microsoft—he wanted to put up an Elle Macpherson poster, but we had a house meeting and voted her down. So he settled for scanning her and downloading her into a screen saver, which was fine because your screen is your space."

Speaking of screens, several pod members, including Lisa, the herbalist, lesbian activist and former Sandinista; Bindhu, the engineer from India; and Terence, the Buddhist monk appeared to be in some sort of meditative state in front of theirs. Maria was reassured by the fact that their 150 MHz workstations included built-to-the-hilt power towers that could handle up to 24 processors and generate 3-D graphics in a wink. The machines were, so far, the only things that indicated what these people were really all about when they put their minds to it.

Suddenly Maria picked up on the intense tranquility of the place. And Enya was cooing sweetly, like a mourning dove, from the Bose speakers.

"They're trying to create a whole new language," Ethan, the elder, whispered. "The first step is to begin imbedding new speech patterns, mostly irrational, subconscious patterns that come not just from the brain in the head but from the other brain in the gut. It's been proven, there are two.

"Our operating system must come to embrace this if we are to have a truly creative platform. We literally seek to approach this as an infant approaches life, without rationality obstructing our emotional initial introduction into the world. So the goal is to turn the client-operator into a pure pursuer of light. Pretty basic, huh? It's the basis for all artificial intelligence. You have to be able to introduce random and unpredictable hits into the process, otherwise you'll never stray from an altogether too narrow course of binary reasoning. You'll never have a smart computer, just an obedient one."

Maria had heard her fair share of psycho-technobabble slung around the Valley in her relatively short time. But she couldn't remember ever hearing anything so patently screwy yet compelling.

"Wouldn't it be nice," Ethan said sweetly, "if you booted up one day and began to compose a flamer on your word processor or e-mail, one that the computer instinctively cued into your enteric nervous system and knew it wasn't really the rational you but simply an irrational projection of your anger and one you might come to regret at the end of the day? Wouldn't it be nice if your system's 16-bit stereo came back at you with something like: 'You know, Maria, people might not think kindly of you for this. Why not allow yourself an opportunity to reconsider before you compose? For everyone's sake?' "

This sounded to Maria like a level of intimacy the nuns used to try to achieve when she was at Catholic grammar school. She didn't know how she would feel about dealing with that all over again.

Lisa intervened.

"Hi," she said, extending her hand. "I'm Lisa, Lisa Rose DeNiccolino."

Maria almost froze. *RoseD.* The laptop bombshell? An avowed lesbian having e-mail sex with at least two guys at work?

Lisa extended her hand further. Maria took it and noted how long Lisa's fingers were and how powerful her hands felt. She noticed Lisa's T-shirt. It said DYKES ON HIKES.

Their eyes met and when they did, Maria looked for something in them. She didn't quite know what, some sort of cynicism or something. And found none.

She found the dark, empathetic and very intelligent eyes of someone she felt she liked, right off the bat.

"Hey, a bunch of us are going to the ocean on Saturday, to Ano

Nuevo, to see the elephant seals fight and mate and undulate or do what they do. We've got an extra slot and we're also planning a potluck picnic. You free?"

Without a second thought, Maria heard herself say, "Sure."

# chapter 27

## It was probably an adolescent male.

That would explain why he lacked the guile and the fighting skills to hold his own against an older, larger hunk of a male who might have gone 5,000 pounds, maybe more.

In any case, the younger elephant seal, probably weighing around 3,500 pounds, had made a feeble sortie at a clutch of females basking on the windswept rocks at Ano Nuevo on the

central California coast on this Saturday in early January. What he
didn't know was that the females were unavailable. The larger,
older male who claimed them as his harem had sounded a this-far-
and-no-farther signal, a huge and grotesque snort emerging from
his grotesque, gnarly snout—which delighted the tourists who had
paid $4 each for the show.

"Yes! Fabulous!" Lisa Rose DeNiccolino shouted. She and Maria
and the other women on the sea elephant watch were standing no
more than twenty-five feet from this spectacle. "Sex, violence,
mayhem, who could ask for more?" It was an amazing sight. A
9,000-pound collision, blubber rippling, six-inch canines gnashing,
blood spewing.

"The wounds will be superficial," Ken, the ranger, reassured the
group. "You've got to cut through a foot of fat there. The real
wounds will be psychological. The loser will probably take to the
ocean, at least for this year, and find a quiet beach—probably a few
miles south of here—to contemplate his failure and his sorrow." As
the battle raged, Lisa, Maria and the four other women in the
group stood transfixed. Lily Watanabe was among them. She had
been a last-minute addition to the group when Lisa had mentioned
to Maria that one of the original group from work had to fly to
Japan to look over a new chip design.

"J.P. suggested they call it the 'Penultimate,'" she whispered.
"An in-your-face counterattack against the Pentium." Lisa had
asked if anyone knew of someone who might be available, and
Maria had called Lily, who jumped at the chance, especially when
she heard the name of the group leader—Lisa Rose DeNiccolino.

RoseD. The e-mail flamethrower. Of course she could come.

The others, Susan from Human Resources, Tara from Marketing and Pam from Accounting, appeared to be longtime acquain-
tances of Lisa. Maria wondered at first if they were also gay. And
she had chided herself for wondering if she'd be uncomfortable.
But her apprehension and her guilt evaporated when Lily accepted
the invitation to join.

They assembled in the company parking lot in Cupertino and
climbed into Lisa's nifty VW camper, which was fully equipped

with a fridge and sink. The trip over Highway 17 to Santa Cruz was a blast. Gossip was encouraged; disclosures of past relationships, especially disastrous ones, open for group analysis, were particularly encouraged. Maria found herself hooting and hollering along with the rest of the gang as the camper climbed the grade to Summit Road and descended toward the ocean.

Lily, who was ostensibly not in this loop, stayed pretty quiet, but Maria could tell she was taking mental notes. And she seemed to be studying Lisa.

The plan was to take the two-hour tour at Ano Nuevo and then head down the coast to find a nice, sheltered beach for the picnic, to which each had contributed. Maria had spent the better part of Friday night making an assortment of tapas: almond-stuffed green olives, carrot salad with oregano, a potato-saffron quiche.

Lisa had packed a camping cookstove and dehydrated ingredients for what she promised would be a "killer minestrone with basil." The others brought salads and breads and, somehow, there seemed to be more than enough chardonnay to survive.

"Watching mammals do battle over sex always gives me an appetite," Lisa exclaimed as the younger bull elephant seal withdrew from the field of battle, undulating forlornly over the boulders and tide pools and into the water. The women watched him head into the surf. Once into deeper water, just as the ranger had predicted, he headed south.

This was in the direction of the beach where Brad and Elizabeth, their two kids and their golden retriever were seeking their own picnic spot, just leeward of the crest of the dunes and below the massive sandstone cliffs.

Brad had suggested that they spend the day at the beach just after Maria had mentioned that she was going on the elephant seal trek with Lisa Rose DeNiccolino, the new coder in the Affirmative Action Pod.

Brad had tried to control his facial features and keep his breathing in check when her name came up. He purposely didn't ask any details. And he wondered if this had been too obvious to Maria.

RoseD. They hadn't spoken since his laptop had blown up during one of their more intense e-mail conversations. No, that was not quite true. He had spoken to her, sent forth Cupid's arrows from his keyboard and tried to conceal his own jealousy after learning he had been electronically cuckolded by Jason what's-his-name, that low-life programmer. But RoseD did not respond, which aroused his obsessions all the more.

So around the office, she went by Lisa, not Rose. This explained why she was not listed in the company phone book or in Human Resources.

Now she was about to make herself evident at the beach.

"Hey, guys, let's go see the elephant seals," Brad had said, convening a family meeting in the kitchen and trying to sound enthusiastic, like Jacques Cousteau or one of those wizards from *Nova* on PBS.

Both kids shot him you've-got-to-be-kidding looks.

"Those things are smelly and gross," protested Alexus, screwing up her face for emphasis. "Besides, it'll be cold over there." Damien dismissed it with his normal sullen silence and pulled his ubiquitous black watch cap down further on his head. Elizabeth said he looked more like a mugger or carjacker than a Palo Alto High School student. "Skateboard look, Mom. OK?" he said.

"Sure," she had said. "Lose your hair." In fact, Damien had nearly shaved it all off with a custom buzz cut, "just to save you all any trouble."

"C'mon, guys, we'll take Winston, and maybe some secrets of the deep will reveal themselves to us," he said, reminding everyone not to forget their rain slickers.

"Yeah, like a great white shark," Alexus said, firming up her defenses.

Brad appealed to Elizabeth.

"We haven't done anything as a family for a while. C'mon, OK?" Elizabeth hadn't seen her husband's domestic application running in some time. She checked her DayPlanner. No apparent reasons for running up billable hours on this particular Saturday revealed themselves. So she agreed.

Elizabeth had even gone, with Alexus in tow, to the deli at Draeger's to load up the Crate & Barrel faux wicker hamper they'd had for a couple of years but never used.

They had no reservations, so they were turned away when they arrived at Ano Nuevo. Then Brad got furious and insisted that they have their picnic right there in the parking lot. If that wasn't weird enough, Elizabeth thought, Brad was scanning the trail leading to the point with his binoculars and entirely ignoring the seals.

Finally, she and the kids and the dog overruled Brad and decided to establish a beachhead further south. They drove for about five miles until they came upon the first stretch of accessible sand. It seemed to stretch forever and offered a buffer of about forty yards between the cliffs and the water's edge, where spectacular winter breakers were depositing tons of foam and several vanquished and exhausted seals were coming in on the tide.

This was all lost on Brad, who trudged through the sand like a man possessed, all the while scanning the dunes for a perfect picnic/vantage point from which to observe anyone along the beach.

"She's got to come this way. C'mon, RoseD, come this way. C'mon, c'mon," he kept repeating to himself, in tune with his stride.

Because they are granite-gray and so still once they land on the beach, elephant seals in repose can be mistaken for massive boulders—even from a short distance. Especially if you are looking at something else or for someone.

In this case, Brad had begun to walk more or less backward. He was focused northward, in the direction he hoped RoseD would be coming, when he nearly banged into one of the behemoths.

Suddenly the gray mass rose twelve feet in the air.

Alexus screamed. Winston barked. And Brad fell back, looking squarely into the gaping mouth of the terrible, bellowing blubber. He was almost overcome by the putrid breath.

But the monster seemed content to merely register a warning. It folded back down and seemed to fall fast asleep, as still as a rock, except for occasionally opening one eye and fanning its posterior fin, which it used to scoop sand over its body.

"Way, way cool," Damien said, shedding the headphones connected to his portable CD player. It was the first sound he had uttered that had any direct bearing on the events of the day.

Even Alexus was generally impressed with the show and how close her father had come to a fantastic end, until she spotted the wounds on the beast's neck.

"He's sick," she shrieked. "He's probably washed up to die. We've got to find a vet." It was at that moment that Brad heard a familiar voice.

"They come up on the beach to rest. The ranger told us. He'll be fine." It was Maria.

"C'mon, join us. Damien, Alexus, go on and help them with their stuff," Brad insisted. And he started toward the dune.

When Maria's group reached them, she introduced everyone. She could see that Lisa was annoyed with the pending circumstances.

Brad was visibly taken aback by Lisa's flamboyant hair, which crackled like lightning bolts from beneath her NO FEAR baseball cap. Still, he started to take her by the arm and steer her toward the top of the dune. Lisa wrenched herself from his grasp.

"You're not quite what I pictured," Brad whispered, looking, for the first time, directly into her eyes. He saw nothing in those eyes coming his way.

"Don't worry. No one knows. I won't blow our cover," he whispered. "Trust me."

Brad turned to the group and immediately took command, directing where the picnic blankets should go, where to place the food and drink.

"I know we can't see the ocean," he retorted to Alexus's protest. "But this is out of the wind. You want sand in your food?"

Meanwhile, the surging tide reached the slumbering beast on the beach. It raised its head, leaned its body toward the dunes and began a slow, inexorable undulation toward drier territory.

It is a remarkable fact that elephant seals will sometimes heave themselves for one hundred yards across the sand to reach a spot out of the wind and away from the water just to snatch a nap.

This particular bull got it in his mind to do just that. And this inspiration struck at precisely the moment that Lisa Rose DeNiccolino began firing up her Coleman stove and Tara from Marketing was popping the cork on the first bottle of chardonnay, a '94 Congress Springs, and Brad was holding forth on surviving his encounter with the monster from the deep, and the kids were making "I'm-so-bored-I-could-scream" faces to each other.

It took more than an hour, with several naps along the way, for the huge pinniped to ride its undulating blubberlike tractor treads to the crest of the dune. In that time, several bottles of wine had been consumed, and the separate picnics seemed to be merging into one. Everyone, except the kids and the dog (who had taken a walk down the beach), seemed to have been lulled into having a decent enough time.

Things seemed boisterous enough that Brad felt bold enough to sidle up to Lisa, who was making menacing noises about doffing her clothes and running headlong toward the water.

"I'm happy to finally meet you," Brad whispered, keeping an eye on Elizabeth. "Why have you been avoiding me?" Lisa shot him a look of pure incomprehension.

"C'mon," Brad insisted. "Go ahead. Take off your clothes. I'd love to finally see my RoseD in the altogether instead of on a flat screen." She hissed something at him. Something so severe Brad wasn't certain he'd actually heard her correctly.

"Rose," he whispered louder than before. "Please. C'mon." This was possibly overheard by some of the others or possibly it was Brad's body language that set things off. Or maybe it was Lisa's body language, because she started to turn. In any case, something was definitely set off. Silence suddenly hit the picnic like a stiff wind. All eyes were on Brad.

Fortunately for him, his intemperance had set something else off as well.

From atop the dune, the 3,500-pound elephant seal pointed its terrible head downward. Instinctively, it folded its flippers like an airplane retracting its flaps. And, with one mighty undulation, it let gravity set its course—right for the picnic blanket.

Down the dune it came like a giant toboggan, and later Maria would tell her colleagues she actually thought she had seen a look of wild glee in its eye.

Someone said it was like watching a tree fall toward you, or rather standing at the base of an avalanche. At first, everything seemed to hang in an altogether virtual state of suspension. But then, as it started to gain momentum, you began to appreciate the mass involved and became aware of the damage it was about to do.

Lisa had the presence of mind to grab her cookstove and a half-full bottle of wine. Elizabeth reached wildly for her Crate & Barrel basket. Brad grabbed for his binoculars. Others grabbed what they could and clawed at the sand, stumbling and crawling out of the way as the elephant seal slid to the bottom of the dune, coming to rest atop the picnic blanket, as Rickey Henderson might arrive at second base. There it sighed deeply and fell fast asleep.

# chapter 28

**Brad and Jason what's-his-name** were surfing on Jason's illegal cell-phone monitor when they stumbled across some chat that was almost too hot to handle.

They had been hoping to pick up the 49ers' team doctor. At this time every week, he cell-phoned the results of his player examinations to his secretary for the files.

The Niners had begun the week as ten-point favorites over the

Packers in Sunday's playoff game at Candlestick. Tapping into the team's fitness report would be almost as cool as stealing the team's playbook.

Actually, Brad had come by Jason's after work for a different reason. He wanted to dangle a hint that he had come face-to-face with RoseD, the object of his and Jason's e-mail fantasies. If things had turned out differently, if she had bolted into his arms when they had met on the beach on Saturday, Brad would have felt no qualms about delivering the news. He would have posted it right in Jason's face.

But RoseD did not transmit even one pixel of connectivity. And then an elephant seal had crashed the picnic. And so Brad decided to take a more circumspect approach with Jason.

They sipped Pete's Pale Ale and munched blue corn tortilla chips and eavesdropped on cell-phone chats while Brad tried to think up a clever segue into the topic of RoseD.

And then Jason's monitor landed on a teleconference call. "Jeez, they sound like terrorists," Jason said.

There was some squelch, suggesting the parties were almost out of range or behind some hills. The conversation had something to do with botched ambushes of some Silicon Valley tech execs. One had taken place in San Jose, a couple up the road in Fremont.

"Why do you think I gave you guys guns?" said one of the voices. There was no mistaking the reproach. "To shoot at a god-damned grille?"

"Sorry, sorry, sorry, boss," another voice answered.

A chorus of "sorries" chimed in.

"Look, we blocked this guy's SL right outside his gate. OK? So what's the dude do? He slams it in reverse and leaves us standing there. I thought, we thought he'd stop when we fired those shots across his car."

"But noooo," came the chorus.

Jason and Brad looked at each other. Once, not long ago, they had overheard some police chatter about a failed kidnapping of a chip maker outside his home in Fremont.

"So far, we've had three screwups and the best we've done, as far as I can tell, is provide gainful employment for local bodyguard companies," said the voice that obviously belonged to the boss. It sounded youthful, almost adolescent, and deliberate, as if it was acting out the part.

"OK, OK," the voice continued. "We've got an even bigger job coming up. If we pull it off, it could be the first and last best job. Ever! I'm talking Bill Gates." Jason took a huge swig of beer. His eyes grew wide. Brad reached for a notepad and leaned closer to the monitor. There was something in one of the voices, not the boss, not the chief underling, but in one of the voices in the chorus. He thought he recognized it.

"Look, in a couple of weeks Gates is coming to Stanford to dedicate some zillion dollar wing of some new computer science department or something," the boss voice said. "So we get his schedule and pick him off while he's bopping around the campus or visiting The Gap at Stanford Shopping Center or looking at real estate in Woodside or Los Altos Hills, whatever. You with me?" The monitor was silent.

Brad and Jason were silent.

Something this big took a while to download.

"What'll we do with him? Where do we take him?" one of the voices asked. It sounded even younger than the others. It was the one Brad recognized.

"We've got a couple of weeks to figure that out," the boss voice said. "The main thing is that we don't ask for cash. We don't ask for stock. All we ask for is that Gates order the Wintel army to retreat from the shelves of Fry's and Circuit City."

"And the Mac and Infinity operating systems will be saved!" shouted the chorus. "We'll be heroes."

"Jeezus, sounds like a musical," Jason said, munching furiously on the chips. "If it weren't serious."

"What about the gun? Still got it?" the boss voice asked.

"Got it," answered the chorus.

"And I'm not afraid to use it," said the member of the choir

Brad recognized. There was no question he recognized it. It was the voice of his own son, Damien.

Brad nearly upchucked a big swallow of ale. Some backflowed through his nose—not burning the way Coke did but still causing a call-911 magnitude hops overload.

"You OK, man?" asked Jason.

"Aarrghh!" Brad said.

"Look, man, I think we should go to the Santa Clara cops," Jason said.

"Hang on, hang on," Brad stammered. "What are we going to do? Tell them we stumbled into this nest of kidnappers while using your highly illegal cell-phone monitor? . . . Besides, they're not talking about nabbing Steve Jobs or Larry Ellison or J. P. McCorwin or the chairman of Infinity Computer. They're talking about Bill, as in our mortal enemy, Gates."

Jason considered the conundrum seriously for a moment. Brad was relieved to be gulping air again, rather than foam. And relieved that he would at least get a chance to confront his own son before the cops did.

"OK," Jason said. "But what about J.P.? Shouldn't we clue him in? I think we should get him to sign off on this."

"Let's sleep on it," Brad suggested. "The exec-nappers were talking two weeks. We've got some time. Just keep monitoring. We might even bust this thing ourselves."

Jason went to the fridge and grabbed two more ales.

"OK, dude, we sleep on it," he said. "But we probably already missed hearing the 49ers' team doctor. What a drag."

# chapter 29

**J.P. was into heavy-duty phone con-
nectivity** when Maria walked into his office. It was 8:10
A.M.

He was nervously sipping Volvic natural spring water and staring at the ceiling before he began his side of the conversation. She
guessed he was probably being interviewed. And she could also tell
by the name John, which he kept repeating at the beginning or

end of every point he was trying to make, as in "John, you and I both know . . ." or "precisely the point, John," that the person on the other end of the phone was either the John from the *Wall Street Journal* or the John from the *New York Times*.

*WSJ*, J.P. jotted on a legal pad. He motioned for Maria to sit. "John, I am not at liberty to say whether Infinity is about to dump its entire R&D on us. You know how things work. Just put me down for a no comment, John," J.P. said. He made startling big eyes at Maria, from which she gathered that her boss was actually hearing news from the reporter rather than the other way around.

"All I can say is what should be obvious to someone with your experience in the business, John. Infinity has got to get its engineering and marketing act together. They've got to go with their instincts instead of business-schooling themselves to death on every decision. And I think the reason they chose us to develop new applications for them illustrates that point precisely, John."

J.P. always reverted to the word "precisely" when he was being deliberately vague.

"John, look, any discussion of a takeover is purely off-limits," he said, trying to sound as though he was speaking from within the loop in answer to the question that was on the minds of everyone in the Valley. "Why ask me? Ask Scott McNealy at Sun. Or Larry Ellison at Oracle. Or someone at Hewlett Packard. But, as long as you are asking, the Infinity name recognition alone should be worth $44 a share. Got it? $44 a share, John.

"John, you're welcome. OK, sure, but I don't do lunch much these days. Too busy trying to improve our and Infinity's position. But you might bag me for a game of racquetball early some morning, say around six? Or is that when you're just getting home?"

J.P. laughed and winked at Maria when he hung up the phone.

"They're fishing," he said. But a look of concern spread from his eyebrows to the corner of his mouth. "Jeez, a takeover and we're dead. We'll never get a chance at the VCs and investment bankers. Where's Infinity on the NASDAQ?"

He swiveled quickly in his chair and clicked two or three mouse commands to his incredibly masculine turbocharged Infinity 150 MHz processor with the built-in graphics accelerator. Immediately, NASDAQ numbers were dancing across the screen.

```
InfinityC . . . on 55611 sales . . .
       31¹/₈ . . . + ³/₈
```

"They're trading. But it's holding," he said. "The vultures are circling on the rumor that it's for sale. People are looking for a score. Boy, if they only knew what we knew, they'd be calling their brokers and putting in their short orders."

This puzzled Maria, but she did not want to convey her ignorance.

If they only knew what we knew? she thought. What *do* we know?

J.P. clicked again.

```
Microsoft . . . on 28200 sales . . .
      91³/₈ . . . + ⁷/₁₆
Netscape . . . on 12166 sales . . .
      167¹/₄ . . . + 8¹/₄
```

He whistled: "Let's get Marc Andreessen over here for lunch. Just an informal thing. But make sure the press hears about it. . . . Let's leak the rumor that he may be interested in consulting on our Web construction and browsing app—and maybe moving a little Netscape money our way."

He clicked one more time.

```
SunMicr . . . on 49969 sales . . . 44³/₈ . . . − ³/₈
```

"Ha," J.P. shouted. "They're betting hard that it is Sun and their shareholders don't like it. Now, if we've done our work and the

*Journal* takes our bait and runs with it, we should see a bigger drop in Sun stock by around noon tomorrow.

"Meanwhile, we've got to keep Infinity stock prices up," he said, taking a big swig of bottled water. "I know that McNealy's over there licking his chops and primping himself as the great white knight. I also know that he ain't gonna budge for more than $23 a share. You can see how touchy the market is. His shareholders would kill him."

Maria nodded. She was fueling up on J.P.'s kinetic energy. And his ability to manipulate the market through the press.

"You know what else? Infinity and Sun hate each other. All this talk about a merger of corporate cultures is garbage. McNealy's no flower child, he's the son of a car salesman, that's what. Everything's bottom line with him. It'll be a hostile."

Maria said she had certainly picked up a sense of corporate hostility when she worked at Sun. She definitely would not describe Scott McNealy as a flower child—frat boy was more like it. His father wasn't just a car dealer, he was vice-chairman of American Motors. McNealy grew up rich and spoiled and carried around a huge case of arrested development. The whole company did. Those macho company slogans—"Have lunch or be lunch"—and the company hot-tub parties . . . very retro.

"Sun and Infinity actually talked about a merger back in '88 when Sun was trying to get into the desktop PC business and IBM and Hewlett Packard were threatening to bury them," J.P. said. "They were actually in the same room at Infinity's campus. The deal was to fuse Infinity software with Sun's open chip standard and operating system. The technology would have spanned everything from PCs to mega-workstations. Even the stock swaps were agreed upon. A lot of people were gonna get rich, especially the Sun people because their stock was relatively low.

"You know what happened? McNealy said he wanted to run the whole thing. My boss, the president of Infinity and the chairman both just looked at him. I swear, I thought the chairman was going to spit on the floor. But they just folded their briefcases and walked out. . . . Leaving McNealy standing there looking like an overgrown woodchuck. It was pretty cool and I've got to tell you, I've had my differences with the chairman and the president, but I have a soft spot in my heart at the memory of that moment."

Maria appreciated the peek into the Valley's behind-closed-doors history. In fact, it was intimate moments like these that actually endeared J.P. to her. He had experience and he didn't mind sharing. It felt good to be back in the loop.

"We're racing against time and the market," J.P. continued. "Infinity can only ride its cult wave so far—and that includes whatever cachet I lend them. Announcing they've turned to us to bail them out gives them some legs. But they can't leverage my name forever. Unless they have something to show, the shareholders are going to get the heebie-jeebies again. We've got to stay ahead of them. If anyone's going to be in position to sell short, it oughta be us."

Baba RAM DOS walked in without knocking. And J.P. kept talking as if Baba had been part of the conversation all along.

"You think McNealy's not going to try to stampede them? Or that Bill Gates or Andy Grove aren't just gonna ask people to compare the relative values of their companies to sales? Infinity gets killed in an arena like that. We've got to get control of the arena—get people to focus on the technology Infinity is about to develop, not the embarrassing relative market value of the company. We've got to keep pushing the technology concept to keep stock prices up."

Maria sat erect. Baba extended both hands against J.P.'s large picture window and leaned hard against it, as if he were doing isometrics or emulating the posture a great leader might take when weighing a momentous decision such as bombing a Third World nation back into the stone age.

J.P. said they could count on having lunch in. Right here. Chinese for six.

"Let's bring in Brad from Marketing and the R&D guys. We're gonna start drawing up a business plan and ordering T-shirts. And, one more thing, call DeAnza College and the San Jose Convention Center. And call the one in Santa Clara, too. Let's book a firm date for a product unveiling. . . . And call Regis McKenna. He knows how to throw a promotion. . . . He'll know where to get those ash-blond assistants in short black skirts to deliver cool informational packets."

"For when? September? October?" Maria asked, registering but not commenting on the evidence of J.P.'s innate sexism. Maybe he trusted her not to call him on every little misstep.

J.P. looked at her queerly.

"God, no. Sometime within the next sixty days. Before the end of the quarter," he said. "And that'll include two weeks' rehearsal time. . . . Actually, find out when Bill Gates is coming to Stanford to dedicate that new engineering building. It would be fabulous if we could stage our show-and-tell the same day."

# chapter 30

**J.P. did not consider himself a stick-
ler for compulsory attendance** except on
certain occasions—such as this.

"A revolution does not march a straight line," he told his disciples just minutes before the big event. "It wanders where it can . . .
and, above all, is possessed of enormous patience."

"Vintage Mao," Lisa hissed to Maria.

She had a point. It was 3 A.M. There was no moon, no sky. There was only cold fog as J.P.'s employees gathered for this thirty-mile trek from the Santa Cruz Mountains to the sea.

This was to be the company's first mandatory, fully experiential Zen odyssey to "confront the enemy within," as Baba RAM DOS characterized it. Recently named the company's wellness director, he had passed out mirrors to every employee.

"Some of you will be weary. You will question your own strength and stamina and patience and, yes, even your allegiances during our journey together," Baba told the marchers. "When you do, we only ask you to hold up your mirrors. Look within yourselves—not at others—to assist you or gripe to."

"Hmmm, heavy," Lisa muttered, holding up her mirror. "Marin, mid-'70s."

Maria stifled a giggle and zipped her Patagonia pile jacket up tight against her chin. She exhaled and could see her own breath rush like a blue vapor geyser against the headlights of the four-wheel-drive van Baba had rented. In it he'd packed bandages, salves, maps, a Field Guide to Pacific States plants, natural juices and an assortment of inspirational tapes. Baba would not be walking the walk. He would be monitoring and dispensing.

Just then, Jason what's-his-name whipped alongside and stopped, balancing on a mountain bike as if he were treading water. His Gore-Tex shell was spattered with mud, which also nearly obscured the miner's light on his racing helmet. Jason was breathing hard. "Been halfway down and back already. There's a flood, mud, crapola, impossible slop, everything you could ask for. . . . Whatta rush!" he screamed.

Jason had been jazzed ever since Baba invited him to mount his silver Cromoly-steel Bontrager Racelite mountain bike and scout the route, which was known to bikers and hikers as Skyline-to-the-Sea.

"The bike's cool," said a muffled voice from out of the dark. "Come with a heater?"

It was Brad. His voice sounded as if it were coming from some dark place. He had on an enormous, stiff hood that made him look medieval, like a penitent on a pilgrimage.

"You gonna turn that thing into a tent if things get rough?" Lisa asked.

"Depends," Brad responded.

Lisa cleared her throat and started to say something to Brad—Maria guessed it would be harsh—but J.P. appeared and handed out Night Ranger high-resolution night-vision binoculars.

"Take these, and remember, we are all joined, each of us, all of us. We are all lead dogs and we are all part of the pack. That way, everyone has the best view as we move through the forest and from darkness to light."

Their route, according to the United States Geological Survey topo map projected on the company's whiteboard the day before, was to follow a southwest course from the Saratoga Gap, 2,600 feet above sea level and near the headwaters of the San Lorenzo River, through Castle Rock State Park, descending through Big Basin Redwoods State Park, a popular hangout for naturalists and campers, and on to land's end, which they hoped to reach before dark.

"What about cougars?" Brad asked.

"And weirdos?" Jason added. "Wasn't there some guy who used to hang around here and like kill people?"

"Trailside killer," Lisa answered. She pulled out her mirror and thrust it in front of Brad.

"He was arrested years ago," Maria added quickly. She sensed she'd better intervene, or their long day would end before they had even taken their first steps.

"All right, let's do it," J.P. shouted, circling a flashlight overhead. And the marchers, twenty-five in all, led by Jason on his mountain scout bike and trailed by Baba, who stuck to the blacktop in the van, stepped from the parking lot to the narrow trail and descended into the darkness.

The fog muffled sounds and seemed to draw the forest ever tighter around them as J.P. and his disciples filed, one by one, along the switchback trail. Occasionally, there would be the discordant heavy thump of a misstep, followed by a curse, followed by laughter up and down the line.

When they had dropped about 600 feet and nearly cleared Castle Rock State Park, the morning light began to show them the way through the feathery redwoods and the mood shifted.

"When's breakfast?" Brad asked. He was directly behind Maria. Brad's stomach was emitting sounds normally associated with large forest mammals.

"I don't know," she said. "I hadn't thought about it."

"I sure hope someone did," Brad said. He hollered for J.P.

"Hey, J.P. Wh-at's for break-fast?"

J.P. answered with silence.

Brad tried again.

"Halt!" J.P. commanded.

The line stopped.

"Gather up!" J.P. ordered.

The group bunched. As they did, the fog seemed to lift like a curtain, and J.P. took the stage. He spotted a tree stump and hopped up. He was grinning puckishly.

"I have thought about breakfast. Baba and I both did," he said. "We thought about it and decided against it. Lunch, too. Meals pollute. Our goal is purity . . ."

There were groans, the shuffle of feet, furtive looks, the first hints of insurrection.

"You talking about fasting, man?" asked Rick Raptor. "Cuz if you are, I'm glad I brought a stash of Power Bars."

"No, I am not saying we won't stop to eat," J.P. countered. "We will take breaks as opportunity presents, foraging breaks. The forest will provide opportunities for each of us to test our resourcefulness. Let's encourage each other, help each other and rely on ourselves. In fact, Baba and I whipped up a Dijon vinaigrette and we have Odwallas and spring water in the van."

"That's it?" Raptor asked. His voice was cracking. "That's it? Shoots? Sprouts? 'Shrooms?"

Things got quiet, except for the squelch from a gang of blue jays, who seemed equally disappointed with the announcement of no food.

Maria could feel the others pressing in and around J.P. She could feel herself pressing forward, too.

But then came a voice, as if on cue.

"As I understand your leader, you are here to discover. Do I have that right?"

It was a voice Maria had never heard. It was melodic and it came from a grove across the path. "Discovery is within, unless you allow yourselves to be blinded."

An elfin, graceful man danced out from behind a redwood. Maria guessed him to be Asian-American and in his twenties. He bowed toward J.P., who bowed back.

"Permit me," the young man said, approaching the group. He was carrying a pack over his right shoulder. He bowed to the group and knelt, opening the pack wide before them.

Out spilled a colorful array of edibles suitable for the kitchen of Chez Panisse.

"Over one hundred varieties of delicious mushrooms in these mountains," he said. "Chanterelles, tan oaks, portobellos, white caps. And, of course, many more that you eat at your own risk. But you should always sniff them. If they give off an almond odor— they can kill."

He produced fiddlehead ferns and bracken ferns, which he described as delicious and safe, as these were, in their unfurled, fetal positions. There were nettles for tea, roots for peeling and boiling for brews.

"Here are clovers and chicories, evening primroses, fennel, nasturtiums, wild asparagus," he said. "You can flavor them with the nectar of columbine and primrose. Here, you try."

He held out a fistful to Raptor, who recoiled. And then to Lisa, who accepted. Maria watched, waiting for an expression. And Lisa obliged.

"Not bad," she said. But then she was a herbalist herself.

Others, Maria and most of the members of the Birthing Pod,

joined in. And before long, they formed a convivial circle and munched away while the young man who said his name was Kato, regaled them with the do's and don'ts of foraging. Kato, who allowed that he was an independent programmer, told of spotting a mountain lion with a cub just the week before.

J.P. seemed pleased with the return of order. After conferring with Baba, he invited Kato to join the group for the rest of the hike.

"I can show you a secret deeper in the woods," Kato said, expressing his gratitude.

After much walking, Kato guided them to the secret. It was in a clearing guarded by trees and heavy brush, as if nature had exercised great care to protect it. There were maybe three dozen hearty green plants, and each stood at least eight feet tall. They were dense with long, toothy leaves that were hairy underneath and dripping with resinous stuff that reflected the sun.

"Holy shit!" Jason whistled. "Whatta score!"

Kato smiled and then bowed as J.P. reached the patch. J.P. did not smile. He circled, silently assessing. He wore a look of severity, even as he stood back and measured the height of the plants. Then, without comment, he reached into his right rear pocket and pulled out a cell phone.

Maria could tell by the tone of his voice that J.P. was conferring with Baba and that the two were taking this very seriously.

J.P. punched the sign-off button and retracted the antenna. He looked, expressionless, at his disciples. He turned back to look at the plants. Then he turned to his disciples again.

This was a matter of great gravity, Maria could tell.

Then J.P. bowed to Kato and said: "Mr. Kato, we would like to offer you employment as company herbalist."

And the others applauded. All except for Lisa, who was hoping for the title herself.

# chapter 31

**Brad was concentrating on the lat-
est published strategies** for generating market warmth for inapplicable applications. The chapter he had
bookmarked was "Sustaining a Vanishing Species of Vaporware."
He was highlighting away with a yellow Brite Liner when he got
a call from the reception pod, telling him he had visitors.

There were two, a guy with an open, friendly face that reminded him of Howdy Doody and a slight, intense-looking Asian woman he vaguely recognized.

"Mr. Roth, I'm Agent Smith and this is Agent Watanabe. We're with the Federal Bureau of Investigation. May we have a minute?" the Howdy Doody guy said, smiling widely and extending his hand.

A thousand dreads drummed through Brad's mind: Was it his online betting? His online relationship with RoseD? Jason's kinky virtual massage parlor? Lurking on Jason's illegal cell-phone monitor? The huge patch of marijuana they had all discovered on J.P.'s nature walk? Any one of those was enough to bring on the feds.

He felt the impulse to say he had to go to the men's room and then run like hell.

"Sure, come on into my office," Brad said. His voice sounded like an echo. He could feel blood making a squishy sound behind both ears.

"It's about your son," Agent Watanabe said before Brad could even offer them chairs or had a chance to close his door.

"Agent Watanabe is assigned to the Unabom task force," Agent Smith said. "You probably know that the manhunt turned up a lot of public attention. It also generated a huge budget, and with it, we were able to arm ourselves with the most sophisticated surveillance technology imaginable. We can spy on just about anyone . . ."

"What Agent Smith is saying . . . by the way, my name is Lily, Lily Watanabe. I was on that picnic when we were interrupted by the elephant seal," Agent Watanabe offered, smiling. "What Agent Smith is saying is that the task force is onto the trail of more than one terrorist. . . . During routine surveillance of certain cell-phone conversations, we came across something very distressing."

Agent Smith stood and checked the door to ensure that what Lily was about to tell Brad went no further than this office.

"We have reason to believe a local gang is planning to kidnap a very high-profile business executive—in fact, one of the most influential business executives in the world," she said.

"Who, Bill Gates?" Brad said, trying to sound as if he were

joking. It was purely reflexive, a desperate attempt to cover up what he already knew.

Both agents looked astonished.

"How did you know?" Agent Smith said, leaning forward. His face had lost its goofiness.

"A joke, a joke, I swear," Brad stammered.

"Brad," Lily broke in, "we have reason to believe your son—Damien, isn't it?—is involved in this plot."

Brad sat back, trying to make himself appear more horrified than he already was. Hell, he had been trying for days to figure out how to confront his son without revealing that he had overheard him on Jason's illegal cell-phone scanner.

*I mean, what kind of adult hypocrisy would that be?* he had thought while rehearsing his opening lines. Now he had to play an uncertain role for an even tougher audience. If he let on that he already knew, that would probably make him an accomplice to the conspiracy. If he let on how he knew, that meant that Jason could get busted, and one thing might lead to another. He, too, could get busted for gambling online.

"You're joking" was all Brad could muster.

"No, Mr. Roth," Agent Smith said, narrowing his eyes. "We are here to enlist your help so that Bill Gates, one of the most important men in the world, and your son do not become part of a bigger problem. You get what I am saying?"

Brad swallowed air. "Coffee? Tea? Mineral water? Juice?"

"We're here to ask your help," Smith said, ignoring Brad's offer. "For the sake of your family."

"We want assurances of your cooperation," Lily said. "Look, we're certain your son is not the ringleader. From what we have overheard, he's part of an organization that seems to be based in Palo Alto or Saratoga. They communicate by cellular phone. And every time we tap them, it sounds as though your son is taking orders. . . . On the other hand, we must tell you, they have indicated that they are armed . . ."

"Mr. Roth, does your son belong to any left-wing groups? Or

militia-type organizations? Does he wear any emblems or tattoos or clothing that might be connected with gang affiliations?" Agent Smith asked. "Does he seem sullen at home or hostile or unresponsive to authority?"

"Brad, here's what we're asking," Lily interrupted. "Just act normal, OK?

"But try to keep close tabs on Damien without seeming too conspicuous. We'd also like a list of his friends and we'd like to check your phone records, for starters. We also ask that you tell no one, not your boss or any friends or even your wife."

"Also, don't be alarmed if you see unfamiliar vehicles parked in your neighborhood," Agent Smith said. "We have you under surveillance."

"What's gonna happen?" Brad asked. He felt faint.

"I'm afraid we cannot disclose that," Agent Smith said, with exaggerated relish, Brad thought. "That would be a breach of bureau protocol. But, we can assure you, the bureau will be sensitive to the potential for injury to innocents."

"And my son? Damien?" Brad asked.

Agent Smith shrugged.

Brad turned to Lily.

She raised her hands and turned both palms toward him as if to deflect his angst.

"Just cooperate with us, Brad. We'll do our best," she said, handing him a business card. "There are some special, secure numbers on the back. Call us anytime."

"But remember," Agent Smith said, standing and thrusting out his hand to Brad, "do not confront your son or try to help him. He could be armed and dangerous. Do you understand? Do we have your assurance, Brad, that you will not attempt to intervene?"

Brad nodded yes and held the door open for the pair of FBI agents. He was desperate to be rid of them. He hurried them back to the reception pod and to the top of the stairs.

As they shook hands once more, Kato, the new programmer who had presented his credentials in the forest of the Santa Cruz

Mountains, was walking up. He seemed startled when he came across the pair of FBI agents, and they seemed startled as well. Brad also thought he detected a look of mutual recognition exchanged between the programmer and the agents.

Weird, he thought, and made a mental note to tell Maria about it. And then thought, No. They told me to leave everybody out of the loop.

# chapter 32

### Brad and Maria got simultaneous
**e-mails:** Come in quick! (J.P.).

Baba was already in J.P.'s office. So was Kato, the newest member of the R&D team. He was wearing a black T-shirt that said READ ME. WRITE ME. EXECUTE ME. And he was standing over a round conference table under a sign that said LOGIC IS THE ULTIMATE WEAPON.

"We're in business," J.P. said. And beckoned his executive assistant and his marketing director to the table.

On it was what looked to be an off-the-shelf, big-memory Infinity 5000 computer. Nothing about it looked unique except for the Minicam mounted atop its monitor and the keyboard, which was thicker than most and the color of a rotten avocado—which was to say, government-issue olive drab.

Even the Minicam was not all that unusual. Monitors had been used for teleconferencing for a couple of years. In fact, they had become so mainstream, Maria had seen them advertised on television commercials.

The keyboard was another matter. It looked as if it belonged in a stealth bomber.

"Sit down, Brad, play with this thing a bit," J.P. said. "Show him, Kato."

Kato booted up the machine and asked Brad to log onto a program Brad had not seen before. J.P. sat behind his own desk, and Maria noticed he was booting up a similar machine.

"Just use your own password," J.P. said.

"OK," Brad said, when he was on.

"OK, now we're going to ask you a series of questions. I mean, I'm going to write some e-mail and you just answer," J.P. instructed. "Simple. Straight-on."

Maria took a chair next to Brad. Both Baba and Kato leaned over the marketing director. They watched Brad's monitor.

```
Where'd you work last? (J.P.).
Redmond, Washington, for Microsoft. (BRoth).
OK, what's your dog's name? (J.P.).
Winston. (BRoth).
OK, do you ever fantasize about playing shoot-
ing guard for the Seattle SuperSonics? (J.P.).
Sometimes, yeah. (BRoth).
```

Maria did not get the point. But she could tell by the way that Baba was beginning to fidget that the point was about to be made.

```
OK. Brad, do you ever download dirty Net sites?
(J.P.).
```

Brad hesitated. He looked over his shoulder at Baba and then at
Kato, who was grinning. Kato nodded, urging him to answer.

```
No. (BRoth).
OK, OK. Ever had an e-mail relationship?
(J.P.).
```

Brad didn't hesitate this time.

```
Nope. (BRoth).
```

J.P. stood and flashed Brad a smile that said: "We know better
than that, don't we?"

"Whaa?" Brad protested.

"You're fibbing, Brad," J.P. said. "Come over here, all of you,
and take a look."

He scrolled the dialogue and when he came to Brad's answer
about downloading pornography, the word FIB blinked directly
underneath.

"Oh, Bradster," Baba said, mockingly. "You have a double life."

Maria giggled.

Brad made an exasperated gesture toward the screen.

J.P. scrolled further and when he came to Brad's response about
e-mail sex, the screen responded with THAT'S A CROCK.

"Wow!" Maria said.

Even Brad was impressed, forgetting for a moment Baba's immediate response, which was *"C'est un sacre menteur,"* but sounded
to him more like *"Sacrebleu!"*

"The point is that Kato has developed a technology that not
only detects falsity, it differentiates the degree of falsity, or at least
registers the respondent's false disposition," J.P. started to explain.

"Permit me," Kato said, grinning even more broadly than before. "It measures the respondent's visceral reaction to certain interaction, in this case, an interrogative from an authority figure, the boss.

"It is based upon two time-tested interrogation principles," Kato said. "The first is that certain facial expressions are universal and that you can therefore standardize them. A professor at the University of California at San Francisco has developed this theory by traveling the world and taping facial expressions of people responding to questions that are designed to stimulate a variety of emotional responses: joy, sadness, triumph, defeat, submissiveness, resentfulness and even lying. This recognizes that not all people respond similarly to the same stimuli, meaning that a headhunter might not register remorse when asked about his victim the way you or I might. . . . But he has found that generally, when people are feeling a certain emotion, say anxiety or the need to lie, their faces signal their disposition. This can be standardized."

"What about a poker face?" Brad asked.

"That's where the keyboard comes in," Kato said. "See, the keyboard measures GSR. That stands for galvanic skin response or how much you sweat. We all send electronic impulses through our pores, depending upon our emotions, through molecules of sweat. In essence, these molecules are the atomic versions of facial expressions. They change according to how we internalize stimuli and react."

"Sort of like a lie detector then," Baba said, not to Kato but to Maria and Brad.

"Precisely," Kato said. "In fact, this keyboard is a lie detector, a virtual barometer of our inner information."

"Only better, right, Kato?" J.P. said.

"Oh, much, much better, boss," Kato said. "This keyboard is coated with a special silica composite, a smartskin that makes it a kind of superconductor. The FBI uses it . . ."

It was the second time in a couple days Brad had encountered a reference to the Federal Bureau of Investigation, and both times Kato had figured in obliquely. That was weird, he thought.

"The really neat thing we have developed, or, I should say, Kato has developed, is a software program that downloads the camera's monitoring of facial expressions and measures them against standards for facial expressions established by the professor from UCSF," J.P. explained. "Likewise, it downloads the electrical impulses off the fingertips onto the keyboard and measures them against the standard established by lie detector experts . . ."

J.P. put his arm around Kato.

"We have a breakthrough," he said, and he sounded very emotional. "Think about it. This is a system that can beef up law enforcement. But that's not the only application. Consider its use as a standard for administering employment applications, consider how it would work in business negotiations, even globally. Hell, consider how it would work in diplomatic negotiations. To achieve peace. Not only does it detect whether someone is lying, it could, with certain refinements, detect how someone is feeling about themselves on any given day or in any given situation. In other words, you not only know when someone is lying, you know when they are feeling inclined to lie or to be depressed or feeling like they are getting the best of you. It's the next best thing to seeing the cards of everyone else in the game."

J.P. slumped in his chair, appearing exhausted but elated, as if he'd just managed a team to a World Series win or a startup through an IPO.

"When do I do a marketing plan?" Brad asked eagerly, happy to find the attention deflected away from his transgressions. "It'll make a hell of a show for the software vendors . . ."

J.P. stood. He sauntered to the window and stood silently. He stood that way for a long time. So long that Maria began to feel self-conscious. She ran her hands over the keyboard. It felt as if it had scales.

"Should I begin dropping hints that we're onto something?" she asked demurely.

J.P. turned. He looked first at Baba and broke into a broad smile.

"No. Patience, buttercup. Ooops, sorry. Lost it for a sec.

"We're onto something. That's all. This is just the start. Remember what we are after? Remember why you all signed on? We are here because we intend to build the last best thing. So far, we've only laid the first beams of a framework."

"But it is an amazing framework, no?" Baba said, picking up for J.P. "With this idea, this platform, we can now move toward total interconnectivity between hardware, software and the final frontier—human beings—wetware. We can begin to develop a completely intuitive technology, one that will manage personal information sites as we, ourselves, would if we had the brain capacity, the patience, the care, the foresight."

J.P. jumped back in, "What we are saying, guys, is that we have unclogged the gateway to not just artificial intelligence but artificial wisdom. Once technology can measure our moods, can find truth, can determine our needs, can read the minds of others and determine their needs, then technology can surely be fashioned to serve us."

"Awesome," Brad said, sounding as if he really meant it.

But he was still troubled by the FBI reference Kato had so easily come by, not to mention the smartskin keyboard itself.

Where'd he get that stuff? Brad wondered privately and congratulated himself for showing some self-restraint. Maybe, he thought, his survival instincts were finally kicking in.

"In any case," J.P. said, "I'm going to have tech services facilitate the whole company with these systems. We will begin product testing ASAP. Think about it, the whole company organism will be its very own prototype."

"A type of technosphere," Baba said, rolling the last word around in his mouth. *"Trés élégant.* It should prove very interesting, in more ways than one."

It sure will, Maria thought. I can't wait to use it with certain people in this room.

# chapter 33

## The news of Kato's big breakthrough

did not sit well with the guys in the Pentagon Pod, especially since it arrived with the surly tech services team which began retrofitting every work station with the new *truth tubes*.

"You're breaching our security," Rick Raptor, the Pentagon chief, protested.

"Look, dude, we're just doing our jobs," the chief tech replied. "You got a problem with that?"

Raptor responded by headbutting the guy just the way he had seen Dennis Rodman do it to an NBA referee on the sports reruns. In fact, Raptor had declared Rodman, the NBA's leading rebounder and acknowledged alternate personality, "a pure genius and my modern-day hero." He had even dyed his hair the same flaming blood orange color as the Chicago Bulls' forward and begun hanging out in gay bars and declaring himself destined to be the father of Madonna's unborn child, which did not please his parents one bit.

J.P. was tolerant enough, but it did not please him that Raptor tried to impose his hair color on other members of his R&D team as a sign of solidarity, although Jason what's-his-name was the only one willing to go along.

Raptor had been invited in for an audience with J.P. and Baba, and Baba, as company wellness director, had diagnosed him with severe adjustment disorder with mixed competitive anxieties thrown in, but found nothing to impede his progress toward coming up with a killer app.

The headbutt, though, was a bit beyond the pale. It had drawn blood.

J.P. took the tech services chief's complaint very seriously and had wanted to suspend the Pentagon Pod from the juice bar and support services for an entire week until Baba pointed out that they, too, might be onto something and that Raptor might be suffering from J.P.'s neglect, saying, "He's just young and restless. Like we were once *au temps jadis.*"

"Well, let's see," J.P. said, suggesting by his tone that violence would only be tolerated as a means to an end. "I was just about to order my broker to short some Infinity stock. . . . I figure we can bounce them around a bit before we virtually come to the rescue . . ."

But he told Baba to tell the Pentagon Pod to get its act together by early the next day.

Naturally, Raptor and his crew leaped at the chance.

They worked through the night, not only preparing an alpha run but transforming the Pentagon Pod space into a virtual south of Market–style industrial-strength nightclub.

"Showtime," Raptor announced. He was wearing eyeshadow, black leather and a rapacious grin. He pulled back some black velvet curtains and delivered J.P., Baba, Maria and Brad to a cadre of leather-clad, long-legged vamps who escorted each by the arm to their assigned leather love seats. Maria felt a little self-conscious about this, especially when her escort spoke to her in a coquettish but unmistakable tenor. Still, J.P. and Baba seemed to be at ease. As for Brad? She could only guess.

They sat for what seemed to be ten minutes or more, making small talk and small jokes with their escorts. Maria was trying her best but it was hard to suspend disbelief in the whole scene—especially since she could overhear harsh words, such as "I can't get the goddamn router locked in" and "Forget it, we'll go with what we got" hissing like amp rush from the blackness behind the makeshift stage.

Finally, there was a distinct crack of a whip and out stepped Jason, recognizable only by his signature skateboarder's shuffle-strut and the Mohawk ponytail. Otherwise, he was a picture of the quintessential dominatrix. Like Raptor, he wore heavy black eyeshadow. He had on a black leather tank top with silver-studded shoulder straps that crisscrossed, bandoleer-style, across his chest. He had on black leather chaps and—Maria couldn't quite tell, but it looked to be only a leather codpiece and black boots with spiked heels. Best of all, he was carrying a long bullwhip, which he cracked as he approached center stage.

"What'd you expect, Brooks Brothers or Laura Ashley?" he asked.

"Victoria's Secret," J.P. called out, laughing heartily.

Maria had not expected J.P. to be so giddy. And she found this a little upsetting.

Another crack of the whip brought on an overhead spotlight to reveal the apparent star of the show, another off-the-shelf Infinity 5000 and an ordinary-looking keyboard. Behind it was a giant whiteboard and a projector, not unlike the one J.P. normally used for his own dog-and-pony shows.

"As you know, our goal all along has been to be faster, smaller and more powerful," said a voice that was obviously Raptor's. "The problem, historically, has been how to compress these goals into the smallest available space. And that has been only part of the problem. The other is to do it economically and perhaps, and this was unthinkable until very recently, to do so as a constant motion, in other words, to make this power perpetual or self-renewing."

The lights came up higher. Jason sat down at the keyboard and as he did, Raptor appeared. He was wearing a blue denim jacket over a denim workshirt adorned by a very expensive-looking tie. "The Steve Jobs look," he said. He was also wearing a thin tube microphone that wound around his neck to the front of his mouth, making him look like an airport traffic controller or a rock star.

"Now, a demonstration. Jason will boot up, sign onto the Internet, book an airplane reservation and get confirmation, all within forty-five seconds—an exercise in speed, precision, sorting intuition and how fast his fingers can move."

Raptor asked Jason if he was ready. Jason nodded. A digital clock appeared in the upper right-hand corner of the whiteboard. So did what appeared to be a projection of Jason's monitor.

"Where do you want to go today?" Raptor asked, mocking Windows 95's slogan.

"Cape Town," Jason shouted, "mondo surf."

"Go!" Raptor shouted.

Jason's fingers flew furiously at the keyboard. Nothing happened.

Raptor stood with his hands on his hips, glaring at Jason, who sat back and crossed his legs demurely, a concert pianist with no music to play.

"Excuse me," Raptor said. And went backstage.

Maria could see the curtains bulging and knew lots of frantic activity was taking place back there. Meanwhile, J.P. was making pleasantries with his escort, who brought him an Odwalla carrot juice and half a Noah's blueberry bran bagel.

"Sorry, folks," Raptor was back onstage. "The first act was brought to you by Microsoft."

Brad and Maria both laughed. J.P. did not.

"I've heard that before," he said, which made Baba laugh.

"OK, OK," Raptor said. "Ready, set, *go!*"

Again, Jason's fingers pounded away at the keyboard. The initial result was a blur, then static, then, incredibly, an array of gates that opened and closed and then columns of airline schedules from San Francisco International, showing connections through London or Frankfurt or Madrid.

Jason highlighted a connection through London and a schedule appeared. He chose an 8 A.M. flight leaving SFO, arriving in London's Heathrow Airport at 1 A.M., and clicked. Then he typed Connect Immed Cape Town and the cursor ran through another column of connections until it settled on a 2:50 A.M. departure time.

Name? the screen asked.

Jason wrote: Jason Fillmore.

It was the first time Maria learned that he actually had a last name.

"I wish I was named after the auditorium," he said. "You know, Janis Joplin, Jefferson Airplane . . ."

"Keep going," Raptor shouted.

The screen was asking Seat selection?

Window if available Jason wrote.

Within a blink, the vacancies were scanned and Jason was assigned Row 16, Seat A.

Method of payment?

Jason paused. "I don't have any credit cards."

"Take mine," Brad shouted and gave him his Mastercard number.

"Thanks, dude," Jason said and flashed Brad a brotherly look harkening to their online joint betting ventures.

Declined the screen said. Cannot verify card number with seat request.

"OK, OK," Raptor shouted. "Check the clock."

It showed that thirty-seven seconds had elapsed.

"You guys get the point?" he asked.

"Fast," J.P. said. He was smiling.

"Mondo fast," Jason said.

"The fastest," Raptor said.

"Good show," J.P. said. "But can you make it work without a backstage backup?"

# chapter 34

**As Maria discovered, the Pentagon Pod's demo was all an illusion,** slapped together with some Net Objects software Jason had pirated from Steve Jobs and driven by some hefty 3-D Indigo stuff one of the pod's buddies at Silicon Graphics had managed to make available in return for two center-ice tickets to the Sharks game against Montreal.

But Raptor's virtual alpha run to Cape Town did demonstrate two important points. The first was that speed was everything, especially when navigating the Net. And the second was that any demonstration, even a phony one, must come across as high-concept performance art before any audience, whether vendors or VCs, would take things seriously.

"You've achieved something," J.P. told the Pentagon Pod warriors. "You've set a standard for performance for when we finally go live before a big audience at the MacWorld convention or Internet World or even in front of some potential investors."

For his part, Raptor was not above seizing on J.P.'s approval to advance the cause of his group, which was, he reminded everyone, "to come up with the ultimate killer app. We'd like to call it 'Brute Strength,'" he said, imploringly, urging J.P. to process the very sound of the concept "Brute Strength" like a sommelier eagerly waiting for the connoisseur to finish the exploratory swilling of a recommended Sonoma cabernet and pronounce it "fit."

"Brute strength?" J.P. said, winking at Baba. "What you showed us is more like *petit sirah*."

Baba chuckled. So did Brad. So did Maria.

"Actually, we, we're onto something," Raptor said. His eyes were bulging and his ears were turning red.

Guy's in a rage, Maria thought.

"We just couldn't get it ready for the alpha run," he said. "So we thought a little smoke and leather would at least get your attention."

"Well, zen," Baba said, impatiently. "What is zis keeler app?"

Raptor looked sheepish. But only for two or three seconds.

"Let's show 'em," he said, addressing his fellow warriors.

There was a wild scurry as the Pentagon Podsters leaped around like stagehands between acts and quickly disassembled the previous props and replaced them with new ones.

Maria recognized the mainframe. It was another Infinity 5000. But attached to it was a square black box, about six inches by six inches. The box emitted a trace of something, an odorless foggy essence, suggesting that what was inside packed a lot of power. She associated it with the emissions of a booster rocket she'd seen on TV prior to a shuttle launch.

"Liquid nitrogen," Raptor said. "We're supercooling."

"Ah, so," said J.P., moving in for a closer inspection.

Baba moved in closer, too.

Taking the cue, so did Brad. But Maria hung back, not certain their safety could be guaranteed, especially since this was Raptor's venue.

But J.P. seemed to grasp the point immediately.

"Vapor."

"Exactly!" Raptor said.

Maria thought she detected an urge in both men to embrace each other.

"Huh?" Brad said.

"We're talking superconductivity, Bradster," Raptor said, emboldened by J.P.'s quick take. "See, just a week ago or so, I go out of my condo. Remember the morning after the big storm?"

Brad nodded.

"The wind knocked a big Monterey pine down, huge thing, right across a power line. And I go outside and the line is down and arcing all over the place, you know, beating around like a rattlesnake in heat. Every time the line hits a puddle, all hell breaks loose. Sparks fly everywhere," he said, his eyes growing wide. "It's like so obvious."

"What is?" Maria asked.

"Come on," J.P. said. "Think about it. What's the greatest conductor of all?"

"Water!" Brad answered with the alacrity of a quiz show contestant.

"Exactly," Raptor said. "Water . . . or some property of water."

"You got water running through that Infinity system?" Brad asked, clearly getting the scent of the point Raptor was about to make.

"Close, but not exactly," Raptor said. "But we have moisture circulating through it in a closed system.

"We can supercool it out here with liquid nitrogen," he said, laying his hand on the black box. "Project it inside and through the circuit board . . ."

"Thus making your own superconductor right inside the system, am I right?" J.P. said. He folded his arms across his chest. A look of childlike wonderment crept across his face.

Maria was not exactly getting the point.

"So?" she said.

"So! So! Is that what you're saying? You don't get it?" Raptor banged his knuckles against his forehead.

"When you can supercool your circuit board, you boost your superconductivity. In other words, you potentially double your clock speed," J.P. said. "So, with this add-on, you could, say, load in an off-the-shelf Pentium chip and go from 200 megahertz to 400 megahertz without having to buy any upgrade from Intel. . . . Even better, you don't need Pentium. You can go faster yourself."

"Without Intel inside," Brad added, already seizing the marketing concept.

Maria guessed this was one of those rarefied moments people come to the Silicon Valley in quest of.

"Oh, boy, oh, boy," J.P. said, rubbing his hands through his hair.

But Raptor was not through.

"See, the key is the fridge, the box. We run liquid nitrogen from it and through the system, and we will soon be able to completely control its temperature," he said.

"But the real key is miniaturizing it, yes?" Baba asked.

"Yep," Raptor answered. "We've got to shrink it. We've got to create a microfridge so that we can get rid of this clunky box. Once we get the cooler down to the size of a circuit board, we can load it into the system and lessen the distance the coolant has to travel and have more control."

"So you can supercool it or bring it back to room temperature?" J.P. asked.

"That's what we're after, boss," Raptor said. "If we can do that, we can not only generate our own superconductivity, we can even increase the speed of the circuitry by running water through the system."

"I still don't get it," Maria said.

"Not really water," J.P. said, "but just think what happens when something goes from being incredibly cold to incredibly warm in a short time—in this case a nanosecond?"

Maria was stumped and felt embarrassed.

"Vapor," Raptor said, grinning hugely. "We run on vapor."

"Beautiful," Baba said.

"Beautiful," J.P. affirmed.

"Beautiful," someone else said, and suddenly everyone in the Pentagon Pod was talking at once.

"We're having a heady experience," Maria quipped. Everyone laughed.

"Vaporsoft, that's what we'll call it," Brad piped in. "Vaporsoft."

A second of silent recognition swept through the pod as everyone repeated Brad's phrase: *Vaporsoft*.

Unbidden, one by one, Brad's colleagues turned to him and bestowed upon him a collective look that borrowed from pure awe and worship. For a moment, Brad Roth was afforded the status, at least among his colleagues, of a pure genius.

# chapter 35

**Brad was pretty hyped when he got home** and so it was a good thing no one was there to greet him except Winston.

The thing was, he and every employee had taken a mandatory vow of nondisclosure, to black out even family members, which was a routine way for any company to indemnify itself against the loss of trade secrets. In Brad's case, nondisclosure was all the more necessary since his wife was a securities lawyer. It could just turn out that Elizabeth or her firm might be representing a potential underwriter, or worse, a direct competitor or would-be ally of Microsoft—which would include just about everybody but Apple and Infinity or Larry Ellison.

Things had really gotten spooky around the Valley ever since an exec at Intuit, the Menlo Park software maker, shared the secret of a possible takeover by Microsoft with his wife. The wife passed this along to her son by a former marriage, who passed it along to someone else, who passed it to someone else, who bought up a bunch of Intuit stock—and then sold short not long after the Intuit exec passed his wife another secret, that the deal was probably not going through and she, in turn, started the ball rolling again. The net result was that the person at the end of the daisy chain got it coming and going. And the exec got the ax.

Brad was happy to be denied the temptation to do something that would have gotten him fired for the second time in six months. But he also needed a moment to gloat.

"Winston, boy, we're onto something. Big. I mean real big, boy, bigger than Windows 95," he trumpeted to the retriever. "We're going to blow people away. And you know what we're going to use to blow people away, boy?"

Brad knew from experience that dogs could not appreciate rhetorical questions. Which was why he accelerated his speech and exaggerated the tone of the word *boy*—to achieve the result he was looking for.

Winston obliged. He wagged. He cocked his ears. He made big appreciative eyes. He chewed his tennis ball furiously.

*"Vapor!* That's what. We're using vapor!"

Brad put the Stones' *Hot Rocks* on the CD and danced a little jig and then sparred with his dog, who was dancing too. He feigned jabs at Winston's jaws in a mock effort to separate Winston from the tennis ball, which drew a low growl that Brad hoped was playful, but he was not completely certain.

Truth be told, Brad had no real affinity for pets. And he and

Elizabeth had been through a batch. They'd had a couple of whiny Siamese cats, who insisted on sleeping on their bed. The cats became irritated whenever Brad got up to get a drink of water or go to the bathroom and took it out on him with well-timed and well-aimed coordinated swats. The kids had rats and hamsters and turtles and things, all of little interactive consequence except when they escaped.

Once, though, when Damien was around twelve and they were living near Redmond, he brought home a ferret from school. The class had adopted it from some indeterminable source, but the night custodian objected to being alone in a room with "a god-damned weasel," and the principal backed him and ordered the thing sent to the Woodland Park Zoo in Seattle. So Damien intervened and promised a good home and apparently stated unequivocally that it would be okay with his folks, which wasn't the first time he had lied.

Anyway, Henry, which was the name of the ferret, had evil pink eyes and yellowish gray and brown fur and slinked around and made his nest in unlikely places, which included Brad's favorite golf cap and, when Brad evicted him, in Brad's underwear drawer.

"It occurs to me that Henry seems to have bonded with you, Brad," Elizabeth observed one night. That was before Brad was really on to her sarcasm. In fact, he still felt pretty good about his wife—or at least the possibilities ahead for them as a couple.

To demonstrate, one night when he was certain the kids were asleep, he took Elizabeth in his arms and told her, "Hey, babe, I really love you."

She murmured something back that Brad interpreted as encouragement—and he went for it.

By now, though, the ferret was nesting behind the curtain on the windowsill over the head of their bed. "Just so he could be closer to you," Elizabeth was to say later, months after the attack.

In retrospect, the animal had obviously become aroused by Elizabeth and Brad's lovemaking and, with perfect timing, at the worst imaginable moment, Henry leaped from behind the curtain, landing directly on Brad's head, where he draped himself "like a coon-skin cap," Brad would say, adding that not only did Henry adhere to him by using his claws, "he bit me right on the forehead."

Brad dined on this story for a while and he was certain Elizabeth did, too, although he guessed she left a few things out. But the important point was that he really had little use for pets, even Winston, unless he found himself alone.

So Brad danced with the dog and played tug-of-war over a tennis ball and even got Winston to bark every time he shouted, "Vaporsoft!" and was actually enjoying and congratulating himself, when Damien walked in.

"Dad, you know Mom doesn't like you to roughhouse with Winston," his son said, frowning, and headed directly for his room. He was wearing a faded plaid flannel shirt untucked over baggy black shorts that Brad guessed were resting halfway down his cheeks, which caused him to saunter in a slow, lethargic, amoebic way.

He looks like a low-pressure area, Brad thought, and suddenly he felt a knot in the pit of his stomach. But how could he be a terrorist?

It's like I'm in the middle of something . . . Kafkaesque, Brad thought, pausing for a sec to appreciate just what he was appreciating. Finally, he understood the meaning of what his artsy friends had been referring to all those years. This was bizarre and damn scary.

"No, it's unbelievable," he said out loud to Winston, who was starting for Damien's room. "It's just unbelievable. Our son wouldn't . . ."

And he stopped himself and wondered if, in fact, he hadn't caused this, whatever it was . . . this angry rebellion, the sullen clothes, the mopishness. Brad used to blame it on Seattle, on the weather, on Kurt Cobain. But this was California. Even better, Palo Alto, California.

And yet, when he and Elizabeth checked in with the other parents, they found common ground. Just a stage, the parents agreed all around. Adolescence. That was the explanation. In fact, when it came down to it, when Brad and Elizabeth matched other parents story for story, Damien came out a little on the nearly tolerable side of the scale.

What am I gonna tell the other parents when they see the news and see my son being led away or in some hostage situation? Brad wondered. He looked out the window, wondering when Elizabeth would be coming home but glad she wasn't there yet.

How could he keep from blurting it out? From barging into Damien's room right now and making a father's arrest or whatever they called it? Or throwing his arms around his son's shoulders and leading him off into the night? What would that make him?

An accomplice, Brad thought. Damned if I do, damned if I don't. If I can just get a handle on this . . . I can get back to the FBI and clear things up. My son just wouldn't . . . couldn't . . .

He felt like a hostage himself.

And he found himself opening Damien's door.

The CD was blasting, and, judging from the disk cover, it was the Beastie Boys. Damien was lying on his stomach, looking bored and thumbing through *Rolling Stone*.

Brad walked over and sat on the bed. Fortunately, Winston joined them and lined himself up to be patted by both father and son.

"So," Brad said, feeling the pain in his stomach.

Damien kept turning the pages.

Brad reached over and turned the CD down. Damien rolled his eyes and gave him a glance that said, "OK, I'm preparing for your best shot."

"So," Brad said again. His mouth felt dry. "How's it going?"

"OK."

"Just OK?"

"I guess, yeah," Damien said. "Yeah." And started to turn the CD up.

"So-o-o," Brad said for the third time. "Something bugging you?"

Damien rolled his eyes again to send the message: "Isn't it obvious?"

But Brad persisted. "So what's cool in *Rolling Stone* this week?"

"Last week's, Dad, last week's," Damien corrected. "There's this sucky piece on Bill Gates. They're wondering if he's like gonna buy up the rights to all the Beatles' music and put it on Microsoft digitals, just like he's doing to all the photo images from all over the world."

Damien sat up.

"The piece talks about Gates trying to own all the sights and sounds ever photographed or recorded. That really sucks. . . . I can't believe you ever worked for him."

"Well, you saw what happened," Brad said, brightening at the prospect of actually interfacing live with his son.

"Yeah, you got fired," Damien shot back. "Let me ask you something, Dad, OK?"

"Sure."

"Do you hate Bill Gates? Do you?"

Brad pondered the question and started to equivocate.

"You know my new boss, J. P. McCorwin? He got fired by Infinity. Now we're trying to save them," he said. "So I can't say I actually hate Bill Gates . . ."

"Well, I do. If he wants to control all the audio that's ever been recorded, I think that sucks. That's what I think. I hate the sonofabitch."

Brad had never heard his son utter such a hostile expletive, at least not when it was obvious it would be overheard by an adult.

"That's a pretty strong opinion," he gulped.

"I'm entitled," Damien said sharply. "A lot of us are entitled. A lot of people are afraid of him. But I'm not. Neither are friends of mine. I can tell you that."

He cranked up the CD and turned back on his stomach. End of discussion.

Yeah, you're entitled, Brad thought. We're all entitled. But not to grab the guy. And what? Hold him hostage?

His stomach was getting the better of him. He felt his nerve letting go.

"Well, guess I better start dinner, buddy," Brad said, weakly, and stood to go.

"Dad, would you mind closing the door?" Damien said.

Brad did not mind. For an irrational moment, he considered trying to lock it from the outside.

# chapter 36

**At 1:50 P.M., Pacific Standard Time,** the floor in J. P. McCorwin's Cupertino headquarters rippled once, not violently but just enough to cause people to stop whatever they were doing and ready themselves for what was to come next. The instinct was primordial and not based upon any experience. It didn't involve ducking or running. At this point, it was all mental.

For a few seconds, there was nothing. And then the quake could be heard outside, coming. And when it hit, the floor shook like a sheet on a clothesline. People froze. They stared into each other's eyes, imploring their colleagues, anyone, to make the damn thing stop.

And it did. And there were no aftershocks.

Someone turned on KCBS, the all-news radio station, and the wall speakers announced that instruments at the U.S. Geological Survey in Menlo Park placed the epicenter along the Calaveras Fault, about eighteen miles southeast of San Jose. A USGS seismograph had recorded the strength at 4.7, the newscaster said.

"Just a chimney twister," she said, sounding disappointed. "But we'll update you if we find any real damage."

If one measures a quake by relative numbers, then 4.7 on the Richter scale is not all that impressive. But what is impressive is the look people get in their eyes. This is primitive. The look is of pure, unadulterated, untweaked animal terror.

In San Jose, a man, thinking that someone was breaking into his home, stuffed a loaded handgun into this pocket, vaulted up the stairs to save his elderly mother and shot himself in the foot. In a Milpitas office building, a worker kneeled directly under a glass skylight and began to pray. On a nearby golf course, a ball stopped dead two inches from the cup and then rolled in, sending the entire foursome shrieking to the clubhouse.

But even more impressive is how most animals act during the moments, sometimes hours, even days, leading up to a quake. Birds become agitated and then fall silent. Squirrels scurry. Dogs bark at the sky. Lovers quarrel. People do goofy things. It is said metaphorically that life in California is lived under one continuous full moon. This is only partly true. Earthquakes add another measure of ticklishness.

It was during the hour leading up to the quake that J.P., Baba and Maria were being held hostage in JP's office by a young man who called himself Robert and who was offering himself up as a developer-licenser for the last best thing. Which was balanced on the bridge of his long, narrow nose.

He wasn't large or imposing, which was probably how he got through the door in the first place, although J.P. had insisted there be no security guards. But there was something messianic about him—he reminded Maria of Steve Wozniak or Elton John—something about his body language and how he kept spitting out the words *ignore me at your peril* that told all three—J.P., Maria and Baba—that they'd better not make any sudden moves.

"I have a 128-bit accelerator packed into this baby for both receiving and transmitting," he said, adjusting the oversized dark glasses on his nose. A thin cable attached to one of the earpieces led down the back of his collar. "In other words, total interactivity." Maria noticed the guy had one hand in his right pocket and was obviously holding something. Baba was noticing this, too. Baba looked alarmed. Like a bank teller, Maria thought.

"So, Robert, what does your system do?" J.P. started to ask. Maria could tell he was trying to sound sincere.

"Let me finish, please," the guy snapped. "You got a problem with letting someone else speak?"

J.P. shrugged and shook his head.

"All right, all right. . . . With these, you have interactive video? OK? Only you don't just record, you influence. You transmit digital signals to the gates of any common system—telephone switchboards, alarms, light switches—even traffic lights."

"But Bill Gates is already working on that," Baba said, inappropriately.

"Beel Gates, Beel Gates," Robert said, peering over his glasses and mocking Baba's French accent. "Do not interrupt, OK?

"See, the beauty of my system is all in the eyes. You scan, you see whatever it is you want to influence, you focus. And . . ."

He paused, allowing his audience to catch up with the concept.

"You blink. Instead of pointing and clicking, you blink. Instead of a mouse, you have your eyes. Just point and blink. It's much safer than any hand-held device, especially in, say, a car. You come up the driveway and blink open the garage door. You hit a traffic light. It's red. You blink and . . . turn it to green."

He removed the glasses and blew on the frames.

"I call it the FlameThrower. So what do you think?"

Baba, who seemed recklessly overripe with malapropisms on this particular day, began to whistle "Three Blind Mice."

"I'm offering you the killer app, the world's first truly inter-active media," Robert repeated. His voice was growing squeaky with frustration. "You want me to take this system to Gates? To Ellison? To Trip Hawkins? Do you? I'm warning, mock me at your peril."

Maria could feel the barometric pressure fall.

"Please, be our guest," J.P. said, beckoning toward the door. "Actually, we were hoping for something with the word *Net* in it. To froth up the venture capitalists."

"No! Uh uh," Robert said. "I know you guys got $10 million from Infinity. From what I hear, you haven't developed a damned thing. I'm gonna give you a chance to earn that money . . ."

"What do you have in mind, Robert?" J.P. asked. He sounded very deliberate, very nonalarmist, like a 911 operator or his own hostage negotiator.

"Let's take a ride. We'll hit Stevens Creek Boulevard. You can drive. Or she can drive," he said, leering at Maria. "We'll deliber-ately hit the red lights. And, in the blink of an eye, we'll change traffic patterns and make history. What do you say?"

This was not a question. Maria could tell, and her guts began to rumble.

Outside, there was a rumbling sound, too. And the floor quiv-ered.

Robert put his glasses back on and started to scan the room, cocking his head as though he were listening for something with his eyes. His breathing grew rapid. And then the floor shook very earnestly.

"Oh, oh, oh," was all Robert could muster. "I can't breathe."

He turned, he stumbled, he crawled out the door, fell flat on his face, regained his footing and dashed down the hall and then down the steps.

They could still hear him screaming, "Oh, oh, oh," as he dashed out the door.

J.P. was the first to regain composure.

"Well, thank goodness for nature," he said. "There was a moment there when I was sorry we voted against that woman in R&D, what's her name? The one who wanted to bring in her AK-47?"

"Lisa Rose DeNiccolino," Baba said.

"Right," J.P. said. "I was sorta thinking we could have called her for help."

Baba chuckled. Maria did not. She was still too fazed and still waiting for the aftershock, or for that guy, Robert, to come back.

Just then, a human force burst into the office. It was Jason what's-his-name.

He looked wild-eyed and Maria started to say something to calm him down.

"Jeez. Is this way cool or what?" he said.

"Personally, I don't like earthquakes," Maria said.

"Quake? Oh, the quake. Well, personally, I love 'em. It's like earth-surfing," Jason said.

He was holding something in each hand. In one was what looked like the black plastic cover to something about the shape and size of a hand-held Apple Newton. In another was the guts of the thing. Maria recognized a small circuit board, the 3.5-inch disk and various other mini-arrays.

"This is sooooo cool!" Jason said. "The quake hits, right? And this dwerb comes running down the stairs and out the door. Only before he leaves, he drops this thing. . . . It's lying there on the carpet and I pick it up and the first thing I see is . . ."

Jason cradled the device like a priest would a chalice, offering it around the room—first to J.P., then Baba, then Maria.

"My God," J.P. said. "It's a micro—refrigeration unit."

"You got it boss," Jason said. "The guy's got a supercooler."

"And therefore the capabilities for creating superconduction," J.P. said, joyfully. "He wasn't kidding when he said he had a 128 accelerator. . . . We've got it. We've got it.

"Jason, get back down to R&D, let's load this baby into one of the Infinity laptops. One with just a 133-megahertz processor and 16 megs of RAM. Let's see if we can make it fly."

"But it's that guy's intellectual property," Maria pointed out.

And things got quiet for a sec.

"Nope," J.P. said. "His intellect. Our property. He dropped it, we caught it. Think about it."

# chapter 37

**J.P., Baba, Brad and Maria were hud-
dled over their "Computers Do a
Brain Good" institutional ad cam-
paign,** which was spread out on an oval table in J.P.'s office.
Brad had thought up the idea as a way of creating international
goodwill and perhaps getting Vice President Al Gore or California
governor Pete Wilson hip to pitching in a little government subsidy.

"We can even design a mouse that Bob Dole can hold for photo ops instead of that pencil he always carries," Baba said darkly.

J.P. and Brad both laughed but Maria thought this in totally bad taste and could tell things were starting to get out of hand when the hooves of a thundering herd sounded in the hallway.

Jason what's-his-name burst into the office first, so excited he didn't bother to knock. Rick Raptor was right behind him, followed by other members of the Pentagon Pod, including Kato, the newest member.

"Jeez, jeez, this changes the whole ball game," Jason said, gasping for breath. "This changes the whole world. This just plain kills Intel and Oracle and Sun."

"No, this obliterates them," Raptor said, moving in ahead of Jason. He was, after all, the head of the Pentagon Pod. "This, this reduces them to silicon dust."

"What does? What does?" J.P. asked.

The Pentagon Pod had been well-drilled by Raptor. They moved as a unit to the oval table. Raptor, with one sweep of the hand, cleared Brad's ad campaign off the table. And Jason moved forward and placed a little box down. Maria had seen it before.

"Ah, the micro–refrigeration unit, the supercooler," J.P. said.

"The microfridge and then some," Jason said and started to explain. But Raptor bumped him out of the way again. Like a surgeon, with a tweezer in one hand, he leaned over the device and plucked from its insides a microcircuit with a surface about the size of a thumbnail. In the other hand, he held a magnifying glass.

"Come here and take a look," he said, motioning to J.P.

J.P. bent over and peered through the magnifier. He peered and peered, and suddenly his knees locked. He stood straight and then turned to Baba. His face was like a rubber mask, all contorted. Maria hardly recognized her boss.

He rolled his eyes, he licked his lips. There was a knot in his throat. He was making gargling sounds, obviously groping to put into words the enormousness of what he had just observed.

"It's a superchip. . . . No, no, that doesn't even describe it. It's bigger than that. Take a look," he said to Baba.

*"Formidable,"* Baba said. "It is so *petit.*"

"Roughly the thickness of one six-hundredth of the diameter of a human hair," Raptor said. "Mr. Kato here discovered it."

Kato did not step forward. He just bowed his head slightly and smiled.

"Mr. Kato also discovered that there are about 120 million transistors loaded into this baby—that makes it about twenty times faster than Intel's Pentium Pro," Raptor continued. "It also means that this little piece of silicon reduces the need for other chips in normal PCs by up to 90 percent. It's virtually a complete processing system in a single chip."

"And when you combine it with the superconductivity of a micro–cooling device?" J.P. asked.

"You got the A-bomb of electronics," Raptor said proudly, looking very much like he was to the manor born. He looked very much as if he was born to repeat his own lines: "The A-bomb of electronics."

"Have we actually tried it out?" J.P. asked.

"Yep," Jason said. His baseball cap was turned backward, making him look as if he was about to enter a wind tunnel. "You remember the trick we tried, using the dummy system to book airline reservations?"

J.P. nodded.

"Well we were actually able to get up and running on the Net and book the entire Pentagon Pod to London and even rearrange other people's seating reservations so that all of us could sit together both coming and going—the complete round trip—in under a minute," Raptor said.

"Whew," Brad said.

"Wow," Maria said.

"What this does is make Larry Ellison's cheap little black box that he wants to hook to a TV and call it a computer actually legit." J.P. was thinking out loud. "Can you imagine what he'd pay for the license?"

"It gives really high-octane possibilities to everything that guy Robert was telling us about, even changing traffic signals," Brad added.

"Yeah, yeah," Raptor said. "Quicker deals with ATMs that like recognize your face or fingerprints."

"Instant recognition of human speech patterns," Baba suggested. "Or other cognitive pattern recognitions, such as linguistic parsers for filtering e-mail to separate the spam from the essential, eh?"

"Or as flamer retardants," J.P. added, looking at Baba, who returned the look. They both laughed.

Private joke, Maria thought. I don't get it.

"And think what it could do when you combine it with the truth technology . . . you know, the galvanic skin response filtering system Mr. Kato is working on for electronic conferencing," J.P. said.

"And, oh by the way, Maria, regarding the intellectual property imbroglio you brought up yesterday . . . let's avoid it. Let's find that guy Robert and just hire him."

Brad and Maria winced. Even Baba winced.

"Let's give him some little job," J.P. said, "just to get him on board. So that when we go public with this thing, he can't go screaming to the lawyers that we stole his intellectual property. Remember, he dropped it on us. We'll hire him and let him work on making improvements. If he touches it at all while he's here, we can claim it was work for hire and that we own it."

Baba nodded approvingly. Easy for him, he didn't have to find the creep.

"Kato, would you mind working with him?" J.P. asked. "You two would make a good team. He's obviously brilliant. But he could benefit from your calming influence."

Kato bowed again and just smiled, looking very, very pleased with himself and the situation he found himself in.

# chapter 38

Ooh, baby-baby! (RoseD).
Baby, baby, oh! (JasonWHN).
Ooh, baby, ooh, baby, ooh! (RoseD).
Hubba-hubba-hubba! (JasonWHN).

**Around 10 P.M. in the Pentagon Pod,**
Jason what's-his-name approached an Infinity FirePower laptop
computer wearily, as a matador might confront a bull at the moment of truth. After all, he'd been burned once before.

He was explaining all this to Kato, how he had tapped into
e-mail and met this person—RoseD was her screen name. That's
all he really knew of her, except that she gave hot chat and he had
been hooked and then, one night, when things got really hot

between them, his laptop had detonated and he had lost almost all his chest hairs, plus his favorite aloha shirt.

"That made an impression, lemme tell you, dude," he said.

Kato nodded.

"Did you ever try to contact this RoseD again?" he asked.

Jason shrugged. "Naw. I thought I'd let things cool down. Besides, I'm developing my own multimedia babe. She's like totally interactive. Close to perfect. Come on over to my apartment in Santa Clara and I'll introduce. Actually, I've got a lot of cool stuff over there."

"I'm certain you do, Mr. Jason," Kato said, contemplating the invitation. "But why not try to contact this RoseD again, especially since we have the assistance of such a potentially powerful and fast system coupled with the lie detector keyboard I am developing?"

Jason thought about this for a long time, which, for him, was about twelve seconds.

"Cool," he said.

"Great," Kato said. "I'll get the keyboard."

Actually, there are a bunch of things I'd like to ask RoseD, Jason thought. Like, who is she? And how did she make that laptop go *blooey* when I thought we were having such a great time together online?

And there are some things I'd like to ask Kato, too, he also thought. Like, just *who* is he? How come he was out in those woods all by himself that morning we all took the company hike? What's his background? Where'd he get his engineering experience? Not that it matters . . . but there's something about him. Like . . . he's kinda different.

"Here we go," Kato said, hooking the drab-looking keyboard with the lizard-skin texture to the alternate keyboard port, which was one of the lesser options among many that made the Fire-Power potentially predominant in the marketplace.

He flipped the mainframe over and, with a tiny Phillips screwdriver, unfastened the sleek cobalt plastic cover, exposing the guts of the machine. With practiced precision, Kato then extracted the motherboard, removed the chips and inserted the single, incredibly powerful chip.

"Hey, man, you got good hands," Jason observed. "So, like where you from originally?"

"I'm second-generation Japanese-American, grew up in Sunnyvale not far from where Steve Wozniak grew up," Kato said. "In fact, I used to hang out in video arcades and Woz was my idol. Man, he had real hand-eye coordination . . ."

Kato continued to work as he spoke, soldering a couple of tiny wires in place. "Then a couple of guys and I decided to build our own games. That's when we learned about programming."

"So you're more or less self-taught, like me?" Jason asked.

"You could say that," Kato answered.

"Put her there, dude," Jason said, extending his hand.

"Gimme the micro—refrigeration unit," Kato said, all business.

It seemed to fit perfectly between the motherboard, the disk drive and the cooling fans, so Kato connected it to the circuit board. Within minutes, the system was complete and Kato was buttoning things up.

"Now, the moment of truth, so to speak," he said to Jason. "Let's go find RoseD."

"Should we go out there on the Net? Maybe she's in orbit somewhere," Jason said. "In fact, let's run Microsoft's Explorer. It's fast."

"No," Kato commanded. "Let's use clunky old America Online. The key is to see how much acceleration we can give even the slowest systems."

"OK, dude," Jason said. He tugged at his baseball cap, pulling it down harder on his half-shaved head, and signed on.

And he was there in the post office before he felt his finger finish clicking.

"Wow, I mean whoa!" Jason said, pulling back from the machine. "Fast, huh?"

Kato said nothing. He pulled up a chair and positioned himself to monitor every single event.

"Now go for it," Kato instructed.

"Uh, this is kind of personal," Jason started to protest. "I mean we haven't interacted in a while, you know. It may take me a while to warm her up, OK?"

Kato nodded, not taking his eyes off Jason's hands or the screen.

"OK, OK," Jason said, and composed his mail.

```
TO: RoseD
Rose?
```

No response.

```
TO: RoseD
Rose? You out there?
```

Still no response.

Jason sat back and exhaled deeply. Kato sat back, too. He was thinking.

"Do you remember exactly the words you used to first contact her? Do you?" he asked. "Try to remember."

Jason took his baseball cap off and rubbed both hands along his scalp.

"I think she called me up first," he said. "Yeah, she hit on me first."

"But she hasn't since the fire, right?" Kato asked.

"Right," Jason answered.

"Let's try something else," Kato said. "Do you remember what was in the Subject box on the e-mail?"

"Sure," Jason said. "Sex. S-E-X."

"Do it," Kato said.

Jason wrote the word, followed once again by the plaintive words RoseD. R U there?

The response was immediate.

```
Well? I'm waiting in People Connection.
(RoseD).
```

"Yes!" Jason shouted, waving a fist in the air. "She's on me, man."

He clicked to the chat room and asked her to go private, saying, "That's our thing."

"Ask her a personal question. Let's see how our lie detector keyboard works," Kato said.

```
JSon: Hey. Where you been lady?
RoseD: Like the cut of your Calvin Kleins.
```

"Jeez, that's what she said the very first time we met," Jason said. "It's like déjà vu or something. It's like we're meeting again, for the first time."

"Go on," Kato said. "Advance things."

And Jason obliged, jumping right in. He and RoseD went at it hot and heavy. Boosted by the super-microchip, which was in turn boosted by the supercooler, they managed to contemporize *Kama Sutra* within about two minutes.

And frankly, Kato was getting a bit embarrassed. He could feel himself flushing about the time Jason suggested to RoseD that they consider a virtual coupling position that, in Kato's mind, would have to be followed by at least a week in traction at Stanford Hospital.

Kato could feel his own breathing being altered. He was having trouble swallowing and began eyeing the big cooler of spring water when it happened.

"Aaiieeghh!" Jason wailed. "Aaiieghh! She's frozen up on me!"

Kato snapped his head around. Jason was standing and appeared to be playing the keyboard like Jerry Lee Lewis at the piano.

"Help, help," Jason screamed. "My hands are stuck. I'm freezing."

About 2 A.M., after he had helped unstick Jason and taken him to the trauma center at Valley Medical Center for the treatment of his freezer burn, Kato dialed a special number.

"Agent Watanabe here," came the sleepy reply.

"It's Kato," he said. "I've met RoseD. She's back, only this time she's turned into an ice queen."

# chapter 39

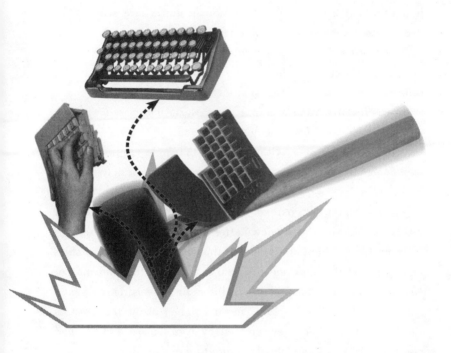

**J.P. started out the evening expansively.** "Have anything you want," he told Maria. They were sitting at a recessed table facing a big picture window at the Bella Vista up on Skyline Boulevard. From the outside, the place looked like an aged roadhouse set among the redwoods, which was logical since it had gotten its start back in prohibition days when it was located astride a prime bootleggers' route from the stills of Woodside to the speakeasies of San Francisco. On the side opposite the road, the view side, was the San Andreas Fault, which offered, depending upon your perspective, the dizzying possibility of total catastrophe or, if the fog broke, a breathtaking view of the Valley floor, nearly 2,000 feet below. In either case, it was enough to make anyone swoon.

Inside, it was about as formal as you could get and still be in the redwoods. The waiters wore tuxes and carried an aura of haughtiness that matched the traditional country fare, which nodded, without apology, toward the heavier side.

Maria ordered abalone amandine, which came in a light chardonnay cream sauce. J.P. had salmon Wellington, *en croute*. He also ordered a bottle of 1993 Far Niente chardonnay.

It was the first time in a long time Maria had talked with J.P. without Baba RAM DOS along.

"He's out to dinner with a couple of Apple engineers," J.P. explained. "We just might get lucky and take advantage of the brain drain."

At first, Maria felt guarded. But he had whisked her up the hill in his 600 SL with the top down after taking her past Neil Young's place on Kings Mountain Road and then John Sculley's old stables and then past the big stone entrance to the place the chairman of Infinity Computer, their client, was intent on converting to a venue site for the Olympic Games. They'd laughed about that, just as they'd laughed when they whizzed by Neil's place and J.P. had cranked "Harvest Moon" loud enough to serenade all of Woodside.

Maria was beginning to relax by the time she took her first sip of wine. The view helped ease things, too. The lights below were coming up and she could make out Highway 101 and the illuminated grids that formed office parks and shopping centers and suburban tracts that had all sprung up on the Peninsula even before the chip was invented. Now though, the entire grid looked like a circuit board. She was thinking this when J.P. clinked her glass.

"So," he said. His eyes were aglow. "I got a call today from a big shot at Kleiner Perkins. They were fishing, but fishing hard. They wanted to know if we'd be interested in an alliance. You know what that means?"

"They want to add us to their portfolio?" Maria asked.

"That's the easy way of looking at it, I suppose," J.P. said, twirling his wineglass against the candlelight. He looked as if he was trying to hypnotize himself. "I call it something more like colonization.

"We've got speed, maybe more speed than anybody right now. That's like finding God," he said. "They know we're onto it."

"How do you know they know?" Maria said.

"I made damn good and sure they know. I made damn good and sure a lot of people know we're onto something," he said.

"How so?"

"I told my barber," J.P. said, showing his teeth in an uncontainable grin that started out as a smirk. "He's the barber to the stars. He does all the guys—Ellison, McNealy, Sanders, Jim Clark, used to do Sculley and still does half of Sand Hill Road. When it comes to dealing information, the guy's a virtual human Web site. Plus, you should see his portfolio. He's onto an IPO while it's still a gleam in the founder's eye.

"Soo, I just planted a little seed. . . . It beats dealing with those dunderheads in the press."

"And the next thing you know, the phone rings and the venture capitalists are starting to swarm, is that it?" Maria asked.

"That's what we're here for . . . aren't we?" J.P. said, leaning back in his chair.

Maria felt a mild wave of revulsion and J.P. obviously caught the look in her eye.

"What? You really think this about changing the world?" he asked, a little too indignantly, Maria thought. "You think this is about info for the masses or some nice, tidy concept you picked up at Stanford Biz School? You think Silicon Valley is Fantasyland? You think we're busting our keesters eighteen hours a day to provide gainful employment to a bunch of video arcade dropouts and incurring huge overhead expenses that will eat us all, you and me both, alive?

"No way. We are in business to make only one thing—money. Our business plan is to make news and push the hot buttons of the guys with the up-front bucks. That's the only way we can indemnify ourselves."

Now it was Maria's turn to sit back in her chair. She took a long, slow sip of wine and said, "I thought you really wanted to change the world. I thought you wanted to turn the workplace into a pure democracy."

"I did, once," J.P. said wistfully. "But let me tell you something. When I was at Infinity, I was running a small team—Baba was on it—we had carte blanche. So we came up with a keyboard that was going to change the world. It was going to prevent repetitive stress. Baba and I and a few others were going to prevent a disease that afflicts millions. You could customize this keyboard to fit your own hands and strength."

"And?" Maria asked.

"And, and we were told we were asking too much. We wanted the keyboard built in the U.S., to provide jobs for U.S. workers, instead of sending business to sweatshops offshore. That meant the cost per unit would have been about 10 percent more. We also asked that we be allowed a certain percent of the sales, since it was our idea.

"The answer was 'no way.' Our ideas were Infinity property. We were owned by the supposedly enlightened, democratized Infinity Computer, the workplace of the '90s. I'll tell you, it was like being held hostage and we were supposed to be grateful for it. You know what the Stockholm syndrome is?" he asked.

Maria did. It was a situation in which hostages, out of fear or by virtue of being brainwashed, actually sympathized with their captors, and in some cases—Patty Hearst, for instance—became soldiers for their captors' cause.

Maria twirled her glass in the candlelight. She gazed out the window once more and focused on the dazzling lights below.

"Is all that an illusion?" she asked.

"Obviously not," J.P. said. "But those streets weren't paved, or the circuits wired, with changing the world in mind. They were built on money with one explicit purpose—to make more."

Maria started to protest. But J.P. interrupted.

"Look, I don't want to have this big company and lots of employees. I'm not into that. I'm not into upgrading every six months or facing extinction and laying off a bunch of people with high hopes in between," he said. "I want to manage ideas floated by the brains of a few good people who will be handsomely rewarded, up front, not down the line. . . . And we have a chance to pull that off, maybe the only chance in our lifetimes."

He's always twisting things, she thought. Everything he says or believes probably has a twist in favor of his rules, his view of the world, his sense of right and wrong. He makes it up as he goes, or as the money flows.

She averted her eyes and sipped her wine so that she wouldn't betray her indignation.

"Maria," J.P. said, leaning across the table, pushing his face toward hers and coming as close as he had ever come to her. She wondered if his feet were still on the floor, he was leaning so far. She looked around, embarrassed. "I want us to begin something together. Starting tonight or early tomorrow, if you're game."

She felt flushed. Tried to blame it on the wine. But also couldn't take her eyes off his.

"I want us to start working on a prospectus for an initial public offering. See, I think that once the word gets out, we're going to be seeing the investment bankers in our parking lot. But we can head them off at the pass. We can, in my humble opinion, draw up a prospectus on what we already know—using speed and the best of intentions and a hell of a lot of bandwidth to boot. We can go public without any real product in hand. Only a promise . . . OK? Just think about it."

If she'd forecast the evening or even rehearsed her reactions, Maria could have imagined J.P. hitting on her, and she'd have reacted if and when he tried . . . but she was not prepared for this. She was both dazzled and frightened.

"I just have three questions," she said, surprised at her odd boldness. Or maybe it was the wine. "The first is: What about Infinity?"

"Their stock is dropping faster than their market share. They're losing a manager a week. There is a rumor that the chairman is dumping stock. It's chaos, utter panic. Which is fine, as long as they hang on long enough for us to launch an IPO. If not, we'll want to be in position, casting off before the mothership sinks."

Maria nodded. "My second question is: Just when do we get a name?"

J.P. winced. "The guy at Kleiner Perkins wanted to know that too. I said we were kicking around the name MacroHard. The guy said: 'Why that?' And I said, 'Cuz it beats being small and soft.'"

Maria guessed J.P. was not ready to be pinned down. "My third question is this: Just who the hell is RoseD?"

J.P. gazed out the window.

"If I tell you, will you work with me on this?" he asked.

She hesitated, gulped and said, "Yes."

J.P. stayed silent for a moment. Then he turned from the window, looked directly at her and said, "I can't tell you exactly right now. It wouldn't be right . . . the fires in the laptops and all. But I can tell you this.

"We go back a long way."

# chapter 40

**J.P. and Maria were cruising the S-turns** halfway down the hill from the restaurant when the car phone sounded. Since J.P. needed both hands on the wheel, he used the conference mode on the cellular, allowing Maria to listen in.

It was Baba calling.

"Hi, Pete," J.P. said, reverting to his old friend's former first name. *"Ça va, mon vieux?* How'd dinner with Capps go? He interested in coming on board?"

Maria knew that would be Steve Capps, the legendary developer of the Macintosh program for Apple Computer. Only recently, he had jumped and let it be known that he was "looking to pursue other opportunities." The hot rumor was that Microsoft was coming after him with all its guns blazing.

"That is not why I am calling," Baba said. "I am calling because theez guy Mr. Kato called to interrupt me at the restaurant. By the way, the *medallions d'agneau* were superb, especially with a Jordan cabernet."

"What year?" J.P. asked, leaning into a curve.

"Eighty-seven," Baba said. "Not bad for California."

"Sonoma, Baba, Alexander Valley," J.P. corrected. "So, what's up?"

"Oh, yeah. This guy Kato called to say that Jason whatever his name is, you know, the surfer guy who got caught on fire? He is now in the hospital with freezer burn."

J.P. laughed.

"Kato called to tell you that?" he asked.

"It happened in R&D," Baba said, sounding stern. "While he was using one of the laptops. It froze up on him."

"Did anybody see what happened?" J.P. asked quickly.

"Kato was a witness."

"What?!"

J.P. tromped on the brakes so hard that Maria's shoulder safety harness emergency tensioning retractor locked, preventing her from being catapulted from the Mercedes convertible. But the impact knocked the wind out of her. She was gasping desperately to catch her breath.

"Get him into my office. ASAP. We need to download what he saw," J.P. said without even turning his head toward Maria.

Baba said he would do what he could and J.P. started down the hill again.

"Aren't you even going to ask how Jason is?" Maria said between gasps.

"Oh, yeah, Baba. How's the surfer dude?"

"I don't know," Baba said. "I forgot to ask."

Maria exhaled loudly, making her distress obvious.

"You OK?" J.P. said. "These antilock brakes are great, eh? Nose of the vehicle stayed straight as an arrow. Shows you what 70K will get you."

Maria asked if she could use the car phone and J.P. obliged. She called the emergency room at Valley Medical Center in San Jose and asked about Jason. The ER operator said she couldn't locate him, until Maria said: "Guy with freezer burn."

"Oh, that dude," the operator said. "We're keeping him for the night. He'll be OK, but he's all bandaged up and a little stressed out right now. He says a computer caused it. Can you believe that?"

"Hang up," J.P. said firmly. He was staring straight ahead and going a little too fast, Maria thought, judging by the squeals the tires were making at each turn and how her stomach felt.

"He must have been using one of the *old* laptops," J.P. said. "Jeez, I thought we got rid of them all after Hopkins got burned."

"You mean Harry Hopkins?" Maria asked, already knowing the answer. She started to tell J.P. about the name on the return address —RoseD—on the laptop-size package that had been sent to the Atherton venture capitalist, but caught herself. No, she wanted to talk to Jason first.

They sped through Woodside and J.P. roared up the on-ramp to 280 without another word exchanged between them.

He's really agitated, Maria thought, and decided right then and there that once J.P. dropped her off she would go see about Jason.

"You don't need me to hang around while you talk to Kato, do you?" she asked.

J.P. was silent, driving hard south in the fast lane, although he could have used any lane this time of night.

"No, no, go ahead," he said, patting the steering wheel. "Don't worry. We'll clear everything up. Besides, I want you fresh for tomorrow. We start working on the prospectus, remember? In six months, you'll be able to afford one of these babies, trust me."

Strange last words, Maria thought, locking them away for future reference. She also felt a chill, and it wasn't from the air rushing by at seventy-five mph. *"Trust me."*

They were in Cupertino within twenty minutes and Maria arrived at the emergency room at Valley Medical Center in San Jose in another twenty. It was 12:52 A.M. Definitely not visiting hours.

Maria checked first at the ER and was told Jason had been transferred to a room, which she found after much wandering.

"Jason, you OK?" she said, bursting in the door of his room just ahead of the night nurse, who threatened to call security.

"Gawd, this TV sucks," Jason said, manipulating the channel changer with his toes. Both hands were swaddled in bandages. But otherwise, he was sitting up in bed sucking on ice water through a long flex straw and looking pretty much normal.

She asked again how he felt.

"Rejected," he said. "I mean like I load in all the ammo—the new superchip, the supercooler—into the FirePower and I go to call up this old friend—her name's RoseD—and pretty soon we're yakking away, you know, and like I look down and there's vapor coming out of the keyboard and then my fingers are stuck there. I'm like iced."

He looked genuinely bewildered and held up his bandaged paws as proof.

"Did Kato see all this?" she asked.

"Kato? Yeah, Kato, he's a heck of a dude. Anyway, he had me use one of the lie detector keyboards and asked me to call up RoseD. I don't know how he knew her. But he did. So I go, 'Sure.'

"It's like I haven't really talked to her since after the fire, you understand. But anyway, just when things were getting back to normal . . . I get the big freeze. You know, I'm starting to get a little depressed about me and Rose."

"What did Kato do?" Maria asked.

"You mean besides drive me to the emergency room?"

"Yeah, besides that," Maria urged.

"Nothing. Except he asked me not to tell anyone about this . . ."

"What?" Maria asked.

"You know, he asked me not to say anything about RoseD," Jason said. "Which was OK by me, not wanting the big boss to know I have this, like, um, friend I have been talking to on company time."

"I think you're right," Maria said, staring out the window, and then said rather cynically, "I'm certain J.P. wouldn't want to concern himself with anyone else's dubious liaisons."

# chapter 41

**Kato was already in the reception pod** when J.P. arrived the next morning. And with him was Robert, the guy who looked like Elton John and who had dropped the super computer chip on his way out the door during the earthquake. He was wearing a fresh pair of oversized glasses.

"Come in, come in," J.P. said warmly, ushering the two in just as Maria came around the corner.

A pair of Smurfs, Maria thought, as she knocked politely and stepped through the threshold. And Robert is wearing the same shirt as yesterday, probably the day before that, too. She nodded at the two and then looked quizzically at J.P.

J.P. rubbed his hands together.

"Robert, I want to apologize for being rude to you the other day . . . but, well, a computer contained in eyeglasses, especially controlled by the wink of an eye, was . . . how shall I say this?"

"A little much?" Robert asked.

"Precisely," J.P. said, reverting to a well-worn phrase reserved for when he found himself in situations calling for the utmost in disingenuousness.

"And now that you've seen it you are considering it?" Robert said. "Am I right?"

J.P. nodded.

"Well, what if I told you I went directly over to a VRML conference at the Fairmont Hotel and crashed a sushi fest being hosted by Mitsubishi? What if I told you I ran into a guy by the name of . . . uh, name of . . ."

He reached into his pocket, presumably fishing for a business card. But it still seemed a menacing gesture to Maria. The guy gave her the creeps.

"Here it is. His name is David Rose. He says he's been writing you about a hand-held Web browser."

J.P. shrugged and looked at Maria. She shrugged back.

"Anyway, he's got this agreement in principle with Mitsubishi to develop it. He showed me the cocktail napkin supporting the hand-shake deal. So I told him about my operating system and we got to planning. End result: He shook my hand . . . in fact, we even sketched out a tentative deal for my OS on another napkin . . . it's right here."

He fished again in his pocket.

"OK, OK," J.P. said quickly. "We're prepared to make you an offer. We'd like you to join our company . . ."

"I'll need 25 percent of all new product line profits that launch as a direct result of my system," Robert said firmly.

"Robert, that could add up to more money than you'll ever need," J.P. said boldly. "We'll give you 8 percent of the first million in profit and fifteen percent after that."

Maria did some quick calculating and figured it was more or less the same type of deal J.P. had promised her—only hers would come in the form of stock options.

"Fine," said Robert. "When do we start?"

"Today," J.P. said. "First, why don't you hang out in the kick-back quadrant for a bit? Try out our new juice bar. . . . Kato, would you stay a minute?"

Maria knew that J.P. wanted her to escort Robert out, but her instincts told her to stay. So she just pointed the way and returned just as J.P. was starting his interrogation.

"First of all, how did you find that wacko?" J.P. asked.

"Not hard," Kato said. "I simply checked the conference schedules, made a few calls and tracked him down. He was staying in the Holiday Inn in downtown San Jose. He had taken a Greyhound to get here."

"Well done, Mr. Kato," J.P. said. "You possess a range of talent that this company will come to value, I assure you."

Kato nodded.

I wonder what kind of deal *he* got? Maria wondered.

"Now, about last night. What happened to Jason? Did you see what happened?" J.P. asked.

"Not exactly," Kato said. "We installed the supercooling device and the superchip. It was amazing how easily things slid into place. And I loaned Jason one of my keyboards—one with the smartskin to register skin responses. Oh, and he made some joke about wearing latex gloves to ensure safe chat . . ."

Kato looked at J.P. and then Maria, hoping for at least a little laugh as he said this.

J.P. only looked solemn. And Maria took her cue from what Jason had already told her about the hot and heavy exchange with RoseD—with Kato urging him on. She *felt* very solemn.

"Anyway, he was just downloading some stuff, nothing out of

the ordinary—except that he was pulling things down real fast. I mean we were both amazed how quick the responses were. It was real, real exciting . . ."

"And?" J.P. said. "Go on."

"I don't know," Kato said, dropping his eyes and shaking his head. "I went for a drink of water and next thing I know, Jason is dancing a jig and screaming and his hands are caught on the keyboard. It's like he's caught in a bear trap, only his hands are frozen to the laptop."

"Your analysis?" J.P. asked quickly.

"We got a power surge and suffered some sort of circuit aneurysm and the supercooler burst," Kato said.

"But, the important thing, Mr. Kato, is that you saw the system work initially."

Kato's eyes grew large. "Definitely."

"Great. Great," J.P. said, rubbing his hands through his hair. "Now, Mr. Kato, can you work with Robert—separate R&D unit, away from the Pentagon Pod and away from those hippies in the . . . what do they call it? The Birthing Pod? No budget constraints. Fly your own flag. But get something out, something that won't blow up or freeze up, like right now?"

"I can only try, boss," Kato said, smiling.

There was something in that smile, Maria didn't know what to make of it. And there was certainly something in Kato's answer to J.P. Not what Jason had told her the night before. No mention at all of RoseD.

"Fine, then," J.P. said, taking Kato by the arm and guiding him through the door. "Because Maria and I plan to dedicate a full day today to drawing up a red herring that will make the venture capitalists drown in their own saliva."

That's a rather hostile way of viewing the gift horses, Maria thought as she accompanied Kato out the door.

"Do you think this thing can really work?" she asked Kato.

"Eventually," he said.

Maria noted his facility for circumspection but still asked the question that had been plaguing her all night since she had talked to Jason in the hospital.

"Kato, what really happened?"

He stopped. He turned and looked directly up at her for what seemed to Maria like a minute or more. She lost track. He was so much shorter and yet his gaze met hers and she could feel his eyes pushing through her own, searching for something. And yet, she did not flinch. She felt . . . transcendental.

"Maria, let's just say we are *both* onto something," he said softly. "That is all I know. But trust me. It will soon become known to both of us."

Strangely, Maria did not feel taken aback. She felt calm for the first time in weeks.

"Thank you" was all she could say. And it was barely audible when she said it. As Kato left, Maria turned back toward J.P.'s office, took a deep breath and walked in.

# chapter 42

**"FBI, Agent Watanabe,"** Lily said, as she always did when she picked up the phone at work.

"Listen, I'm not giving you my name. Just listen. . . ." It was a male voice, deep and insistent and rapid-fire.

"My barber has big-time Silicon Valley connections. So he tells me he's trimming up this VC, guy's well-connected, lives in Atherton, plays racquetball at the Decathlon Club, does aikido with Larry

Ellison and so forth. And the guy says, 'Didja hear about my neighbor Harry Hopkins? Damn near got his whole body barbecued by a laptop computer.'

"So a bell goes off. I'm like the next guy in the chair. And the barber tells me what he hears.... Just thought you'd like to know ..."

Click.

The caller sounded smart. Lily ruled out trying to trace the call. Instead, she dialed the Atherton Police Department and asked for a URL for a home page with hyperlinks to crime reports.

"Sorry," the voice came back politely. "We have a home page we're very proud of, but our computer's down right now. How about settling for a fax?"

The report arrived about two hours later, as did the report from the Menlo Park Fire Department.

She scanned the Atherton police report first. No mention of an exploding laptop, only that one of the officers had suffered mild smoke inhalation attempting to rescue a pet bird. The effort to save the bird was unsuccessful, the report added. A copy of a letter of regret from the department to the Hopkins family was attached.

She turned to the fire investigation. The top was pro forma. But then her eyes fixed on a paragraph well down the page that said:

Victim was suffering burns and smoke inhalation and was vague and disoriented when interviewed. Victim indicates he was in kitchen area working with laptop computer when fire broke out. Victim repeated words fire power. Reference unknown at this time. Requires follow-up interview.

She rifled through the pages, looking for the follow-up. There was none.

She called the insurance company and was put on hold.

Still, it was enough to build her own conclusions. And Lily was planning to interview Harold Hopkins herself when one of the secured lines rang.

"OK. He's inside," the voice said. "He's hired. They want him to start working on an application for the superchip right away."

"Great work, Kato," Agent Watanabe said. "Everything else OK?"

"Yeah, except that I think that J.P.'s executive assistant is beginning to smell something," Kato said.

"Maria," Lily said.

"Right," Kato said. "Actually, she seems OK. She may be the only one . . ."

"Careful, Kato," Lily said. "Stay cool, OK?"

There was a laugh at the other end of the phone. "You mean don't go near RoseD, the ice queen?"

"Keep up the good work, Kato," Lily said, and rang off.

Days earlier, he had proved his worth to the bureau by locating one Joseph Robert Giggs, the guy who called himself Robert, an engineer and former employee of Texas Instruments in Dallas. It seems that TI was missing a beta version of a superconductor it was developing, a chip that its engineering team hoped would be light-years ahead of the competition—speedwise. Joe Bob was a member of that team. But he was also missing.

Those circumstances tend to draw attention—through various channels, that is. Theft was one thing. That's a local offense. But suspicion of taking a trade secret across state lines or possibly international borders was definitely federal.

So when Kato called Lily in the dead of night to report that a superchip had been dropped off at his company's doorstep and conveyed what he had witnessed—Jason's hyper-speed connection to RoseD and then the freeze-up—Lily Watanabe had already been alerted by the FBI's special wire (bizcrime.com), as had thousands of agents throughout the world, as had Interpol and, most likely, the CIA or at least someone with national security and Wall Street credentials. It was that serious, especially when the technology had such high-speed potential and obvious weapons implications.

Boy, wouldn't the Iraqis or Wintel love to get their hands on this? she thought.

"Kato, you've got to find him," Lily said. "Then we've got to turn him. We might be able to utilize his brilliance provided we offer an incentive, such as making certain that TI knows we know where their chip is and making certain that he knows if he doesn't do what we ask, he could be making license plates instead of superconductors."

So Lily almost shouted with glee when Kato called first to report that he had located the guy, now calling himself Robert— no last name—trying to peddle secrets at a trade show in San Jose.

And, when he called a second time to say he had secured a job for the guy in J. P. McCorwin's company, Lily did finally let go— that is after she hung up the phone.

"Yes!" she shouted, clenching a fist in the air. "Awright, big guy. We're just about in place. . . . The hunt for RoseD is about to begin."

And then she stood, looking at the Japanese watercolor on her office wall.

Maria has one like it, she reminded herself. Maria worries me. She's OK, I think. I'm almost sure of it. But we can't let her get in the way.

And then she picked up the telephone and dialed (415) 555-1212.

"Hello, operator. Atherton please. Harold Hopkins's residence."

# chapter 43

**"God, I love the Valley!"** J.P. was pacing like a racehorse in a stall. "So much money out there. And here's where we take poetic license to print our share."

It was 10 A.M. They were already three hours late getting started drafting a red herring, which was essentially a huge sales brochure designed to grab the attention of investment bankers, venture capitalists and potential partners and signal a potential public offering. When it came to generating bucks, a red herring was as much a commodity as the very technology it announced.

*MacroHard*—just go with me on the name for now. It's not permanent. We'll come up with something inspirational"—J.P. dictated, and Maria wrote—"was organized in June 1995 to design, develop and implement comprehensive enabling technology for all Infinity Computer operating systems."

He rubbed his hands through his hair and continued: "Then you get the stuff about putting out the fires in the laptops, etc., etc. It's all pro forma company history stuff to get through the gates of the SEC," he continued. "Then, and I'll help you with this, we say we are positioned to lead an emerging paradigm shift away from text-based, less interactive applications, even from the Mosaic-style WWW browser, toward wide-open, highly interactive, easy-to-use, intuitive, multimedia systems that will utilize the Internet and telecommunications, blah, blah, blah.

"You get what I'm after?"

"You want me to fill in about one hundred pages worth of blah, blah, blah. Is that it?" Maria answered.

"And don't leave out high-speed hardware and virtual language modeling software," J.P. shot right back.

He was in his "J.P. Rules!" mode, which meant 50 percent visionary, 50 percent insufferable—and Maria could add, about 100 percent of a few other things. Nonetheless, she picked up on his vibrations. She got a contact exhilaration high from the role J.P. had asked her to play.

"What about risk factors?" she asked. "You want me to handle that?"

"You mean like our alliance with Infinity Computer and the fact that we have a limited operating history and don't exactly have a working application even as we draw this thing up? Naw, I'll handle that," he said.

"You just go down and mix it up with the R&D folks and then paint a reasonable picture—kind of coagulate"—he had loved that verb ever since he heard Steve Jobs use it at a product demonstration—"everything everyone is doing in one nice coherent preamble to the document that's going to be designed to launch maybe two and a half million shares and land us nearly $40 million faster than you can open a bank account."

Maria thought for a minute and asked: "At this point, shouldn't we highlight our enhancement relationship with Infinity—you know, the way Microsoft did with MS-DOS for IBM?"

"Brilliant," J.P. said. "Brilliant. . . . I knew from the get-go, and I told Baba this . . . that you weren't just another . . ."

"Stanford MBA," Maria said sharply.

"Definitely not," J.P. said, grinning. "You got too much moxie. . . . By showing that Infinity is beholden to us and that we can expect a steady stream of royalties from them, it doesn't make us look like beggars at the table. Also, make certain you use key words like . . ."

"*Propriety* and *standardization?*" Maria asked. "And imply that we will be in position to use our standard, which will be another way of saying *monopoly,* to capitalize on for future applications and licensing?"

J.P. bounced on his toes. "And *enabling,* don't forget enabling. The VCs love that word. People are gonna want, no, absolutely gonna need our system. See, it's all about practical positioning. You see that, don't you? You see that it isn't the technology exactly, it's the *selling* of the notion, the concept. The technology actually comes later—just look at three-fourths of the crap that's on the Web. . . . You tell me, what exactly *is* Yahoo!? And what's their stock trading at? It went straight from the IPO to the stratosphere."

Maria laughed, and then said, "By the way, where is Baba?"

"Still out there looking for Mr. Kato, I guess," J.P. said.

His mood changed. Maria could see it. He looked slightly bewildered.

"Baba and I put this team together. We consider diversity and political correctness and still use a strenuous application process based on the Microsoft employment application. We ask our people to wade through absurd abstractions—How blue is the sky?—How much water does the Colorado River hold?—to test their analytical processing. We even ask permission to talk to anyone's dealer ... And yet, the people who come up with the killer app could be the two guys who just walked in off the street.

"Or out of the woods, in Mr. Kato's case," Maria reminded her boss.

"Weird," J.P. said, rubbing his hands through his silver-blond hair.

It is weird, Maria thought to herself. But she had concluded that some time ago. All we need now is for the bewitching RoseD to show up for the party.

"I wish Baba would get here," J.P. said, starting to pace again. "I need him to start drawing up the fine print, like our plan for using the proceeds—you know, for capital and overhead, such as R&D."

Maria was glad to hear that someone else would be working on the necessary but boring ingredients that had to be poured into a prospectus to satisfy not only investors but the Securities and Exchange Commission. She also knew that lying or embellishing in a prospectus filed with the SEC amounted to perjury or fraud.

This made her nervous. It probably made everyone nervous. It probably even made Jim Clark nervous when he took Netscape public. But this business, all of Silicon Valley, was a cauldron of raw nerves. Besides, the lawyers would obviously vet the whole thing before it went public.

Just find out what these guys are doing down in R&D and tell the story, she told herself. Plow straight ahead. Believe in it. You just have to believe.

And then J.P. broke into her reverie.

"By the way, did you ever schedule that product demonstration? You know, to coincide with Bill Gates's visit to Stanford?"

She hadn't forgotten.

"One month from today at the Santa Clara Convention Center," she said. "Provided we have something to show."

"Oh, we will. We will. You tell those guys down in R&D we

need a working beta version of at least something by the end of the week."

J.P. sighed and looked out the window. Maria could see he was staring past the parking lot and the strip mall next door. He was staring out toward the foothills.

"You know, I have a feeling that RoseD is gonna drop in on us one of these days," he said.

Maria whirled. She stared at him hard. Had he been reading her mind?

"Really," J.P. said. "She can be a big help. Wait and see."

"Wouldn't miss it for the world," Maria said, trying not to sound either startled or sarcastic.

# chapter 44

**"Stop, right there!"** Rick Raptor, the supreme allied commander of the Pentagon R&D Pod, stepped in front of Maria, refusing to let her in. "Top security. You got clearance?"

"I'm J.P.'s executive assistant, is that enough?" Maria said, wondering if the guy was really serious.

"Sorry, I'll need something more than that," he said, guiding her back into the hallway. "But I can tell you this. We'll annihilate the competition . . ."

He looked left and right and then said: "I can also tell you this. And you can tell J.P. Our goal is to be able to download and hyperlink the entire Library of Congress in about fifteen seconds."

"When can I see a demo?" Maria asked.

"After I see one," he said, shrugging. "I said it was our goal, not our beta version."

Maria made a mental note to ask J.P. to review the Pentagon Pod's operating budget. They're being unrealistic and paranoid, she thought.

Meanwhile, the Affirmative Action, or Birthing, Pod was into companionable yet transcendental, quasi-intuitive computing that would probe the user's alter ego and make him or her feel good about experiencing a whole process involving the brain, the soul, DNA and whatever sixth sense the software could reference as an energy source.

That's what Maria was told.

The whole thing was designed around the birthing experience. Lisa Rose DeNiccolino had insisted on this.

"Go ahead, boot up," Ethan, the pod leader, urged.

When Maria did, a soft, warm, honey-colored glow began to pulsate gently from the screen. This was accompanied by a cradling background sound of water. Not waves or a rushing river, softer, much softer.

"The river of existence," she could hear someone say softly in the background.

Maria could imagine herself being rocked to sleep, gently, gently. Her eyes felt heavy . . .

"That's as close to amniotic fluid as we could get using 150 megs and a 1028-by-1024 resolution monitor." Ethan was speaking. "Naturally, with some more RAM and speed and pixels, we could virtually return you to the womb."

"And then launch you into the universe," Lisa said. "Go ahead, sign on."

Maria did and a small litany of instructions floated down the screen. Maria pointed and clicked as directed and suddenly the screen changed. She felt as though she were being pulled by the hand of God right into the screen. Colors exploded and whooshed by, surrounding her, it seemed, as though she were in a meteor shower. She felt totally out of control, but calm, too. No, not out of control. Connected. Connected to her innermost being. It was the calmest she'd felt in days, since the last time she rode Fuego. She felt a rush of exhilaration and primal curiosity.

And suddenly, she burst forth and it was as though the universe had been pulled down or, rather, gravity had been suspended and she felt catapulted upward. She was alone with her own amazement when a voice sounded—it was reassuring, strong and wise. She recognized the voice immediately.

*Use the Force, Maria, go with the Force.*

The voice was unmistakable. It was Obi-Wan Kenobi, the great Jedi Knight/philosopher, speaking to her as he had spoken to Luke Skywalker.

*May the Force be with you, Maria.*

Maria stared into the monitor, only it was no longer a monitor, it was the entire universe. That's how she felt. Enormous.

"Actually, we could give you Maya Angelou or Gloria Steinem, whatever audio avatar works," a voice broke in. It was Lisa.

Maria snapped back into consciousness and felt a bit annoyed, as if she'd been cheated.

"You see? You see?" Ethan was dancing around her. So were the others. They held hands and circled around Maria as if she were a Maypole. "It works. It works. It moves you into your most primitive mode. It invites you to use the Force."

"What's the Force?" Maria asked.

"Yourself," Lisa said. "I mean, you're standing there intellectually and psychologically naked. Now, you're ready to use your own curiosity and all the intuitive powers Mother Earth gave you to multitask in pursuit of—the truth."

"Or whatever else you're after in a particular personality window at a particular moment," Ethan said. "Or maybe not after, at least not consciously?"

"You mean it reads your mind?" Maria asked.

"No, not just your mind, your inner being," Lisa explained. "It taps into your entire self as an operating platform. Not just memory or experience or ambition or gender or some socially conditioned template you've been traditionally operating from. It's powered by total human experiential possibility."

"In other words," Ethan said, "wetware. The ultimate human potential movement."

They were all looking very self-satisfied and Maria didn't have the heart to ask the obvious question, which was: So what? Or, So what happens next?

But Bindhu, the young Sikh engineer, anticipated the question. She stepped forward and said simply: "We are working on the application. It will involve a voyage—most likely through the World Wide Web—that will allow you to intuitively select and sort information that will be actually useful . . ."

"Life-enhancing is more like it," Lisa interrupted. "It will not simply answer questions you might pose but will ask questions you could never have conceived of on your own or by using some old standard digital system. And it will give you *the* answers.

"Use it and it will make you wise, not just clever," she continued, obviously pleased with her explanation. "Use it and shift your center of gravity. Sail over the horizon, onward to an entirely new hyperlink between your RL and the universe."

"What's an RL?" Maria asked.

"Real life," Lisa answered, high-handedly.

"Nice theme," Maria said. "I should mention it to Brad in Marketing."

Lisa pursed her lips as if she'd just sucked a lemon.

"There are *some* people it just might not work for," she said. "Some people are still setting fire to their RLs."

Everyone shared a laugh.

But Maria wondered if Lisa wasn't telling her something. She wondered if it didn't involve Brad and the combusting laptop. And she wondered, despite what her own common sense had told her was next to impossible, if Lisa might, in fact, be RoseD.

# chapter 45

**Maria gave Kato and Robert a few days** to get their act together, and then she dropped in.

"Hi, guys, how's it going?" she asked and immediately flashed that some serious creative tension had settled over their pod because neither one looked up from the design table.

"Quiet, they're operating."

It was Jason, back from the hospital, complete with bandaged hands.

"Can't use my hands, so I'm here strictly as an adviser," he explained. "But I don't know, these guys are really out there. They've left me in the dust."

The way Jason explained it, Robert was trying to grow a new chip, based on the design of the superchip that Kato had installed in the laptop that froze up on Jason. But the chip was too far gone, along with the laptop.

"So, they're back to the blueprint based on Bob's"—it was apparent that Jason and Robert had forged a casual affinity for each other—"memory of his previous design," Jason said. "Then they'll transfer it to a piece of silicon and grow another chip."

"A vastly improved one," Robert said, tilting his head. He was wearing a light like a coal miner's strapped to his forehead. "We're going to introduce even more circuits to enable us to take advantage of our micro–cooling booster system."

And then, at Kato's urging, he turned his attention back to the table.

Jason took Maria aside.

"You know what Kato wants him to do?" he said. "He wants him to set up a new MUD—multiple-user domain—and try to contact RoseD. Kato wants him to start a relationship with her."

Maria started to ask why, but Jason interrupted her.

"Fine with me. Believe me, from now on, it's hands off," he said.

"But why does he want to contact RoseD?" she asked.

"I dunno, something about changing identities through the Internet," he said. "Kato says it's a good way to test the speed and versatility of the system. But I don't quite get it.

"Anyway, that's just one thing they plan on doing. They've got a zillion ideas. See, they're going to develop a really smart multifunctional system with unbelievable input and output capabilities..."

"There, we have it," Robert said. "We've got circuitry—more than ever."

He wiped his brow and took a moment to explain.

"We'll run these circuits first through a block of silicon to be certain we have order. And then we will hook up to some software I have already coded to receive, store, sort and interact with any and all stimuli—e-mail, human speech, Internet servers, television and radio signals, faxes, anything digital and even any new MUDs that we might create for the sake of keeping company."

Maria was having a hard time fathoming this.

"We've designed a bot, you know what that is?" Robert continued.

She had heard the term and vaguely remembered that it was short for *robot*. More specifically, it was a program written to supposedly respond to typed conversations in e-mail or on the Net. She said what she knew and was embarrassed she didn't know more.

"Well, that's a pretty simple explanation," Robert said, putting his hands on his hips. He stamped his right foot and made a big pouty face. "And she's the executive assistant to the big guy? Sheesh."

Kato spoke up. "Robert is working on something a bit more complex, so please forgive the tantrum. You see, it will not only interact conversationally in multiple-user domains, it will define other domains and respond. For instance, it will pick up a phone message or an e-mail or even a news bulletin and answer back, or even act on it. At least that's the theory, right, Mr. Robert?"

Robert continued to pout. But he was also busy. He held a fistful of wires, which he waved at Maria, and then began connecting from the lump of silicon crystal to virtually every electronic port in the pod, including three big Infinity desktop 5000s.

"Oh, man, are we gonna get wired tonight, or what?" Jason was singing.

Kato only smiled.

Maria smiled too. She had a date that night—sort of—with some women friends. One of them, Kate, in marketing at a Mountain View startup, had won a pool on a Niners game and the prize was an overnight in a suite, room service included, at the Fairmont in downtown San Jose. Maria hadn't been to a slumber party since she was seventeen. But she looked forward to this for reasons she couldn't quite put her finger on until one of her friends said, "We could all use a little therapy."

"I'm sorry I won't be able to be here," she told Kato. But offered her beeper number, "in case there are any major technical frontiers crossed," and regretted it immediately.

Even Robert looked disappointed, although Kato just kept smiling.

Jason walked her to the door.

"You know what they're really after?" he whispered. "They're laying a trap for RoseD. Don't ask me why, it was Kato's idea, just like it was his idea to have me call her up and try to talk her in. Anyway, it's all pretty weird, if you ask me."

"What are they going to do?" Maria asked.

"I dunno for sure," Jason said. "But it has something to do with creating a bunch of MUDs to see if they can lure her into one. Then they plan to question her real hard and try to identify her. I guess I could understand it if they were cops or something. But they're hackers, just like me. You know what I mean?"

"Not really," Maria said, patting Jason on the shoulder. "Listen, keep your head up and your hands off the keyboard. And call me if anything weird happens, OK?"

"What could get weirder than this?" Jason said, grinning.

"Just call me if it does," Maria insisted and turned and left with a big nervous knot in her throat.

# chapter 46

**Maria held her breath when the hotel elevator reached the twentieth floor.**

"Welcome to the top of the world, ladies," the well-heeled baggage attendant said, adding, "The president and Mrs. Clinton stayed here. So did Bob Dole . . . and Barbra Streisand."

"Who was with whom?" Kate asked, sounding genuinely incredulous.

This unleashed a torrent of laughter from the other three guests, Maria included, even though it was a silly rejoinder.

But it was OK to be silly. Here they were in a penthouse suite of the Fairmont Hotel, looking down on all of Silicon Valley from the vantage point normally reserved for expense account millionaires, usually from Japan or Taiwan or Singapore. In this case, it was at the courtesy of Kate's startup. The whole thing was extravagantly silly.

"So why not?" Kate said. "We've earned it."

"Check the ceiling," said Loretta, an associate attorney specializing in securities at Williams Skofield Bagley and Strauss, one of the Valley's hottest law firms. "See if it's made of glass."

Maria had known Loretta since grad school at Stanford when she'd come over from the law school for a little "cross pollination, so I can learn how to be a rich bitch." She was not a bit pious, like so many other law students. Maria liked Loretta for that. Plus, she, too, came from a farm family. From outside of Birmingham, Alabama. Loretta was black and on scholarship, She'd also been a hot ticket when she got out of law school and was pretty much able to sass any of the recruiters "I ain't particularly in love with."

She also happened to be in the same law firm as Elizabeth Roth, the wife of Brad from marketing.

"One part self-anointed feminist goddess, the other part stone bitch," Loretta said, when Maria asked for an assessment of Elizabeth. "Like last Friday—it's dress-down day. We're in khakis and polo shirts, and here comes Elizabeth clackety-clack down the hall. She's wearing this Galliano knit pantsuit number that's got to have cost her at least a thou.

"And one of the other women partners says: 'Hey, Elizabeth, you forget something? It's dress-down day.'

"And she bats her eyes at the senior male partner and says: 'I know, I know, I came just as I am.'

"And I say: 'Well, at least you left your necktie at home.'

"But what I wanted to say was: 'Did you loan your husband

your necktie?' I'm telling you, she is the quintessential white male.... What's her husband like? Got to be a dufus. Am I right?"

For a moment, Maria felt sorry for Brad. But still, she answered, "You got it."

"Hey, no more work chat, OK? We're here to get decadent and dangerous," Kate said, plopping herself down at the baby grand piano. She started playing the theme from *Il Postino* and then popped up and dialed downstairs, first saying, "Who else wants a massage?"

Sally, who Maria knew from their days together at Sun Micro, but who went back even further with Kate at Hewlett Packard, jumped at the offer. But Loretta said she'd rather stay and enjoy the view "from the lap of luxury." Maria elected to stay with her and went to the corner windows to take in the panorama.

Amazing, she thought, how everything is so spread out and in such a short time. She tried to pick out familiar landmarks, old ones, like the Mariani fruit orchards in Sunnyvale. But they were gone, just like the canneries, just like the old Harte's Department Store, where everyone shopped in downtown San Jose until the shopping malls strangled business to death. Maria was around four or five when it closed. But she could remember her mother taking her there. She could still smell the popcorn and the odor of fabric that greeted her when she walked through the door.

"OK, OK," Loretta said as soon as the other two were out the door. "So when's the IPO? How many hundreds of thousands of shares you gonna start with, girl?"

Maria was startled. "What? How'd you know?"

"Elizabeth. Married to Brad. Hel-lo?" Loretta said. "Brad's got a big mouth. Elizabeth's got big ears and big ambitions. Of course, she can't officially work on any of this... but she still gave us a heads-up. So we may be working together.... Or we may be working with the underwriters.

"So how much you figure to make right out of the blocks?"

Maria fidgeted. She picked up the room service menu and blanched at the prices.

"Uh, I don't know much of anything, I really don't..."

"For Jiminy Christ . . . confidence, girl. You got to get con-fi-dence," Loretta said. "Whatcha in this game for?"

"That's a very good question," Maria said. "So far, it pays for my horse."

Loretta wasn't buying the brush-off. "Look, we both know what happens when the well dries up. Someone comes calling. Our daddies got to pay attention when the boss calls, right? And when the boss comes calling and says, 'Sorry, we're going dry,' or 'Sorry, gonna turn that field into a shopping center,' in other words, 'Sorry, you've been good with the plow, but now it's time to plow some real money into this land,' what happens?

"You've seen it happen. I've seen it happen. You've said it ain't gonna happen. So've I. No downsizing of me, sister. Not if I own a piece of something. It doesn't matter what. It's the only real insurance policy there is."

Maria could see the flash of anger in Loretta's eye. "Look, Kate's right," she said, trying to sound assertive. "Let's enjoy ourselves with a vengeance."

And they did.

They hit the sauna. They ordered creatively from room service, poured each other champagne and then chardonnay and poured their hearts out to each other as soon as *Friends* was over. Gossip, dissing old bosses and boyfriends, relationships with their fathers and mothers—all were fair game. Laughter, tears, brooding silences, consolations, approbations, hugs. They were all the collateral of the night.

And Maria smiled to herself when she finally looked at the clock, which said 1:30, and announced softly to the others: "Nicest time I've had in a long time. Love you all."

When her beeper sounded, it was still dark. She stumbled to the bathroom and turned on the light to get a better look at the number, which she recognized immediately. From the bathroom phone, she called the office. Jason picked up immediately.

"Man, oh man, Maria you're not going to believe this," he said, breathlessly. "You've got to get over here quick. Hurry, before I call 911."

# chapter 47

**At first, it looked as if the parking lot had uplifted** and formed a mountain overnight. But when she got closer, Maria could tell it was really a pyramid of pizza boxes, stacked haphazardly, blocking the front entrance.

"When I last counted there were six hundred and seventy-four —all pepperoni!" It was Jason's muffled voice coming from behind the obstacle.

"What the heck?" Maria said, and started to laugh uncontrollably. "Whose joke? It's not like it's J.P.'s birthday or anything. Did Larry Ellison send them? Or Jerry Sanders?"

"No," Jason said, sounding unamused, even desperate. "RoseD."

"What?" Maria shouted.

"I'm serious," Jason shouted back. "Come on in. Here, on the left, there's a passage. You can crawl through."

Maria did, although she was almost overcome by the gummy aroma. She was probably one of the very few people working in Silicon Valley who was actually repulsed by pizza.

"I should have sent a canary into the cave first," she said as Jason held out his hand and pulled her through. "Looking at you, I'm not so sure it's safe to go in."

"You got that right," Jason said. "But you also haven't seen anything yet."

He took her right down the stairs to R&D. The door was partly ajar and Jason approached it gingerly. Inside, Maria could hear voices—Kato and Robert.

"OK?" Jason whispered through the door.

"OK," Robert said. "We've got her quieted down."

Maria followed Jason through the door. And the first thing she saw was another mountain—this one of fax paper piled to the ceiling. And there was another huge pile of FedEx envelopes and UPS boxes next to it. They all said EXTREMELY URGENT: PRIORITY OVERNIGHT and were from all over the world. As far as Maria could tell, they were all addressed to RoseD.

"We've also got dozens of airline tickets and hotel reservations for places like Kamchatsky, that's in Siberia, I looked it up, and Qandahar, Afghanistan," Robert said. "You guys thinking about opening a couple of offshore factories? Is RoseD like a site scout or something?"

Maria shook her head. She grabbed a phone and called J.P.

"Better get down here quick," was all she could say, because Jason was pointing to something that took her breath away. It was something awesome and grotesque and made absolutely no sense, as if it had been manufactured in a nightmare.

"Tell me I'm not still back at the hotel, guys," she said. "Tell me I'm not dreaming."

They stood silent. Even Kato had dropped his ever-present smile.

On the work table, where Robert had wired up a matchbox cube of silicon less than twelve hours earlier, there was now a misshapen crystal bigger than a human fist. The wires were still in place and each one still led to the port of some electronic device—computers, the fax machine, telephones, the television, a stereo amplifier, even the thermostat.

"We all went out for beers around ten or so," Robert said. "And we left the power running and all the com ports open so we could have input and output. The idea was to see how many impulses we could send through the circuits."

"So we get back around midnight, or maybe it was closer to 11:30," Jason said, "and we find out that this thing is not only conducting—it's virtually paying attention."

"Huh?" Maria said.

"Yeah, it was actually listening to us and decoding through all the stuff we've got it wired to—two-way audio, video, the Web, the fax, the phone," Robert jumped back in. "It's like doing our will, picking up on everything we say and acting on it."

Maria felt stunned, unable to ask even the simplest question.

"See, just before we go out, I say something like: 'Boy, I'm starved, I could eat six hundred pepperoni pizzas,'" Jason said. "And so we get back and . . .'"

"RoseD moved a mountain, is that what you're telling me?" Maria said, incredulous.

"That's not only what I'm telling you," Jason said. "That's what you just crawled through."

"But the beauty of the thing is that not only did she pick up on our casual conversations and take them seriously, she began looking around on the Web, searching for the fastest and the cheapest eats," Robert added. "She's like the complete personal digital assistant, the last best PDA.

"I remember I was having trouble making certain circuit connections. I guess I said something like, 'Where in the world can I find a good, cheap, reliable router?' Well, we get back and sure enough, they start coming in from all over—Japan, Taiwan, Korea. I look on one of the PC screens and she's talking to some dealer rep's software in Singapore and bargaining him down—if we buy by the lot."

Maria shook her head as hard as she could, as if she was trying to dry her hair. Only she was just trying to clear the air. But the obvious question just fell out of her mouth.

"But 'RoseD'? What's that all about?"

The three were silent again.

"Can't say," Kato said. "Except for the fact that I did call her up in one of the MUDs—using both fire- and cold-protective gloves. We actually had a safe and pleasant chat."

"Until you asked her to come on down to R&D and give you a kiss, dude," Jason said reproachfully. "I think that got her going."

"What did she say when you asked her that?" Maria asked.

Kato smiled sheepishly, but said nothing.

"I'll tell you what she said," Jason said. "She said, 'Kato, I like the cut of your Calvin Kleins.' Same thing she said to me before she burned me. . . . And that's not all she said, cuz you asked her again, right, dude?"

Kato nodded.

"You go, 'Don't make me repeat myself. Please come down and give us a little kiss.' And she goes, 'Why? Did your dog leave you?' Am I right, dude?" Jason was laughing so hard he began to cry.

"That's not important," Robert said. "What is important is that we have discovered in this pod a truly interactive, multidimensional interface that not only recalls, it recognizes, reacts and makes contact with other sites, causing them to react. *That* is what I would call a breakthrough."

"But where does RoseD come in?" Maria asked.

"What breakthrough?" It was J.P., looking moderately horrified. He was wiping tomato sauce off his black Armani jacket. "What the hell is this?"

More silence.

Maria started to say something, but Robert beat her to it.

"Tonight, we grew intelligence. We wired up a silicon crystal, left the building and when we returned we'd given birth to a seven-year-old," he said, pointing to the swollen mass of silicon. "Somehow, we actually programmed and supported an internal will to expand."

When put that way, Maria thought, it did look a bit like a human brain.

"Can we clone it?" J.P. said. "Much less sell it as an application? From the looks of things, you've accomplished about as much as if you'd turned loose a gang of chimpanzees on the place."

Maria thought of blaming it on RoseD. But what would she say? Still, she wanted to test J.P.'s reaction. But just then, Brad stepped through the door. He was smiling and munching on a slice of pizza.

"Maybe we don't ask people to buy these things. Maybe we should build a plastic bust around it—it could be anything: Michelangelo's *David*, Antonio Banderas, Juliette Binoche, Einstein, even your own kids—and ask people to *adopt* them. . . . Think about it—we turn a section of Fry's or CompUSA into a computer placement agency."

"You all think about it," J.P. said, clearly losing patience. "Real hard. In about ten days, we're having a product demo for Infinity and other potential developer clients. About ten days after that, if we get enough buzz, we're gonna have an IPO. So think real hard. I want ironclad possibilities, not mountains of cardboard."

He turned, tore off his jacket and tossed it to Maria, "Get this cleaned, will you?" And stalked out the door.

Maria stood still, too surprised to be furious.

And finally mustered some words: "Guys, things are starting to get serious around here."

# chapter 48

**J.P. was on the phone.** Baba was sitting on a corner of his desk writing instructions on a yellow legal pad.

"Mr. Chairman, that's exactly right," J.P. was saying when Maria walked in. "I am telling you that we are about to coagulate all human knowledge—not just the stuff stored in digits. We think we can develop an engine that will probe and provoke even more knowledge. No more browsing, we're gonna plow and reap, if you know what I mean."

Baba wrote furiously and J.P. craned over his half-glasses to see. He studied the script and then said, "No, sir, I'm not talking about an interface indexing agent like Yahoo! Compared to us, they're nothing more than a card catalog."

J.P. smiled and winked at Maria.

Baba continued to scribble.

"What I'm talking about is a metagalaxy, a 1,000-terabyte techno-utopia, where our computer interfaces for us. . . . No, sir, I said it is not like Yahoo! or some other little startup in Los Altos. They're all static URL collectors. Ours works in real time. It changes with moods . . . adapts.

"That's right, sir, if someone has PMS, our system will respect that." He winked again at Maria.

She made a sour face back. And felt the better for it.

"I would say we're within two weeks of a demo, maybe even sooner," J.P. continued. He leaned back in his chair and planted both Rockports on his desk, forcing Baba to move over a little. It was a signal that J.P. had things under control. "Sure, I've still got a ton of work to do. We've got a bunch of R&D pods all working on separate systems. I'm merging them. Don't worry. The finish line is in sight.

"And if this doesn't blow you away, nothing will," he said, forming a huge silent laugh. "No more exploding laptops. We got that solved. Am I right?"

Then J.P. listened. He listened for longer than Maria had ever seen him listen. He nodded his head and said only, "I understand. . . . Sure. . . . Uh-huh. . . . Of course. . . . We'll do what we have to."

And finally, after this had gone on for about five minutes, he said, "Very well. Sure, have your PR person, what's her name— Gloria Godsend? Have her leak it to the press. Sure, I think you can now say you anticipate a major new product announcement. Go ahead. Let's see if our play-and-plug guys can drive the Microsoft spooks back under their rocks. And let's see if we can move the market our way again . . ."

Finally, he closed: "And you too, have a good one."

J.P. slumped in his chair.

"The chairman said the board is talking seriously about down-sizing over there. He said he sees no way to expand. Microsoft is blocking every move. He says there is serious talk about Infinity becoming a *niche* company, can you imagine?"

"So you slung a little yahoo his way," Maria said.

J.P. looked sternly at her.

"You've seen what we're doing downstairs. We gonna come up with the last best thing. All that's left is to channel. . . . Do you understand?"

Maria could not say honestly that she did. She shifted her feet. She looked at Baba and then back at J.P.

"Do *you?*" she asked.

"More than you give me credit for, I'm afraid," J.P. said.

Something in Maria shook. Was this a menacing message? Was he seeing her as an obstructionist? Was she even necessary any-more? As in off the bus?

"So, tell you what," J.P. said, standing and stretching his arms behind his head in a yoga exercise. He half-winced, half-smiled, showing the exquisite strain he was imposing on himself. Maria could see his dimples. "Let's start giving the VCs—Kleiner Per-kins, Robertson Stephens, Sequoia Capital—the heads-up. And the investment bankers, too. It's time to bring this racehorse around the turn and run for home."

From a pay phone in the Vallco Fashion Park, Kato called a number he had been given in San Jose.

"FBI, Agent Watanabe," the voice answered.

"Yo, Lily. It's Kato. I found RoseD."

Lily Watanabe closed the file on Harry Hopkins. She pulled a clean pad from across her desk and started taking notes.

Kato told her everything that had happened the night before and on into the morning. He told her how Robert had hotwired the chunk of silicon and how he, Kato, had cruised through a bunch of MUDs before stumbling onto her.

"What was she like?" Lily asked.

"She has a pretty crude sense of humor," he said. "In fact, she's almost one-dimensional. She even made a crack about my Calvin Kleins. Heck, I wear Dockers. I don't even wear Calvin briefs. I wear Gap boxers..."

"Get to the point," Lily said.

"Well, the point is that Jason what's-his-name, the guy who got burned and then iced by RoseD, tells me she used the same opening line with him... something about liking the cut of your Calvin Kleins. Heck, I wouldn't even want to guess what he wears."

Lily noted this. And underlined it twice.

"What else?" she asked.

Kato regaled her with the incredible morphing of the silicon chip and the deluge of stuff that got dumped on them—the 600-odd pizzas, hundreds of faxes, e-mails—courtesy of RoseD. And he even confessed to being genuinely impressed by the way she seemed to get along out there on the Web, although he had to admit, "She's really outrageous."

Lily noted this and then asked, "And Robert, is he still with us?"

"Well, he's a little out of control himself," Kato said. "Pretty crazy. But yeah, I think he knows what the score is."

"Yeah, like ten years in federal prison. Do we have to remind him?" Lily asked.

"Nope. He says he reminds himself every day," Kato answered. "I'd say he's definitely with us."

"OK," Lily said. "What's happening over there now?"

"We've been told we have less than two weeks to get a demo ready for Infinity and some developers," Kato said. "And J.P. mentioned something about filing for an IPO about two weeks after that—provided we pull off the demo."

"Will you?" Lily asked.

"I don't see how," Kato said. "Would you want something that was capable of ordering six hundred pizzas every time you left it alone with the power on?"

"No. But if it was dinner from Chez Panisse, I might be interested in at least seeing the demo." Lily laughed.

And then she turned serious.

"Kato. We both know who RoseD is, don't we?"

Kato didn't answer right away. And if she could have seen him, she would have seen the smile on his face.

"You're a pretty smart cookie for a boss," he said.

"Thanks, Kato," Lily said. "And by the way, nice work."

# chapter 49

## Brad was flummoxed.

He hadn't meant to make a bad joke. He only tried to put a good spin on a situation that was obviously out of control.

After all, he'd walked into work just in time to hear one of the R&D geeks talking about developing a computer with the maturity of a seven-year-old—borne out by the electronic order for 600-odd pizzas—and heard J.P. ask how they were ever going to sell the system. He, the marketing manager, had offered his suggestion.

"Don't sell them, get people to adopt them," he repeated to the ride-along diamond-lane dummy on the drive home to Palo Alto from Cupertino. "It was purely from a marketing perspective."

But when he played the tape back in his memory, Brad could work himself up into a pretty good froth over the frostiness with which the others received his idea of molding faces around every Infinity cabinet and then offering them at computer outplacement centers—literally for adoption—on a monthly contract.

"Hey, I'm a marketing guy. It's what they hired me for," he repeated out loud to the dummy, which just stared straight ahead. Brad was too self-absorbed to even acknowledge the double take on the face of the driver in the next lane over as he and the dummy whizzed by in the diamond lane.

But he did remember the look on J.P.'s face. It was the same look the waiter had given him a while back, when he was still at Microsoft, when he cracked the bad joke about Windows 95 and was told his company credit card had been rejected. That was an hour or so before he got fired.

"Jeez, how could I be so stupid?" Brad said, banging his head on the steering wheel. He banged it so hard and so often on the way home that a big red indent had formed by the time he walked in.

"Hey," said Damien. "You into body mutilation now, too?"

It was rare and unnerving for Brad to see his son actually roaming out of his room at a nonmeal time. Brad felt his blood pressure take a tick upward.

Better seize the high ground. "Hey, son, whatcha up to?" And immediately he regretted asking the question. Brad knew what his son was up to. He was up to kidnapping Bill Gates.

"Oh, me and some other guys were just hanging around University Avenue terrorizing people," Damien said, almost too casually.

"Terrorizing people?" The words stuck in Brad's gut. "Terrorizing?"

He detected a sneer. Hell, Brad was terrorized, too.

"On our skateboards. . . . Oh, got to tell you. I got a job," Damien said. "It's not really a job, it's just a gig for half a day."

"Oh, yeah?" Brad asked.

"Me and some of the other guys are going to work as waiters and busboys at a big happening over at a venture capitalist's spread in Atherton a couple of weeks from now. Get this. It's a lunch for Bill Gates. We get like fifty bucks each for a couple of hours' work."

Brad felt his knees get weak. He started to stagger.

"No!" he shouted, taken aback by the sound of his own voice. He'd meant to say, "No, c'mon, really?"

This set off Winston, who launched into deep-throated woofs and careened around the living room, rearranging the throw rugs and even a small table while frantically searching for his tennis ball.

"Yeah, there was an announcement at school. They were look-ing for waiters and car attendants. It was the best deal I could get. I'm only fifteen, right? So I can't go and like park cars or anything," Damien said. He appeared to be smiling widely, which drew a beam of overhead track lights to his orthodontia.

Jeez, he looks like Hannibal "The Cannibal" Lecter in *Silence of the Lambs*, Brad thought.

"This way, though, I might actually be able to get close to the big man, Bill himself," Damien said with undisguised sarcasm. "I'll probably be able to get closer to him than you ever did, Dad.... Hey, did you ever like even get to see or talk to him, yourself?"

"Not really," Brad said. "Oh, sure, I saw him ..."

"Weird," Damien said. "You never even actually got to talk to the guy who fired you?"

He had a point. And Brad was thinking up a rejoinder when Elizabeth burst through the door. Alexus was with her. Elizabeth was still in her "war clothes," she called them. In this case, a dark blue Versace blazer and skirt that hit just above the knee. Alexus was wearing a tap-dance number and looked exhausted.

"Gawd," Elizabeth said, dropping her Bally briefcase in the front hallway. "We had twelve minutes, just twelve minutes between soccer practice and dance lessons. I actually ran a red light. But we made it."

"And a stop sign, Mom," Alexus said. "And how about the guy you flipped off? That was so embarrassing. Mom, Dad, it's all too much of a hassle. I really don't want..."

Elizabeth cut her right off.

"Lexi, we've already discussed this. You are not a quitter. We are not quitters. You know very well that we have already paid through April for your dance lessons. We have paid the dues for the soccer league, not to mention shoes and insurance," she said. "Quitting is not an option."

Alexus staggered down the hall and into her room.

"What's for dinner, Dad?" Damien asked.

A little too cheerful, Brad thought. He's covering his tracks.

"I made an all-veggie lasagna last night for tonight," Elizabeth said, going to the fridge. "We'll mike it just as soon as your father and I have a glass of wine. We have something to discuss."

Whenever she said that, Brad's stomach churned. He immediately felt guilty, like he felt sometimes pulling up to the customs station coming back from Mexico, whether or not he had anything to declare.

"So, Brad," Elizabeth said, pouring them each a glass of Souverain cab that would go well with the lasagna, which had a marinara sauce. "When's the killer IPO?"

"Huh?" Brad said.

"C'mon. We got a call from an underwriter today. They've been talking to J.P. for a month. They even have a rough draft of the red herring. Their application is called Rosebud and it's supposed to have something to do with interactivity."

That was news to Brad. Sure, J.P. had mentioned a possible public offering. But that was after they had something to offer. As far as Brad could tell, and judging by what he'd experienced just that morning at work, a product, much less an IPO, was certainly not within reach. And Maria hadn't said anything about it.

Would J.P. have something going that his marketing director

doesn't know about? he wondered to himself. Maybe I'm the only one who doesn't know. Maybe J.P.'s esc key's got my name on it. Maybe they're getting ready to jettison me.

"Well, we have been running some alphas," Brad said, trying to sound composed. "But I've been sworn to nondisclosure. You know the score . . ."

"Here's the real score." Elizabeth whipped it on him. "Stock flotations are hot and getting hotter. But the analysts give the market maybe another couple of months to stay insane. One guy I talked to says ninety days, tops.

"So, the way I see it, you've got about half that time to get out there—to at least compete for the mind share before you actually have to launch something that will generate revenue and market share. You following?"

Brad was trying, but he didn't know what to say. He obviously wasn't in the loop—even in his own home. Hell, two doors down the hallway, his terrorist son was lurking, probably putting the finishing touches on the scheme to snatch Bill Gates sometime between the smoked chicken salad course and the barbecued salmon course right out from under the royal noses of a bunch of the Valley's biggest hoo-hahs.

"So, you want to tell me what Mr. J. P. McCorwin and Mr. Baba RAM DOS are up to?" Elizabeth said firmly. "Does your so-called killer app do anything besides start fires in laptops? Or maybe you guys and Infinity Computer can enter into a strategic alliance with a charcoal company."

That hurt. Brad felt the pain throb where his forehead had met the steering wheel. Rosebud? Rosebud. That got something to do with RoseD? he wondered. I gotta talk with Maria. She's close to J.P. She's got to know what's going on.

# chapter 50

**Normally, Maria would have blown it off.** With Brad, that was easy enough to do. But there was something in his voice, something so imploringly pathetic, that she agreed to meet him for lunch.

She suggested dim sum.

"No way, Maria," he said emphatically. "I do not want to be interrupted by waiters. Please, this is important."

They agreed to brown-bag it at Rancho San Antonio County Park, just off Highway 280 north of Cupertino.

"Separate cars," Brad insisted.

His Porsche was already in the parking lot when Maria arrived.

He looks a little frantic, she thought as she got out of her 325i, and immediately began to sniff the wind to see if she could pick up on any of Brad's runaway hormones. If he was still trying to hit on her . . .

"God, thanks, Maria," Brad said, breathlessly. His white deli bag was crimped and crumpled. Maria guessed he'd been kneading it nervously while he waited for her. "We . . . I . . . I've got big problems. . . . Can we take a walk? I'm a little nervous."

He gestured toward a footpath leading upward to the gentle, folding hills that were part of a great Spanish land grant just 150 years before. Maria certainly knew this land better than he did. If he tried anything funny . . .

I can spin him around and be back in the parking lot before he even knows which direction to go, she thought. And so, against her better judgment, she agreed to walk.

When they reached the first bend, Brad stopped. He faced her squarely and asked, "Am I on my way out?"

Maria laughed.

"I'm not joking," Brad said. He looked scared. He was searching her eyes. "Am I?"

"Why would you ask that?" she said.

"Because, because," he stammered. "It's like I'm the only one who doesn't get it. First, I come up with a name for the company and everyone gives me the you-know-what. Then I suggest a way to market an operating system that clearly J.P. wants modeled after humans. And you saw what the response was. It's like—I'm chopped liver."

Maria nodded. Which caused Brad to step back in alarm.

"So I'm gonna be eighty-sixed?" he asked.

"Sorry, I didn't mean to," she giggled. "I mean I was just thinking how crazy it was the other night with Kato and Robert and

Jason turning on the system and it ordering over six hundred pizzas."

"Here's what's bothering me," Brad stammered. "I hear through my wife that J.P. has already launched a draft of a red herring to selective investors and investment bankers. He's talking like we already have a product."

Maria stopped giggling. It was her turn to search Brad's eyes.

"Does he?" Brad continued. "Do you guys have something I, the marketing guy, don't know about? Or am not supposed to know about? Are you guys cutting me out of the loop? I really think I deserve a straight answer, Maria. I mean like you're paying me six figures to stay in the dark. It's weird."

Maria was suddenly conscious of how hard she was focusing on Brad's eyes. They looked panicked. They were searching for answers.

"It is weird," she said. She looked upward toward the top of the next hill and felt herself fighting to gain clarity. "It's very weird . . ."

What should she say? What *could* she say? What did she know? When it came down to it, not much more than Brad.

"I don't know what to tell you," she said.

He turned, angrily Maria thought, and started back toward the car.

"Thanks a hell of a lot," Brad said.

"No," Maria said. "I'm serious. I don't know what to tell you because I don't know myself."

And then she told him what J.P. had instructed her to do— make sub-rosa contacts with the money boys and get them lathered about a launch of an operating system that was going to blow Wintel back into the analog age.

"So you guys are onto something," Brad said. "You *have* contacted the VCs and investment bankers."

"Not yet," Maria said, shaking her head. "At least I haven't."

They both stood silently looking at each other. Then, unbidden, they walked on. They found a big ancient oak with gnarly branches close to the ground and sat together. Brad offered to share his grilled eggplant with mozzarella and basil on a baguette. Maria declined, but offered him some of her hummus salad in pita bread, which he accepted.

They sat quietly and ate and watched red-tailed hawks circle overhead. Occasionally, an ugly black vulture swept into view, ruining the picture.

"What if there isn't any last best thing?" Brad asked.

Maria almost gagged on her sandwich. She was thinking the exact same thing.

"What if this so-called killer app isn't anything but vapor? What are we supposed to do?" he continued. "I don't get it. Do you?"

Maria took a big swig of raspberry-flavored diet iced tea. "What if the deal isn't to come up with the killer app at all?" she said, as much to herself as to Brad. "What if . . . what if the last best thing isn't a thing at all . . . just an illusion to come up with the killer IPO?"

They looked at each other again.

"Jeez," Brad said, wiping some cheese sauce off his tie. "Wouldn't that be like an SEC violation or something?"

"I guess," Maria said. "I guess. I think so. I dunno. The lines have gotten really fuzzy lately. It's like IPOs are the '90s equivalent of the frontier land rush. You're bound to wind up with nothing but sand and sagebrush now and then."

"Then it's not just me who has a problem?" Brad asked.

Maria had never heard him sound so straight-on.

"I don't quite know what to say," she said, for about the third or fourth time.

"Listen," Brad said. "Can I tell you a few more things?"

He told her what happened just moments before the laptop blew up and what had led to those moments—how someone by the screen name of RoseD had e-mailed him and how one thing had led to another—"all electronically, you understand." And how Jason had confided to him that he was also having a relationship with RoseD. One that ended like his had, in flames and then finally in ice.

Maria, in turn, reminded Brad that she was not RoseD, but did tell him about the visit from the FBI and the subsequent meetings with Lily Watanabe.

This led Brad to break his promise to the very same FBI agent.

"Maria, I've got to tell you about another problem. It's major," he said.

And then he told her about the plot he and Jason and, to his horror, the FBI, were onto. "My son and some of his buddies are planning to kidnap Bill Gates when he comes to the Valley in a couple of weeks. . . . The FBI wants to set up a sting. I'm not supposed to say or do a thing. I'm supposed to stand by and do nothing while my son . . ."

Brad fought back tears and then confessed to feeling browbeaten by his wife, Elizabeth, who made him feel stupid and adolescent and inadequate.

And Maria would have actually felt sorry for Brad if her own panic weren't washing over her like a flood tide. She had put her own stock option money down on the company, had borrowed from her 401(K), had persuaded her father to chip in $15,000 for an equity share.

"We've got to be smart about this," she said to herself. It didn't matter that Brad was listening, looking to her to come up with the next move. "We've got to get some control . . ."

"Before we lose it all, right?" Brad said.

"Yeah," Maria said, looking directly at him. Until now, she'd considered him a dufus. Now they were aligning for mutual survival. "It's scary, huh?"

# chapter 51

R You Rose?

## "Are you RoseD?"

Lisa Rose DeNiccolino squinched up her face at Maria's question.

"You're not the first to ask," she said coolly. "But I got to tell you, I'm getting damn tired of the question."

But Maria pressed on. "I have to know. We could be in big trouble because of her, all of us."

Lisa looked at her, hard at first, irritated. But then her eyes softened.

"No, Maria. I am not RoseD. It's not even my nickname. Although J.P. sometimes calls me that. When he does, I just say, 'Knock it off, OK?' And he does. He can be kind of a wimp, if you challenge him."

Maria straightened in her chair. They were in the company kick-back pod and a few others were hanging out two tables away. So she kept her voice down.

"So exactly how well do you know J.P.?" Maria asked the software programmer.

"I can't say exactly. I'm not certain anyone except Baba knows him well," Lisa said. "I've been to his house a few times. It usually starts out as a social invitation, just friends, or so I think, cuz he knows I'm gay. . . . But it's always like after one glass of wine, he's hitting on me for all kinds of information."

"What information?" Maria asked.

"Well, you all know I specialize in speech recognition artificial intelligence, right? But he knows, I'm not sure you do, that I worked on some of the follow-ups to the ELIZA project."

Maria vaguely remembered hearing about ELIZA when she was at Stanford Biz School. "Wasn't that some study that proved the limits of artificial intelligence?"

"Sort of," Lisa said. "It was an MIT experiment to test the capabilities of a machine to interact conversationally. But it was really dumb. It could like recognize certain strings or patterns of phrases and respond with similar phrases. But it didn't know what they meant. . . . Kinda like a dog that sits obediently on a street corner when told to, but doesn't have a clue as to why."

Maria started to ask another question but Lisa cut her off.

"The capabilities or limits of ELIZA weren't the interesting part of the program, though," she said. "What was interesting was that people took it so seriously. They were clamoring to interact with it, to be left alone with it, to tell their innermost secrets to it. It was more powerful than a mirror for anyone with narcissistic tendencies."

Maria sat back, wondering where this was going.

Lisa navigated for her.

"The MIT scientist gave up, saying he wanted no part of a culture that valued engineering over human heart and sensitivity. But then there was this Stanford professor, a psychiatrist, Kenneth Colby, who kept developing the program. He saw it as a convenient tool for therapy. . . . You come in, you sit down and tell the computer everything. It listens and says things like 'I understand.' And you pour your heart out.

"I was an engineering graduate student assistant on various knockoffs associated with Colby's work. And J. P. McCorwin was one of the student guinea pigs."

Lisa paused, giving Maria time to sort out the context for what was to come next.

But the leap was easy. Maria had already made it. "Let me guess," she said. "J.P. got hooked."

"Did he ever." Lisa laughed. "It was like he couldn't get enough. Late nights, early mornings, he'd be outside the door of the lab. 'I just want to come in and talk things out,' he'd be saying. And he had this wild look. We couldn't get rid of him."

"What happened?" Maria asked.

"We'd play the programs back, look at the dialogue between J.P. and the machine—that's all it was, remember, just a machine— hardware and software. J.P. would be telling it things you wouldn't tell your best friend. He would be asking for things that were . . . impossible to program in a machine."

"Like what?" Maria asked.

Lisa looked hard at her again. "Let's just say that a warm and fuzzy childhood must have eluded him," she said, her eyes twinkling. "But we all signed nondisclosure statements. I just can't tell you more than that."

Maria folded her hands under her chin and leaned forward, intent on hearing more and encouraging Lisa.

"I can tell you that he was getting so dependent that we had to limit his visits. He didn't like that. He's got a paranoid streak, in case you haven't noticed. So we gave him a floppy disk and told him go home," Lisa continued.

"And?" Maria asked.

"And then I heard he went off to Xerox PARC and was a big success, and then to Infinity, where he drew a lot of attention to himself and then got bounced. I bumped into him once when I was doing massage therapy for stressed-out execs. He was in a rage. Then years go by, and the next thing I know, he's calling me up and asking if I would like to join him in a new venture built around interactive artificial intelligence.

"Well, it beats hell out of writing code for computer games or accessing databases," she said. "Especially since he says he's got some money and knows where there's more."

Maria hadn't taken a single sip of the double cafe latte with low-fat milk she'd ordered. Suddenly she remembered it. She swirled the ingredients with a swizzle stick, finally licked the cold foam and sat back in her chair, trying to frame her next question.

"And now?" she asked.

"He's got me writing code for linguistic parsers to create intelligent language filters—for recognizing appositions and trigger words and flashpoint phrases, or verb forms and their objects within a certain number of words. Also he wants me to measure velocity in speech patterns and program those in for emotional responses."

"So," Maria said, "he has you tinkering with the stuff you were working on years ago?"

"More than that," Lisa answered. "Much more. He believes we can create programs actually tailored to convey intimacy. Which, I guess, was why he's so excited about the polygraph program Kato is working on and the powerful supercooled semiconductor Robert laid on him."

Maybe Lisa misunderstood Maria's blank expression. Maybe she was thinking Maria wasn't quite following, because she said, "It's one thing for people to be involved with their computers, you know. But it's another for computers to form a relationship with them—like they can discuss friends together, or family, or experiences, frustrations, fears—or just sit down and share a good cry."

"This is what J.P.'s after?" Maria asked. "A computer buddy?"

"Yeah, one that judges you without being condescending or makes you feel better about yourself without being disingenuous. One that doesn't try to con you or turn its back on you. That's always there for you."

Maria twisted in her chair. "In other words, loves you?"

"You might say that. Certainly in J.P.'s case, I would say that's true," Lisa said, laughing. "He's pretty needy."

"How close are you, I mean we, to this?" Maria asked.

"A long way, baby," Lisa said.

"So if we were to leak it out there that we're working on this?" Maria asked.

"People would say we're crazy, we wouldn't get a dime in VC money," Lisa said. "Look, artificial intelligence, at least so far as it interacts with humans, is considered passé. It's like having a pet lying around compared to what you can do with the Internet."

Maria started to object, and Lisa anticipated this.

"Unless we can teach an old dog new tricks, program human experience, knowledge, problem solving, even reasoning with emotion and combine them with humanistic communication skills and then turn it all loose on the World Wide Web," she said.

"This is possible?" Maria asked.

"Not only possible," Lisa answered, "J.P. says he can virtually *feel* it."

Maria wondered what she meant by that but thought better about asking.

"So exactly why are we in trouble?" Lisa asked.

"To put it bluntly, the whole thing could blow up in our faces," Maria answered, wishing she knew precisely why she answered the way she did.

# chapter 52

**J.P. and Baba were howling and bouncing** like a couple of schoolkids when Maria walked in. She felt almost embarrassed for them, which effectively blunted any urge she had had to confront them for putting her out of the loop. For a moment, she almost wished that Brad and Lisa had never revealed to her just how far out of the loop she was.

"We've done it! By God, we've done it!" J.P. was yelling and alternately whomping Baba on the back and hugging and dancing around with him.

"Ahrremm." Maria cleared her throat to announce herself.

J.P. flew at her, causing her to take two steps back. He threw his arms around her. He hugged her tighter than she'd been hugged, at least since she reached her thirties—maybe ever. Then he led her to his workstation.

"Boy, oh, boy," he said, rubbing his hands together. "We hooked him, we got him."

"Who?" Maria asked.

J.P. clicked on *Post Office* and pulled down the *Mail* menu to *Check Mail You've Read:*

```
SUBJ: ALLIES
DATE: 96/01/19 11:06:40 EST
FROM: BILLG@MICROSOFT.COM
TO: J.P. McCorwin
Hey. Heard UR onto something. Congrats. Coming
to Stanfoo next week to dedicate new computer sci
bldg named after me. (Gave $6 mil). Tight sked.
Lunching Atherton, etc. Cud squeeze some time to
talk possible alliance. U interested?
    Bill
```

Maria stepped back from the screen.

"What do we have that they could possibly be interested in?" she asked.

Both J.P. and Baba reacted alike. As if they were horrified by her dimness.

"Buzz," J.P. said, moving close to her. He put his arm around her shoulder again. "We got buzz."

Just then the phone rang. J.P. leaped to his desk and hit the conference button.

"J.P.? Ambrose here, returning your call."

Maria recognized the voice. It was Ambrose Boyce, J.P.'s broker.

"Hang on, buddy," J.P. said, and then punched up a stock quote search and typed in InfinityC. Immediately it came up:

INFINITYC——INFINITY COMPUTER
Last Price: $21^3/_8$ at 10:40 EST
Change: Down $^1/_2$
High: $21^7/_8$ at 9:40 EST
Low: $21^3/_8$ at 9:50 EST
Open: $21^5/_8$ at 9:30 EST
Previous Close: $21^3/_8$ on 1/18
Volume: 468,700

J.P. punched in another request and retrieved a quick synopsis: Company recorded 35 percent drop in sales over 2-mo. Christmas season previous year. Also reports 50 percent drop in unit shipments of its FirePower laptops from quarter ended Dec. 31 from same quarter previous year.

"It's looks like a death spiral," he said. "Good enough to cover ourselves. OK, let's put in for ten thousand shares. Got that?"

"Got it, but what's up?" the broker asked.

"Some news is going to hit the market," J.P. said, winking at Baba. "The news is that Microsoft wants into our game."

"Ah," the broker said.

"But why would that drive the price of Infinity up?" Maria asked.

Together, J.P. and Baba shot Maria glances she was learning to hate.

"Because if Gates is interested in elbowing Infinity out of the way to get to us, it says they think we're really onto something," Baba explained impatiently. "And if we're onto something, that means Infinity will benefit, according to our agreement."

J.P. was clearly getting impatient, too.

"Look, Ambrose, I want to be able to short this stock in about two weeks, after we inflate it, got that? Be ready to sell off these shares and then short another ten thousand, OK?"

Maria heard a sigh come through the receiver.

"J.P., you're a rascal," the broker said. "OK, I got it."

"Thanks," J.P. said. And hung up.

"We'll take the money from R&D. In other words, from Infinity," he said.

He turned back to Maria just as she was forming the words to ask about the leaks to the investment bankers. J.P. was obviously reading her mind.

"You heard that we've got the VCs and bankers whipped up, am I right?"

"I've been hearing lots of stuff, J.P." she said, surprised at her own boldness. "But I'm not seeing a thing."

"You're gonna see the market go up," he said, attitude radiating from his eyes, "just as soon as our friends at the *Journal* and the *Times* hear about this and report it. You're gonna see the chairman of Infinity breathing a little easier for a few more weeks. You're gonna see Bill Gates knocking on our door. You're gonna see the investment bankers circling our parking lot. You telling me that's nothing? Let me remind you, Microsoft is a $6 billion company. That's probably twice the entire defense budget of NATO. Nine out of ten personal computers in the world operate with their software. That's muscle."

Maria exhaled and rolled her eyes. She didn't need the lecture.

"We're talking leverage here, woman. We're giving Infinity a little bounce for their money. We're giving Gates a little encouragement. We're giving ourselves a little more notoriety. In other words, buzz. With buzz comes the bees and with the bees comes the honey."

Maria winced. "Bad metaphor, J.P."

"What he is trying to say is that we can look forward to another round of capital from Infinity coming our way, just to make certain we don't throw over with the enemy," Baba said.

"What about shorting the stock, though?" Maria asked.

J.P. shook his head. "Good news can't last forever."

Maria cocked her head. "What's that supposed to mean?"

"Never mind," J.P. said. "We're still going ahead with the demo on the same day Gates is in town."

"You're not going to meet with him?" Maria asked.

"No, you are," J.P. said. "And take Brad along. He'll finally get to meet the guy who fired him. Nice irony, eh? We'll wangle an invitation to the Atherton luncheon. It's at Harry Hopkins's place. I'll take care of everything."

"He's better since the fire?" Maria asked, trying to disguise her voice so as not to reveal what was churning inside her. Brad's son was supposedly planning to help kidnap Gates from that very luncheon. Suddenly Maria couldn't breathe.

"Well enough to host the richest man in the world, I guess," Baba said, chuckling. "By the way, I think we should have something to show him, don't you?" he asked Maria.

"You mean like a real prospectus with a real system to back it up? Like the same thing we're going to have to show the SEC and eventually demonstrate?" she asked.

"Yeah, something along those lines," J.P. said. "I think we should load up a FirePower laptop, give it everything we have. Treat Mr. Bill to a personal demo. . . . Better than a dozen roses, wouldn't you say?"

Maria felt her throat tighten.

Baba chuckled once more.

And it sounded evil.

# chapter 53

Ooh, baby-baby! (RoseD).
...aby, baby, oh! (BRoth).
...h ...aby, ooh, baby! (RoseD).
...hhba-hubba! (BRoth).

**"Don't panic, OK?"** Maria wished she could abide
by her own admonition. But the main thing for now was to buck
Brad up.

To say that he hadn't taken lightly her e-mail that they would
be joining Bill Gates for lunch—the very same venue his own son
had apparently chosen for kidnapping the Microsoft king—would
be like saying an exploding laptop was only a system error.

And she hadn't even told him about J.P. and Baba suggesting that she and Brad demonstrate the new FirePower—the infamous combustible laptop apparently driven by the devil and the remote RoseD—for Gates. No. She couldn't do that by e-mail. She told him right to his face.

Predictably, Brad looked around her office for a place to throw up.

"Take it easy, just try to take it easy," she said, helping him to a chair.

He was pasty and sweating. His eyes bulged.

"We've got to call the FBI!" he said, too loud.

"Shhsshh," Maria said. "Not here. Let's take a ride."

Maria drove. They eased onto Stevens Creek Boulevard and quickly found The Oaks, a pleasant, leafy minimall, and pulled up outside of A Clean Well-Lighted Place for Books.

"Might be nice to hang out in there," Brad tried to joke, "if either one of us was still into reading. . . . You remember reading, Maria, it was a primitive exercise. . . ."

"Let's go get coffee," Maria cut him off, beckoning toward a Hobbee's nearby. It was a preferred power breakfast spot, but her watch said 9:40. She felt confident they'd miss being spotted, and put her hand in Brad's back and more or less pushed him through the door.

Kato and Robert were just leaving. Brad slammed on the brakes and started to spin around.

"Oh, hi," Kato said, sounding equally startled. Robert seemed startled, too.

"We were just drawing up some installment patterns for the new chip and the supercooler J.P. wants us to put together for a demonstration," Robert said. "Plus some new software he says he's developing personally."

"For the big product demo at the Santa Clara Convention Center?" Maria asked, trying to sound all business.

"No," Robert said. "Apparently it's for one very special potential customer. You know anything about this, Maria?"

"No. Not too much," she said, doing her best to cover up and shield Brad as well. "J.P. told us he'd fill us in just as soon as we touch base later today. Brad and I were just going over some prelaunch strategy."

"Right," Kato and Robert said in unison.

Maria thought Robert looked especially nervous. Maybe she'd infected him with her own nervousness.

"Right," Maria said. "See you guys later."

"Right," Kato said, grabbing Robert by the arm and leading him out the door.

"Man, those guys are weird," Brad said. "You know, it's funny, but when the FBI came to tell me about my son and the plot to grab Gates, Kato bumped into them. And it was like he knew them. And the smartskin treatment on the polygraph application he's developing? Remember? He said it was inspired by the FBI."

Maria did think that strange. Even stranger was the obvious fact that J.P. had deputized those two to arm the FirePower that she and Brad were supposed to present Gates. Stranger still, if it was true, was that J.P. was writing some special software himself.

The waiter took their order and Maria absentmindedly asked for a double latte without specifying low-fat milk, which was her custom, especially since she'd been working out less lately. Brad asked for the same.

"Listen, Maria, I've got to state my case," Brad said, when the waiter had come with their coffees and gone. "How can I just sit there talking biz and munching away on some wild rice and arugula thing when I'm like sitting on a time bomb?"

Maria choked on her drink.

"Not literally," Brad said. "But, here's my son, about to snatch Bill Gates right from under my nose. And the FBI probably has a SWAT team surrounding the place. Tell me, what am I supposed to do?"

"Get a grip, Brad," Maria said, wiping flecks of foam off her Jones New York suede vest. "I'm trying to think."

She thought. She sipped. She thought some more—of the fires

in the laptops, the crazy message someone sent to the FBI's Unabom task force using her e-mail address, of the visits with Lily Watanabe, of all the secrets J.P. was keeping from her, of this hell-bent race to the killer IPO, of all the money her own father had invested in the company. . . . No, in her, as a matter of faith.

"We've got to get to the bottom of this," she said.

"No fooling," Brad said, sarcastically. If it had been Elizabeth, sitting across from him instead of Maria, he'd have probably said something far more severe. "Like we've just discovered gravity."

"You know how we're going to do this?" Maria asked. She felt lightheaded.

"Yeah, we're going to call the FBI and tell them everything we know," Brad said. "And then we're going to ask them to warn Gates and spare my kid . . ."

"And, what exactly do we know?" Maria asked. Suddenly, the fog was clearing.

"I know what I know," Brad said. "That laptops are turning on their operators. That this witch RoseD is ruining people's lives. That J.P.'s floating stuff to the money people about a last best thing to end last best things and neither one of us has any idea what that is. That my son is either gonna commit the crime of the century or get busted right in front of me trying. . . . Is that enough?"

"The FBI knows the same stuff," Maria said. "And I bet they know a lot more."

"What's that supposed to mean?" Brad said in that I-feel-sorry-for-myself voice that really tried Maria's patience. Sometimes she could empathize with Elizabeth.

"It means that there's a lot more to learn. The FBI's not going to help. We've got to learn this on our own," she said.

"So? What do we do?" Brad asked.

Maria took a long sip of coffee and when she was through, she banged the cup down on the table, causing the waiter to appear.

"Sorry, we're OK," she said, waving him off. Then she leaned across the table and grabbed Brad's hand. "We're going to get this out of J.P. once and for all. Even if we have to string him up by his heels. . . . Remember, our butts are on the line, too."

Brad pulled back, shaking his head.

"Brad, c'mon," she said. "At least for the sake of your son."

He drummed his fingers, fidgeted, started to say something and stopped. Then he said: "When?"

"Tonight," she said without hesitation. "You and I are going to pay J.P. a surprise visit. Are you with me? Cuz if you're not, I'm going alone."

Maria could see a lump form in Brad's throat. She could see him struggling and thought he might be having trouble breathing.

"OK," he sputtered. "OK. Tonight."

# chapter 54

I am RoseD.

**Jason's phone call killed any second thoughts** Brad and Maria might have had about making an unannounced house call on J. P. McCorwin.

"This is crazy, dude. I'm like surfing cell-phone calls on my scanner and what do you know, I get the FBI.... That's right, the FBI. Well, not exactly the FBI. First, I get this voice. It's Kato..."

Jason had phoned Brad as soon as the call ended.

Brad was relaying all this word for word to Maria, who had shouted, "Tell me again, exactly what did he say?" as they sped in her car up Highway 280 toward the Woodside Road exit to J.P.'s.

"He said he heard Kato talking to a woman. Lily, he kept calling her. Got to be Lily Watanabe. And he kept insisting that he and Robert were working on a bomb, on J.P.'s orders."

"J.P. was ordering them to actually build a bomb?" Maria couldn't believe it.

"Not exactly. According to Jason, who overheard it from Kato, who was speaking to Lily, they were packing a huge electrical charge into one of the laptops. Kato was like afraid that if it got set off by the wrong commands . . . that it might go blooey."

"That's what Kato said?" Maria asked. " 'Blooey'?"

"No," Brad answered. "That's what Jason said. He said 'blooey.' He should know. It happened to him. Just like it happened to me. We know all about 'blooey.' "

As Brad repeated the conversation, it turned out that Jason had heard much more.

"Kato apparently told Lily he knows where RoseD is. At J.P.'s. She told him to meet her there. That's when Jason called," Brad said.

They could see the turn-off sign coming up, and Maria swung into the right-hand lane.

"You sure you want to do this?" Brad said, his voice quivering.

"Of course not," Maria answered. "So don't ask."

She signaled and slowed for the turn, stopped briefly at the stop light to let a generic made-in-America sedan pass.

"Do you think the FBI uses unmarked cars?" Brad asked, craning to identify the driver.

"How would I know?" Maria answered, pulling out and accelerating west toward Woodside. "You think I go around chasing the FBI?"

She slowed down to obey the 25-mph speed limit through the town, which consisted mostly of real estate offices, and steered her BMW convertible past the little shopping center where she and

Brad and J.P. had rehearsed their visit with the chairman of Infinity Computer just weeks before. Then she headed west along the unlighted road, made even darker by a canopy of oaks. When she got to Kings Mountain Road, she turned right and slowed even further, trying to spot the driveway.

"Don't you know which house it is?" Brad gasped.

"No, I don't. It's not like I'm . . ."

"RoseD?" Brad said, forcing a little laugh.

"Yeah," she said, coming upon a hedge and stopping. "This is it. This is it."

A white stone archway shone in the headlights. There was a wrought-iron gate, but it was open. Maria pulled in.

"Jeesus, oh jeez," Brad said, slipping down in the seat as the convertible started to crawl up the long driveway. It curved slightly uphill through redwoods and oaks. "Maybe the FBI's already here."

A few dim lights pointed the way and Maria turned off the headlights. When they came to the first curve, Maria pulled slightly off the gravel and turned off the engine. They could see the big, gabled redwood house perched on a butte above them. It was all ablaze with lights, as if someone had already started the party without them.

"Let's go," Maria whispered, silently closing her car door. She could see her breath's vapor against the lights of the house. It made her think of black-and-white spy movies and she wondered just what she and Brad had gotten themselves into.

The gravel crunched loudly beneath Brad's feet, startling both of them. Maria grabbed his arm and swung him onto the grass beside the driveway. And they crept, step by step, in unison up toward the big house.

The parking area was bathed in spotlights and Maria immediately spotted J.P.'s 600 SL with the LUVBYTS license plates. She also spotted Baba's motorcycle. No other vehicles were in sight.

"We've beat the FBI," she whispered.

"And RoseD," Brad added.

But they could hear voices coming from within. One was Baba's, easily identified by its French accent. There was another voice, a woman's. Neither Brad nor Maria recognized it. Both voices were coming from the second story, which Maria remembered was the living area, where J.P. had his workstation and home entertainment center. They sneaked to the back stairs leading to the deck and listened harder. Still two voices, Baba's and the woman's. No J.P. No FBI.

Maria squeezed Brad's arm and took the lead up the stairs. Halfway up, she turned. Brad hadn't taken a step. She waved for him to follow. He hesitated, looking up at the lighted second story, then over his shoulder at the parking area and the driveway behind.

Maria got a bad feeling and started to descend. But Brad took a first step up. And then another. And was suddenly right behind her.

"Does he have a dog?" he whispered.

Maria couldn't remember and suddenly felt a jolt of panic. But the voices inside became louder, particularly the woman's voice. And curiosity overrode fear.

"Bill, oh, Bill, oh, sweetie, you could have it all," the woman said. And her voice seemed to have dropped half an octave and sounded very passionate and private. "Just go with it, Bill. Lose yourself in me."

"Bill? Who's Bill?" Brad whispered.

"Let's see," Maria whispered back. She put her hands out and began feeling the last stair, crawling inch by inch, to the landing, where she disappeared into the shadow of the spreading oak tree the deck had been built around. She stayed in the shadow all the way to the trunk of the tree. When she reached it, she motioned for Brad to join her. From this vantage, they could see through a huge picture window right into J.P.'s living room. The vaulted ceilings of rosy heart redwood gave the enormous room a cathedral-like appearance. The fact that it had very little furniture made the room look all the more enormous. And right in the middle sat Baba at a workstation. He was facing the picture window, but it was clear he was not looking out. He appeared to be looking at a computer screen. And he was typing at the keyboard as he talked.

That might have been normal, except for the female person who had draped herself over the computer monitor like a lounge-act chanteuse. Her back was to the window and Maria and Brad could see that she was wearing a long, backless, organdy evening dress that seemed from another era. Her hair fell to her shoulders in dark, grayish tresses that bunched up like bouquets and seemed, too, altogether not exactly contemporary California.

"Oh, Bill, Bill, don't be so uptight," she said throatily, floating her hand outward toward Baba like a butterfly. "Oh, Bill, you sweet little geek. Oh, oh . . . you make other men seem so, so inadequate . . ."

"Who's Bill?" Brad hissed. Too loud this time.

Baba stopped plunking at the keyboard. Alerted, he raised his head above the monitor and looked out, squinting to see into the dark. Then he stood, moving to the window, and started for a sliding glass door.

Brad rose and started to bolt.

"No. No." Maria grabbed him and stood herself just as Baba stepped out onto the deck.

*"Bon soir,* Baba." Maria pushed herself into the light. Brad sort of tumbled out, too, and fell in next to her.

"Good evening to you, too," Baba said, clearly startled. "To what do we owe zees leetle surprise?"

"We, we, we came to meet RoseD," Maria heard Brad stutter, and felt bolstered just as her own knees were about to buckle.

"We have guests? Baba, dear? Do bring them in. It's so cold out," Maria heard the woman say. Her back was still turned to the window, as if she hadn't moved an inch despite all the commotion outside.

Baba sighed. *"Oui, ma belle,"* he said, and took Maria by the arm, giving her a painful squeeze. "Whatever you say. Perhaps it is now time you met."

Maria stepped stiffly into the room, aware of every step and every movement her body was now making. Aware of her own urge to turn and run. Somehow, she forced herself to thrust out her hand as if she was going for a job interview and headed directly toward the person.

"Maria Cisneros," she said. "I'm J. P. McCorwin's executive assistant." Baba flew past her and took the woman by the arm, helping her turn as if she were an invalid, or in some stupor. And as her face rotated toward hers, Maria lost all control of her breath.

"May I present RoseD," Baba said.

Faintly, Maria heard Brad's voice behind her: "Oh, God, oh, jeez, oh, jeez . . . J.P.?"

# chapter 55

**The dress was stunning, but the makeup,** particularly the dark lipstick, was overly dramatic, and the wig was cockeyed. J.P. looked so ridiculous in drag that it gave Maria the momentary reassurance that this must be a joke.

She had to laugh, wanted desperately to laugh.

"J.P.?" she asked, just as Brad had. "J.P.?"

Her boss did not answer. He stared without blinking and his

eyes looked like old coals, seeming to register nothing. His mouth was frozen in a stiff, idiotic grin.

This was becoming scary.

"J.P.? Please," Maria pleaded.

"No, Maria, not J.P. At zees moment, RoseD," Baba said softly, exaggerating his French accent.

At the sound of Baba's voice, or maybe it was from hearing the name RoseD, their boss turned and leaned again on the computer monitor, saying coquettishly: "Play it again, Baba, in C + + ."

"Theez calls for an explanation," Baba said. He went into the kitchen, leaving Maria and Brad alone with their own fright.

"J.P.?" Maria said again. "What's going on?"

"What is going on," said Baba, returning too quickly with a bottle of Opus One and three glasses, "is the last best thing."

"RoseD?" Brad asked.

"Not exactly," Baba said, pouring the pricey cabernet, which turned deep amethyst as each glass caught the light. He motioned them to a futon-sofa piled luxuriously with linen pillows in assorted muted colors and urged them to sit. "It is what RoseD creates."

Brad started to protest: "No, thanks, Baba, we'll stand."

"But please," Baba insisted. "It eez no short story."

Maria had heard some of the story from Lisa DeNiccolino, but Brad looked stunned as he heard how J.P., as a Stanford student, had volunteered for a controversial psychological-technological experiment on artificial intelligence and interactivity. How he had not only become convinced that total interactivity was possible, but had actually bonded with the program.

"This was better than going to confession," Baba said of the onetime Jesuit novitiate, "because there was only the computer, no disapproving priest behind the confessional curtain."

But what didn't track was what Baba said next.

"At first, J.P. questioned this technology, you know, this software that presumes to have a dialogue with you. So he tried to trick it. He changed his stories, he lied about his past, his present, even his gender. And when the computer could not see through this, J.P. grew frustrated and tried to teach the computer to be smarter.

"This is where he got into trouble, at least with the experiment. After hours, J.P. would go in, learn the code and then rewrite it to interact with him. If he wanted to be, for instance, a whacked-out veteran suffering from post-traumatic stress disorder, he would program the computer for various unpleasant experiences that might register in the computer's memory when it was interacting with someone. You get where I am going with zees?"

Maria thought for a moment, then slowly nodded as she replied, "Yes, he was working both ends of the software. He was interacting with himself..."

Baba sensed where she was taking this and interrupted. "That's what the Stanford people thought. They thought he was corrupting the program. So they kicked him out.... Which is how he ended up at Xerox PARC." He sipped his wine and looked away for a moment. "He tried to persuade the people there to let him continue his research, but they laughed and he left."

Brad fumbled with his glass, drank a bit, then blurted, "And at Infinity?"

"Eventually, it was the same thing. He wanted money for research. They laughed and we both left.... We went to the venture capitalists asking for assistance. They thought we were mad, like zee mad scientists. They said we were complete narcissists..."

"And?" said Maria.

"We were not. Believe me. I am French, I know about true narcissism," he reminded her. "We were only trying to download our complete selves on zee software so it could be empathetic and intuitive."

"And that is the last best thing?" Maria asked. "Not RoseD. It's J.P. or you. Or whoever decides that their sensibilities and experiences and egos will be the judge, jury and executioner, so to speak."

"That eez an uncharitable way of putting zees project into perspective," Baba said, obviously feeling underappreciated and resorting to his accent.

"So why the big noise about putting out the laptop fires for Infinity?" Brad asked. "And what about Infinity? And what about the ultimate killer app that you have everybody working on?"

Baba twirled his glass in the light. He glanced over at J.P. or RoseD, whoever he was supposed to be. "We needed to get back into the loop in the Valley. With a brief success, we felt we would gain more backing. With more backing would come more money to finish our research and conduct our program."

"Then you really don't give a damn what happens to Infinity?" Maria said angrily. "All this talk about beating back the Wintel Axis and restoring Infinity's market share and corporate self-esteem was pure vapor."

"We care very much," Baba replied. "We, J.P. and I, possess deep in our hearts, to quote the Scottish writer Thomas Carlyle, 'A heavy hatred of scoundrels.' "

"Meaning Infinity?" Maria said, unable to take her eyes off J.P., who remained motionless, seemingly in a trance.

Baba nodded solemnly. "And the others who mocked us, including the venture capitalists who withheld a means to prove our program wise and true and deny us the honor we deserve."

Maria stood, rage coursing from her abdomen to her eyes. "So you'd have us all beat our brains out to get you the last best round of financing, to pull off a killer IPO to get you the money you need to keep your secret pet project alive? You were ready for us to commit securities fraud? Is that what I am hearing?"

Baba smiled. "Zees is done all the time in zee Valley. Besides, *ma petite fleur*, there will be something in it for you, somezeen very nice. And who knows, we may actually come up with an alternative—a true killer app. That's the beauty of it all."

Maria felt as if she was being buried alive. She was having trouble breathing again.

Brad leaped to his feet. "So what about the fires in the laptops? What about my hands? And Jason's? You guys building bombs or what?"

Baba smiled. "Pardon. A little mistake. We only meant for a

*petit* poof. You know, just so we would know the program was working."

"What program?" Brad asked.

"Zees one, Brad," Baba said. He moved to the workstation and held up a disk. He patted J.P. on the shoulder and kissed him on the cheek. "RoseD."

"You mean she is nothing but software?" Brad gasped.

"Precisely, my friend. How do you tell your wife, Elizabeth? Is that her name? How do you tell her that you are not only having an *affaire de coeur,* you are having it with zees?" Baba shoved the disk in Brad's face.

Brad sputtered like a bottle rocket in a bucket. "So the RoseD program set off the fires in the laptops. Wha—what about Hopkins, the venture capitalist?"

"Unfortunate, the house going up in flames. But zen, he does not give us money for the project, so we give him a dirty little secret: RoseD. Somezeen to hide from his leetle wife, no?"

"So you nearly killed him while trying to embarrass him, just to get revenge?" Maria asked. "Is that it?"

Baba shrugged and looked nonplussed.

And J.P. started to stir. "Baba? Baba? Let's get back to Bill."

"My God," Maria said. "They're going to give Bill Gates a charge of RoseD."

"This requires zee utmost in sophisticated interactivity," Baba said, moving back to the keyboard. "You see, the beauty of zees, of all technology, is that you move in and out, from zee impersonal to zee personal, from anonymity to intimacy. You change locations, colors, personalities, including your own. You can be anything, anywhere, anybody . . ."

"And a man becomes a woman," Brad said.

"Or you become a big jock hero, Brad," Baba retorted, and began punching away at the keyboard. "The trick is to draw you in, get you to look deeply into the screen, into the looking glass . . ."

Maria turned to Brad. "So J.P. has transcended into the program. He and the program are the same."

"Precisely. It is necessary to create the perfect interactive program," Baba said, smugly. "And when we are finished here, J.P. will return as J. P. McCorwin, legendary Silicon Valley visionary. . . . And, I might add, our boss. Beautiful, no?"

"Not really," Maria said. "Baba, I've got to tell you, it's sick. And I've also got to tell you something else. The FBI's on the way. I think a lot of this stuff is going to make them sick, too."

Baba glanced up from the keyboard, incredulous. He looked at J.P. and then stared back at Brad and then Maria. He looked as if he'd been shot and was about to fall in a heap.

*"Crétins, imbéciles,"* he shouted, staggering to his feet.

"No time for speeches, Baba," Maria said firmly. "The FBI is on the way. For all we know, it may be the whole Unabom Task Force, plus a SWAT team.

"And"—this was the clincher—"they might have SEC investigators and even investment bankers with them. One sight of J.P., excuse me, the last best thing and . . . think about it. . . . No, on the other hand, you haven't got time."

Baba stood stiffly, clearly stunned, clearly indignant. And then he gathered up a luscious pigskin mailbag he said he'd had since his days as a boulevardier. He began stuffing it with disks. Then he started to unscrew the back of the machine, saying, "We must get the hard disk . . ."

Suddenly, Brad turned to the window. "Someone's coming up the driveway."

They could see headlights bouncing off the redwoods.

"You better go, Baba," Maria said. "Like now!" She could feel Baba's look of hatred. But it didn't matter.

He slung the bag over his shoulder, tenderly grabbed J.P.'s arm and guided him, as if J.P. were sleepwalking, out the sliding glass door and down the stairs.

Maria and Brad scrambled to the deck, and from there they could see Baba load J.P. into the rear seat of the Mercedes. Baba climbed in, started the car, backed it into position, narrowly missing his own beloved motorcycle, and gunned the SL down the driveway. They could see the approaching headlights swerve to let the speeding Mercedes pass and they watched the lights continue toward the house.

There was no time to rehearse stories or even ask each other how much trouble they would be in when the FBI found them. Brad and Maria could only stand and watch the headlights approach as if they were frozen by the beams. They listened to the car careen to a halt in the gravel under the lights.

"It's Jason!" Brad shouted, leaning far over the railing. "Not the FBI."

# chapter 56

**"She here? Is she?"** The words flew from Jason's mouth after he had breathlessly described how "J.P.'s Benz almost zapped me in the driveway."

"No, she's not," Maria said, trying to sound calm as much for her own sake as for Brad's and Jason's. "She was with J.P."

Then, together, she and Brad related their stunning introduction to the world of RoseD while Jason poured himself some of the leftover Opus One and circled the workstation, shaking his head and repeating: "A guy? I was like having a virtual relationship with *a guy?*"

"Software," Brad reminded Jason, as much for himself. "Not anybody real. Only software. No big thing."

Jason looked at him reproachfully, as if to say, "Wrong. A very big thing."

"Did they get the hard drive?" he asked suddenly. "Everything's got to be there."

"No," Maria said. "Baba started to pull it, but then we saw your lights." On cue, a flash shot through the window. More headlights were heading up the driveway.

"Quick, get it," Maria told Jason. "I'll stall them." She took the stairs two at a time and stood alone, composing herself in the parking area next to Baba's abandoned motorcycle just as three plain-looking sedans pulled up. Lily Watanabe got out of the passenger side of the first vehicle. She wore a windbreaker with big yellow letters: FBI.

"Hello, Maria," she said, looking surprised. "Is J.P. at home?"

The doors to the other vehicles opened and seven or eight men, all wearing baseball caps and windbreakers that said FBI, leaped out and took up stations around the base of J.P.'s house.

"We have a federal warrant, Maria. We're going inside."

"J.P.'s not there," Maria said. "He must have left just before we arrived." She could hear her heart pounding and only hoped that in the semidark, Lily couldn't see the lie written all over her face.

"And what exactly brings you here tonight, Maria?" Lily asked, all businesslike. "Presumably, you weren't invited."

"The same thing that brought you, Lily," Maria said, holding her ground. "We wanted to meet RoseD."

Lily tried to look directly at Maria, but one of the spotlights was shining in her eyes. She shifted and then kicked at the deep exit marks J.P.'s Mercedes had made in the gravel.

"They left quickly," she said.

"Apparently," Maria said, and figured by now the guys upstairs had had enough time to extract the hard disk. "You want to come in? Come in."

Lily beckoned for two other agents to join her, and Maria led them up the stairs. Jason and Brad were standing near the fireplace, looking a little too relaxed. Brad gave her a quick wink, which Maria did not acknowledge, fearing that Lily was looking for any sign of conspiracy.

"The place is a bit sparse," Lily said, looking around. Then she took some official-looking documents out of her briefcase and laid them on a work shelf flanking the terminal where, moments earlier, Baba and J.P. had been performing their RoseD routine.

Immediately, the other agents began consulting the documents and tagging various objects in the house, most prominently, the entire workstation.

"This is a court order allowing us to confiscate certain things," Lily explained. "I'm sure you understand. You do, don't you?" It was hardly a question. And Maria merely shook her head, affirming what Lily knew that she, Maria, probably knew.

"Out of personal courtesy, I must also tell you that you will all probably be subpoenaed as witnesses," Lily said. "So you should be thinking of retaining counsel. But, obviously, there is one question I would appreciate knowing the answer to right now. . . . Anyone know where J.P. went?"

All three shook their heads no.

"Not surprised," Lily said. "OK. We'll just leave two agents here to greet J.P. when he returns. Otherwise, I think we can be going." Maria escorted Lily downstairs.

"Can I ask you one question, Lily?"

"Sure, but understand I may not be permitted to answer," Lily said.

"Kato?" Maria asked. "Yours?"

Lily hesitated, and then said: "He's very good, isn't he?"

"And Robert, the guy with the chip—yours, too?" Maria asked.

"I guess you're going to learn this when the case breaks—by the way, we're charging J.P. with several counts of conspiracy, bomb-making, assault and accepting stolen property that crossed state lines . . .

"No, Robert wasn't ours. He is a heck of an engineer, though. He works for Texas Instruments, in Dallas, or did, until he skipped out the door with the specs for a superchip he was helping develop.

"We got onto him," Lily said. "And turned him. . . . So, yes, you could say he was working inside for us. And we have reason to believe that J.P. knew the chip Robert had dropped off was stolen. . . . We think he was going to use it to build smarter bombs."

She doesn't know everything, Maria thought. She doesn't know just how deeply connected J.P. and RoseD really were. That's what J.P. wanted a faster, more powerful system for. He wanted to virtually recreate himself. She shuddered.

"You OK?" Lily asked.

"Just cold," Maria said, walking her to the government car.

"We'll touch base," Lily said. "Maybe, when this blows over, we can get in a workout together."

Maria stood, watching the agents wind down the driveway. Then she walked back upstairs and summoned Brad and Jason, who were, by now, on a first-name basis with the remaining agents. She told Jason to hurry finishing off the wine, and when they were together outside, she whispered, "Give me the hard disk."

"I'd like to take it home and give it a spin on my operating system," he said. "See, I've already got some cool stuff and if I can integrate this with what I've got, we could be in for the greatest last best thing ever."

"A climactic best thing," Brad said, laughing. He'd experienced what Jason had waiting at home.

"Give it to me," Maria hissed.

Jason handed over the disk.

"Did you install another?" she asked, putting the packet in her coat pocket.

"What am I, like just another CGI Joe?" he asked, insulted. "Of course. I replaced it with a really hip Seagate they had sitting in reserve. I even ran off data transfers to make it look worked-in."

"OK, OK," Maria said. "Let's get out of here. Meet me in my office tomorrow at 7:30 A.M. We've got to sort things out quick. And, I guess we better hold a staff meeting before this thing completely blows up."

"What are we gonna do?" Brad said as they drove back through town.

"I don't know," Maria said. "Sleep on it, I guess."

Brad was still asking, and she was still answering, "I don't know" when she dropped him off in Palo Alto.

But before she turned toward the freeway, Maria swung her BMW up Embarcadero Road, across El Camino, into the Stanford campus. She could see the landmark Hoover Tower on her right as she swung left away from the tower and the nearby business school where she had done time and changed her life. She drove past the football stadium and then turned west toward the far end of the campus, winding along some familiar side streets until she reached a parking space near Lake Lagunita.

She climbed out and hiked quickly up a short berm to the edge of the lake. In the spring, it was a major hangout, a great place to practice windsurfing and work on a tan. Now, on a late winter night, she had it to herself.

She stood on the berm and listened to the water lapping at the bank. A pair of ducks murmured as they swam toward her and then turned away. Across the way, from one of the frat houses, the Sex Pistols blared. From another she could hear the competing voice of Patti Smith.

"Must mean books are closing for the night," she said out loud to herself. "God, Maria, just a few years ago. That's all you had to worry about. That's all."

She thrust her hands into her coat pockets and felt the hard drive in her right. She pulled it out, holding it up against a distant streetlight. And then held it higher, over her head, against the sky.

"You wanted it all, Maria. All of it," she said. Tears started to form and she sniffed hard, fighting them back. "Is that it? Is that what you are about? You just go along, never questioning, never saying: 'That's it, I quit'? Is that what you've become?"

She wiped her nose with her sleeve. Then she looked toward the middle of the lake. And cocked her arm and launched the hard disk—J.P. and RoseD—as far out into the deep water as she could.

# chapter 57

**Brad knew he had no chance of slipping in the door unnoticed.** In fact, he didn't want to be unnoticed. Right now he wanted to talk, needed to talk. He let the front door bang closed behind him. Elizabeth was waiting in the kitchen, but the look on her face told him she might not be his best audience.

"You look guilty as hell," she said, pouring herself a hefty glassful from a Zaca Mesa chardonnay bottle that was already three-fourths empty, as far as Brad could tell. She didn't sound agitated, which would have been normal. In fact, she sounded slightly giddy, loopy even, very abnormal for Elizabeth.

"I've got something to tell you," he said gravely.

"And I've got something to tell you," she said, over the top of the glass, which she held like a microphone.

"OK," Brad said, gulping, "here goes." He edged over to the buffet counter and hopped up, trying to find some high ground. "It's all a sham. . . . J.P., Baba, the killer app, the prospectus, the public offering. Pure vapor."

Elizabeth crossed her arms, but still held her wineglass to her lips meditatively. "Infinity, what about Infinity?"

"They didn't want to save it. They just wanted to pick over its smoking carcass for the sake of their own credibility," he said, and half-caught himself thinking, Jeez, Brad, you're sounding clearer than I've ever heard you in a long, long time.

"Does the chairman know?" she asked.

"No one knows, except for Maria, Jason what's-his-name and"— he lowered his voice—"the FBI."

"My God," Elizabeth whispered. "This will sink them."

"Who?" Brad asked.

"Infinity," she said, looking horrified. "And we were getting ready to handle their part of the alliance with J.P.'s company, including representing the underwriter, who's picking up a seriously big block of shares." This time she gulped from her wineglass. "We, the firm, are supposed to get in on the IPO. Are you telling me there will be no IPO?"

Brad felt himself recoil. Anger seized him and took hold.

"Elizabeth, this is not about getting rich. It's about credibility," he snapped.

"Credibility? You're one to talk," she snapped right back.

"Yeah, credibility," Brad answered. "I'll tell you something else, for the sake of clearing the air. . . . I was having an affair . . ."

He checked himself, tracking her eyes, seeking to measure her reaction. And saw only a glare. And that she'd crossed her arms tighter. Still he pushed on.

"Only it wasn't really an affair. It was an online relationship with someone I hadn't met until tonight," he continued. Then he gulped again, gasping for breath. "It turns out that this person, RoseD, was simply a figment of J.P.'s perverse imagination." Now he wished that he had some of the wine. "It was only a piece of software. . . . An interactive computer program."

Elizabeth took a long sip. She appraised Brad, looking for a long time into his eyes. And then the corners of her mouth turned up.

"You mean . . . you mean you were in love with software?"

"Not exactly in love. I would call it more of a casual relationship," Brad said sheepishly.

"Software stole your heart? You were hitting on a floppy disk?" She burst out laughing. She laughed so hard she spilled some of her wine. She took another long drink, but she was still laughing so hard that she spat it down the front of her Eileen Fisher silk blouse. Brad wondered if the stain would come out while Elizabeth laughed so hard that tears began running down her cheeks.

"Brad," she said, suddenly freezing. It was her turn to gulp. "I've got something to tell you," she said, dropping her gaze. What she said next was barely audible. "I am sexually attracted to someone. And it's not you. And it's not software. He's a real person. He's a senior partner at a big venture capital firm and he's got real money."

Soft as they were, the words hit him like a slap. Brad felt his insides roil. He felt as if his entire self were being flushed down a drain.

"Jeez, Elizabeth, can we talk about this?"

"Brad, I have been to see a divorce lawyer," she said. "It's the next step after rock-climbing."

He tried to force himself to laugh, as if it were a joke.

"Soooo, just what are you going to do?" she said defiantly.

Brad stared at the ceiling. He counted the track lights. He stared down and counted the tiles on the floor. He traced the tiles on the counter with his fingers. He couldn't think. He didn't know what he should, what he could, do now.

"Can I borrow the Range Rover?" he sputtered.

"You think I'm going to turn over the keys to you for a safari to Napa or Santa Cruz at a time like this, when you're obviously more than a little bit out of your mind?" she asked.

"I don't need to go anywhere. Just unlock it for me and I'll take an air mattress and a sleeping bag and camp out there tonight. And don't worry, I'll be gone early," he said. "Got a big meeting."

Ramon Cisneros was propped against a pillow on the couch with only one eye open to the Sports Channel when Maria knocked twice and came through the door.

"Papa!" she said. "Is it too late? I started to drive home from the Peninsula and somehow, I don't know, I ended up here."

"East San Jose is a long way from Los Gatos," he said, with the equanimity Maria knew she could count on. "So you must want to talk."

"*Sí*, Papa. *Sí*," she said. "I have a problem."

Suddenly, the door from the kitchen opened and Maria's mother, Catalina, trundled in. She was wearing a housecoat and rubbing fatigue out of her eyes.

"Mama, Mama." Maria embraced her. "*Cómo está?*"

They held each other until her father tired of this and said, "Are you two going to make a statue or something? Catalina, get Maria a drink, me too, *tequila superior.*"

She returned with two tumblers.

"And the bottle, too, *esposa,*" Ramon said, waving her back into the kitchen. "Maria and me need to talk."

She returned with a bottle of Sauza Commemorativa, which was usually reserved for special occasions. At Ramon's urging, she kissed each good night after extracting a promise from Maria that she would come for dinner on Sunday.

"So, *qué tal?*" Ramon said.

And Maria could not hold back her tears.

"Papa, I'm so sorry," she buried her head in his chest. "Your money, my money, I've probably lost it. It's gone . . . "

Ramon pushed her head away and held it in both hands.

"What? Gone? What about Mr. J. P. McCorwin, this great visionary you work for? What about this big new company that's gonna make us all rich, eh?"

"He's gone Papa. There never really was a company. It was all . . . how shall I say this? *Una ilusión grandioso,*" she said, wiping the tears from her eyes.

It took some explaining and Maria tried to go slowly and carefully, and in doing so, she sorted some things out for herself. Meanwhile, Ramon smoked and sipped from his glass, which he refilled several times.

Maria could see the fire start to build in his eyes and counseled herself to remain circumspect so as not to incite him.

Slowly, she painted the picture of chicanery for her father, being careful to include him among the crowd of sophisticated financiers and tech execs who had been either taken in or were on the verge.

And when she was done telling him the story, Ramon poured each of them another drink and lit another cigarette. Maria hated the idea of his smoking. She knew it had cut into the time he had left, but she loved to watch him inhale, especially in the night, when the ash glowed and grew long and the smoke curled upward like some spirit.

Ramon held the cigarette, examining the ash himself, and then dashed it out.

"Let me ask you this, daughter. Are there any smart people at this place you call a company? Are there any honest people?"

Maria said "Yes" to both questions.

"Are there any smart-honest people, one and the same?"

"I think so," she said.

"Do you consider yourself one of those people?" he asked.

Maria looked at her father for a long time. She couldn't answer. Ramon jostled her. "Eh, what do you say, my daughter?"

"That I am your daughter, Papa," she said.

"You are honest and I think sometimes smart. But there is one difference," Ramon Cisneros said. "All my life, I worked for someone else. I was honest and sometimes smart, but never smart enough or brave enough to test myself."

"Maybe you never really got tested," Maria said.

"Maybe not," he said, taking another sip. "We had it pretty good. We had land, horses, you kids. We got along."

"Until the land went away," Maria reminded him, putting her head back on her father's chest.

"So, where is this cyberspace, then? Is it a new land?" Ramon asked. "Or an illusion?"

"It's still being explored," she said.

"And people are paying to be guided?" he said.

"Not exactly. People are paying big money to companies that are promising to guide them."

"Up front?" he asked.

"Yes, to companies making these promises," she said.

"Isn't that what J.P. was promising? Isn't that why I put down money and others did? Isn't that what Infinity Computer was counting on?"

"Yes, sort of," Maria said.

"And you have people in your company who can do this?" he asked.

"I think so, Papa, with time and resources," she answered.

"Then you still have a company, am I right? We haven't lost our money yet, have we? Unless J.P. and the other *bandidos* get to the bank before you do," he said. There was a twinkle in his eye. Maria could see it through the smoke.

"Go home daughter. Sleep. Get up with the crows. Tomorrow is a work day, eh?" Ramon Cisneros said, putting the cap back on the bottle of tequila. "You have smart, honest people waiting to hear from you."

# chapter 58

**Maria delivered the news** to the chairman of Infinity Computer from her car phone just in case she had to make a run for it. "Sorry to call you so early, sir, but I'm afraid I have to tell you there is no killer app, at least not at this time," she said, checking the digital clock in her BMW. It was 6:15 A.M.; she was already on Highway 85, heading north from Los Gatos, as were hundreds of others on their way to work in Silicon Valley.

The chairman allowed as he'd been up for fifteen minutes, ever since his broker called to tell him a sell-off of Infinity stock was under way right from the opening bell.

"J.P.," Maria said. "He's shorting."

"What?" the chairman said.

Maria told him the rest of the incredible story and concluded just as she reached the parking lot of what had been J.P.'s startup in Cupertino. She pulled in and braced for the chairman's reaction.

"You mean to tell me that the fires in the laptops were all J.P.'s doing, at least the latest rounds?" he said. "And that technically, our problem was with the batteries all along, even before J.P. got hold of them? That J.P. simply engineered a software interface to make them combustible? Is that what you're saying?"

"Yes, sir," Maria said, reluctantly, looking up at the three-story building that was supposed to be the fountainhead of the last best thing. She waited for his reaction, waited so long that she wondered if the chairman were still on the line. "Hello?" she said meekly.

"I'm thinking," he said gruffly. "I'm thinking that we forked over ten million dollars and severely scaled down our own R&D, based purely on J.P.'s vapor. I'm thinking that our credibility has fallen as fast as our stock. Even Scott McNealy won't touch us now, and believe me, I have considered a fire sale." The chairman chuckled at his own words.

Is this a good sign, or has he gone bonkers? Maria wondered.

"We have no choice," he said suddenly.

Maria held her breath, waiting for the ax to fall.

"We've got to push on. Somewhere out there is an application that will recapture hearts and minds and pocketbooks. Hell, these twenty-something-year-olds are coming up with them right and left," he said. "How old are you, by the way?"

"Thirty-two," Maria said.

"In other words, old," the chairman said. "But not quite over the hill, at least when it comes to running a startup."

Maria pushed the phone closer to her ear. "What do you have in mind?" she asked.

"No, the question is, what do you have in mind?" asked the

chairman. "Throwing in the towel or coming up with the last best thing?"

"Is that an offer?" she asked.

"I said we haven't much choice," said the chairman.

Maria felt the rush. She clenched her fist and shot it in the air. "Mr. Chairman, I think we can proceed with a demonstration. It might not be the end-all, be-all last best thing, but I think we can ride with what we've got."

"Get on with it then, Maria. I assume J.P. hasn't snatched all the R&D money?"

"I'll secure it, sir," she said.

"Very well," he said. "On with the demo, then." And he hung up.

Maria's hands shook as she picked up the telephone in her office. It was now 6:40 A.M. Business hours for some people.

She called Texas Instruments in Dallas and persuaded the president's secretary to put her through. She told Jerry Junkins, the president, what she had discovered: that her company was in possession of a stolen TI chip prototype. She also told him she knew everything the FBI knew. And she told him the rest—that J. P. McCorwin was probably going to be charged with receiving stolen property.

"But there's one thing you should also know," she said. "Your chip can be made to work. We've done it."

She did not tell him the net result had been an order for more than 600 pizzas.

"We can give you a demo," Maria offered. "No strings attached. And believe me, I'm not calling on behalf of J.P. I'm calling on behalf of the people I work with. They're smart, honest people and they've already done what your people haven't been able to do. At this point, they don't even know J.P.'s missing."

Without hesitation, the president said he would send someone out for a demo. And then he added something else that made Maria's palms sweat: "If all goes well, maybe we can talk about an alliance."

Next she called a broker she knew in New York.

"Where's Infinity?" she asked. The answer was $20^3/_8$, down from $21^3/_4$ at the opening bell, a ten-year low. "Good, buy ten thousand shares. Charge them to our company account."

She hung up, saying to herself, We'll take the money out of R&D.

Next, she called the offices of the big cheeses at Pacific Bell, AT&T, General Magic, even MTV and *Wired* magazine, and left the following message: "We are developing a revolutionary new software platform for content parsing and interactive site development on the World Wide Web. A demonstration will be given on January thirtieth at 4:30 P.M. at the Santa Clara Convention Center. We will be available afterward to discuss possible strategic alliances."

When it came to the RSVP, she said, without hesitating, "Pegasus Technology," and gave the street address of J.P.'s former company in Cupertino.

Pegasus, the winged horse. How'd I come up with that? she asked herself. And then she called Mountain View and asked for the office of Netscape president Jim Barksdale and got his voice mail.

"Hey," she said. "We've got what you need. We're talking quality content that'll make your Navigator look clueless. Come by the Santa Clara Convention Center next week and check it out."

She was on a roll now, hardly conscious how fast her fingers were dialing.

"Federal Bureau of Investigation," the voice said.

"Agent Watanabe," Maria said.

"I'm sorry, she's not in just yet, would you like to leave a message on her voice mail?"

Maria said she would.

"Lily? Maria. I have a couple of questions. What happens if neither Brad nor Jason nor Harold Hopkins files a complaint? And what happens if Texas Instruments makes no claim against our company for receiving stolen property? . . . Just think about it."

She hung up thinking, Come on, Maria, you're sounding like J.P. already.

And then she turned to her PC and composed mail:

```
SUBJ: CHALLENGE
DATE: 96/01/23 9:56 EST
TO: BILLG@MICROSOFT.COM
Our software can whip your software at chess.
Care to play? How about later this week when you
come to Stanford?
```

And she was there to greet Brad and Jason when they arrived. She ushered them into her office and told them that Infinity's chairman was still behind the startup and what she had decided.

"We've still got a chance to kick some butt. But anyone who wants off the bus can check out with Human Resources no later than 4 P.M.," she said.

"I'm in," Jason said.

"I've got no place else to go," Brad said, quite literally.

And they helped direct each of their colleagues to the company kick-back pod and stood ready to dress the multiple wounds that would surely be inflicted by Maria's announcement of J.P.'s departure.

"He believed himself to be the last best thing," Maria said. "He wrote his own rules. Even now, with frontiers of technology being pushed further and further out there, some people apparently think it is OK to suspend the fundamental rules of humanity. But I want to emphasize something: As long as we're in business, we're going to operate smartly, honestly, truthfully, with regard for each other and with due consideration to the consequences of what we create. And we will create . . ."

She had more to say, but cheers interrupted her. The cheering lasted so long she finally had to wave her arms to break it off.

"This isn't a celebration," she shouted. "It's a call to all our brains. Let's go use 'em."

She felt like crying but held back the tears, and when she returned to her office, she was relieved to see two dozen phone messages, including one from Bill Gates, another from Larry Ellison, one from Ted Turner, whom she hadn't even called, and two from Lily Watanabe, all waiting for callbacks.

"I'll get to them later," she told her assistant. "First, I'm going for a ride in the hills."

# chapter 59

**January thirtieth dawned clear** and there was much relief on the Peninsula, particularly at Stanford University, where Bill Gates would be dedicating a new computer engineering building at an outdoor ceremony.

There was even more relief at the Atherton home of Harold Hopkins, who was hosting a poolside luncheon after the ceremony for Gates and sixty Silicon Valley heavyweights. The menu included barbecued sea bass in jade sauce with caramelized baby carrots, complemented by a 1994 Santa Cruz Mountains chardonnay made by Hopkins's cardiologist friend Tom Fogarty, followed by a ginger crème brûlée, accented by fresh raspberries ordered especially from Draeger's in Menlo Park and cappuccino made with Starbucks coffee, of course.

Like Gates, Hopkins had grown up in Seattle and attended the private Lakeside High School, where he was still on the board of directors. That was their connection. It was not, each insisted, based on money, which was laughable, since Lakeside's tuition nearly matched Stanford's.

This would be Hopkins's first public outing since an Infinity laptop had tried to toast him. It had severely burned him and incinerated part of his house. Now, his hands were nearly healed and the structural damage had disappeared just as quickly. Some things were based on money, at least according to his contractor. The luncheon would provide a nice platform to show everyone that Harry Hopkins was back in the game.

Unknown to any of the guests, including Gates, even to Hopkins himself, was that by 10:15 A.M., a two-block FBI perimeter was in place. Agents disguised as gardeners, tree pruners, dog walkers, joggers, housekeepers and FedEx delivery people were already assembled and a fleet of motley vehicles was at the ready.

Agents Watanabe and Smith had chosen a previously owned Chevy half-ton pickup the INS had seized in a raid for their command post and had taken up a position under an oak tree on one of the pathlike streets just a couple bends up from the Hopkins estate. Lily and Agent Smith were each dressed in Oshkosh B'Gosh overalls and wore floppy hats to conceal their radio earpieces.

It was through the earpiece that Lily received the news that J.P.'s 600 SL had been ID'd at the Reno Airport earlier that same morning, which explained why he and Baba had never returned to J.P.'s place in Woodside. They were, in the vernacular of the FBI, considered fugitives. And soon the alert would go out to every major law enforcement agency in the world.

In the meantime, Lily and Agent Smith ran communications checks with the various agents at their posts, including another dozen stationed at the Stanford campus to prevent what would be, if they didn't stop it, the most sensational kidnapping ever. They also listened to a special wideband scanner that was set up to intercept and monitor all cell-phone traffic within a two mile radius.

At about 10:30, the caterers arrived. And they were followed by an open Jeep Wrangler with five teenagers who, Lily supposed, were part of the event staff—valets, waiters, dishwashers.

"All clean-cut local kids," Agent Smith remarked as the Jeep sped by. "But so were the Chowchilla kidnappers."

Lily searched their faces, trying to identify who among them might be a terrorist, specifically Damien Roth.

Two more cars passed, carrying more teenagers, and turned toward the Hopkins place. Lily thought she recognized Damien from a photo Brad had loaned the bureau. But she couldn't be certain.

Ninety minutes later, a voice cracked over the radio. "Stanford all clear."

"They're on the way," Lily said.

Fifteen minutes later, a phalanx of vehicles approached. Each was of sufficient size and luxury to suggest that whoever was behind the wheel held the future in his or her hands. Harry Hopkins led in his Lexus. Lily recognized Gordon Moore in the next car, and Nathan Myhrvold, Microsoft's applications chief, was with him.

"There goes Wintel," she said. She also recognized, Regis McKenna, the Silicon Valley marketing guru, and George Shulz, the former Secretary of State and now a Stanford big shot, whose major existence was to give benedictions at events such as this so that particular people would be inspired to cough up endowment money.

The cars kept coming. Among them Lily spotted Brad Roth's Porsche followed by Maria's BMW.

"Duck," Lily said, feeling suddenly conspicuous in her disguise as the cars tooled by.

As they turned into the driveway, Brad and Maria passed a black-and-white Atherton police vehicle, and Brad, taking measure of two officers inside, smiled, waved and said through gritted teeth, "Armed, dangerous and after my son."

Officers Chip Meyers and Pierce Cullen smiled and waved back. They were the perfect models of comportment, having been chosen to ensure that the Gates event would come off with the perfect order and security and privacy the Atherton police were paid to uphold.

Once inside, Brad relinquished his Porsche to a grinning sixteen- or seventeen-year-old and immediately looked around for Damien.

"He's probably in the kitchen," Maria said, stepping out of her car. She took Brad by the arm. But their way was blocked by other teenagers, who asked their names and issued tags to match and made certain they were routed around the outside of the house and across the back patio toward the pool. There, ten round tables had been set up, and ushers were waiting to escort them to their assigned seats.

Maria was amazed to find she had been seated across from Hopkins, Gates and Andy Grove, right in the center of the luncheon. Brad had been relegated to a table in the outer ring.

Meanwhile, the guests filtered in, mingling by the pool. When Brad was handed a glass of champagne, Maria could see his hand shaking as he took it. She asked for a soda water and stepped into the crowd, immediately bumping into the chairman of Infinity Computer.

"Ready to go with the demo?" he asked, clinking her glass.

"It's why I'm drinking mineral water," she answered. "I'll save the champagne for later."

Others read her name tag and made the association with J. P. McCorwin's startup, which meant that Maria finally had to invoke the refrain she'd been practicing all morning: "No, J.P.'s on an extended trip looking for developing talent in the Third World."

Finally, there was a flurry. The French doors swung open and

Harold Hopkins, looking none the worse for wear except for his horribly discolored hands, and Bill Gates, the richest man in the world, stepped out of the house and onto the patio. Brad caught a glimpse of his son inside and felt a shudder of helpless terror.

Gates squinted, even in the winter sunlight, and Maria thought he looked incredibly pasty. Some old Seattle cliches immediately came to mind. But she didn't have long to revel in them because Gates came right toward her. He read her name tag and said, *"En garde . . .* I understand that this afternoon we have a chess match to attend."

Maria smiled, extended her hand and introduced herself.

"I know," he said, sounding slightly irritable. "You've got the name tag to prove it. . . . And by the way, about your name, Pegasus? We've already attached it as a code name to a prototype for PDA software. We're not in the public domain yet, and you obviously are, but I'm certain our lawyers can work things out."

What a jerk, she thought. Or maybe he really thinks he owns everything. . . . Or maybe he just gets nervous in social situations. . . . But he couldn't be as nervous as I am.

The servers brought lunch and Maria listened patiently to Gates deliver a history lesson about great powers controlling shipping lanes. "The key is to not only control Internet servers as one would the Suez and Panama Canals, but to virtually set up toll booths," he said, and repeated the same when Hopkins asked him to stand and deliver some short remarks.

He concluded by asking Maria to stand and repeat the challenge she had e-mailed to him.

She felt weak and her mouth went dry. But she stood and even cracked a joke about winner-take-all, which drew laughs, and invited everyone at the luncheon to drop by.

At that moment Brad Roth saw his son Damien start out the door. He carried a tray of crème brûlée and headed right for Gates's table.

From his perch in a neighbor's redwood, an FBI agent saw Damien, too. He spoke quickly into a cellular radio. "Viking is approaching Lion. Viking is carrying an undetermined object that could be a weapon or a bomb."

In her Chevy truck, Lily picked up the message. Lion was Gates. Viking was Damien. And she was excited. She switched to the command radio to shout the command, "Go!"

Agent Smith turned on the ignition and stepped on the gas. Gravel flew as the old truck spun onto the pavement and careened around the first bend in the road. Garden tools flew out the back and the tires squealed, which was enough to alert Atherton police officers Cullen and Meyers.

As the pickup rounded the final bend, with Hopkins's driveway in sight, Officer Cullen guided the black-and-white patrol car directly into its path. The truck stopped inches short of the Atherton police shield on the side of the vehicle. But by then, the Atherton officers were out with their weapons drawn.

"FBI!" Lily shouted, fumbling in her garden overalls for her ID.

"Right, Fat Bug Ick-sterminators," Cullen said, deliberately mispronouncing the last word. "Out of the vehicle, turn, stand, legs apart, hands on the roof. *Now!*"

Meanwhile, Damien had cleared the first ring of tables and was starting toward the inner circle, looking directly at Gates. Maria picked him up out of the corner of her eye.

She shifted her look toward Brad, but he had already left his seat. There was a flash of motion, a collision, two bodies tumbling, chairs and a table turned aside and the bodies fell right into the pool.

"Dad! Dad! What are you, crazy?" Damien screamed when he and Brad surfaced.

"I can't let you do this, son. The FBI, they'll kill you," Brad screamed back and started to shove his son under the surface, certain that black helicopter gunships would be circling overhead any second.

"What? Do what?" Damien sputtered.

"Kidnap him," Brad shouted meekly, when his head broke the surface again, and he pointed at Gates. "Gotta stop you . . ."

The water was only chest-deep. After scrambling for a moment, both father and son were able to stand. And suddenly Brad was aware of all the guests gathered around the pool. And then he was aware of his son striking the water.

"It's a school project, Dad, a school project. . . . A civics project. . . . We just wanted to see how close we could get to the richest man in the world. . . . We just wanted to see if we could breach security. That's all," Damien shrieked. "A school project."

Brad stood, dumbfounded, blinking at his son. "This was a school assignment? That's all?"

"You can call Mr. Dorgan, my teacher. Go ahead, he's waiting to hear how close I could get . . ."

Brad looked up. Gates was peering down at him. So was Harold Hopkins. Hell, so was half of the pantheon of Silicon Valley. Brad straightened his sodden tie and started toward the pool steps, already rehearsing his apology.

"A civics class?" Gates asked Damien. "Were you going to serve me crème brûlée or toss it in my face? Seriously."

"Seriously?" Damien asked. "We'd talked about tossing it."

"Cool," Gates said. "Wish I'd done something like that when I was a kid. . . . But noooo."

And then he turned to his host and said, "Harry, you got a pair of swim trunks I can borrow?"

# chapter 60

**With all the mayhem at Hopkins's luncheon,** Maria barely had time to get to the Santa Clara Convention Center ahead of the audience. But she rehearsed her speech along the way and checked in with the R&D crew every five minutes by cell phone.

"God, Maria, you sound like a little girl going to confession!" she hollered at herself. But it was a confession. Before the toughest audience she'd ever faced. And she knew she was going to have to come clean.

"There is no last best thing!" she hollered even louder. "There is no more J. P. McCorwin . . ."

And then, as if in a daze, she was pushing through the big front doors and trotting down the aisle past row after row of empty maroon seats and bounding up the steps to the stage of the convention center.

Jason, Raptor, Ethan, Lisa, the whole R&D team, was swarming over an Infinity 9500 laptop like a pit crew at Indy.

"Loaded?" Maria asked.

"Loaded," Raptor answered. "But still not test-fired."

"Not one run-through?" she asked. She felt her insides about to burst. "That's fatal."

"No time," Jason said, stepping in. "Look, we've been through some of this stuff separately. We got the new chip in. We got the supercooled vapor accelerator."

Lisa put her hand on Maria's shoulder and said, "We've given it personality."

"But will it all work at once?" Maria asked hoarsely.

"We're about to find out," came a sneering voice from across the stage. It was a Microsoft tech, a tall, muscular, Nordic-looking guy with a beard and aviator glasses. He wore an unbuttoned flannel shirt. Underneath, a T-shirt said WINDOWS 95 RULES!

He was also making the finishing hookups on a Hewlett Packard Vectra desktop system.

"Dual processors," he said, patting the tower cabinet. "Two hundred megs of Pentium power, 64 MB RAM, 2-gig hard drive. We can download a billion moves a minute. Want to surrender now, gracefully?"

"You don't have the authority to demand our surrender," Maria said, recalling something out of a history book.

She turned back to her team. Terror radiated from each of their faces.

"No time for stage fright, guys," Maria said. Her voice was elevated and reedy, betraying her own fright.

Brad waved and trotted down the aisle. Damien was with him. So was Lily Watanabe.

"They're on the way," he said breathlessly. "Everyone—the chairman; Gates; some big shot from Texas Instruments; Grove; Harry Hopkins; Ed McCracken from Silicon Graphics; Regis Mc-Kenna; John Doerr, a Kleiner Perkins hot shot; some guy from Pacific Bell; some guy from AT&T. Even some scouts from Apple."

Maria looked toward Lily, expecting her to intervene, half-hoping that she might mercifully arrest them all before they made further fools of themselves.

The FBI agent stepped forward, extended her right hand and squeezed Maria's arm.

"Go for it." That's all Lily said.

"You guys ready?" Maria asked her crew one last time. She couldn't help glancing again at the powerful and proven HP desktop system. Compared to their puny-looking Infinity laptop, it looked like Goliath.

Raptor nodded. "We're wired and plugged. Let's play."

According to the rules, the dueling systems would be required to interface through the Net, which meant finding each other and joining up on opposite ends of the field of battle—a multiple-user domain, in this case a chessboard in cyberspace. It was a nifty little wrinkle that was supposed to demonstrate the quickness of each system's hardware and the selectivity protocol of their respective interface software.

Once the two systems had each other in their sights, the chessboard would appear on each screen and it would be projected to a giant screen onstage. At that point, only one more keystroke would be allowed by either side. After that, the software was to take over.

As for the match itself, it would be two out of three. The format would be classical, meaning each side had two hours to make forty moves, two hours to complete the next twenty and then an hour to end each game. This was the same format to be used in two weeks in a highly publicized match between an IBM computer and Gary Kasparov, the world champ. The word was that IBM geeks had been working on a chess program, with some help from Microsoft, for six years. And Kasparov all his life.

Maria's crew had been working for less than six days. She only hoped that, if things went beyond her wildest dreams, her side would at least be able to open or employ one impressive defensive move.

Still, she boldly told the one hundred or so people who filled the front third of the theater, "Since this tournament could take all night, we have arranged for accommodations nearby as well as two catered meals, but no movies."

To herself, she said, I wish . . . that J.P. were here.

Then she told the audience what she had been dreading.

"J.P. is gone," she said, and waited for the gasps to subside. "And he's probably not coming back. I know a lot of you have been curious as to what he's been up to. Some of you are expecting the last best thing . . ."

She took in a breath and let it out: "I have to tell you. There is no last best thing."

There were more gasps. Then, worse, heavy silence. She could see people shifting their seats. She expected them to pelt her with boos, expected them to leave. Wished Lily would come down the aisle right now and take her away.

"Maybe there never will be a last best thing," she continued, lowering her voice. "I'd like to think of that proposition as fortunate. Because to search for the last, or ultimate, best thing is to suggest that one day, there could be no more quests. That would be a black day, not just for Silicon Valley, and I include Redmond, Washington, when I say that. . . ." She tipped her head toward Gates, who waved decorously. "To cancel the quest or even to postpone it or preempt it, would be to stand in the way of social development. It would be inhumane and unpardonable. I hope none of us in this room possesses the greed or arrogance to work toward that end or even think it possible."

Maria had said what she had to. And so she closed, "In truth, we haven't even run a full alpha on our system. We've run some applications and are pretty excited about them and we'd like to disclose them to you. But we are not yet ramped up and running. We don't really know what we have. We're just a collection of people who are working hard to try to stay in the game. We don't care about controlling the shipping lanes or even about killer apps. . . . But we do feel deeply that technology should be integrated with humanity so that the world will become an even smaller place . . ."

She started to back up and was looking for the stairs when the chairman of Infinity Computer rose and said, "Candor is a rare commodity in this Valley, Maria. And I haven't heard the word 'humanity' outside an ad in as long as I can remember. . . . Thank you."

And he led the applause, which lasted until Maria descended the stairs and found her seat next to Brad and Damien in the front row.

The theater lights dimmed as Jason took the stage. He was wearing a pair of blue jeans and a black polo shirt—for him, the equivalent of dressing for a state dinner. He cracked a couple of corny Windows jokes, but otherwise was pretty straightforward. Maria felt some relief.

And then Jason said, "Ready? *Go!*"

The room filled suddenly with the sound of gently swirling water and the big screen projected what the Infinity laptop monitor showed—soft, honey-colored pulsations that suddenly burst like a meteor with the light in the core of the screen intensifying and seeming to come closer.

"Wow," someone in the crowd said. "Like a roller-coaster ride."

"No. Like being born," someone corrected. Maria recognized Lisa's voice and felt even prouder, because the Windows 95 logo hadn't even showed up yet.

The light at the center of the screen grew even more intense and everyone in the audience had to feel as though they were emerging into . . . something. Suddenly there was nothing but blue sky before them, then blackness and stars. And the reassuring voice of Obi-Wan Kenobi came out of the surrounding darkness. "May the Force be with you, each and every one of you."

This drew howls, which turned to raspberries when the Microsoft logo finally appeared and the theme song "Start Me Up" drowned out Obi-Wan.

By then, though, Maria's software had already sped through file checks, hitched onto an Internet server and had located a multiuser domain for the chess match. It waited patiently for Windows to catch up, and when it didn't, it went back and provided the URL address.

"See, it has real-time empathy," Lisa said.

The audience laughed, warming to what they were seeing.

Maria looked over at Gates. He was leaning forward, appearing to be thoroughly engrossed. Beside him, Nathan Myhrvold, his chief content honcho, was furiously taking notes.

The two sides lined up opposite each other, and Maria's Pegasus system stole the initiative by selecting a protocol that allowed it the choice of white or black—offense or defense. It chose black, a surprise.

And the rest went downhill from there. Windows opened with a classic white pawn to the center, clearly out to seize the high ground. Pegasus replied cautiously by playing a black pawn along the side.

And the difference in tactics became immediately apparent. Windows was marching into battle. Pegasus saw every move toward it as a threat and was intimidated and deferential.

It was not a chess match, it was a chase. Windows quickly brought up its knights, bishops and queen into attacking positions and Pegasus retreated, even refusing obvious Windows sacrifices, which it recognized as "gambits" or "traps" and said so in messages scrolled across the screen before each move.

That showed an even greater difference between the opponents. Microsoft pushed ahead, silent and unyielding, using all its lethal tactics—pins, the skewer, the knight fork, double guard, doubling attack. And Pegasus read these assaults and announced its reasoning before parrying or retreating with every move.

By the end of the first thirty minutes, sixty moves had been made and the outcome was not much in doubt. Windows owned the center of the board and seemed unstoppable. Pegasus seemed to be orbiting the outside lanes, its king and offensive pieces ducking and running.

"Coward," someone yelled.

"You gonna run scared all night?" yelled another.

Sounds like a boxing crowd, Maria thought, and slumped in her chair.

"Resign," someone else yelled. "You don't have the heart for this game."

Maria sunk further.

"Wait a minute." Gates rose. He climbed the stairs and gangled toward the big screen. "Are you guys seeing what I'm seeing?"

"Yeah, that Pegasus thing is showing its tail and getting it kicked," said a sharp voice Maria recognized to be that of a venture capitalist J.P. had once introduced her to.

"No, wait," Gates persisted. He stood before the screen, which now showed the shadow of his head and shoulders. "I'll tell you what I'm seeing—"

"No. I'll tell you." It was Lisa, approaching the stage. "I'll tell you because I've been working on this, on and off, for more than fifteen years. You're seeing fear . . . in other words, we've managed to program—"

"Emotion?" asked Gates. "You've morphed software into actually being scared?"

Maria stood. "We don't know for certain, but we're working on intuition that runs along the lines of human intelligence and actual, not virtual, emotion."

She approached the stage and looked up at Gates. Even in the dark, she could tell. He was blown away.

"Awesome," he whispered, wiping his glasses. "Absolutely awesome. And you've done this with capital constraints?"

The lights came up, the programs shut down. The crowd pushed in. Maria could feel hands patting her on the back. She could see business cards being thrust at her.

Could hear voices saying, "Call me tomorrow, will you?"

Could see Lisa in tears and Rick Raptor shaking his head, saying, "Fear? Fear? We gotta work on this thing."

"You're right, we do," Maria said.

She asked Jason to dismantle the laptop even as Gates was circling it and asking for a personal demo.

"How about dinner?" he suggested. "I'd like to talk strategic alliance."

"No, thanks," she said. "I mean on dinner. It's been a long day. I'm tired."

Jason handed her the laptop and she tucked it under her arm and made her way through the venture capitalists and developers and corporados who looked hungrily at what she was carrying.

"Call me tomorrow." She heard it a dozen times on the way out the door.

In the parking lot, she hooked up with Brad and his son.

"Awesome," Damien said.

"You're right, awesome," she said back.

"You want to come for pizza with us?" Brad said.

"No, thanks," she said. "You two need some time alone." Then she jumped in her BMW 325i convertible, put down the top, threw her head back and closed her eyes. She had planned to head north on the Great America Parkway to the freeway, but she was too keyed up to go home just yet.

She punched in her favorite Mary Chapin Carpenter tape and turned eastward on Tasman Drive, entering what was now part of the Golden Triangle—the epicenter of high-tech that touched the borders of San Jose, Santa Clara and Sunnyvale. She passed Agnews State Hospital for the mentally disabled. She passed an office park that had once been a field where Lily Watanabe's father raised flowers.

Half a mile later, she pulled onto a dirt road and came to the bank above the narrow Guadalupe River. Maria got out, looked down into the slow-moving water and let her gaze follow back upstream. She imagined the source way off in the east foothills near where her own father tended someone else's orchards. She remembered the fishing trips they'd taken with her sisters, remembered once actually seeing a salmon spawning in this river. She also wondered where J.P. was.

She returned to the car, grabbed the laptop and walked back to the water's edge. She stood, holding the device and then opened the case, booted up and let herself be born according to the software program, and was still mesmerized by what she saw on the screen.

"Pretty damn good," she said. She could feel the tears running down her cheeks. "Amniotic fluid. Lisa's idea. Like being born.... A computer that has emotional intelligence. Pretty damn good.... Pretty damn scary."

She crouched, cradling the laptop on one knee. She thought for a second, then said loudly, "To real live human beings," and typed this is for you, Papa.

She stood, looked out across the water and raised the laptop over her head as if she was hoisting a champion's sterling cup she had just won at a Grand Prix aboard Fuego.

And she imagined throwing the laptop into the water, as she had thrown the hard drive with the RoseD program. She imagined watching it settle, imagined seeing flame as the computer fluttered like a coin toward the bottom. And the flame would not go out.

She stood for a long time, holding the laptop and looking down into the water.

"You can't stop the fire, Maria. You just can't," she said. She lowered the machine, snapped the lid closed and carried it back to her car.

On the way home, Maria turned the tape up real loud and she felt elated and terrified at the thought of tomorrow. And she passed the Highway 280 turnoff that would take her to work in a few hours, she shouted at the top of her voice, "You're right, guys, this thing needs a lot of work!"

# and then . . .

**The Valley chilled as winter pushed into spring** and summer turned even chillier as one new company after another went public and was frozen in place by a suspicious market. The season of the killer IPOs, J. P. McCorwin's dream season of harvesting vapor, had turned into a slaughter— particularly for companies that launched stock without products or earnings to show investors.

Maria Cisneros had seen the chill coming and wisely postponed the public offering that her former boss had promised would make everyone, including Maria's father, very rich.

"Not until we have more than concepts to point and click to," she told her team and her investors.

Maria's former boss, J.P., had not been heard from—at least not directly—since the night Baba stuffed him into the back of his own Mercedes and roared out the driveway ahead of the FBI. Pegasus had nearly been the victim of a couple of mysterious but not very well disguised intranet hits for money, but Maria had already alerted Finance to require her personal signature or electronic code to authorize any amount over $10,000. And so the mysterious requests had failed to get at the company coffers.

There were sightings—or at least reports of sightings—of someone who fit J.P.'s description. One report had him sporting a beard and living a hermit's life in a shack in Montana. Another said that J.P. was hiding out on an island off British Columbia claiming he could induce razor clams to produce pearls. There were other, more uncertain sightings on Ibiza, on the Rue Jacob in Paris, on the night train to Venice, on a mountainside in Japan, on the Steppes of Mongolia.

The police followed each lead and only one panned out—the one about the hermit in Montana. He turned out to be the suspected Unabomber, which held no small irony for Lily Watanabe or anyone else on the Unabom Task Force connected with the investigation of the combustible Infinity laptops.

And so even as J.P.'s company soared without him, J.P.'s name remained on "the most wanted" data bank of every major law enforcement agency in the world, even as the Unabomber sketch, complete with hooded sweatshirt and dark glasses, came down. Everyone at Pegasus watched alt.jp.fugitive and bet on where he'd show up first: *Cops* or *America's Most Wanted*. Privately Maria figured that he had the money and the means to morph into any identity he chose, but she kept that to herself. She felt like she owed him that much. No more.

And what about Maria? Her every move was now widely re-ported. One big reason was her successful legal battle with Micro-soft, which had tried to claim the name Pegasus as its own, reasoning that it had been using the name for a widely reported secret prototype PDA software it was developing.

"They can't own everything," Maria said in a postvictory press conference. She knew she was holding the cards, in other words, the public domain on the name. It was classic. She argued that she owned the name because she had stepped into the daylight with it first. And a federal district judge in Seattle agreed.

Microsoft then offered to buy the name for $10 million. Or that was the rumor Bill Gates and Maria no-commented.

There were other rumors, too. That Gates offered her big-time money and stock options to leave Cupertino for a key position in Redmond. That Gates had also offered a huge amount, in advance, for whatever it was Maria's people were working on. "Planting a flag in cyberspace," was how Gates supposedly described the gam-bit. And there was a big buzz over that—including a downtick in Microsoft stock and a huge uptick in interest in whatever it was Maria and her folks were doing over at Pegasus.

Investors knocked on her door and Maria found ways to accom-modate them. There were also rumors that the chairman of Infin-ity had countered Gates's proposition by offering Maria the president's slot, which she turned down.

In any case, Maria resisted all offers except for those from private investors she trusted. Her R&D budget swelled, as did the rumors that Pegasus would launch a new best thing before the end of the last financial quarter. Maria did her best to appear to soften the rumors without killing the buzz. And she was so good at it that romantics around the Valley annointed her as a "rising star," a mantle she wore like a silk scarf. Watching her, Valley romantics quietly reminisced about the good old days, saying things about her that would have embarrassed (or even appalled) many of the industry's other hot young things. They called her things such as "credible" or "honorable," even "cautious"—words that had been consigned to storage since the rush of IPOs that stormed the Valley like Visigoths.

And the romantic sentimentalists weren't the only ones talking. Words like "renaissance" and "rebound" and "turnaround" were also popping up whenever the name Infinity Computer came up. Indeed, its hemorrhaging had apparently been staunched and its losses shrunk for two consecutive quarters. The news pushed Infinity stock upward again, and as the stock passed 22, then 25, then 27, the ratings became more favorable; and as they did, the stock punched through 30. Because they had invested at the bottom, Pegasus Technology and Maria both made a tidy profit on the surge.

"It's all pretty heady, Papa," she said one late-summer evening. She had called ahead and asked her father to join her for a drive. He was delighted, of course, especially when Maria put the top down and they headed west on Highway 880 and then north on Highway 280. They approached the turnoff for De Anza Boulevard and Maria turned on the blinkers.

"Where we going, *hija?* To your office in Cupertino?" Ramon Cisneros asked. "You finally gonna show me the last best thing, eh?"

Maria smiled and turned the car in the opposite direction, heading toward Sunnyvale. They turned left on El Camino Real and Ramon cursed all the fast-food joints and strip malls.

"All this garbage. This is what your Silicon Valley makes, eh?" he said, lighting a cigarette. He drew in deeply and then exhaled straight up into the air.

Maria knew her father was enjoying himself.

"Do you remember when the Silicon Valley wasn't invented yet?" he asked. "No. You're too young. But do you remember the orchards? Ah, the cherries, the apricots, plums, prunes, peaches. . . . When it was called the Santa Clara Valley, only that, not the Silicon Valley."

"And the Valley of the Heart's Delight," Maria nodded and smiled. "People think that sounds corny now."

They came to an intersection just beyond the civic center and Maria turned right heading into a maze of side streets. They passed small, tidy bungalows and then doubled back toward El Camino, where the houses grew bigger and farther apart. They passed an occasional postage stamp orchard, no bigger than half a square block, and Ramon recognized them all.

"The Marianis still own those cherries, or what's left of them," Ramon said. "And the apricots, too, oh *los huevos del sol,* we called them. Remember? And that cherry orchard over there? Belongs to old man Johnson. But I heard they're trying to sell. . . . Next time we come by it'll probably be one of those ugly glass-and-steel monstrosities where they're making something none of us will ever figure out how to use."

Maria could feel her smile growing wider as she circled the block. Ramon drew another drag on his cigarette. "Do you remember the springtimes when this whole valley was a flood of blossoms, one side to the other? The tourists would take trains down from San Francisco, just to smell the air . . ."

Maria stopped the car. She turned the key and hoisted herself half out of her seat for a better look at the orchard.

"I do remember, Papa," she said, looking out across the orchard. Then she reeled in her gaze and caught her father looking imploringly at her.

"What is it my daughter?" he said. "You are about to tell me something. What is it? Go on."

Maria took a deep breath and said simply this: "The last best thing, Papa," and nodded toward the orchard. "I put money down on it this morning. It's ours."